# SHARKS
# IN THE
# TIME
# OF
# SAVIOURS

## KAWAI STRONG
## WASHBURN

CANONGATE

This paperback edition published in 2021 by Canongate Books

First published in Great Britain in 2020 by Canongate Books Ltd,
14 High Street, Edinburgh EH1 1TE

First published in the United States by Farrar, Straus and Giroux,
120 Broadway, New York, 10271

canongate.co.uk

1

*British Library Cataloguing-in-Publication Data*
A catalogue record for this book is available on
request from the British Library

ISBN 978 1 78689 651 3

Designed by Richard Oriolo

Printed and bound in Great Britain by Clays Ltd, Elcograf S.p.A.

MIX
Paper from
responsible sources
FSC® C018072
www.fsc.org

**Kawai Strong Washburn** was born and raised on the Hamakua coast of the Big Island of Hawai'i. His work has appeared in McSweeney's, Electric Literature and *The Best American Nonrequired Reading,* among others. He has received scholarships from the Tin House and Bread Loaf writer's workshops and has worked in software and as a climate policy advocate. He lives in Minneapolis with his wife and daughters. *Sharks in the Time of Saviours* is his first novel.

kawaistrongwashburn.com

~

'Beautifully written'
*Vogue*

'Brilliant'
*Financial Times*

'Mixes hardscrabble Hawaiian reality with flights of wonder
and the supernatural in a way that is wholly original'
*Vanity Fair*

'Old myths clash with new realities, love is in a ride or die with grief,
faith rubs hard against magic, and comic flips with tragic so much they
meld into something new. All told with daredevil lyricism to burn'
Marlon James, author of *Black Leopard, Red Wolf*

'A brilliant novel and one of the most engaging and memorable books I've
read this year. Sentences sparkle, the narrative voices remain distinctive and
complete, and the deep notes of magic sound under the realism of poverty
and loss. I didn't want it to end'
Sarah Moss, author of *Summerwater*

'With prose that can be breathy and sweaty in one paragraph before gliding
softly and tenderly into the next, this passionate writer cries out for us to see
Hawai'i in its totality: as a place of proud ancestors and gods and spirits, but
also of                                                            )f mystery and

'Unputdownable. Washburn is an extraordinarily brilliant new talent'
Tommy Orange, author of *There There*

'Epic in scope, it throbs with magic realism and urban misery . . .
Told with such loquacious vigour that the reader is swept along, utterly rapt.
It marks Washburn out as a writer with talent to burn'
*i*

'A story of trauma passed down through the generations, of how poverty,
grief, and broken dreams weave their way through the lives of one family. Yet
it is a story told with joy, even humour, in lyrical, hypnotic prose that will
stay with you long after you turn the last page'
Tahmima Anam, author of *The Bones of Grace*

'Richly imagined and evocative . . . I was enthralled by the world captured in
its pages and, once I turned the final page, found myself wanting more'
*Los Angeles Review of Books*

'Washburn has written the great Hawaiian novel . . . A volcanic powerhouse
of a debut'
Benjamin Percy, author of *Red Moon*

'One of the finest debut novels I've read in years, a story about the
resilience of family and resilience of home – a story at once lucid, original
and transcendent'
Omar El Akkad, author of *American War*

'The story of a family, a people and a legend, all wrapped in one. Faith and
grief, rage and love, this book pulses with all of it. Kawai Strong Washburn
makes his debut with a wealth of talent and a true artist's eye'
Victor Lavalle, author of *The Changeling*

'A lush, virtuosic novel with breathless scope and lasting depth. Kawai
Strong Washburn's vision is searing, his talent explosive, his heart beating
loud and proud on every page'
Claire Vaye Watkins, author of *Gold, Fame, Citrus*

*For Granny, who drove me eighty miles round-trip*
*to get the next book in the series*

# PART I

# DELIVERANCE

# 1

# MALIA, 1995

## *Honoka'a*

WHEN I CLOSE MY EYES WE'RE ALL STILL ALIVE AND IT becomes obvious then what the gods want from us. The myth people tell about us might start on that liquid blue day off Kona and the sharks, but I know different. We started earlier. *You* started earlier. The kingdom of Hawai'i had long been broken—the breathing rain forests and singing green reefs crushed under the haole fists of beach resorts and skyscrapers—and that was when the land had begun calling. I know this now because of you. And that the gods were hungry for change and you were that change. In our first days I saw so many signs, but didn't believe.

The first came when your father and I were naked in his pickup truck in Waipiʻo Valley, and we witnessed the night marchers.

We'd come down into Waipiʻo Valley on a Friday, pau hana, with Auntie Kaiki babysitting your brother at home, and me and your father both knew we were going to use this childless night to screw our brains out, were run dumb with electricity just thinking about it. How could we not? Our skin rubbed dark by the sun and your father then with his football-days body, me with mine from basketball, the two of us feeling our love like the hottest habit. And there was Waipiʻo Valley: a deep cleft of wild green split with a river silver-brown and glassy, then a wide black sand beach slipping into the frothing Pacific.

A slow descent to the bottom of the valley in your father's bust-up Toyota pickup, hairpin turn after hairpin turn, a sharp cliff to the right, cobbled tar underneath, the road so steep it caused the truck cab to fill with the smell of the engine's burning guts.

Then a jarring road of silt and waist-deep mud puddles at the bottom of the valley and we reached the beach and parked the truck right up against the freckled black eggs of rock that rimmed the sand; your father made me laugh until my cheeks prickled with heat and the last shadows of the trees were pointing long toward the horizon. The ocean boomed and sizzled. We unrolled our sleeping bags in the bed of the pickup, over the gravel-smelling foam pad your father put down just for me, and once the last teenagers were gone—the thick buzz of their reggae bass fading into the forest—we took our clothes off and made you.

I don't think you can hear my memories, no, so this won't be so pilau, and anyway, I like to remember. Your father gripped a small fist of my hair, the hair he loved, black and kinked with Hawaiʻi, and my body began to curl into a rhythm against his pelvis, and we groaned and panted, pressed our blunt noses together, and I pulled us apart and straddled above and came back onto him and our skin was so hot I wanted to store it for all the times I'd ever felt cold, and his fingers traced my neck, his tongue my brown nipples, this gentleness that was a part of him that no one ever saw, and our sex made its sounds and we laughed a little, closing our eyes and opening them and closing them again, and the day lost its last light even as we kept on.

We were on top of our sleeping bags, the cool air minting our dampness, when your father's face got serious and he rolled away from me.

"You see that?" he asked.

I didn't know what he saw—I was still coming out of some sort of fog, still rubbing my thighs together for the tingle there, the last of the oiled rush of our love—but then your father jolted to a sitting position. I rose to my knees, still sex-drunk. My tits swung in against his left biceps and my hair fell down across his shoulder and even though I was scared I felt sexy and almost wanted to pull him into me, right there, never mind the danger.

"Look," he whispered.

"Come on," I said. "Stop messing around, lolo."

"Look," he said again. And I did, and what I saw yanked me tight.

Out on top of the far ridge of Waipi'o a long line of trembling lights had appeared, slowly dipping and rising as they moved along the valley's crown. Green and white, flickering, it must have been fifty, and as we watched we saw the lights for what they were: fires. Torches. We'd heard of the night marchers but always assumed it was only a myth, part of a hymn of what had been lost to Hawai'i, these ghosts of the long-dead ali'i. But there they were. Marching slow on their way up the ridge, headed for the black back of the valley and whatever waited there for undead kings in all the damp and darkness. The string of torches plodded along the ridge, winking between the trees, dipping, then rising, until all at once the flames snuffed out.

A loud, creaking groan sounded out across the valley, all around us, the sound I imagined a whale would make before dying.

Whatever words your father and I had choked in our throats. We were up and off the pickup bed and jerking on our clothes, toes in gritty black sand, us hopping and gasping and yanking into the cab, ignition, and your father had the engine loud as we tore back through the valley road, the headlights flashed over rocks and mud puddles and bright green leaves; the whole time we knew those ghosts were in the air behind us, around us, if we didn't see them we felt them. The truck bounced through the rutted wreck of the tar, the windshield showed trees and sky and back down, into the muck, up and down as we bounced, everything black and blue but what our headlights could flash over, your father making the truck race between the lurking trees and up the long road to the exit. We came up out of the bottom of the valley so fast that there was nothing below now but the few speckles of house lights farther back in the valley, the outlines of the sunken taro patches gone white in the midnight.

It wasn't until we got to the lookout that we stopped. The cab was full of panic and mechanical effort.

Your father blew a long breath and said, "Jesus fucking Christ."

It was the first time he'd talked about anything holy in a while. And there were no more torches; no more night marchers. We listened to our blood thump in our ears and it told us *alive alive alive*.

Just one of those things, is what me and your father told ourselves, soon after and for many years. After all, there were so many people in Hawaiʻi that had seen similar things; we'd talk story in full kanikapila mode at a beach barbecue or back lanai house party long enough, and plenty similar stories came up.

THE NIGHT MARCHERS—you'd been conceived that night, and all through your first years there were stranger things. The way animals changed around you: suddenly subdued, they'd nuzzle you and form a circle as if you were one of their own, didn't matter if it was a chicken or a goat or a horse, it was something instant and unbreakable. Then there were the times we'd catch you in our backyard, eating fistfuls of dirt or leaves, flowers, compulsively. Far beyond the dull curiosity of other keikis your age. And some of those plants—the orchids in hanging baskets, for example—would bloom in the most incredible colors, almost overnight.

Just one of those things, we still told ourselves.

But now I know.

DO YOU REMEMBER HONOKAʻA IN 1994, not so different than today? Māmane Street, both sides with low wood buildings from the first days of cane, front doors repainted but inside still the same old bones. The faded auto-mechanic garages, the pharmacy with the same deals always on the windows, the grocery store. Our rented house on the edge of town with its layers of stripping paint and cramped bare rooms, shower stall patched onto the back of the garage. The bedroom you shared with Dean, where you started having nightmares vague with sugarcane and death.

Those nights. You'd come quiet to the side of our bed, still partially tangled in your sheets, swaying, with your hair smeared every direction, sniffling in your breath.

Mama, you'd say, it happened again.

I'd ask what you saw, and you'd start to talk in a spill of images—black fields cracked and empty, cane stalks shooting not from soil but from the chest, arms, eyes of me or your father or your brother or all of us, then a sound like the inside of a wasp hive—and while you talked your eyes were not your own, you were not behind them. You were only seven years old, and the things that were pouring out of you. But after a minute of talking this way you'd come back.

They're just dreams, I'd tell you, and you'd ask what I was talking about. I'd try to repeat some interpretation of the nightmares—the cane, the reaping of your family, the hives—but you never remembered what you'd just been telling me. It was as if you'd just woken and found yourself in front of me while I told you someone else's story. The nightmares happened every few months, then every few weeks, then every day.

The sugarcane plantation had been around since before we were born, our whole side of the island shagged with fields of cane, mauka to makai. I'm sure since the beginning people had been talking about the Final Harvest, but it seemed like it would never come: "Hāmākua's always hiring," your father said, dismissing the rumors with a flap of his wrist. But then, so soon after your nightmares reached their daily cadence, along Māmane came the low of the cane-truck horns, that September afternoon in 1994, and your father was one of the drivers.

If I could be above our town, looking down, I would remember it this way: Into the town came the tractor trailers, many with the chain-link-style beds, empty loops like the ribs of neglected animals, swaying as they made their way past the Salvation Army, past the churches, past the empty storefronts that used to hawk bins of cheap plastic imports, past the high school across from the elementary school, past the football-baseball-soccer field. As the trucks passed, blowing their horns, people left the bank and grocery store and gathered in rows on the sidewalks, or the shoulders of the streets. Even those inside that didn't come out must have heard the truck horns moaning, the air brakes bleating, the hymn of an industrial funeral. It was the sound of a new emptiness coming. Because they would never be in the fields again, the trucks were polished to a mirror-shine, none of the dirt of work on them, and for all the Filipino-Portuguese-Japanese-Chinese-Hawaiian families that lined the streets, the chrome threw back a slippery quicksilver reflection of their dark-brown faces and the new truth settling there.

We were in that crowd, me, Dean, Kaui, and you. Dean stood still and stiff like a little soldier. His hands were already so big at nine, and I remember the dry sheath of his palm wrapped around my hand. Kaui was drifting in between my legs, the breathy tickle of her hair against my thighs, a few fingers pressing after. You were at my other hand, and unlike the confusion and anger thrumming along Dean's fingers, his stiff neck, unlike the four-year-old's dreamy spin of apathy coming from Kaui, you seemed completely at peace.

Only now can I guess what you'd been dreaming about—whose was the death, our bodies or the sugarcane. In the end it didn't matter. You'd seen the end coming before any of us. That was the second sign. There was a voice inside you, wasn't there, a voice that was not yours, you were only the throat. The things it knew, and was trying to tell you—tell us—but we didn't listen, not yet.

Just one of those things, we said.

The cane trucks made their turn just before the grocery store, ascended the steep hill out of town, and never came back.

A few months after the plantation went under, we were completely stretched. Everyone was searching; it was no different for your father. He was driving for hours across the island, chasing a paycheck that moved like obake: here and gone. Sunday morning in the orange light bouncing off our old wood floors he'd be at the kitchen counter, clutching his favorite coffee mug spreading its Kona steam and sliding his fingers over the "help wanted" section, lips moving like a chant. Days he found something, he'd slowly cut it from the page and take it with just the tips of his hands and place it in a manila folder he kept near the phone. Days he didn't, the sound of the newspaper as he crushed it was like a flock of birds taking flight.

But that didn't stop your father's smile; nothing would. He'd been that way even when things were steady, even when you all were in hanabata days, upper lips crusted with baby-leak, just learning to walk, and he would fling you into the air so your hair would flap open and your eyes would squint happy and you'd squeal your brightest. He'd throw you guys as high as he could—aiming, he said, for the clouds—and when you'd come back down so would my heart. You've got to stop, I'd say, especially when he'd do it to Kaui.

I not gonna drop 'em, he'd say. Besides, we can make another one if they break their necks or whatever.

Other times, in the morning, he'd stay in bed later—mostly he'd been an early man, that still continued after the cane trucks stopped—and he'd curl up close to me and start giggling through his thin mustache, and I'd try to scramble free from the covers before he'd rip a good fut and trap me in the cave of it with him, the ripe cheesy-beany stink of whatever was burning in his gut.

Almost taste better going out than coming in, yeah? he'd say, and giggle again, like we were back in high school goofing off in fifth period. I remember once he did his fut-under-the-covers thing and asked that same question and I said I don't know, let me test, and slipped a finger up inside his boxers, just into his butthole, and he squealed and jerked away going, Eh, that's too far, that's too far, and I laughed and laughed and laughed and laughed. There was something about your father, and me, and us, and how we'd push each other, that went good with the quiet times, us in the bathroom watching each other brush teeth in the mirror, or juggling the one car we had (we traded the bust-up pickup for a bust-up SUV just after you were born) to get you all to science fair, basketball practice, hula performances.

But if we could've poured our money into a cup that cup would be half empty. Your father lucked into a part-time thing at one of the hotels, like everyone else wanted, but he couldn't get full-time or the good tips at the restaurant, only working the room crews, and he'd come back and tell me about the barely touched plates of ahi on the balconies being picked over by a mass of mynahs and the volcanoes of clothes on the hotel room floors. Those haoles got two pairs of clothes for every day of vacation, he'd say, Two for every *day*.

And it felt like almost as soon as that hotel job came, it went, Seasonal Restructuring. And my hours at the mac-nut warehouse got slashed. Our dinners got simpler, never mind the food pyramid. Your father did everything he could, a house-painting job here, some landscaping there, a couple days bent over at a friend's farm. I picked up a few nights at Wipeouts Grill. We came home with backs splintered with pain, aching legs, and blood-drumming foreheads, and we'd pass each other and hand you kids off while one person's shift ended and the other's began. But those shifts were less and less on the calendar, until suddenly we were at home using the calculator to find out how much time we really had.

"We can't do this," your father said to me. It was late in the evening, after you all were asleep. Dogs were barking down the road, but the sound was soft and we were used to it. The gold light from our desk lamp made our skin look honey-coated. Your father's eyes were wet. He wouldn't look straight at me, and I realized I hadn't heard a joke from him in so long. That was when I was really afraid.

"How much?" I asked.

"Maybe two months until trouble," he said.

"And then what?" I asked, although I knew the answer.

"I gonna call Royce," he said. "We been talking."

"Royce lives on O'ahu," I said. "That's five plane tickets. That's a whole different island, a *city*. Cities aren't cheap." But your father was already standing up and walking toward the bathroom. The light went on, and the fan, then the water hissing and spattering in the sink, the wet sucking and spraying of his breaths as he washed his face.

I wanted to break something, it was so still and quiet. Your father came back in the bedroom.

"So I think," he said, "I'm gonna sell my body. The mahus get my okole and the ladies get my boto. I'd do that for us."

"I'd do that for *you*," he followed, after pausing a moment.

He had his shirt off and was looking at himself in our long mirror. "I mean, check 'um, yeah? All the sex waiting in this body."

I giggled and hugged him from behind. I spread my hands over each pectoral and ignored the way they were starting to sag a little toward bitch tits. "I'd probably pay money for these," I said.

"How much?" Your father grinned in the mirror.

"Well," I said, "what's included?" I let my left hand drift down, worked it into his waistband.

"Depends," he said.

"Mmmm," I said. "What I'm feeling's probably worth two or three dollars."

"Hey!" He pulled my hand out.

"I'd be paying by the minute," I said, shrugging my shoulders, and your father snorted. But then he paused.

"We're going to have to sell more than my dick," he said.

We both sat down on the edge of the bed.

"We've got Kaui and Nainoa wearing Dean's old clothes," I said. "They get free school lunch."

"I know."

"What did we have for dinner last night?" I asked.

"Saimin and Spam."

"What did we have for dinner the night before?"

"Rice and Spam."

Your father stood back up. He walked to our desk and leaned down on it, placed his palms on it like he was going to push it this way or that.

"Fifteen dollars," he said.

He stood, sighed, laid his palm on the dresser. "Twenty-five dollars."

"Forty," I said.

"Twenty." He shook his head.

He went this way, touching each thing he could see: a seven-dollar lamp, a two-dollar picture frame, a closet full of five-dollar clothes, the sum of our lives not more than four digits.

AND I WAS never good at math but I could see the other end of this and there were dark lights and payment plans and bucket showers on the other side. So three days after those calculations we got you kids to school and I was at the roadside, hitchhiking with your father's hunting knife in my bag, getting forty miles to Hilo on no cost just to walk in the sweaty rain to the Section Eight division of County of Hawai'i and start our application. "What brings you here today?" the woman at the counter asked, not unfriendly, and with her dark and freckled arms, the extra folds of skin outside her sleeveless blouse, she could have been my sister, was my sister.

"What brings me here," I repeated. If I had the answer I wouldn't have been standing there, steaming Hilo wet, begging for the housing vouchers.

AND THAT WAS how we were when the third sign came. We couldn't cut any more corners. But Royce had come through, as simple as a phone call to your father and a phrase, "I think I got something for you, cuz," and suddenly everything pointed to O'ahu. We'd sold some of our stuff and then we sold more, roadsiding it in Waimea, by the playground, across the street from the Catholic church, where all the trees grow up over the parking strips and everyone has to drive past if they're headed to the beach. We'd made enough from those sales, the food bank's help, and Section Eight to get a cushion, enough for five tickets to O'ahu with something still in the bank.

Your father had a plan for the rest of the money—a glass-bottom boat cruise on the Kona coast. I remember telling him no, we couldn't do that, we needed to save every last penny for O'ahu. But he'd asked what kind of father would he be if he couldn't give his children relief?

"They deserve more than they get," he said, I still remember this, "and we gotta remind them that things is gonna get better."

"But we don't need some tourist cruise," I said. "We're not that kind of family."

"Well," he said, "maybe just once I wanna *be* that kind of family."

I had nothing to say to that.

So Kailua-Kona, Ali'i Drive, small stone walls and swerving sidewalks fronting the scoops of sugary beach and luminous ocean, then all the little storefront tourist traps, leading back like breadcrumbs to the beach hotels. Your father and I stood at the Kona dock, each holding a ticket for the boat ride, plus one for each of you kids, and we watched the tides surge and all the clean glossy boats rock and dip and shine slick with each swell. The pier was long and blacktopped and spined with fishing poles, and halfway along the dock's edge a group of local boys were pitching themselves off, into the water, over and over, exploding into the ocean-froth of the boy who'd jumped before, *chee-hoo*'ing and slapping their wet feet across the wood steps back to the edge.

Then we were out away from the dock of Kona, sitting in a plush jointed couch on the *Hawaiian Adventure*, a trimaran like the types we always see drifting in the haze of the Kona coast, especially at sunset, boats with slides off the back and lobster-colored tourists jabbering on the covered decks. But this one had a middle hull with thick glass in the bottom that let us look down into the ocean, and as the engines pushed a mellow vibration again and again across the deck, the water went from something green-blue to a deep, almost purple color, and the coral grew up thick and knotted, in sections stuck out fingers or bloomed brains and the spiked red fans of sea anemones, swaying like the tide was a wind. I could smell the sun, the way it heated the old sea salt on the edges of the boat, and the sharp too-sweet fruity Malolo syrup in the fruit punch, and the sting of diesel fuels belching from the grinding engines.

Mostly we sat inside, all five of us in a row right down front in the plush stadium seating, looking through the glass bottom, me telling stories about which animal was which god, how they saved or fought the first Hawaiians, your father cracking jokes about how his Filipino forefathers only eat dogfish or the black fish with long noses, and the sun slanted in under the ceiling and the motor kept churning its hum up through our seats. I was somewhere warm and slow and Kaui was asleep in my arms when I woke without knowing why.

You and Dean and your father were gone, in fact no one was in the viewing cabin. Voices were rising out on the deck. I shifted Kaui from my lap—she complained—and I stood. The voices were clipped into basic commands: We're going to make a turn, keep pointing, get the preserver. I remember feeling like the sounds were coming from the other side of a cavern, so far away and cotton-stuffed in my head.

I grabbed Kaui's hand. She was still rubbing her eyes and complaining, but I was already bringing her with me as I climbed the stairs from the viewing cabin to the sundeck. Impossibly white. I had to shade my eyes and squint so hard I felt my lips and gums lift. People were gathered along the cabled rail of the slick white deck, looking into the ocean. Pointing.

I remember seeing your father and Dean. They were maybe thirty feet away from me and Kaui, and I was confused because your father was wrestling Dean back from the rail and Dean was screaming *Let go*, and *I can get him*. One of the deckhands in a white polo shirt and baseball hat pitched a red life preserver into the air, and it wobbled and wheeled out into the sky with the rope whipping behind.

Did I run then to your father? Had he pulled Dean off the rail? Was I gripping Kaui's hand so hard it hurt her? I can assume, but I can't remember. I only remember that I was at your father's side then on the blazing-white deck, rising and falling with the waves, and all our family was there, except for you.

Your head was bobbing like a coconut in the ocean. You were getting smaller and farther away and the water was hissing and spanking the boat. I don't remember anyone saying much of anything, except the captain, calling out from upstairs: "Just keep pointing. We're turning. Just keep pointing."

Your head went under and the ocean was flat and clean again.

There was a song playing from the speakers. A tinny, stupid-sweet Hawaiian cover of "More Than Words," which I still can't listen to, even though I liked it once. The engines churned. The captain was talking from the wheel upstairs, asking Terry to keep pointing. Terry was the one who'd thrown the life preserver that was floating empty in the waves, moving away from where I'd seen your head.

I was tired of being told to point, being told to wait, so I said something to Terry. He made a face. Then his mouth was moving under his mustache, words back at me. And the captain was calling again from above. Your father started in, too, all four of us saying things. I think I finished talking with something that made Terry start, so that his face flushed around his sunglasses. I saw myself in those mirrored lenses, me darker than I thought I was, which I remember made me happy, and my shoulders from basketball, and that I'd stopped squinting my eyes. Then my feet were up on the railing and Terry's eyebrows were raised and he started to open his mouth at me. He reached for me—I think your father did, too—but I leapt into the big empty ocean.

I hadn't been swimming long when the sharks passed under me. I remember them first as dark blurs, that the water told me the weight of those animals, a shove of wake against my legs and belly. They passed me and all four of their fins punched the surface, knives on the summit of dark swells, cutting for you. When they reached where your head had been, the sharks dove under. I started to swim after them but the distance might as well have been to Japan. I dunked once to try and see. Underwater there was nothing but a vague darkness and froth where the sharks were. Other dark colors. Pink and chummy ropes rising from the froth—I knew those would be next.

I didn't have any more breath. I broke the surface and choked in oxygen. If there were sounds, if I yelled, if the boat was closer, I don't remember. I went back down. The water where you were was all churn. The shapes of the sharks were thrashing, diving, rising, something like a dance.

The next time I went for air you were at the surface, sideways, prone and ragdolling in the mouth of a shark. But the shark was holding you gently, do you understand? It was holding you like you were made of glass, like you were its child. They brought you straight at me, the shark that was holding you carrying its head up, out of the water, like a dog. The faces of those things—

I won't lie. I shut my eyes as they neared, when I was sure they were coming for me, too, and if everyone was yelling and crying out, as I imagine they were, and if I was thinking anything, I don't remember any of that except the black of my closed eyes and my prayers without a mouth.

The sharks never hit. They passed again below, around me, wake like a strong wind. And then I opened my eyes. You were there at the boat, clutched to a life preserver. Your father reaching down for you—I remember how angry I was at how slow he went, all the time in the world, and I wanted to say, *Are you a fucking pau hana county worker? Grab our child, our alive child*—and you were coughing, which meant you were breathing, and there was no red cloud in the water.

This wasn't just one of those things.

Oh my son. Now we know that none of it was. And this was when I started to believe.

# 2

# NAINOA, 2000

## *Kalihi*

HEAR THE BLOOD HUSH, THEN RUSH, THE THUD OF IT coming along my knuckles. Cracked knuckles, swollen knuckles, bloody knuckles. Bloody knuckles used to hit and hurt, not because I wanted to but because my brother made me. This was New Year's, Black Cat Crackers up and down the cul-de-sac, *pop pop pop*, whole families in green plastic chairs in their driveways, sidewalks smooched with char and red shreds of paper. The fireworks were going and Skyler and James went behind the garage to play Bloody Knuckles with Dean, and since Dean went, I went, and since I went, Kaui went.

Years already I'd been trying to understand what was inside

me, while the rest of the world was trying to tear it out. Especially my brother sometimes. This was one of those nights where he hated me.

Skyler, James, both of them hapa Japanese, tall and round stinking teenagers. James with his braces, glittering and spitty. Skyler with his floppy hair and cheekfields of pimples. Both with their prep-style clothes, all Polo and Abercrombie. And there was my brother with his jaw-length twizzles of hair, baggy Billabongs and too-small Locals Only T-shirt, surfer-dark skin and pursed thick lips. So obvious we didn't belong, but Dean was always trying to trade up: him and Skyler and James, their knuckles already blistered with blood, laughing and shaking the pain out of their hands.

"Miracle boy's turn," James said through his braces, nodding at me.

"Fully," Skyler agreed, "I think so, yeah, Dean?"

All night my brother had been one-upping them both, James and Skyler. My brother running faster, swearing dirtier, the only one quick enough to cockroach a beer from the adults' cooler. So cool, all for James and Skyler, since their families had glossy SUVs and heavy dark furniture in their high-ceiling houses, everything Dean wanted to be. But how could he get there, I bet he wondered, besides getting rich boys close enough that maybe he could absorb some of whatever they were that we weren't.

And me and my brother both knew I was the only one that had done anything for us anyway, because of the sharks, what came after. We'd been on the news and in the papers and every time Mom and Dad had been talking about how poor we were. So then we were getting donation checks and clothing drives and even free food some places, from everyone that had seen and heard the stories Mom and Dad kept telling, how I was lucky to survive the attack but we were so broke that groceries and rent and bills were going to kill us instead.

And even after the letters and donations, things didn't stop. I talked about the sharks in my Kahena Academy application, the selection committee had probably heard of me, too. So I got into the best prep school in the state—a full scholarship, the same as it was for all Native Hawaiians—even if the school was full of kids far beyond what James and Skyler were.

And my family, especially Dean, could see all the other things happening to me, that I was getting smarter, quickly, that it might as well be magic how my brain was vaulting me past my classmates. And the 'ukulele, too—the songs I could play—*He's some kind of prodigy*, the teachers were saying, and Mom and Dad like the sun when teachers talked about me. They'd started to say I was something special. Even right where Dean and Kaui could hear.

All that happening and my brother here with James and Skyler, then me. They all knew what they'd heard.

"So what, Dean," Skyler said, "I get a turn with him or what?"

Dean stared at me, started to smile, but I swear underneath I saw a flinch, maybe he didn't want it to go all the way, he was still after all my brother. But then the grin spread. "Everyone gotta take a turn, Noa," he said.

Illegal aerials—the type of red and blue and gold explosions only hotels were supposed to launch—boomed in the black above us, tossing our shadows against the stucco walls of Skyler's mansion.

"You've got a hundred pounds on me, easy," I said to Skyler. Like that would help, like anything would help.

"No be like that," James said. "Fairy."

"Get some bloody knuckles," Skyler said, stepping closer,

punching hand still twitching. He aimed it at me, made a fist, the clench was slow and stiff and I could see the flaps of skin on his knucklebones, the bits of blood. Around the corner came the murmur of the party, the sparkling crash of beer bottles piling up, then the firecrackers, *pop pop pop*.

"Cut it out," Kaui said, her voice smaller than all of us, she actually put her hands on her hips. We all froze, every boy, we'd forgotten about her, standing at my side, little sister three years under me.

I looked at Dean again, I wish I hadn't; it shames me now to remember it. How I was thinking he might still step in, say it was a joke, of course a teenager with the body of a man shouldn't be pounding on a middle-schooler.

"Come on, mahu," Skyler said to me. "What, first time punching? Hold your hand up."

I raised my fist. Dean leaned back lazy on the wall, crossed his arms.

Kaui said, "Noa, don't."

"Go away," I said to her. "It's between us."

Skyler put his fist up. Six inches from mine. Our knuckles: his already chewed with punches, mine all smooth and thin, even I saw the ending. Then Skyler moved to punch me; I flinched. "No flinching," he said, punched my shoulder with his other fist, soon there would be a bruise like the day after immunization. "We gotta go again," he said.

So we did, set our fists in the air facing each other. I tried to make my wrist lock, tried to think of what I could be that wouldn't break or bend, statue or train or rock wall, but then he punched into my knuckles. There was a bony slapping sound.

Pain shot to my elbow, I yelped, Skyler hooted. "Gotta go one more time if you cry like that, pussy."

I looked at Dean again, but he made like he was only watching the fireworks, burning in the air above.

"He not gonna save you," James said. "It's big-boy time, sack up, bitch."

My teeth were clenching so hard my whole jaw was a balloon of hurt, something like my knuckles were, don't cry don't cry don't cry. "All you retards can do is punch," I said. "You'll be praying for McDonald's jobs while I'm graduating from Kahena."

James's feet shifted in the grass, I heard the hiss and crackle. "You guys hear this smart-ass?" James said to Skyler. "Maybe we both get a turn for the second round."

"No," Skyler said. "Only me."

My hand was shaking then, all my fingers and my palm whumping with my pulse, but I closed the fingers, felt the pain stretch and burn across my bones. I put my fist six inches from Skyler's again. He punched, harder, like a heavy door slamming closed, my hand still in the doorjamb. An explosion in my hand bones so big it blew through my eyes, everything white for a second, I fell back on my ass in the dirt. When I landed I made an awful wet crying sound, like a puppy.

James and Skyler both laughing, Skyler flapping his punching hand, and out front on the lawn someone must have told a good joke, because all the adults were laughing, right at the same time.

Kaui moved in front of me. "Cut it out, botos," she said.

"What?" James laughed again. "Wait, what?"

"I said enough," Kaui said.

"Maybe it's your turn, then, yeah?" James said to her. "You and me."

Dean stood up from his lean. "James, no be stupid," he said, his pidgin dialed up since he wasn't with Mom and Dad.

"Do it," Kaui said to James.

"Both of you shut up," Dean said.

"Too late," Kaui said. Then to James, "Do it, scaredy cat."

"Watch your mouth," James said.

"You gonna watch it for me?" Kaui said, all ten years old of her. "Do it, pussy." She put her fist out, just as mine had been, her hand so much smaller and rounder, there almost weren't any knuckles.

James set his fist in the air, six inches from hers.

Kaui's face like something carved from koa, little brown sister, bushy hair pigtailed. I didn't know what to say—part of me wanted her to try it, because she was always thinking she could keep up with me and Dean, even though she was five years younger than him and three years younger than me, she should know her place . . . and then part of me didn't want her to try it, because I knew the only way it could feel when it was over.

"Kaui," Dean said.

"Do it," Kaui said to James. She kept her fist out.

James shrugged, locked his arm, pointed his fist at hers. He twitched a fake at Kaui, she didn't flinch. He shifted his weight and threw a punch from his shoulder, but when his fist met hers it wasn't a fist, he opened his hand and grabbed her wrist, laughed. Patted her hand. "Come on, I not going hit a girl, specially not Dean's sister."

Dean laughed, too, he knew he had won, James and Skyler liked him enough, probably because of what he let them do to me. I chose it, I wanted to say. I matter, not you. But the three of them shifted their positions, just a bit closer to each other, me and Kaui outside their loose circle.

"Go," Dean said, waving us away like bees at a picnic. They were all three laughing. I turned, I walked away through the trimmed bright grass, I heard Skyler's voice, dimming—"I got some fireworks," he said—and then I was out of earshot.

"I hate that stupid game," came Kaui's voice next to me, and I jumped a little.

"I didn't know you were there," I said.

"Well, I am," Kaui said.

"You shouldn't have come back there," I said.

"Why not?"

If there was one thing Dean and I agreed on, it was that no one got to hurt Kaui but us. That was what it meant to be her brothers, but I knew what Kaui would say if I explained it that way, so I didn't. Instead I said, "You got off lucky, they didn't hit you. It used to be like that for me, too."

We'd made it back to the sidewalk, two houses down, Uncle Royce's party. Skyler and his family would have hated it here— which is why they'd gone to another party up the street the other way—people here were just in jeans and T-shirts, camo board shorts, the tarry smell of cigarettes, no decorations, beer in cans from half-gutted cardboard boxes. Then another rolling pop of firecrackers.

"If you're tired of everyone picking on you, maybe don't be such a smart-ass all the time," Kaui said.

"You know," I said, "just because you learned a few swear words, that doesn't make you grown-up."

"Whatever," she said. "Bet they'd still be wrecking you if I didn't step in."

"Doesn't matter," I said.

"Things like that with Dean," she said, "it's almost like you *want* to get beat up."

She was right, that's exactly what it was, but how could I tell her? She didn't know, no one knew, how after the sharks I could feel Mom and Dad holding their breath so hard it was almost like they were holding mine, they talked about the 'aumakua, how me having been blessed by the spirits, chosen, meant something. Already I was lucky for them, had brought them things, the donations they got from my story that made our move to O'ahu so much easier, certificates and awards from Kahena Academy, shaka respect from every local that heard the shark story and felt the old gods in it, everything, it was me.

Dean saw it. And he heard, too, from Mom and Dad, could I be the new Hawaiian scientist, or some senator, or the whole renaissance. We all heard, and there were things growing in me that made me believe I could turn into those dreams.

Still I shrugged at what Kaui said. "He's always mad at me. I figure maybe if I just let him get in a few good lickens he'll get over it."

She snorted. "Dean's not so good at that."

"At what?"

"Getting over things."

Then there was an awful whimper, a human sound you just know is bad, me and Kaui both stopped talking. We saw Dean, dark skin shirtless, walking slow toward us on the sidewalk from behind Skyler's house; Skyler was with him, their shoulders bumping. My brother had used his shirt to wrap Skyler's hand and now cradled it. I noticed a new, black smell, almost like after firecrackers, burned paper, but more sweet and smoky, grilled pig maybe. And Skyler had his eyes clamped shut, tears squeezing out in between, him whimpering, my brother telling him that everything was going to be all right, James behind them looking sick.

All the parents and the party shut up.

Dean said, "He tried to let go but the fuse was too short." Skyler was shivering like a horse coming up out of a river.

Dean whispered something to Skyler, Skyler shook his head. But anyway Dean started to pull the cloth back and showed us something like a hand, three fingers that wiggled white, two others that didn't, there were yellow chunks and shreds of skin, then splinters of bone gone gray in the light. The sweet pork smell blew again across our noses. People hissed and turned away.

Then voices came up again, loud and urgent, someone's keys jingling, while I stepped forward and touched Skyler's hand, I didn't know what I was doing, even Dean asked me that, *What are you doing*, but I didn't answer because there was too much in me to speak: I felt the prickly growth of the grass in the lawns all around, as if it was my skin, the beat of the night-bird wings as if I was the one flying, the creaking suck of the trees breathing in the firework air as if the leaves were my own lungs, the drum of the hearts of everyone at the party.

I touched Skyler's hand, my fingers traced the splinters of bone and shreds of skin. And in the space between our hands, something pulled, like magnets, and there was a warmth. But Skyler's dad arrived, pushed me back, and closed the shirt over his son's hand—it was better already, I swear, the skin closing back, the bones stitching themselves, I saw it was better—and suddenly my head felt fizzy, filled with helium, like after running too fast for too long. I stepped away, I tried to lean against the folding table with the mac salad and musubi, but my hand missed the tabletop, touched only air, I ended up on the ground, on my ass, for the second time that night.

From there I watched as two fathers took Skyler into a truck, the square sound of the doors closing, the chatter and roar of the engine starting, and, somewhere more distant, *pop pop pop*.

Kaui nudging my shoulder. "Wake up," she said, and she said

it again and again until I did. Who knew how long it had been. "What did you do?"

I wanted to say, but my eyelids were heavy, trying to make my mouth muscles open was like trying to open a refrigerator with a slug. I didn't know what I had done, exactly. Only that there was a feeling from Skyler's hand, a feeling of wanting to correct itself, and I was part of that feeling, made it larger, if only for a minute.

Dean arrived, looking down on us. "We gotta go."

I could see something burning there behind his eyes. Scared and angry and shamed. This was when it really started, wasn't it. "Sorry," I said, hoping that would be enough, this time, and I think I was also saying it for everything since the sharks had first saved me.

"Sorry for what," he said. "Not like you was the one grabbing a firework you couldn't handle."

I shrugged. "I know. But still."

"But what, you thought you was going fix his hand or something, when you touched it?" Dean smirked and shook his head. "You didn't do nothing."

Mom and Dad were calling to us from across the street. "We gotta go," Dean said.

We got in our dented blue Jeep Cherokee, me and Kaui and Dean in the back, Mom driving us home because Dad was four beers deep and, he said, didn't want us to see him fondle a cop to get out of a DUI. His palm on Mom's thigh and her fingers laced between. Headlights going past us the other way as we came down from Aiea, Dean looking out his side window and every now and then taking deep blowing breaths, all the signs and buildings along the H1. He looked even older, just since we'd got in the car, and I bet I did, too. Neither of us like the

Dean and Noa from Big Island, before the sharks: I remembered us sprinting through Hapuna Beach big-wave advisories, surf booming to our knees, then our chests, we'd dive right under the foaming whitewater. We'd feel the rip pull us sideways along the beach, see who could get deeper under each wave, let the sucking current of the coming set drag us along, the grains of sand gathering and bouncing over our spines, and we'd feel the water start to bend and stand up, tugging on our board shorts, and when the wave crested and tossed its full force directly on top of us, we'd push deep and open our eyes and grin at the yawning curl of gold sand and blue ocean that couldn't touch us. Underwater Dean's eyes were as I think mine were, squinted with joy, and the air rushed from our noses and mouths in silver ropes as we swam back toward the surface, where we'd high-five at our bravery, at what we could beat. Now we were in the Jeep, coming home, Kaui in between us, both boys and our Bloody Knuckles hands, driving toward whatever would come next, while part of me kept checking the rearview mirror for what we were leaving behind.

# 3

# KAUI, 2001

## *Kalihi*

OKAY, SO, THAT WHOLE YEAR. IT WAS LIKE LIVING ON the edge of legend again, just like after the sharks, only bigger. Another numb-nuts boy blows his hand off playing with fire-crackers like every other New Year's. Only this one doesn't end the same way. Blessing said that Keahi said that Skyler-them went to the emergency room that night. And the doctors un-wrapped Skyler's New Year's hand explosion. Wiped away the blood, right, and underneath was nothing but clean strong skin. His hand like it had never played with fire.

Oh, man. You can imagine, if Keahi was telling Blessing, then people knew about it all the way in, like, Saudi Arabia. Old news. Keahi'd talk about the invention of the wheel like it was hot rumor.

But the arrivals were slow. Something about the news stayed quiet. Neighbors came every now and then. Steady but slow. Some local auntie with her just-woke hairstyle, two-year-old son riding her hip, the son with diabetes, and her saying, We heard some things about Nainoa. And can he help. Or the man who came another time, hapa Korean I think, a size-small shirt stretched over a size-large chest, rubbing his arm, saying stage four had spread all the way to his toes. And can your son help.

Those first times I don't think Mom knew what to do, she just listened. Eyebrows all crinkled up with sad and let in who-ever was talking, went to find Noa in his and Dean's room. Then the person would go in there with Mom, but soon enough she came back out.

"He said he could only do it alone," she said that first time.

Later the person would come back out. I don't know what Noa did but I know when people left they were practically reg-gae skanking. Every step a rubber-band bounce. Plus their eyes easy, not like before. So he was fixing something.

And so of course people kept coming. Slow but steady. Never a crowd.

One time I saw this: A grown-up lady, talking about early-stage this or that, when she got ready to leave after her visit, she stopped at the kitchen. Where Mom was. Handed her all this cash. I thought Mom would be surprised, like "I can't possibly take this from you." But no way. She nodded and took it so easy, like she was checking out a grocery shopper at J. Yamamoto.

Me and Dean and Noa aren't stupid, we knew there was al-ways stuff Mom and Dad owed. Phone calls all the time where they were negotiating everything from credit cards to the house.

It became like a prayer at our house, Our Father who art in debt collection, hallowed be thy pay. When I was in, like, fourth grade, I thought everyone had rent parties. Until I was talking about it at school and the teacher got all wet-eyed. Asked me some things after class.

Do you need help is what she asked, with this sad-serious face. Is everything okay in your family.

And I said, "But you're a teacher."

She said, "Now, what does that mean."

And I was like, "You're a *teacher*. What are you going to do, split your food stamps with us?"

But now, with people showing up to see Noa, it's no more Ross Dress for Less at our house. We've even had, like, a family trip to Pearlridge. All of us got to pick out a few things from Gap and Foot Locker. We've had a few good ahi dinners at home, too.

I GUESS MOM let everyone know that we had a family life, they couldn't just visit whenever they wanted. And, seriously, people *listened*. It was definitely a *Lucky you live Hawai'i* moment: no one ever came around after dinnertime, or even just before, just Mom and Dad at the table running their numbers, envelope of cash. Then Dean coming back from his pickup games at the court, announcing himself with the *tamp tamp* of his basketball on the sidewalk, the beat of the ball like probably he was inside, bouncing with jealousy.

Came a night like that when I went to Noa's room. This was maybe four months after people had started coming to see him. He was lying there on his bed, arms limp and hanging. Staring at the ceiling and breathing slow.

"Hey," I said.

He nodded his head. That was all.

"You okay?" I asked. He rolled over away from me, toward the wall. Which pissed me off. Because it was obvious he wasn't okay, but no one else seemed like they were asking. And it was obvious he wanted to be asked, and here I was. "Whatever, then," I said, and started to close the door. Only he said something. Of course. Just as the door was about to close.

"What?" I asked. I came back inside the room. All basketball posters and rap stars on Dean's side, robots and sword dudes clutched by big-chee-chee princesses on Noa's side. "You wouldn't understand if I told you," he said.

I should have slapped him. "Sorry if the new King Kamehameha doesn't have time to talk to one of the villagers," I said.

"What do you mean?" he asked.

"You're the king," I said. "You tell me."

"I didn't ask for this," he said, and sat up. Made it seem like getting up took all this effort. "What do you know, anyway? You don't know what it's like. None of you do."

Oh, brother. It was like he didn't understand how he sounded. "I know you've been going around with your nose in the air like me and Dean don't even live here," I said. Which was true. Like Mom and Dad didn't even ask him to do chores, because he *needed rest*. There'd be times where just him and Mom would go off on a drive to *talk about things*, only it would also be dinnertime, and so me and Dean would get "treated" to Dad's Hamburger Helper special. While Noa and Mom come back smelling like Rainbow Drive-In or Leonard's Bakery, I swear.

"There are—" Noa started. "It's my head. I have all these things inside, they won't stop."

"Like what?"

He asked me did I know how we were living.

I said I did: Mom and Dad were busting their asses, but we were at least better than we were on the Big Island, after the sugarcane plantation shut down. And obviously whatever he was doing now was getting us money, too.

Noa rubbed his face. Hard. Like there was something there he couldn't get off. "See, that's what I mean, you don't understand. 'We' doesn't mean you and me and Mom and Dad. 'We' means Hawai'i. Maybe even more than Hawai'i."

"Okay," I said. "What does that have to do with you?"

"I'm trying to figure that out." He shrugged. "I think I'm supposed to fix it. That's what all this is for."

I squeezed my hands open and closed. Open and closed. "What, only you?" I asked.

He was quiet then. I could see that he was ragged, run wet like the horses back in Waipi'o Valley, the ones we used to ride that I can only remember by their smell and their feeling. The whole land coming up through their galloping muscles. That was what they were supposed to do: run. But when they ran for long enough they got just empty and blown out, right? Couldn't even do the one thing they were supposed to. "Yeah," he said. "Only me."

And okay, so he was tired. It was hard, because I felt sorry for him, but he was doing that thing where he wanted me to feel like it was my fault—that he was feeling the way he was, and that I couldn't fix it, and that he was special—all of it my fault. He did that feeling to people a lot, I think. And it worked, mostly, even on me. Except that time it didn't, because all I could hear was what he thought of me and Dean: nothing. Because he thought he was special.

Part of me believed him. But part of me didn't. I left his room like a whipped junkyard poi dog. The feet that were moving my body didn't feel like my own. My hand that touched the knob was not my own. Maybe he would be exactly what Mom and Dad thought, Hawaiian Superman. Fix the islands and protect our family. It didn't matter. There was no space there for me.

Back in my room, on my desk, pre-algebra and life sciences and English in a stack. It wasn't the only thing I wanted to do, but it was the first thing I saw. I could get B-pluses just by farting. Not good enough, not anymore.

I started my work.

TURNS OUT I WASN'T the only one thinking that way, right? Something had changed in Dean after New Year's, but especially after people started coming around for Noa. Most days Dean would be home just to drop off his backpack, swap his clothes, then he'd be out beating his basketball on the sidewalk, the sound fading away as he went to the court. Sometimes I'd sneak down there, too, follow way behind. On the court he'd be going at high school seniors, guys in college home on break. Him with the basketball bouncing and rocking and shooting under his hand. His dancing knees. He'd take the ball and drive right at their chests, like a bull in a ring, like the pictures I saw of Spain in the summer: browns and reds and knives in the sunlight. I bet everyone else at the park thought he was just a hothead, but I knew what he was really charging at.

He was already good on the court. He got better.

My grades were already solid at school. I got better. Plenty people would probably say I should be happy enough just to be at Kahena Academy. But, okay, it wasn't enough. Noa was there already. Ahead of me in all the halls and stairways. On the fields and in the textbooks. Everywhere I entered, a breath later, I was *Nainoa's sister, the shark one, they say he can do crazy things.*

And I could bring home another perfect score on a test and Mom and Dad would smile, rub my back. But I could see in their eyes it wasn't the same as when Noa came out of his room, finished taking people for the day. They practically fell over the tables trying to get to him. To touch him and coo and bring him water and snacks before dinner.

I figured it didn't matter what Dean or me did, then. Turns out I was wrong. By the start of the full school basketball season, Dean was so good he was getting his own sentences, nothing about Noa. "Division One potential" and "guaranteed all-state." And suddenly the whole family started getting dragged to his high school games. I hated basketball. ("I told you to get ready," Mom would say, coming into my tiny room, seeing me still on the bed with my books, in my boro-boro clothes. I would say, "He has games like twice a week." Mom would say, "This is your brother," like it explained anything. Like I was stupid. I would ugh and ask, "How long is basketball season? I should get extra days to hang out at Crisha's house for every day I have to go to his stupid games." Mom would say, "Kaui," and shake her head, "act right.") Then sitting up in the woodchip-and-popcorn-smelling upper rafters with the squawking, hoop-earring platform-wedge girls. All that heat from the lights and our butts on the sticky planks of seats, while down on the wood court sweaty boys panted around each other and watched a little ball fall into a little hoop. The horn going off for time-outs or whatever. Grown men with serious faces hollering at teenagers. And each other.

Noa got into it at the games, too, yelling until his voice was sawed apart, jumping and bumping Mom and Dad. I think Noa just wanted things to be how they were before, when him and Dean and me used to get knotted up in the worst wrestling battles you could imagine, us all elbows and sock-stink, trying for arm bars and rear-naked chokes. Angry and laughing at the same time, hurting each other enough you know it could only be love. Back when the sharks were almost just a story and everything looked like it would stay tight. I bet Noa thought if he cheered hard enough he could get that back.

And Mom and Dad, too: I saw. Full of yelling, excitement. They had ideas for Dean the same way they had ideas for Noa. So, yeah: Nainoa was *becoming* and Dean was *becoming* and I was invisible besides. But I was still *becoming*, too. I was. Okay, no one saw but that doesn't matter. There were all sorts of things inside me (like, when we had to build bridges out of toothpicks as a school project, I stole two extra boxes of toothpicks from the school, researched about truss and span design, built a bridge that could hold two more bricks than anyone else's . . . or when we had the school survivalist competition, and I figured out how to turn the tarp into a small tent and guessed at how a shirt could be used to filter water, I was the one that survived the longest from my class . . . every project like that, I could feel things in me growing strong and steady), and I felt like more and more I could do whatever I wanted. If I wanted it bad enough.

BUT OH, MAN. Then things started to unlock themselves. This one day, another basketball game. Dean had made the varsity team and it was preseason or something. Us back up in the stands and the clock just barely starting to tick down toward halftime and all I was thinking was, If I have to stand up here and clap for one more hour.

"I'm going to the bathroom," I told Mom. She hardly even looked my way. Which was perfect, right, because it meant I had plenty of time, and once I was out of sight of the court and down the hall toward the bathrooms I just kept going. To the fire escape and the old-brown-paint steel door that creaked me outside. Far on the other side of the parking lot, a cigarette tip danced orange. A little light laughter.

But then there was something else. Chanting. It was faint, and I turned around and around to try and catch the direction. It was a woman's voice and there were runs of choppy speaking that started almost like a yelp but then her sounds were more punchy as she said short sentences. Then, at the end of some of the chanted lines, there would be a long-held note, a song and a gut-cry at the same time. It echoed and echoed. It was across the street, what looked like the cafeteria. Cream-colored paint over thick brick and blocky columns. Groaning metal doors propped open against the thick air.

I stopped just outside the edge of the spilling light, where no one could see me. The cafeteria floor wobbled with the reflection of overhead lights. All the chairs and tables were pushed back to the walls. There was a line of three older women, sitting cross-legged on blankets with their hourglass-shaped ipus, right, thumping them against the ground. Slapping and rolling their knuckles and palms across the hollow shells. And in the middle of the room there were three rows of girls—all older than me, it looked like—dancing hula.

Just ordinary girls in ordinary clothes. I had heard hula chants already before. But this was different somehow. I could feel something true and old in it, something that was opening all over me, gave me chicken skin.

I stood just outside the door and watched the whole practice. Sometimes the kumus would stop their ipus and the song and then holler out things like, "Nani, you gotta fix your hela, it's way off from everyone else," or, "Jessie, your arms is limp on the kaholo," and then the song would start over. Three lines of girls, stepping and turning and bouncing. The ipus thumping and finger tapping and the women chanting their song. It got inside me, okay? Deep down. Got me all twisted with something I didn't know the name of. It went that way and I watched until, behind me, there was the final countdown of the basketball clock. I heard the crowing from the stands and turned, started to walk back down to the gym. Dean and another win, I figured, but it sounded like the game was close. Like maybe everything was unsure, right until the end.

I DIDN'T HAVE much time to think about it right away, though. What happened was the next day a man turned up at our house. It started with him pounding a fist on the door. Noa was in his room but for sure he heard.

Dad was the one to open the door. The man came pouring in, almost landing on his face.

"Where is he?" the man asked. His whole body was moving. Eyes blinking. Him turning his head toward his shoulder and doing this weird dance-shrug. His hands all butterflies, flapping open and closed at his sides. It was like he was getting gently electrocuted.

"I gotta see him," the man said.

"Yeah, no." Dad crossed his arms so the guy could see the cables of muscle. Dad is, like, surprise strong, usually looks all like a doughy dad body, until he does things like that.

"It's not getting better," the man said. Then he realized he knew where Noa was, started to walk toward Noa and Dean's bedroom door. Dad put a palm against his chest. The man didn't even try to push it off. Just leaned into the hand, like it was a strong wind he could push through if he just kept going. But his body was still doing that same electric wiggle and shake, and Dad's hand stopped his steps.

"Come out," he called then. He yelled it toward Noa's door: *Come out, come out, come out.* Until spit frosted the sides of his mouth.

Dad started to wrestle the man back. To the same door he came in. But, okay, just like that, the man and Dad both stopped their surges. Separated and stared down the hall.

Noa had come out and was standing there. A bald Korean woman with no eyebrows and her face all stretched tight was standing next to him.

"You shouldn't—" the man started. He raised his palms, still shaking. "You didn't stop nothing, see? It's still coming."

He tried to take another step toward Noa, but Dad grabbed him again. "I'm already dead," he said. "Do you understand?"

He shook Dad off him. Then he left, screen door slapping on its hinges. Yelling from outside until his hoarse voice disappeared.

Dad was still in the exact same position. One hand halfway up like he was going to make a point. Or defend himself. Anything. He let his hand fall down. "Maybe we take a break, a little bit," Dad said. Mom was there, too.

But the part that mattered most was what came later. When Dean came home and heard the story. He went into his and Noa's room and closed the door after and of course I went and listened, the cool sludge of the old door paint the only thing between me and my brothers.

". . . I could call up Jaycee-them, we could go wreck this guy," Dean offered.

"What is this, the Hawaiian Mafia?" Noa said.

"Just saying," Dean said.

"No," Noa said. "He has Parkinson's."

"Don't matter if he's got, like, Rolexes," Dean said. "He can't come in here—"

"It's a neurological disorder," Noa said.

"You fucking punk," Dean said. "Even when I'm trying for help, you gotta go and be a dictionary."

"Sorry," Noa said.

They got closer to the door. How I knew is that I could feel their voices buzzing along the ridge of my ear, right through the door.

"But fine," Dean said. "I'm supposed for protect you. You're the one, right?"

His voice like he was tasting something he didn't want in his mouth. Especially not anymore, now that he was flexing into a hot-shit basketball star and suddenly he could hear people talk about him, too, not just Noa. But there in that room he said it: you're the one. And it was like all of a sudden that made it true. Like, we all saw what was happening to Noa, that there was something special. If it wasn't really the gods of Hawai'i doing something heavy, maybe it was a new science. Some sort of, I don't know. Evolution.

Dean and Noa didn't say anything else because Dean opened

the door. Only I didn't realize until the snappy click of the door-knob. Jumped back just in time to not dump at their feet.

Dean snorted. "How's this, she was listening at the door."

"Kaui," was all Noa said. Like he was a million years tired.

"I couldn't hear anything," I said.

"Nothing worth hearing," Dean said. He reached out to muss my hair, pushed too hard when he did it. My brothers split in the hall without another word: Noa with his 'uke in hand, breaking for the garage. Dean to the front room, probably television, whatever game was on, right? And me still there in the hall. Feeling like—in my own house—there was nowhere to go.

EVERY DAY FOR THE NEXT WEEK I went back to the rec center, listening for the chants and the opening of practice. Usually it was on the basketball court instead of the cafeteria, but either way, I could find it. Voices called. I'd watch from outside the door. When it was done: the girls squatting back on their shoes and then cracking into their cliques. Then the kumus opening their gym bags and slipping in their ipus and then rolling and tucking their mats, the ones they'd used for pounding and sitting. Then putting back on their shoes, too. All of them out the doors and then the shined gym floor, and the chants and the ipu stopped echoing in the rafters. All I could hear was the low buzz of the exit sign.

Whatever was there, in that air, I can say it fed me. I'd go there and listen and even dance just a little myself. And when it was over and I went home I'd push harder, fly through the pages of my textbooks. Extra-credit science, I'd collect tadpoles from the culvert near our house. Or extra-credit math, right, I'd calculate dice throws or card games. People would find me after class and ask for help on their homework or always want to be my partner in labs and quiz bowl. And this was *Kahena* I was doing this at.

**STILL, SOMETHING WENT WRONG** with Noa after that Parkinson's guy had showed up. He suddenly stopped taking people in. Mom and Dad would have to go to the door when it knocked and apologize, *Sorry, he not gonna come out today, sick or something, I think*, all refunds and—after it went on for a few weeks—no extra cash. Mom and Dad at the table with their envelope getting empty, doing long division and subtraction. Always subtraction.

Noa wouldn't say what, exactly. Just that he couldn't.

"Let him alone," Mom and Dad would warn, if they saw me sneaking around by the garage door. On the other side he'd be playing the 'uke. Songs all sad and tricky, sometimes with so many notes and chords tumbling along at the same time, it was like he had an extra hand. Later they'd get him out of the garage and the three of them would smash together on the couch. Faces flashed with white and blue from the television. While me and Dean were the ones doing Noa's chores, okay? Sweeping the floor or washing the dishes or cleaning the bathroom.

"Don't do nothing," Dean would say, suds to his wrists while he tried to find the last forks.

Only once I did. Dean in his after-basketball shower, Mom and Dad getting ready for bed. Noa was in the garage, but he wasn't playing. Hadn't been for a while.

When I went through the door he was at the far corner, by Dad's bench, where Dad kept his hunting and fishing stuff. All his car tools and everything. Noa was hunched on a fold-out chair, pants pulled down to his knees. He was facing away from me.

I walked over all cockroach-quiet. The air smelled like old wood and Noa was taking these weird deep breaths. He was holding something in one of his hands. Whatever it was he had it low in his hands, so I kept stepping closer to see. I got maybe five feet away when I kicked a bottle cap. It went skittering and pinging into some dark corner and Noa jumped. "Hey—" he started, trying to cover things with his hands. But I made it in time. He couldn't hide what he was holding.

There was a hunting knife in his right hand, long and thick and teethy. On his left thigh, up high where his skin was way lighter, there was a fresh cut. Blood was weeping out.

We started talking all at once. I wanted to know what he was doing and he just wanted me to go away. But I was tired of going. I kept asking was he hurt and should I go get Mom and Dad.

"No," he said. "No no no. It's not an accident."

"I know it's not an accident," I said. "You see anyone else in here holding a knife?"

He clunked the knife down on the table like it said something. Like that meant this was over. The cut was weeping blood. Noa was just staring.

"Fix it," I said.

"I can't," he said.

"You mean right now?" I asked. "Or, like, ever?"

We watched it bleed. He was staring so hard I thought his face would pop.

"Noa?"

"It's never been like New Year's," he said.

It made everything make sense. How he would only see people with his door closed, all alone. How the Parkinson's man came back. "Noa," I said, "all those people—"

"I still did *something*," he said. "I could feel it most times, almost like I was in their bodies. But there are all these things that keep coming, pictures, commands, I don't know—" And he slapped his palm against his head. Hard once. Then again. Then again, with his eyes clamped closed. And tears ran from the edges of his lids.

I put my hand on his back, but he jerked away like he'd been bitten. "Get away," he said.

I guess I wasn't surprised. So I did what he said.

I WENT BACK to the gym the next day after school. More heat than before. No clouds, making the afternoon almost like a squinty headache. The spitting pop of bus brakes. Voices hollering into and out of the gym. Even the bright *crack* of people playing pool in the front rec room. I watched the hālau from outside the door.

We had an arrangement, okay. Because I never asked my mom and dad about paying to join. I knew the answer. So the kumus said I could still come if I only watched from outside, right? When Kumu Wailoa—the one with her tissue-paper-worn tank tops, vana of armpit hair poking out, chicken-pox forehead and smile like a dolphin—when she said I could learn whatever I saw, I told myself I'd learn everything.

The kumus started the music for the warm-up. Easy soft slaps of the ipu. I did the warm-up, same as the girls inside: 'Ami, 'uwehe, kaholo, hela, the step and swing, arms like lightning bolts sometimes and then like water. Rock and circle of the hips. My back and all those bones. Stiff as a spear. It made me feel right. Like a back-in-the-day Hawaiian woman, the beat of *their* hula. Their scarred, flexy, almost-black skin, I felt it. Closed lips with mana and their naked chee-chees out in the open, no haole dresses. Fisted hands that wove lau hala mats and pulled kalo from the fields.

So maybe Mom and Dad and the gods didn't care about me the way they did about Noa. That didn't mean I couldn't be something. I was still here.

# 4

# DEAN, 2001

## *Kalihi*

THERE'S THIS SAYING AND IT'S A POSTER ON THE WALL opposite the end of my bed so I see it every time I wake up, and I believe it more than anything. It goes like this: Every morning gazelles gotta run faster than the fastest lion or they going get eaten. Every morning lions gotta run faster than the slowest gazelle or they going starve. That's true, that there's just the two types of people in the world. I see it all around me at Lincoln High yeah, kids in boro-boro clothes and crying about how prep school kids just get whatever they want and don't know nothing about real life, but these same Lincoln High kids is only ever just bitching like that and then waiting, palms up. Don't none of 'um ever stand up and take what they want, I figure that makes them the gazelle. There's no gazelle in me, I don't do the scared running. I'm only and always a motherfucking lion.

But even then there's a third type of person I guess. Not a type really, just my brother, and I don't wanna believe in him but most times I do. I do. I seen the sharks, then after, how crazy smart he's getting, people coming to see him because of what they heard happened at New Year's. Mom and Dad, Mom especially, talking about 'aumakua and old gods of the 'āina coming back. When she says it sometimes I get chicken skin, even. So yeah, I believe. I hate it—I *hate* it—but I believe.

Except, plenty mornings I wake up and there's Noa across the way in his bed, drool-sleeping with his faded blue sheets, same like when he used to come find me in my bed, nightmares he'd had, and I'd tell him it's going be all right and let him climb in with me, him hot as a hibachi charcoal. Only now I wake up without him, eating cereal and joking with Mom and Dad, Kaui coming in, and I get them all laughing and smiling, just me. Until Noa shows up, right, and suddenly it's all questions about what's happening with his day and did he sleep okay and here's some thoughts about which extracurricular program he should enroll in at Kahena.

Hard not for get angry at that. I'd feel it like a fist flexing inside my own chest.

Used to be we'd live like this: I'd cup a fart around my brother's nose and he'd go *Quit it, mahu*, and come rolling into me. We'd throw into a wrestling knot, even pull Kaui in, all three of us on the cheap-burn carpets at Old Navy or the steep shore at Sandy Beach. Back then it was all grapples, no hate-spit running from our mouths or us putting our elbows in each other's windpipes, that came later. But when it did it came hard.

Or all those weekend kanikapilas, when we'd both do 'ukuleles on the scratchy red-and-green folding chairs, singing "Big Island Surfing" while Mom's pulling Spam musubi out the cooler and Dad's getting the shoyu chicken going on the grill. That was us, too, until Noa got to be so he could move so fast on the strings and neck of the 'uke, and he'd do it even faster when I was trying for keep up. Just so he could smile and say, Let me slow down and show you.

Shithead. But he could never beat me footracing, or in any sports, and I could see it wasn't like how school or music was, coming natural to him. So I kept balling, with him or without him, until I was nothing but flow on the court, until everything out there was mine. Sometimes I'd get Noa to come to the park and play D on me if there wasn't no else there to play against, I'd even let him score some points, get us in a actual game, before I'd take over and wreck him. For a long time Noa kept coming to those park days, even when he knew he'd never win.

But then, after New Year's, after the sick and hurt and hoping neighbors started showing up, after the Parkinson's guy, each one made Noa a little more and more . . . off. Something breaking, is how I figured it. Sometimes I'd wake up in the middle of the night, no idea why, sure enough I turn over for face the room and Noa's awake, sometimes outside the room, and I can hear him going through the medicine cabinet in the bathroom, probably trying everything in there. Or sometimes he'd still be in our room but crouching into my stash box like he's some Mission Impossible and it's a bomb, next day I run the count and sure enough I'm short. I wonder if he even knows how to roll a joint, or if he just ate it or what. But you could see how something was getting to him, small-kind, kids all whispering in the hall at school like they always do, Mom and Dad almost like it's obvious they think something's wrong with him. Like he's broken. Even though he's still bringing home principal's medals and like that.

Then one day I came home early on a rest day and there was Noa at the counter going through Mom's purse. I asked what he was doing and he said he wasn't doing nothing and so I was all, "You need to get it together." He didn't say nothing at first, which is how I could tell I was right. Me and him both standing there thinking about how there's something going on with him, his abilities. How we know he's not living up to what everyone thinks he should be. Then he was all, "You take her money all the time."

That wasn't fully true. Because yeah, sometimes I'd take from her purse, but it was only when I needed small-kind for important things—a little more to pay back Roland if my sales was slow, maybe some McDonald's for after practice—and I could always make it back four or five times over in a day, once me and Roland got good again. So that's nothing like taking money just to take it.

I said to Noa, "It's not like you need it."

He shrugged. "Sometimes I just want a little something, you know?" he said. "Like one of the Limited Edition Quiksilver board shorts. I mean, even just a Coke from the store, without having to ask anyone."

Of course I knew what he meant.

"Besides," he said, "I've been making us money, from the people visiting for help. It seems like I can have a little bit of it. Not like you."

"You're not making shit anymore," I said. "Not for a while."

"Yeah, well," he said, "I guess I'll just have to try for your C average and study hall, right?" We were standing close and he'd dropped his hand from Mom's purse, then tried to push past me for our room. But I put a hand on his chest.

"Stay straight," I said. "You don't want this."

"Get out of my way," he said. But it wasn't the words that set me off. His eyes was louder than his mouth, and I could see he was fully thinking down about me, like if family was a tree he knew which one of us was the rot.

So I hit him. Full-on false crack—my knuckles, his nose. When he went down I put my knee on his chest bone and got ready for lump him more. But he was yelling and just like that Mom was there, out from the shower I guess. We'd fully forgot about her. Towel-wrapped and her dark Hawaiian skin all slick and still soaped, long hair kinked and shiny, and she tried for hold her towel up with her armpits but also tried for get me off Noa.

The more she pulled at me and hollered to stop the more her hands said who her favorite was—all these years—so I turned and hit her, too. Hard. I'd maybe been in one or two scraps at school and then mostly in like seventh grade or something so even hitting Noa with real heat was something I never done. But no one in our family ever hit each other like I hit Mom right then. I mean when I hit her—when I felt the meaty spark of bone hitting skin—I knew I was turning myself into something ugly and new.

Mom's strong, though. She stood up straight-backed, didn't even touch her cheek, and asked, "What are you doing?" and I tried for say, Fixing him, but then Mom's towel coasted off her body. I didn't want to, but still I saw the stretch marks, the woolly fan of her urumut, and when she bent, her tits lolling down like goat udders. My stomach all spinning with shame. I was still straddling Noa's chest.

"Get off me," Noa said.

"Never," I said. "You don't know what you're doing."

"Like you do?" he asked.

Normally Mom'd be, like, I don't need to keep you boys, I know just where to hide a few dead bodies and me and your dad can make more kids, only this time they'll all be girls, thank God. But she didn't say none of that this time.

I let Noa push me off. He made like he was going to the garage, then changed his mind and slammed out the front door. The screen door wobbled, then the creak of the hinges and the crack of the frame after.

"All right, okay," I said to Mom's stare. "All right, okay, okay, okay, all right," all the way to my room.

THERE WAS THE REST OF THAT NIGHT, then the morning after. We had an away game, and most game days I'd start my morning slow, dream about what I was going for do on the court, like this: me bringing the ball up the floor, all AND1 Mixtape at the top of the key, my shoes chirping and the other team scrambling, they bring the double team but I got a sick crossover that breaks their ankles, mongoosing between two chumps as I spin to the rim, and when I finger-roll for two the net goes swish like a air kiss to the crowd, and the crowd comes back at me with that roar.

But not this time. No daydreams. This time I hid away at home, then hopped the city bus to school without breakfast. School was school, something happened in my classes I guess, but might as well I was standing in a Laundromat, teachers like a bunch of stupid machines churning around me, making noise.

When the game finally came that night, I played like limp dick: passing out of bounds, air balls from inside and outside the arc, crossover bouncing off my knees, turnovers turnovers turnovers. I couldn't feel nothing of my flow. Nobody from my family was at the game, too. It was an away game anyway, and sometimes Mom and Dad had late shifts or whatever, but something felt like no one being there was maybe on purpose.

When the team rode back to Lincoln after, I couldn't say nothing. Normally, I'd get Nic up on my lap, let her put her ass on my legs, her mynah bird laugh, but instead this time it was me just thinking, over and over, Anyone can have one bad game. Looking at my hands. But even then I knew this wasn't just gonna be one time.

When I got home it was only Mom and Dad sitting on the couch. I figured I'd see the same bruise on Mom's face that had been growing the night before but her face was brown and un-swollen. Dad kissed her on that same cheek, stood and looked at me like Later, later, we're gonna catch up on this, and then when he'd passed I heard the fridge opening and closing. The spit and clatter of a beer bottle being opened. Then the wood creaks of him moving down the hall. Whole time Mom looking through me with funeral eyes.

"I'm sorry," I said to Mom.

She shrugged. "You hit like a flight attendant," she said. "I was in tougher scraps at Walmart Black Friday."

"I don't know why I did it," I said.

"I don't believe that," she said. "I think you know why."

She was right. That punch was how many years in my heart and knowing she knew? Might as well I was hitting myself, too.

"He's getting stupid," I said. "I was trying for fix it."

"Trying *to* fix it," she said. "Dean, seriously. Speak the way you were raised."

"The hell is this," I said. "Why won't you let me say I'm sorry?"

"Because you're not," she said, and we stood there, staring at each other until I stopped.

AFTER, THERE'S A Monday-night game against Saint Christopher and I went three for fifteen and brick four from the foul line. Might as well I was a pregnant whale, how I handled the ball. Was a home game but not feeling like home with our crowd quiet as a pop quiz. I tried for shake the feeling I still had, something bruised and queasy every time I thought of Noa, of Mom, of family. But nothing worked, the feeling just clamped on me all the same, all over the court.

Saint Christopher stomped us bad and I got benched while still had five minutes left, on the end of the bench I dropped a towel over my head and let everything be dark and stink and muffled. Just before the towel covered my eyes I saw two scouts up near the rafters, packing up their cameras and laptops and heading for the door.

Maybe they weren't there for see me.

HAD A REST DAY after Saint Christopher, and I was home from study hall watching *SportsCenter*. There was the Top Ten with windmill dunks and over-the-wall catches, holes in one and right hooks for the knockout, all of it giving crowds that roar, same as I used to give us.

Someone entered the room from behind and a sandwich bag of my buds came plopping into my lap. Noa's voice said, "Saw this in one of your shoeboxes."

I rolled my head back since he was behind the couch, so I was looking at him upside down, and I was all, "What, you're going through my stuff now?"

"You need to be more original than a shoebox. Plus," Noa said, "I thought you were done with this."

I rolled my head forward and looked at the lumps of sweet pakalolo inside the Zig Zag papers.

"Don't you got some cancer to cure?" I said. "'Ukulele masterpieces to write?"

"I thought you said you'd quit," he said again.

"I did," I said, which was true.

"If that's quitting then my farts don't stink."

"Might as well they don't, the way you act," I said. "Nose up in the air when you're the one that's all bust-up. Anyway, I bet this bag is short from you lifting buds from it."

"I didn't touch it," he said. "Nothing's wrong with me."

I go back to watching SportsCenter. "Yeah, right. Almost no one coming around our house anymore, yeah? And the ones that does get sent away by Mom and Dad. Goes like this," I said, then in my best Mom and Dad voice, "We've decided it's for the best that he takes a break from helping people for a little while. Please don't come back until you hear from us."

For just a second he was fully surprised, but he fixed it fast. "Yeah, I bet you're happy," he said. "I bet you smile every time you close the door on someone."

"I ain't happy we're broke."

That shut him up. On SportsCenter there was Tiger Woods,

sticking it to everyone else, Vijay Singh just behind him, and I'm all, I bet there's some pissed-off haoles at the country clubs tonight.

After a minute Noa said, "We're still better than we were on the Big Island." The way he said it was almost like he was sorry, like he didn't want a fight anymore. Might as well he just admitted something's wrong. But I couldn't stop myself.

"I mean I guess," I said. "But no thanks to you anymore. Mom and Dad been counting on you."

Then he was all tight and cold. "That's the problem," he said. "That's all you guys think about. Us, us, us. This is bigger than Mom or Dad. Bigger than all of us, bigger than me just making chump change for our family—"

"Ain't nothing bigger than our family," I said. But I maybe said it, too, because I could tell he was right, that the things he was gonna be was bigger than all of us. "That's what's wrong with *you*."

"The drugs, though, Dean," Noa said. Him all rubbing his face like he was talking to a bad dog. "Don't be stupid."

Mom was right, I wasn't sorry. I figured if I hit his teeth hard enough he'd swallow them. "Just shut up," I said. "I oughta knock you out." My muscles was all heat, and the only thing that kept me from hitting him again was how it felt the time before when I did it. So I turned the volume up.

"Dean," he said. "Shit. I'm sorry."

"Whatever," I said.

"It doesn't have to be like this," he said.

"Then what does it gotta be like," I said.

"I'm sorry," he said, and I knew what was in his voice, it was true. I should've said sorry, too, I should've clapped his hand and maybe clowned around or something, tried to go back to before, when we was just brothers. Only I couldn't. There was too much in between. Too much of him.

Watch me rise, I wanted for say, you watch what I do the next five, ten years, you watch me on *SportsCenter*. Won't be nothing bigger, only I'll be it just for our family. But he was gone, and we hadn't finished what we'd started. So I said to the empty room, "And I don't need for sell nothing anymore. I don't."

**THE WHOLE WEEK AFTER,** Coach went at us hard. We kept losing games. Last one that time was to Kuakini by seventeen. Us at practice, maybe a few days before the game against Kahena Academy, and Coach was all, Kahena is going to be on you like it's prison and they're selling your buttholes for cigarettes, and you deserve it, too, if we lose I'm the first one putting up the highlights on YouTube. He dragged two trash cans out from the bathroom and put one at each end of the court and said, We're doing suicides until someone pukes, and then we did, we sprinted back and forth to the touch lines until our legs was all beat to wobble and the blood in my chest was like a whole cave on fire. Every time Coach hollering and keeping his stopwatch, and if we couldn't match the last one he made us run another.

Alika stopped after the fifty-something suicide and palu'd into the trash can. We watched his stomach squeeze and the way his legs wiggled just before it came up and then the spatter as it hit the bottom of the can.

"Now you know how I felt after our game last night," Coach said, standing next to Alika but staring at all of us. "Every time I watch the film of our sorry-ass loss I'm going to be like Alika is now. What's your problem?" Coach asked me. Must've been I was staring at him.

And I wanted for be like: I don't know what happens next.

"I said what's your problem," Coach said.

I could talk big in front of Noa, but maybe won't none of it get better.

"Nothing," I said, hands on my knees, sucking wind. "I don't got a problem, Coach."

I stopped by J. Yamamoto on the way back from practice, even though I had the drunk head of too much workout and not enough water. I was off the bus and walking through the mist from the hot rain that just finished sizzling on the blacktop, and the shopping carts was all hissing and crashing across the lot while the workers lined 'um up and I stood at the huge J. Yamamoto front windows and watched my mom. She was in full-on work mode: green apron, fingers pecking at the keys, and easy wrist flicks to close the register drawer every time after she gave change.

Her eyes would go down and up when she looked from the groceries to the customer. I remember 'um clear, because it made me think of my application days. That first letter, how when it came Mom started with a bright voice, all, Here's one from Kahena Academy! And if the letter was lighter than we thought no one said nothing and then we were all ripping it open and Dad's hand gripped my shoulder and Mom's eyes swooped low with reading and then her eyes came back up wet heavy and she said, Okay. Okay.

How many times I tried for get into Kahena Academy, where Noa and Kaui are now, where they got scholarships for us Native Hawaiians, but you gotta prove you're worth it with a fully juice test, all haole words and useless math. Like just because you can define "catalyst," you get in.

We regret to inform you. Our applicant pool is three to one and growing. We encourage you. Try again.

Seventh grade, eighth grade, ninth, me applying and the letters coming, one every year. And then the try for the next year would start: fat flexy prep books and Mom packing me J. Yamamoto Whole Wheat Crackers and I was all, No Ritz? And Mom was all, It's twice the price and you're only paying for the commercials, and so J. Yamamoto crackers with old peanut butter and me in the cafeteria as soon as school was out, sweating the prep books until practice. All those mornings on the bus to Lincoln, Jaycee-guys would be talking about *Monday Night Football* or *Temptation Island*, and I was all, FOIL method and quadratic equation, and they were all, The hell does that mean, and I was all, I don't know but I feel like I'm having its baby.

Kaui and Noa got into Kahena their first try.

And Dad every week working luggage at the airport with after-dark overtime. And Mom some mornings and some nights and if she's lucky both at J. Yamamoto, her going after extra shifts the way a crackhead goes after batu. And at the end of the night them coming home with work still banging around in their bones, might as well they're saying, Dean, can't you see what we are? And me wanting to say it don't matter if I can't get what they want on some stupid test, guess whose name everyone knows after the arena on Friday night. Guess who can tell you how the girls smell naked at almost every school in our division.

I stayed by the side of the window, near the propane rack. Customers came and went, I could hear my mom and Trish talking with 'um, you could tell when it was a local because there was plenty laughs and names of cousins and grandmas rolling around all relaxed, but when it was haoles usually they were like, Do you know what time the *Arizona* Memorial opens, or

How do I get to Sea Life Park from here. And Mom and Trish answered but you could tell they wanted for be like, Everyone brown is not your tour guide. Mom got hours left of standing, trying for smile, taking people's cards and giving them all the steaks and swordfish and fancy beer they want.

Listen, all of you, I wanted for say: I'm going to take us all away from this. I'm gonna make it so that can't no one order us around for anything. And the way is basketball. Noa might be special but he's not money. I can do it. Here, then college, then pros, and I mean it. I'll make so much money it'll be coming out my okole. I always felt that and then I was making 'um happen.

ONLY NOW EVERY basketball game was worse. Another week just the same. When they're over, when it's quiet and there's space in my head, it fills up with that night, how much I wanted for hurt Noa and Mom both, like really wanted to break some part of them, and the way afterward my knuckles felt like bee-hives, full of all this small pain that's still stinging me from the inside, trying to get out.

But I had that shoebox and I figured why not? and texted Jaycee I was too sick to practice and instead I caught the bus to Ala Moana Park to hang out past the hibachis. To sell. I was over by the part where you still got some of the old-fish stink of the bathrooms but you couldn't see it easy from the street, so I figured it was the safest spot. The ocean was all sagging against the rocks, had that grass starting for die in a yellow way. When I first sat there, for a while before buyers started coming, it was even fully peaceful. No basketball no Noa no nothing and I was actually thankful.

But the buyers came. They always find me. At least I still got my flow for that if nothing else.

I sold until I shouldn't. Until the ocean was ashy from the black clouds mobbing down off the Ko'olaus and a few raindrops slapped my head. I sold until everything was empty. Then I went home.

When I got to the front door at our house, I heard the popping rips of meat hitting oil in a pan and from the half-burned golden smell of breadcrumbs frying I figured it was Mom making chicken katsu. I was home later than I should've been, so I stood at the door trying for think about my story when Mom just opened the door for me.

"I thought that was you," she said, with her tired smile.

I looked over my shoulder. Not like there's anyone or anything back there at the end of the cul-de-sac, but it gave me a second to think about what to do.

"Yeah," I said. "Long practice today."

"Nainoa told me about the new study group you're in after school. Must be hard to do that after practice?"

It took me a minute to figure out what Noa did for me and then I nodded and said, "Yeah. But I'm doing okay."

"Good," she said.

I took my shoes off, put my ball on the ground. It rolled across the slanted-ass floor, toward the hall to our bedrooms. That bent-ass floor. Our tin roof all shot with rust. Our kitchen counter that's got all these black and yellow spots from years of smokers and slackers that had the house before us. We were getting ready for eat chicken, from the sale bin I bet at J. Yamamoto, with the sell-by date way past, so that Mom gotta bread the hell outta it for keep the real taste hidden.

"I'm sorry," I said. Like all of a sudden. Like a guilty kid.

She stopped turning the chicken, looked right at me. "I thought we talked about this," she said. "It isn't about just sorry."

"I can be better," I said.

"I know," she said. "So do it."

"Noa, too, yeah?" I said. "It's not just me."

Mom was getting paper towels out to cover a tray for the katsu. "We need you to support your brother right now. Let him worry about his problems."

It was weird silent after that. I could've said, This is bullshit, making me be his helper, but I thought of Mom at J. Yamamoto. Just didn't seem right to fight anymore. "How was your day?" I asked.

I almost never asked her that, I don't know why. She realized it, too, because I saw her brighten and fully think. Took a minute before she answered.

"My day," she finally said, tapping the tongs on the pan. "My day sucked dick."

"Right, I get you," I said. "What kind of dick, though? There's all kinds, you've got your long horse dick, your furry goat dick, your hot bull dick . . .

"But," I make like I'm thinking, even rub my chin, "that's really more of a balls thing, with the bull."

Mom laughed. It was a good one, too, like it just firecrackered out from a place even she didn't know was there. "God, boys," she said. "You're all so sick. I should know better than to even get you started."

"I'm a perfect gentleman," I said, "once you get to know me."

"A perfect gentleman can help set the table, then," Mom said. She pointed at the silverware drawer.

She asked me to go tell Noa and Kaui that dinner was almost ready, and that I should take my backpack to my room, and then she was back with the plates and the katsu and I did my part before going to our room, me and Noa's.

He was there, head-down into his 'uke, but it fell off the minute I came in.

I was all, You can keep playing, just that it's dinner soon, and he said he was done anyway, then him just sitting there half curled over his 'uke and me holding the doorknob thinking, How come every time now I talk in this house it's like someone caught me kissing my cousin.

"You didn't have to lie," I said. "With Mom."

He leaned back on his arms. "I know," he said.

And I guess that's all we could do.

Then there was dinner, me and him just listened to Kaui or Mom, not much except if we were asked whatever, which was plenty from Mom for Noa, come to think of it. Still wasn't long before dinner was done and we all peeled off on our own, Kaui back in her room on homework and Noa in the garage with his 'uke, back to the crazy stuff he did when he got lost in it, and I tried for work on my econ homework but in the end all I could do was write *The market clearing price is I'm fucked* and then I was on the couch, watching *SportsCenter*, and everyone else was asleep.

I still had hours left before my head would give up, I could tell. So I went into our bedroom and there's Noa's sleep-weight in the darkness, could feel him all heavy and gone in his breathing. In the closet had my Flu Game Jordans and the Allen Iverson Sixers away jersey. I suited up and grabbed my basketball and felt all the places the texture bumps was wearing down. It was way-black in the night, like after midnight. Had the basketball pinned under one arm, carrying my shoes in that hand, when I came back out to the living room and there was Mom's purse.

The refrigerator kicked on and grumbled, ice clattered inside. I could see where Mom's wallet was, right in front, the gold clasp rubbing off to silver underneath.

The cash I was holding all came from someone else—just strangers I sold pakalolo in the park—but, then, that money was mine, maybe the only thing that felt like it. And it wasn't nearly enough for change anything that mattered in our family. The only way I could do that for real was to make, like, haole-kind money, until there wasn't nothing I couldn't buy for Mom and Dad. Noa could become president or a new kahuna or famous doctor or whatever, but the only thing I could be was right there in my hands, that basketball. I put the money back in my pocket. Then I was out the door and down the street, through Kalihi in the dark.

The park was closed that late but that didn't mean nothing, had the backboard all mossy on the edges and streaked with mud from other people balling in the rain from earlier that day. The net was broke in one or two places, sagging and hanging into its own holes.

I bounced the ball a few times, listened to the ringy pound. The wind came on and the trees clattered like applause. I closed my eyes for the first shot, I don't know why. I took my shot, let the ball start with everything coming up through my ankles, jumping clean, but when the ball came off my fingers I knew it was all wrong and then the clang of the rim and the ball bouncing into the chain-link fence. I watched it till it stopped moving.

I went and snagged the ball and took another shot, eyes open, and it swooped in and out of the rim and bounced, bounced, right to the edge of the court. I quick-stepped and scooped the basketball. I cut to the corner and then busted a crossover, turned, bent with my back to the rim like I had D on me, might as well it was Kahena Academy, or whoever else thought they could try for defend me. But can't no one defend me. I was fadeaway spinning for the hoop and I let my shot go high and right at it. I watched it rainbow down. I knew that shot was going in, already I could see it dropping through with that swish, it had to, it had to, just like I'm saying, I'm unstoppable.

# 5

# MALIA, 2002

## *Kalihi*

I CAN'T HEAR YOUR VOICE, BUT I KNOW THAT YOU'RE still listening, always. And so I can tell you: sometimes I believe none of this would have happened if we'd stayed on the Big Island, where the gods are still alive. Fire goddess Pele with her unyielding strength, birthing the land again and again in lava, exhaling her sulfur breath across the sky. Kamapuaʻa, wanting her love, bringing his rain and stampede of pig hooves to break her lava down, make it into fertile soil, the way it is all across the grassy hills of Waimea, down into the valleys, surrounding where you were born. Or there is Kū, god of war, who one day plunged himself into that same soil, turning from a father and a husband into a tree, a tree to bear fruit for his starving wife and children. The first breadfruit. He was a god of war, but he was also a god of life. Sometimes he came as a shark . . .

So I wonder if some of him is you, and if some of you is him, the way the ocean and the dirt and the air here are all made of the gods. It was what I believed at first: That you were made of the gods, that you would be a new legend, enough to change all the things that hurt in Hawai'i. The asphalt crushing kalo underfoot, the warships belching filth into the sea, the venomous run of haole money, California Texas Utah New York, until between the traffic jams and the beach-tent homeless camps and big-box chain stores nothing was the way it should have been. I believed that you could defeat this.

With shame now I see that could never have been the case. But I remember when I was especially full of faith, and it was the day your father and I discovered your graveyard.

Do you remember? You were a junior in classes, although barely sophomore-aged, and still Principal's List and Science Club captain and playing the 'ukulele like you'd swallowed the whole Hawaiian history. And it was good, all of it. Excellent. Though the truth is that, for all the pride we had in everything you were doing, there still was, especially for me, a feeling of failure. We'd pushed you the wrong way after that New Year's, expecting you to fix the people who heard what you were capable of and came to our door, hollowed out with desperation. Yes, I thought, this is it, he'll start with them, and it will grow.

And yes, there was something in it for us, too. We did want—we did *need*—the extra money that came in. I'm sorry.

When you stopped taking those requests, you closed off from us even further. So much about you became a secret, and I don't think you ever completely came back. This we also came to understand after that graveyard day.

Do you remember the graveyard? I do. The rare day your father and I were both home in the after-school hours; we noticed you'd left and hadn't come back.

"He just took that same path he always takes," Kaui said, shrugging when we asked.

It was late. We wanted you back. So we took the path, too. Around the corner and across the street from our house, the brown footpath dropped behind frazzled hedges to an open field. Scummed water trickled through a canal to the left, and beyond, a hurricane fence fronted the dusty backyards of muffler shops and industrial warehouses. Tuna smells bloomed along the path, which continued straight to a distant clump of trees. Along the path, as we walked, we saw cairn after cairn, each rock pile newer than the one before. Only the cairns weren't all stone: they were spiny and flashing with bike cogs, car engine parts, abandoned elbows of pipe. Some were already covered in weeds.

"What are these?" I asked your father. He squatted next to one.

"Look like graves to me," he said, which I had already known would be the answer.

"Augie," I said.

"He's down here," your father said. "Somewhere."

Your father turned toward the trees at the end of the path. From the industrial lots came the sound of metal slicing over itself, the crack of a pallet dropping in the dirt.

We stood and went on along the path, the graves at regular intervals, shin-high piles of rocks and scrap metal. The last cairn before we reached the trees was topped with a half-buried plastic robot, something you had built in one of your incredible science classes at Kahena. The robot was a sun-scalded blue, scoured with animal marks.

I bent and touched it. "This is Nainoa's," I said to your father. It looked like a few brown scabs of blood were clinging to the inside of the robot's arms. What I smelled coming off the cairn was mostly a rocky smell, but underneath, faintly, something of old wet leather and rotting cotton.

"Some of the other stuff, from before, that was from our garage, too, I think," your father said. "Had an old gear from his first bike."

The trees were as close as they were going to get without us going into them. There was a dizzy feeling starting in my head.

It wasn't as dark as I had expected inside, the trees were low with sun breaks. As we walked the dizzy feeling I'd had expanded, running down my skull along each rung of my spine and throat, into my chest. My eyes felt fogged, blurred, and when I opened them wide again, I snatched your father's hand, as if I might fill with whatever I was feeling and float away.

We stopped. There was a clearing on the other side of the trees and you were there, sitting in the grass, your knees kinked up with your elbows resting on them, fingers playing at the air between your ankles, as if you were waiting to be picked up after school.

"Thank God," your father said. "I thought maybe he was back here playing with hisself."

I told him to stop, which never works with your father.

"No, it's okay, I got a few friends that was like that back in the day. Did I tell you about how John-John tried with his dog's—"

"Augie, shut up."

There was a mess in the sky. A dark shape wobbled through

the break in the trees, flapping and tumbling, and smacked into the earth right next to you. A feather fluffed through the air. The shape rose—I saw that it was an owl—and dragged itself toward you, a few sloppy heaves of its bulk before it collapsed at your feet, chest up. We watched that chest swell and shrink, slower and slower.

You closed your eyes and put your hands on it.

"Is he," your father said.

The owl's breathing slowed again, and again. It was such a paper-light thing. Your face tightened and furrowed, sweat rolled down the line of your jaw. The dizziness in me surged. I was weightless, I was in the sky, beating my arms, only they weren't arms, they were the stringy muscle and soaring sheets of feathered wings. I rocketed into the sky, all blue everywhere but for the knobbed ridges of the Ko'olaus getting smaller beneath me. Everything was air, fringed in golden light, and I rose toward the sun like I was riding the fastest elevator, surging and expanding, until everything I was seeing popped, like the lightest bubble.

I was back in the trees, standing with your father, and in the cradle of your hands, the owl had stopped breathing. Without shifting from your kneeling position, you yanked the owl's body up by the wing and pitched the whole body hard back into the grass. A leg flopped crookedly in the wrong direction.

"Shit!" you called out once, your voice warbled and breaking, the true voice of a boy. You clutched your head in both hands and wailed at the ground.

"Don't," your father said, lurching in one crackling rush from our hiding spot, before I could stop him. "Don't!"

You turned at the sound, your face snotted and flushed. As your father moved forward, you scrambled back.

"Don't touch me," you warned, and your father froze in a crouch, arms outstretched to gather you up. Our gazes locked, then moved apart, and I turned mine again to the owl. One wing was jutting up from the limp mess of feathers, and tufts of fluff fluttered when the breeze came through. I wasn't even a little sad, as I'd expected I should have been; instead I was filled with the echoes of what I'd felt and seen just before, golden and rising.

"We just wanted to make sure you was safe," your father said.

You stood, went to the owl.

"Nainoa," I said, because you seemed small and guilty of something, black-brown hair shorter than your brother's with that side part you used to have, and you were still in your white polo and navy school pants, your right arm across your body, gripping the biceps of your hanging left. "Are you okay?"

"Of course," you said. That was when I saw the trowel, you must have brought it from our garage. You yanked it from the ground and began digging.

"Do you want help?" your father asked.

"You can't help me," you said.

And so your father came back to me. We didn't stay to watch you dig the rest. It didn't seem right.

We stood outside the trees, by one of the cairns.

"Did you feel anything in there?" I asked Augie.

"Felt like I was flying," Augie said. "Might as well it was right into the sun."

My mind was just catching up with what we'd felt, what we'd seen. "Augie, my God, how long has he been seeing things like that? Doing things like that?" I wanted to count the graves, to consider how many animals you'd lived their last breaths with, how many times you'd tried, and failed, to make a difference. How many other things you might be seeing and feeling without

us, all of it like running into a wall over and over. The thought
that we'd be able to help you through this, to guide you to what
you were supposed to become, was total stupidity; along with
what we'd been asking you to perform for us, in our home, with
the desperate neighbors we'd subjected you to, the stories we
told you about what we thought you were. It came unspooling
from me as we stood there.

"I use whatever I can find," you said. "When there aren't
enough stones."

You'd come up behind us while we did our own thinking.
You had more to say, and if we'd asked, if we hadn't, it didn't
matter; you kept talking. Waved the trowel at the grave we were
considering. "This was a dog," you said. "Some poi dog, like I
couldn't tell what kind."

You said you'd found it down there when you were out messing around along the canal, skipping stones and taking a break
from everything. The dog had been hit by a car. Probably one of
the shipping trucks or construction monsters that were always
grinding and shuddering along the canal. After it had been hit,
the dog dragged itself, all its broken parts, to the clearing. I can
only imagine the jammy trail of its insides it must have left along
the ground.

You said that you'd tried to fix it, that when you'd laid hands
on it, for the first time you felt something important: all the broken
places in its body. It was like a puzzle, you said, and all you had
to do was put the pieces back together. But you worked in one
place and another would start to die. Then you'd turn to that
place and the part that you fixed before would be unraveling itself, and on and on, until finally you lost. "I was the dog at the
very end," you said, and started shivering. "I was running on this
bright road. Paws ticking into the mud, my body this bouncing

knot of muscles. It was like I was dumb with happiness, I don't know . . . I ran and ran and ran, but everything got weaker and weaker, until I was just . . . floating into darkness."

You'd buried the dog here and sometimes came back to visit. You said it always made you feel better, lighter, as if you were again the dog, running.

And standing there was exactly like that. Later the field would be fenced off and the fence would become a wall and the wall would become another building, storing and manufacturing cement, and the graveyard was gone, somewhere under the foundation. But I remember it as it was then.

You explained that other animals had come after the dog. Flocks and strays, poisoned from antifreeze and wrecked from car strikes and being chewed up by cancer, crawling on their last to arrive here, waiting for you. To give up their last sparks.

"I'm sorry," I said.

"I don't know what to do with it," you said. "I keep messing up."

Augie put his hand on your shoulder. "No you don't," he said.

"What do you mean?" you asked.

"Feels way happy, doesn't it?" Augie asked. "Right at the end. Feels that way to me, anyway."

But you shook your head. "I have to start fixing things.

"I have to fix everything," you corrected.

Whole nights after the sharks, your father and I had been wondering what would happen, what you would be. I believe that graveyard day was the first time we truly understood the scale of you. If you were more of the gods than of us—if you were something new, if you were supposed to remake the islands, if you were all the old kings moving through the body of one small boy—then of course I could not be the one to guide you to your full potential. My time as a mother was the same as those last gasping breaths of the owl, and soon enough you'd have to gently set down my love, fold it up into the soil of your childhood, and move beyond.

I remember leaning back against your father's chest as we sat in the grass. Shadows had moved over the water in the canal, but far beyond that, the lights in Honolulu were winking on. The golden feeling of the owl's last flight stayed with me, even if the vision had long since coasted into the dark.

# PART II

# ASCENSION

# 6

# DEAN, 2004

## *Spokane*

WAY I FIGURE, BEFORE THE FIRST HAWAIIANS BECAME Hawaiians, it was them back in Fiji or Tonga or wherever and they had too many wars with too many kings and some of the strongest looked at the stars and saw a map to a future they could take for themselves. Broke their backs making themselves canoes to cut through forty-foot swells and sails big enough to make a fist out the wind and then they got free from their old land. Goodbye old kings goodbye old gods goodbye old laws goodbye old power goodbye limits. Came a time in all their salty tattoo-muscle nights on the water when they seen the white light of the moon over the new land of Hawai'i and they was like: This. This is ours. All us, all now.

That's me that first night in Spokane. For real I felt all the kings that came before me in a heavy way, like they was right inside my heart, like they was chanting through my blood. I could see them with me, even if my eyes didn't close. We were the same, me and them: I went launching across the big gap of sky between Hawai'i and the mainland, seen the big grids of mainland city lights from the plane window, skyscrapers and highways that just kept going and going, all gold and white. For me they was just like those navigating stars for the original Hawaiians, pointing the direction to what's mine. When I stepped off the night shuttle to Spokane and stood in front the clean lawns and new brick buildings and saw the coaching staff ready to greet me as one of the top freshman basketball recruits in the whole country I was like: all me, all now. King me, motherfuckers.

Before, back in Hawai'i, all everyone wanted was for me to believe in Noa, to raise him up. Like my job was to be his keeper, to be second place and help him get to the finish line.

Hate to break it to you, but I don't fit in second place.

And for what? It's not like Noa ever got us nothing to show for it, Mom and Dad still hurting for money at the end of the month. Same thing all over the islands. Only way you get out of something like that is to be so good the only thing anyone can do is pay you. And pay you big. That's what I knew I was finally gonna do when I got to Spokane.

This started in, what, fall 2004. Only thing that mattered was basketball. Captains ran the off-season work and so we was all in the arena, upstairs where the track is, wall squats and wind sprints, then back to the weight room. Guys was asking if

I'd ever seen a place like this, rows and rows and rows of clean bleachers for thousands of fans, the weight-room facilities with top-end machines and new paint on the racks, and I was like, Just because I'm from the islands you think I never seen nothing like this. But, then, it was true, too, not because the islands but because Lincoln High. I only seen facilities this way when we was playing away games at Kahena or the other rich-ass prep schools. So, yeah, I seen a place like this, but never before was it mine.

All the halls and laboratories and commons like they got fresh paint every other year, pretty little bookshop with all its way-too-fucking-high prices. But everywhere I swear except in the locker room the university was white as milk. I saw brown people on the sidewalk and I was like, Thank God, I was starting for think I was the last one left.

And the classes? Didn't even know what I'd signed up for, serious, someone from the front office of the team took care of registration, and the homework I got help on, guys on the team tipped me off to finding a tutor first week, sophomore girl if I can help it, big eyes toothpick jeans cross around her neck, like that. She'll help out, they said, She'll know who we are. And it was just like they said. I had to write down the numbers and words myself, sure, but if my brain was there it was on the scoop of her elbow, the freckles across her nose. Gotta love college.

But basketball, we went hard. Every day, all the time. Fifteen of us on the grind ten times harder than I ever did back home. Just balling all the time, the *tamp tamp tamp* of the basketball into that polished wood, the perfect chirp of our shoes. We ran one-on-ones, we ran two-on-twos, we ran two-on-ones. Contested mid-range jumpers and turnarounds and arc shooting drills. This was a whole new level, though. Guys on the team was all way quicker and stronger and smarter than anyone I ever played against back at Lincoln, now I'm playing men instead of kids, and for that first year I felt it. They all had a step and an inch more in the air than me, half my stuff was getting blocked or picked, and it was almost like the atmosphere around me would sink and get soft.

Be bigger. Be stronger and faster. I had to.

After practice, there'd be like four or five of us in the cafeteria, knees icing in fat blisters of plastic sports wrap, staring at our plates of limp beef broccoli, no hunger since we was all still on the afterburn of whatever bull-ring-type drill coach had just put us through. The greasy smell of burnt meat filling the cathedral ceiling of the dining hall, the cold of the tabletop, it was all huli-huli in my head. Made me feel faded even though I was sober as a Jehova.

"I think I just fell asleep with my eyes open," Grant said.

"You did," DeShawn said, "I seen it. Me, I'm just trying to keep from pissing myself. How am I supposed to take a leak when I got all this in the way?" He jiggled his ice-packed knees. "They ice up our knees like this, they should give us some diapers, too."

"You're, what, rehydrating or something?" Grant asked, nodding at the XL cup DeShawn was drinking from. "This kid's always trying to rehydrate, but first thing in the morning he's drinking Diet Coke." They was roommates, white-ass Grant with his Stockton wigger thing going on and DeShawn from L.A.

"I need the caffeine," DeShawn said, like he was apologizing.

"Drink coffee, fool."

"Tastes like your mama."

"Come on," Grant said. "I'm tryna relax, here."

"You been relaxing all semester," DeShawn said, "with your

history classes and all that. All I can think about is Business Calc. Midterm in two days and I'm supposed to study tonight? My brain feels like I been hotboxing."

"Like a balloon, right? Like if your neck wasn't holding it on."

"Yeah."

"Grant's head always feels like that," I said. "I bet he was the kid eating glue in the back of the class."

"Him in elementary with his big ears," DeShawn said. "I can see it."

"Elementary nothing," I said. "I'm talking about last week."

DeShawn and Grant both cracked up, like *howling*, bending forward over the table, other guys, too.

That was it—that feeling. I was starting for get inside something then, I was part of those guys. We was out on that court bleeding and scraping and working together, the way they'd say, Good, get that next pass a little stronger, thread that here, or when I did finally sink a few jumpers they was like, That, do that again, every time—I knew they believed in me. They saw what I was, what I was gonna be.

What was back home? I was calling Mom and Dad from the start of the semester, usually sitting on the couch we'd shoved under our lofted dorm bed, the couch all avocado checker pattern with cigarette-burn freckles and the wall opposite with the mini-fridge. Chicken-scratch sound of my roommate, Price, writing out his homework—he didn't get a laptop, just like me, maybe the only two guys at school without computers, it's like I never get a break from being reminded where I came from—and I would talk with everyone on the phone, Mom Dad Noa Kaui, one at a time.

"So, what, how's the weather?" I would ask Dad, every time, because I know he loved to laugh at my cold ass and say, "Brah, it's all good, every day, me and Mom and Kaui and Noa at the beach last weekend, sun in the morning and rain at night, just perfect. How's the land of shave ice? You lick a pole and get your tongue stuck yet?" And then he'd giggle and say, "Nah nah nah. Tell me how's it going."

And he would tell me small-kind something, and then Mom would get on and she'd do the same, but both of 'um pretty quick got to the point where they was all like, You gotta see what your brother is doing back here. Every time, every call, it always got there, no matter what I did. They'd say how even the teachers didn't know what for do with Noa, he was burning through upper-division Kahena classes whether it was chemistry or Hawaiian language or AP calculus like it wasn't nothing. How had him in the *Honolulu Advertiser* for his perfect SAT scores and there was all these fat envelopes and e-mails and calls from colleges storming into the house, how they was trying for get him taking classes at the university already. And they was saying probably Stanford was where he was going.

I hated this part of the call. I wanted for know and didn't want for know what he was doing. Especially what he was *doing* doing, his kahuna abilities, right? But still yet, when Mom was talking to me, she'd usually be all about some award Noa was getting, his new special classes or whatever, and yet they never said nothing about that other part of him, the part we all still didn't fully understand. "Sometimes I wish I knew what was going on inside of him," Mom would say. "Does he tell you anything?"

First couple of times she did that—asked me about him, like me and him were talking with each other behind her back, the way normal brothers do, I guess—I thought she didn't understand how things was.

I snapped this one time. "You know," I said, "maybe I don't believe in him so much anymore. Not the way you do."

"There's nothing to believe," Mom said. "You're going to lie about what you've seen with your own eyes?"

"I'm not saying what is or isn't here," I said. "But how come I never felt anything like that myself? How come if there's gods they're not in all of us?"

"Where's this coming from?" Mom asked. "Haoles getting to you? You never talked this way before."

"It's just I figure you're not seeing the right things," I said. "Full-ride scholarship, Mom. People that come here go early in the NBA draft. Every year. Maybe you're not gonna see it until I bring in that first fat check, though."

"All I asked is whether Noa was talking to you or not," Mom said. I let her squash it. Maybe I don't feel anything the way you feel it because I'm the only one paying attention to how the world works, I wanted for say.

"Noa doesn't tell me nothing special, Mom." Which was true. When me and him talked on the phone—you could hear Mom and Dad make him take his turn—we'd be all like, What's up, nothing, heard there's gonna be some new laboratory at school, yep, I guess you and the team got a road trip coming up, yep, cool, it's raining here right now, which sucks, I wanted to go to the beach, you got any other news, nah, me neither.

But check it: there was always this pause. That's how I knew there was stuff happening inside him that he wouldn't tell no one about. But I couldn't ever cross over from where I'd gone to where he was. I don't know why. Take me back there now and I'd jump that gap in a minute, even if it took some mahu-style crybaby speech, some sort of over-the-phone hug. You take me back now and I'd do it like nothing.

On those family calls usually I would get Kaui last. I bet Mom-guys was bribing her, like she couldn't go Prince Kuhio mall unless she talked to me, but honestly talking with her was the best part. Surprised me as much as anyone.

I remember this one time when she was, like, "Did they do that thing where they start asking you about Noa?"

"Yeah," I said. "Every time! Why do they always do that?"

"I swear sometimes it's like they forget I'm here, Dean," she said. "They tell you how I got on Principal's List at Kahena? Or the National Honor Society?" She was still, what, fourteen or whatever, but I was always like, whoa, because of how much she sounded like she was already out the house. Almost like I could hear her comparing mortgage rates and checking off a packing list for a New York City conference with a glass of wine and Sudoku in one hand while she's still talking story with me in the other.

"I dunno," I said. "I think so."

"Don't lie."

"What about hula?" I asked, anything to have us both not be pissed for a minute.

"Hula's good," she said. "I'm in the performance group. We did a thing at Ala Moana last weekend, and we have another performance coming up at the Hilton. Like we even get paid for it, but we have to give it back to the hālau."

"Sounds like you're mostly dancing for haoles," I said. "You like that?"

"Oh my God, kiss my ass, Dean," she said. "I bet *that* is even browner than your face now. How's the cold weather, making you haole, right?"

"No," I lied.

"And I bet they give you starstruck and Brazilian-waxed freshman girls to do your homework."

Me laughing. "Come on, I was just joking about the haole hula," I said, even though she was right and I was right, and we both knew it. Now when I think about it, seems pretty funny, how we both had each other figured out and we both hated it.

"Everyone's always 'just joking,' right?" Kaui said. "Except when they're not."

"Easy, killer," I said, even though I knew what she had. That hunger, that rage.

I think even talking about Noa, small-kind the way we did, was still something. We had that together, our own way, you know? Mostly Kaui didn't like me, I don't blame her, especially later, when things was bad at Spokane and she was out on her own, college in San Diego, that time she liked me even less. But for a while when it was just us talking on the phone we'd brag a little to each other, hold each other up, stuff that no one else was gonna do for us. And I seen that even if I was the first canoe out to sea, crashing through what we figured was possible for our family, Kaui and Noa was coming right behind.

THAT FIRST YEAR, yeah, I was getting my head up and starting to hang with the other guys on the court, but I was still the backup to Rone, who was the starting two-guard and the guy everyone looked to when the games got tight. By the time sophomore season started, I was doing everything I could not to be his dick rider, hitting the weight room and the stairs and the box jumps, had the ankle weights strapped on every minute I wasn't at practice even, calluses growing around where they rubbed my legs raw when I walked. Started for be like I fell asleep and woke up on the court, bleeding or sweating or spitting over equipment in the weight room, the *cheep* of shoes on the polished court floor, the flow and dip and rise, me and the ball. But nobody, the team, coach, nobody, still knew what I was.

And then there was this one night when we had a home game and they called it Hawaiian Night, where they gave every fan a plastic lei for wear in the stands and had rum punch and pineapple and shitty kalua pig at the concessions. When we stepped into the arena for warm-ups and I saw that some people in the stands must've known beforehand and had their cheap polyester online-bought aloha shirts, straw hats, and those stupid drinks in their hands, I wanted for punch every haole I saw in the throat.

I remember all this like I'm still playing the game right now, like the part that happened next happened in my body and keeps happening every time now, when I remember. We had Duke there that night, huge early-season game where we wanted for show everyone what we could be, but by halftime we were down by twelve and sinking.

When we were standing in the hallway, waiting for come back out for the second half warm-ups, something happened to me. Maybe it was how they had an Iz song playing on the sound system, maybe it was seeing all the aloha prints, maybe somehow the smell of bullshit concession kalua and pōke got the taste of the real stuff from back home going in my mouth, maybe it was something coming from the actual Hawaiians that was in the stand—had more of 'um than I thought in Spokane—or maybe it was just something in me, rising up only because I knew where I was from and what was happening that night.

I don't know. Something in the air. Something green and fresh and blooming, I swear I was smelling the islands, how it was when we was little, back in the valley, ferns after rain and the salty mist by the black sand beach. Almost like there was voices in my head, chanting. That same *king* feeling in my chest, ancient and big.

I got back on the court and I was everywhere, all at once. All the other players was exit signs I was passing on the freeway. I poked the ball away from their slow stupid fingers and crossed over and blitzed and had skyhooks and floaters and threes from so deep might as well I was taking shots from outer space. Everything went in. Like I was throwing pebbles into a lake. Coach was pissed I think because I didn't hardly pass, I was coast-to-coast half the time, got to be that everyone on my team and everyone on the other team just stopped to watch, I swear. Whole arena like, Here he comes again.

Final buzzer goes and we win by ten and I'm right in the middle of our jumping chest-beating mob on the court. Whole place exploding with cheers and noise and all us on the team shoving and screaming in each other's faces, where you can feel the heat and spit of all your brothers, like, We won. And later, when wasn't no one left in the locker room and I started out across the campus by myself, dirty snow and wet brick walls, that feeling from the islands was still inside me, running under my skin like blood, even when the air was so cold had steam cooking off my head and my breath smoking out into the freeze.

I didn't slow down on the court after that. More games went that way. And things started for change, about who knew me and who didn't. Got for be that when I did my phone calls home, Mom and Dad started talking plenty about *me*, Mom saying how people was asking about me when they seen her at J. Yamamoto and the local news stations started following all our games, saying how I was from Hawai'i and look at me now at the university, plenty people on the islands talking already about the playoffs and the tournament, where I'm gonna go in the draft, clapping Dad's back during his airport shifts, How's your son's double-double last night, yeah? Those days, all those games after Hawaiian Night, I was holding that big feeling inside me, what woke that night at halftime, something like a hurricane, and—even if it wasn't the same as what was in Noa?—I knew it was still giant, still powerful enough to yank my family up from that shitty house in Kalihi and set us all down someplace better.

# 7

# KAUI, 2007

## *San Diego*

THE FIRST TIME I MET VAN WE WERE AT THE BLACK throat of a culvert with a slice of cocaine between us and she was asking did I want some. I was still coming down with no oxygen after escaping a skunked and stale house party that had been busted by Campus Safety, same as Van and her friends, and when they saw me on the sidewalk after we'd ran, Van said, I heard what you were playing on the stereo, and she turned to one of her friends and said, This bitch was playing Jedi Mind Tricks! And the friend, Katarina, laughed in a way that made her lip ring shine with the wet flash of her teeth. They were two haole girls and a Vietnamese boy, who had unwrapped his dick from his pants so he could turn away from us and hose a spattering piss onto a sidewalk hedge. Katarina said she wished she'd pissed in the face of this one guy who wouldn't stop talking to her at the party, and Van said that guy probably would have liked it, and Katarina said, Well, I'd poop in it, then, and I knew I'd found my tribe before they even knew my name.

"Kaui?" Van repeated when I told them. She was the one. She had this hacked bob haircut and eyes that were both bored and ready to start a fire. "Yeah," I said. "Volcanoes," she said, "angry natives." And I had to laugh. Partly at least because there was no *Getting Lei'd, get it* or *Do you surf and oh the fruit there is unbelievable it ruined me for everywhere else* or *I'd love to visit Hawai'i, why did you ever leave.* Van had thick arms, right, same as me, only hers jumped with muscle when she did the slightest thing with them. Katarina was the whitest, with sloppy black hair. Skinny like someone had tossed a Nirvana T-shirt on a coat hanger. The pisser was Hao, his blocky Vietnamese torso dressed for yachting, and he joked while he was shaking himself dry that he should start wearing a catheter to the keggers. "Seriously, though," Hao said. "I heard about Hawai'i. There are parts of the islands where they hunt white people for sport, right?"

"Only in the elementary schools," I said.

"I like her," Van said to no one. I was blurred through the fog of four beers and didn't remember how we'd even left the party together, really. The roar and dogmouth steam of the party and then the quiet night like a sheet thrown over my head, and now we were here. On the concrete embankment of a drainage ditch outside the entrance to a culvert big enough to swallow a truck. Above us, cars blew past on the boulevard. I was three thousand miles from Hawai'i and anyone who knew anything about my brother, okay, and I'd never again need to be the sister of a miracle. And there was the cocaine, neat on the back of Van's phone.

"First time?" Van asked.

"Don't worry," Katarina said, and she went, a quick dip and sniff. Stood and sucked in all the air like she was surfacing from deep ocean. She leaned her head all the way up to the sky and stretched out on the embankment. Let the crown of her skull rock against the concrete.

Van sliced another line and didn't say much, and Hao said, "You or me?" and I realized he was asking me. I sniffed up the little mound Van had made and my blood rocketed up into my head and exploded into light. Happiness prickled across my everything. Friendship, I was thinking, right? Love. Feels like this.

Somewhere far away and right next to me Katarina said, "Let's do the culvert. We can do the culvert. Guys, guys," her sharp-teeth smile. A laugh from somewhere.

"The culvert." Was it me or Van that echoed it? "Easy."

And then we were there, down under the city in the gaping culvert, sprinting and whooping in the blackness. Running our hands along the endless baffle of steel ridges while our feet slapped through the murk. In my head I'd be like: *There's a turn just up ahead, if we go far enough we'll see light.* But the culvert just kept getting darker, the smell of batteries and old laundry. So dark my eyes were making things up: globes of red and blue flittering in my eyes when I blinked. Dry scratching and skittering on the walls in front of us, animals departing in the dark. The feeling that something was always just ahead. It could've been a cement wall. A fence of wire coming undone into a sheet of daggers. Didn't matter, said my beating body. We'd boom through whatever headfirst, all hard bones and hot power. Locomotives. What was this train we'd made ourselves into so quickly? It was roaring me away from Hawai'i. Then and now. And yes that was what I wanted: San Diego, yes; goodbye, the islands, the gods, legend of Nainoa.

We did this many times that year. We never found the end but we always found our way back.

I WAS AN ENGINEER AT SCHOOL, or anyway studying to be one. There were books, doorstop books with page-long equations. They chewed into my spine when I set them in my backpack and the titles were profound and sexy, right, like *Fundamentals of Engineering Thermodynamics*. Plus I was always in the labs: places with wood-paneled walls, old glass beakers, peeling tables of commonly used physics equations taped to the walls and corners of desks. And boys. Always, always boys. Whole classes, boys shaped like teddy bears or tree lizards. Always first to pull out their opinions, shove their knowledge at each other. I guess there's many ways engineering could feel but mostly it felt like any place feels where there's twenty boys and three girls. I had to go in with my back like a rod. Be the baddest bitch is what I said, in my head. And then did.

Sometimes I would sit by the other two girls in class— Sarah, Lindsey—but us being together felt like we were all doing it because we thought we needed to. And after a few choppy conversations? They were so haole—Idaho or North Dakota or whatever—it was obvious they'd never even sat that close to a brown person before. Meaning I was on my own, right, but whatever, I liked it. Until a few weeks into class we started group work and since I'd iced out the girls I was grouped with a bunch of boys.

Group work the way I remember: Phillip with his raging

boner for the sound of his own voice, always the first to pipe up with the proposed solution. The rest of us sitting around the table as he drove forward with scribbling on the final sheet. I'd do all the homework problems myself separately—the only way I was sure I'd understand everything anyway—so he and I were always getting into it. It reminded me of Nainoa, the way when we talked now he had an answer for everything, just bulldozed whatever I was going to say until our calls degenerated into snark and cheap shots for the weak places in each other's armor.

In group work it would go something like this: "Wrong frictional coefficient," I'd say. And Preston or Ed would sigh, and here comes Phillip.

"No it's not," he'd say.

"Look," I'd say, and start to write out the equation again, explaining how the final speed he'd calculated made no sense in the given context.

And if it became clear from arguing that I was right, Phillip would start talking about how what I'd said originally was phrased incorrectly, okay, and so what he was *really* talking about was this other thing. Or that he meant I'd balanced the equation incorrectly, not that the final answer was wrong. "The math you were doing before was in the wrong order."

Or sometimes, through just enough grinding him down, I could prove that I was right. But by then Phillip would just come back with, "Calm down." His hands up like I was pointing a gun at him. "You're overreacting." Preston or Ed would shrug and the shrug would feel like a nod and I'd want to fart all over all of them.

"*Call of Duty 4* is coming out this weekend," Preston offered once, as a white flag. Or maybe it was that other kid in the group. Gregory, was it? It didn't matter who said it. They were all capable at any moment of saying something like that, right. I mean they even smelled the same. Cheese that had been licked by a dog and then left out overnight.

I sighed. "What," I said, "is *Call of Duty 4*?"

Quiet for a second. The sense they'd all be happy if only I'd step out of the room and never come back.

"I'm definitely getting it," Preston went on. "I'm going to stand in line tonight at Best Buy."

"Who isn't?" Phillip said, voice full of excitement.

"I'm not," I said.

Silence again. A chair scraped, the circle closing just a little, me on the outside. As far as I was concerned, just go for it, boys. But not Ed. Ed the courageous one. He took his cue, when the others hunkered together. Came over and sat down at the desk next to me. His weak chin and fruit-punch-red lips. "Kaui," he said, like it was a word he had practiced in the mirror. He hunched closer and nodded. "I'm not buying *Call of Duty*, either."

"Oh God, Ed," I said. "I'm not going to let you touch my vagina."


PLENTY DAYS I'D lift my head from one of my textbooks, some opaque corner of the library. Faint smell of paper decaying into must, wood glue, and cold steel. Me greasy with lack of sleep, eyes charred from too much reading. And I'd realize it had been forever since I'd danced hula.

I figured there would never be hula here, but there was. San Diego had hella Hawai'i people, closest you could get to the islands without falling in the Pacific, I guess. I went to find them once, I did. All the Hawai'i kids in the university club. They did hula on the quad in the bright months of the year and it would've been so easy to get wrapped in with them. Their hapa Hawaiian, Japanese-Portuguese-Tongan, Spanish-Korean brown skin under pilling hoodies from high schools whose whole reputation I knew. Mynah-bird laughter and *Nah for real, got musubi we're making tonight* or *You heard the latest Jake Shimabukuro, was nuts, yeah,* and barefoot in their dorm rooms, *Bocha at night of course,* all the other things that were as much a part of me as my bones, but that felt wrong now, somehow.

I knew they'd know Nainoa, or Dean, all the legends I didn't want to be mine. If I stayed with those kids and did my hula, what then? Old Hawai'i life would slip back into me like a sleeping pill. Sludge me down until I was just another member of the club. Just again his shadow, shaped like a sister.

**BUT THEN THERE WAS THE CLIMBING:** That day when in the bland and heavy, pancake-smelling dining hall Van said to Katarina, "I bet you she can climb. You think?" And Katarina said, "Let's find out."

Van's friend had a car he'd gotten on the cheap. A busted-up Japanese sedan from who knows what year, right. Bumper duct-taped and fence-wired back to the frame. All the seat belts cut or chewed or sawed or burned off, a radio that sounded like electrocution. Upholstered in, okay, a vague armpit smell. All that mattered was it had four seats and a trunk big enough for our climbing gear and that Van's friend had this communal key he'd leave around like a treasure hunt and if you found it you could drive the car. If it was still in the lot and hadn't been towed.

It was still in the lot. We took it north. It was a golden early California hour. We had the windows down like you do in Hawai'i and everyone's hair was bucking with the beat of the wind, except Hao, his swirled explosion of spiky hair too short and stiff to move much. We stayed in the left lane all the way, the billboards and the barbed-wire lots and the shitty endless sameness strip malls slipping in and out of view with their stucco white. And the matchstick-brown-and-sagebrush hills. Until Van blinkered us off the 5 and it wasn't until the loop and drift of the turn gave me gravity in my belly that I realized we'd been doing above ninety the whole way.

All the veins of retarred cracks in the road plus pink-gold smogginess of sunup plus the prickled slack palm trees and flat brown rectangles of unused land. Van drove down two wrong streets and past a barely up chain-link fence with frothing pit bulls, barking their guttural balls off.

Katarina and Hao were bantering like the stupidest siblings. Now Katarina was suggesting Hao touched himself while listening to boy bands on the radio. Now Hao said it wasn't masturbation, he was just learning the dance moves. Which brought them back to me, hula, oh God—

"Are we almost there?" I called out to Van.

"Okay, okay," Van said. We all bounced with the sudden potholing of the car. Gravel popping under the tires. "Here we are," Van sang out. She swung a sudden right and locked the brakes into a skid. The dust cloud caught up to us and when it cleared we were looking at the darkened husk of grain silos, columns of cylinders weeping unidentified industrial creams, skeletal crane arms and scaffolding lurking behind them. A small flock of crows ribboned into the breeze, crying out in creaky voices.

And then we were inside the thing. The ground floor of the elevator crammed tight with riveted beams and spears of light, huge pipe joints and all along the train-car-shaped center aisle, rail tracks for whatever carts used to move here. I couldn't believe how holy the air felt.

It was just me and Van standing in there at first, Hao and Katarina still catching up. Van's breaths sounded small and even as she turned to take it all in. She hooted once, softly. The brightness in her face. I said okay, this was okay, only I wasn't talking about the climbing or the elevator. But I didn't tell her that. I didn't tell her how much I wanted what was happening, right now. All around there were so many angles and edges and blunt corners and places to grab and hold on and go up.

"Sometimes this is all I think about," she said. She nodded off to Hao and Katarina as they entered. "I love them," she said. "Let's see if you can keep up."

"You tell me how my ass looks in these jeans when you're watching me from below," I said.

She laughed. We were looking right at each other. Take a match and hold it to the strip, start the strike. Somewhere at the microscopic level there are whole worlds of hot light that gather and jump to the match tip. That's what we were.

"All right, hula girl," she said. "Be a bitch on it."

We climbed. At first just me and Van, straight up our columns of iron, clutching the ridges and edges and using our rubber-soled feet like paws, dancing and moving and pulling, going up together. As we went we spread out, all four of us, grunting and clattering and rising up off the floor, climbing our way into the ribs of this long-dead steel giant. Toward the heart of the thing. I moved closer to Van, Katarina, Hao. I wanted us together, wanted them to feel with me the big nameless thing we'd worked our way into, a silence like the presence of our own private God.

I TALKED TO my parents on the phone but I hated it. They kept me a person of two places, okay? A person of here and there, and not belonging in either place. But if it was a give and take between the two, Hawai'i was starting to lose. I could almost feel the sun and sand and salt of Hawai'i flaking off.

"How's the haole land?" Dad would ask, his favorite way to start calls.

"No one showers and the food sucks," I said.

And Dad straight cackling on the other end of the phone. Almost so I could hear his smile lines. "I knew it!" he said. "I knew it. Fuckin' mainland and its stink-ass haoles. So, what, you're running the campus now or what?"

So you are paying attention, Dad, I thought. Maybe just a little bit.

"You know it," I said. "I started robbing banks on the weekends, too."

"That's what I'm talking about," Dad said—both to me and to Mom, off-phone. "Better be, with the bill they're sticking us with."

I wanted to say I'd cosigned on the loans and it wasn't just him. That some of the kids here didn't have any loans, or if they did, spent them like the future was a certain thing: new laptops and nights out at restaurants and the sort of apartments where the cabinets were, like, Scandinavian sexy. While I was working off scanned pages or library-lifted books where I'd removed the magnetic strip. Quadrupling up on the McDonald's Dollar

Menu to stash enough in our mini-fridge for half the week, then chopsticking bricks of saimin on the late nights. I didn't forget where I was from or how each semester's tuition bill alone felt like I was holding a gun to their heads. And my own.

I clamped my mouth shut. So hard pain cranked through my teeth. "I know, Dad, trust me, I know."

"People these days," Dad said, "it's like everyone's out to get as much money from you as they can, yeah? Like, if they figure the price can be just a little higher, every time, they raise 'um up."

"So life's good at home?" I said. "You and Mom still doing your thing?"

"What, you mean like sex?" he asked. "Yeah, we still oofing. In fact, just last night we was—"

"Dad—"

"No, serious, just last night we went for happy hour at Os-mani Bar, and I was like, 'Babe, no one gonna see nothing in the parking lot, and—'"

"Dad! I'll hang up the phone. I swear to God."

He laughed and laughed. "Only joke! Sheesh, everyone's all uptight over there. We doing good, Kaui, we doing good. I dunno. Working our asses off. Price of paradise and like that. It's home."

We went on for a minute, things here and there about neighbors, a couple of people I knew from high school that Dad saw at the airport, working security jobs or ticket-counter jobs or as flight attendants. There was a training program he was hoping to get into, so that he could move into a flight-mechanic position. "All those guys is badasses," he said. "Marines and all that. I should have gone military."

"So you could be yelled at by haole guys with skinhead hair-cuts for, like, six years or something? Come on, Dad."

"I coulda seen the world, though," Dad said. "Got real skills, you know? They learn things there, at least."

"Yeah, they learn how to shoot other brown people," I said.

"Okay, okay," Dad said. "I get it, you know everything now that you been at college for a semester or two, yeah yeah yeah. I love you. Here's your mother."

The phone tumbled from hand to hand.

"You're doing okay," Mom said, barely a question.

"Of course," I said. "Did some great climbing last week with Van-guys."

"Climbing," she said. "I hope you don't think you're just there to party."

"I just got all this from Dad," I said. "I know what I'm here for."

She cleared her throat. "How are classes, then?"

"Hard," I said. "But I like engineering."

"Good," she said. "At least you're not studying, I don't know, American history of comic books or something like that."

"Right."

"You getting enough sleep? Enough food?"

When I can afford it, I wanted to say. But I already knew where the call was going. It didn't matter what I said, so I stayed quiet, so that we could get where we were going faster.

"You talk to Noa lately?" she asked. There you go. Didn't take as long as I thought.

"I mean, maybe," I said.

"How's he doing?"

"Didn't you just talk to him?"

"We did," Mom said. "But you know, kids don't always tell their parents things."

If only you knew me, Mom, I wanted to say. I've felt the midnight crush at a strip club, me and Van and Hao and Katarina there almost like a joke, but still pulled in by it, the red lights and sweat and gritty beats. Did you know I'd been so many times drunk or stoned or snowed, trying not to trip my numb legs on themselves while walking dark o'clock streets. Or did you know I'd climbed without a rope at terminal heights at least a few times, just me and air and death.

"Don't be worried," I told her. "We're fine."

"I hope so," she said. "We did a lot to get you there, you know."

She had to stick it in, right? She never said shit like this to the boys, only to me. Like I was supposed to be guilty of ambition while they were just living their full potential. "I know, Mom," I said.

"We miss all of you," she said.

And I said I did, too—and I did. But feeling it then, the missing was different than I expected. Less desperate, I guess. And getting smaller all the time.

# 8

# NAINOA, 2008

## *Portland*

**I RECOGNIZED THE HOUSE EVEN THOUGH I'D NEVER SEEN** it before, recognized it even if the two police cars hadn't been there, they were all the same these days (the places we went): the bedsheeted windows, the trash-choked clapboard siding, the greasy scatter of engine parts on the clumpy lawn.

"I love what they've done with the place," Erin said, yanking the ambulance's shifter into park. She dropped the lights and we each pulled a fresh pair of blue latex from the box. I went around back to get the kit, she started toward the officer on the porch, speaking to him in bored tones, preparing for the state of the apparently traumatized skulls inside.

The radios spat, it was otherwise quiet. The officer at the top of the porch bowed, toed open the door. "There's one in the living room near the fireplace," he said. "Looks like the other one fought in the kitchen before he gave up."

Erin stepped up the creaking stairs, through the yawn of the door, a plastic scent like old diapers, a hot bloom of air. I went right behind her.

The light inside was sooty, the wood floor gouged and cross-slashed from years of use, crown molding and naked bulbs. Near a dingy sectional couch was the first patient, skeletal and sallow, with an officer bent over his torso, ramming him with chest compressions.

Erin dropped to the floor by the officer's side and he understood, pulling his hands back like it was time to wash them. "The second?" Erin asked, even as she started compressions, and the officer nodded toward the kitchen. I went, around the corner, into the stench, it was as if a cat had pissed into a moldering refrigerator. The wall above the stovetop was scorched, something like a war bomb burn, and on the floor a topology of discarded cookware and trash bags, organic refuse, and in the back corner, near the refrigerator, the third officer was negotiating a grizzled rope of a meth addict onto a stool.

The addict was breathing like he'd just surfaced from drowning, but he was breathing, through his tangled roots of goat beard, a face pecked with bloody scabs.

"The fuck is this party," he said.

I was confused and turned toward the officer. "He looks alive," I said.

"That's the problem," the officer said, his nose red and swollen, it looked like he'd taken a punch there. He jerked the addict by his shirt scruff into a better seating position.

"Any other problems?"

"My mortgage, my kids, your questions," the officer said. He looked like he was waiting for me to leave. "Maybe check his friend in the living room."

But I was already gone as he said that, back to where we came in, I saw the baseball bat for the first time on the floor, grip tape blackened with palm sweat, the end pink and spiked with bits of hair. There were fist-sized hamburger wrappers balled all over, an empty bookshelf leaning drunk against the back corner, and there was Erin working on the one who'd been beaten, paddles in her hands. The patient was still on his back, his left leg folded wrong, bent sideways and high. Eyes closed, the blue bloom of his lips.

"Hey, inspector, you want to help here?" Erin said, holding the paddles, and I already had an idea. I dropped to my knees, there was no pulse, not a hint at the carotid or ulnar.

"D-fib isn't working because his heart isn't beating," I said. Now the stink of sweat and urine, there his crusty shirt already yanked up around the splay of his armpits, a dollop of gel at the ribs, another at the pectoral.

"I lost it," she said, dropping the paddles. "It was there."

"It's gone," I said.

"I know."

"Airway clear?"

"Fuck you," she said. "I'm not an idiot. It's the bat that did this."

"Maybe the drugs," I said. "Let's try again." I stitched my fingers together, put the edge of my palm into his sternum and compressed, careful to avoid the xiphoid process and the hemorrhage that could follow its snapping. His body: at the beginning it was just him, a man, but my eyes and teeth pinched as I compressed his chest, the oxygenated gasp of everything that moved in him, and then I felt as if I were squinting my brain. He was the him I saw but also a him I felt: I felt the weave of his skin and the buttery chunks of fat underneath, the hush and rush of what could only be his blood, so long and blowing, all of this just a feeling, it was nothing I saw. There were other muddled sensations deeper down, but strongest was an effervescent urge, his body eager to start repairing itself, but even that came and went so quick I still couldn't separate all the this from the that. There were colors I felt, he had the yellow tarry rush of meth's hate booming through his veins, then the jagged red memories of anger that came and went like thunderheads inside his skull, a color I'd felt many times before—and all the while the truth of my hands, chest compressions, shoving blood around his husk. I was on my knees and over the patient, my palms at his sternum, dropping my weight down and letting it come back up, one two three four five six seven, on and on and on. The liquid pop of the already broken ribs went like a clock. Something sparked, it certainly wasn't the compressions, it was only that I was searching, the same as I always am when I do this now, searching and feeling and trying to understand what the injury *was*, at the same time that I understood what his body *should be*. I think something had already started—

Erin was saying my name like a chant, her fingers hooked into my right deltoid, I realized she was shaking me. The look I must have given her as I took my hands off the body.

"It's been five minutes since you started, superhero," she said. "No change. We need to transport."

I was breathing hard, as she had been, and I could feel the slick cool sweat patches at my back and chest. But the addict's body was quiet; everything was finished, wasn't it. The police officers watched us pull back from the body, the still point of sound when everyone understands.

"Transport," Erin said again.

She was gone and returned with the gurney, bashing it up the steps with one of the officers, bright metal crashes as it hit each stair. I was still doing compressions until we lifted him into the gurney, then rolled it back down the stairs and into the wide-open back of the ambulance. Erin legged up into the back with the gurney, and had started to close one of the ambulance doors when the patient sat up calmly, spat Erin's plastic rescue breath guard from his mouth, and said, "Holy, holy, holy."

We froze: Erin reaching for the still-open door, me about to secure the other, we stared across the gap between the end of the rig where we were and the risen body in the back. Even from that distance I could see the yellow-blue flush had left his skin, the wrinkles shallowing, his hair thicker, it was as if he'd been made younger by fifty years. He looked, in a word, healthy. He curled his spine forward and hacked a wave of vomit onto the snow-white sheet covering his lap.

His mouth was slack. He looked down at his mess, then back up at us, wiped his jaw with his wrist. Glanced again at his lap, where the sheet had swelled into a pyramid with a thick knob at the apex.

"I think I have a boner," he said. "What happened?"

IT WAS OUR last call of the shift. We weren't even sure if we should still take him to the hospital, every vital sign was perfect all of a sudden, nothing to report, and what could we have said that wouldn't have put us both in the psych ward anyway. But it seemed even worse to leave him there with the officers, who were already folding the other addict into the back of a car, ready to be done with him and back to their desks, the reports. So we took the risen one to the hospital with a single police escort and ran down the situation to the ER staff, who said, "If he isn't dead he can wait in line with everyone else," and Erin said, "Thank God," and the addict demanded cigarettes of everyone that passed our chairs in the waiting room, until a female nurse said, "Jesus Christ, shut up," and produced a loosey from a desk behind the attendant's window and placed the cigarette in the addict's palms like a dog treat. Erin and I started back for the rig and saw the officer's slow-blinking face and purpling nose as he realized how much longer he'd be the responsible one. We signed our papers and drove out from under it all.

Back at the station Erin cleaned the rig, running through inventory as loud as she could, she wasn't saying a word, but the slapping of tape rolls and trauma shears and intubation packs in and out of their places, the crackle and squealing zip and scratchy Velcro tears, she was still telling me her opinion. Are we doing this again, I thought, so I waited, leaning against the outside of the rig, behind the open back door, listened to her fumbling with a hose as she moved it back and forth, the fold and rustle of a duffel.

"I'm going to go sit down," I said as if the door weren't there. "Maybe just a quick granola bar or something."

She leaned around the door so she could see me. "You go do your thing." She flapped a wrist in my general direction. "The way you always do."

"At least a cup of coffee?" I said. "You look tired."

"So do you."

"But I'm not," I said.

"Right, I forgot, Mr. Invincible."

"Did I do something to offend you?" I asked. I was always the one that had to be the adult this way, although Erin was two years my senior.

"I knew that addict's heart had stopped beating," she said. She moved out of sight, back behind the door, then locked a buckle, the clean clip-sound echoed in the flat morning of the garage, us all alone then for a minute, the other paramedics and EMTs back in the lockers or the kitchen. "And I knew that there was risk to the femoral artery when we were extracting the biker," she went on, "and I knew not to give insulin to the hypoglycemic drinker. But there you were." I crossed my arms and waited, it was always better to let her boil over, there was even something to enjoy in it, almost a taste to her fury, when she'd really get going, when she'd call me a *snot-nosed book rat* or *wonder-boy mansplainer*, all my attitudes and ass-stuck explanations, she'd been here so much longer and why was it so hard for me to remember that. She came back out of the ambulance.

"You always have to say something, don't you."

"Only when I'm right," I said.

"There you go," she said. She was finally looking at me, her cheeks hot, a flex and pulse to her throat. Her eyes were ringed with bruise-colored skin. "I can't wait until you go to med school." She started toward the side entrance to the station, the hall with the bathrooms where every shift we scrubbed off all the remains of everyone we'd touched that day.

"I don't know how he came back, either, Erin," I lied, loud enough for her to hear. "He was almost gone. I don't know how he came back."

She stopped walking, but stayed faced away from me.

"But you were following the right procedure," I said. "The chest compressions."

"You're lying," she said. "You did something."

I turned back to the ambulance, considered all the stinking howling leaking hours we'd spent in it. What did I do, Erin? Even I was still trying to understand, I only knew that when I touched a broken body, I held an idea of what that body *should* be, and that idea became the muscle of a heartbeat, or the fusing of bones, or the electrochemical bolts storming through synapses. I'd felt the addict's body wanting to be repaired, and then the body had done just that, chased the overdose from its own blood and brain.

"All I did was work," I said. "Just followed procedure."

We both knew she'd made a mistake with the paddles, I'd seen it in her eyes, the panicked flex of recognition that I had caught the mistake, as much as she had. "You did what you were supposed to," I said. "I'd say that to anyone who asked."

She was still facing away, but I saw her exhale.

"Okay," she said.

"Get some sleep," I said.

"Fuck you," she said, but I could hear the ease returning to her.

THE NIGHT ECHOED IN MY HEAD, the burning-cat-piss stink of the meth house, the air of hate and rage between the men inside, the stickiness of death and neglect. And something deeper, the trembling understanding of what I was becoming capable of. I was home now, considering my open refrigerator, all condiments and partially finished boxed mac and cheese. A queasy knot in my stomach. I closed the refrigerator and stared at the biology anatomy chemistry textbooks that were propping up the thrift-store television in the corner.

There had been an effervescence under my skin as I'd come home, popping with excitement at what I'd done, but now, as I stood in the center of the apartment, the energy all slithered away, taking so much strength with it, it was all I could do to move toward my bed, my legs slower with each step, the feeling of being underwater. I got enough of my clothing off before I slumped into bed and plunged through the softness of the mattress into darkness.

WHEN I WOKE, it was clear some time had passed. The air had moved from morning crisp into the thicker afternoon, the light already thinning outside the window. I checked my watch, three-thirty, turned to look at my bedside table, where I saw a photo-booth strip of pictures, me and Khadeja and her six-year-old daughter, Rika, clumped together like a bouquet in front of the tiny camera, blown out with black-and-white light. The heaviness in me was gone; only that fizzing underneath, all the ideas of what I'd seen. When I sat up and saw the dim, bare truth of my apartment, the excitement within me felt so suddenly incomplete, so bottled and lonely, that I knew I had to get out.

I had my shower and clothes on and hopped a bus to Khadeja's office.

"YOU'RE OUTSIDE?" Khadeja asked, after I'd called her from the sidewalk.

"Just for a second," I said. "Come down."

The building all glass and steel, polished and blandly imposing, but through the three-story foyer I saw her walking.

Khadeja. The boom of her Afro pulled back in a ponytail pom-pom, eyes full of gleeful intelligence, the draping fabric that floated off her broad arms, the lines of flex in her calves with each clacking step toward me. I can only imagine it was a stupid smile I gave at her arrival, I was stoned for her in that moment.

Five months we'd been seeing each other, met in a bar when she was out for a friend's birthday and I was winding down with two other guys from work, after that it was us meeting at first at strange times, early-afternoon drinks or lunches during the week, all of which I understood later when she finally had me over and I met Rika. And it worked, we worked, and we'd continued; only now did I think there was enough there that I could do this, show up unannounced at her office.

"What is it?" she asked.

I'd expected a gaze that was annoyed and busy contemplating balance sheets and compounded interest, but she appeared genuinely happy to see me. "I know you're busy at work," I said, and she shook her head.

"Company party," she said. "Celebrating another strong quarter."

"Vegetable dip with only the celery left," I said. "Store-brand soft drinks and gas-station wine, a few balloons taped to the sides of the micro-kitchen."

She laughed. "How did you know?"

I shrugged. "It's an accounting firm."

"They were about to start Pictionary."

"You think you could steal some of that wine?" I asked.

Five minutes later and her purse was warming a bottle of low-grade red, we walked along the streets to the North Park Blocks, evidence of a recent peace vigil: shriveled thumbs of burned-out candles rested on every solid surface, then soggy cardboard signs discarded gently against statues and the legs of benches. *Study War No More*, they pleaded, and a few of the larger signs had been repurposed as mattresses by the homeless that haunted the park.

"Not my favorite place," Khadeja admitted.

"What's not to love?" I said, trying for comedy, suddenly scared I could ruin this feeling I had, rather than expand it to hold us both. "I'm sorry. I didn't have a plan. I just wanted to see you, is all."

The simple truth of that brightened us both, for we had both been, when we first met, so much older than those around us, aged with the things nature had asked us to carry—she with Rika, who she'd borne so young, me with my accelerated path through school, the work I was trying to do now—and in that state it had been that much more exciting to find someone else that understood true circumstances, and how much more important that made a present tense *you me us we are doing just this* that could exist only briefly before we were dragged back into those circumstances.

"Well," she said with a flash of her teeth, spreading her arms, "I'm here. Entertain me, Mr. Flores, and you better make it fast."

"So," I said, scooting over next to her where we sat on the steps of a statue, "did you know I have powers?"

She touched her tongue to her top teeth, still smiling. "That's right, we're doing that thing where we still have secrets from each other. Go on, go on."

"It's quite simple, actually," I said, with no idea what I'd say next. "It will require wine." We'd neglected a corkscrew, but I showed her how to finger the cork back down through the neck until it bobbed in the wine below, we each took a pull straight from the bottle.

"I'm connected to things no one else can see," I said. I took her lower back into my hand and gently guided her snug against my hip. "Listen," I whispered into her ear.

And we were quiet, and she heard the birdsong that was emerging, as I had been hearing for blocks at a time already, over the city noise rather than under it, because of what I was. I didn't think there was any way to amplify it, but I told her again, "Listen," and what was in the trees came back bright and clear.

"It sounds like they're searching for each other," I said. "But if you listen closer . . . none of them are actually lost."

Khadeja was perfectly still. She had her eyes closed. We both listened, the bird calls went, bouncy and bright. The smell of wet bark, rich and papery, from the recent rain.

Khadeja listened a minute more, then opened her eyes and looked at me. "That's one of your things," she said. "Animals."

I shrugged. "Maybe."

I noticed that she didn't move, stayed close. "I'm serious," she said. "Maybe it seems negligent, but when I first saw you act that way—what was it, our second date or something, remember the little dog outside the restaurant, that woman all in yellow that was far too drunk and looking for the elevator?—you did this thing," she said. "Where you crouched down and just barely brushed the dog. It was going nuts, and when you arrived, it went so calm it might as well have been drugged. That was when I knew you'd be good with Rika."

"Because I petted a dog gently, I was going to be good with your daughter?" I said. "That *is* negligent."

And she laughed. "Don't tell Rika."

With a hand gripped on the neck of the wine bottle I gestured off the sidewalk. "Look," I said. I pointed down to massive puddles that had formed in the soggy ground, bad drainage, and to a cluster of ants there that had made themselves into a lumpy ball, each ant linking to another ant with nothing more than smell and touch to understand the need to survive, and that to do so they'd have to weave together into a fabric thick and solid enough to repel water, and float that way for as long as the water carried them, and that some of them would drown for it. I was narrating it all as we sat there, pulling from the wine, warm and corky, the bits of it that tumbled along our tongues. We both kept spitting the crumbles into the dirt. I was still talking about the ants, I wondered what the world would be like if we were even a fraction as mighty as they were, to build our bodies into a raft for each other—

"That's it," Khadeja said, and shook her head, though she still smiled. "That'll do, Mr. Flores. I didn't come for a biology-and-holiness seminar."

I realized how much I'd been talking and was immediately embarrassed. "I'm sorry," I said. "I didn't—"

"Just be quiet," she said, "just for a second." Then she tilted her head and leaned in to me, our lips finding each other, again and again, until we left the rest of the bottle on the steps and found ourselves wandering back through the damp spring park. We'd made something, just sitting there together, meeting each other over and over, and now whatever it was we'd made echoed off the streets and buildings around us as we walked, our arms hooked into each other and cuddled so fierce that it was almost as if we'd created new bones that joined us at the ribs.

# 9

# KAUI, 2008

## *San Diego*

SUMMER BREAK WAS COMING AND THERE WAS NOTHING in me that wanted it.

Summer break in Hawai'i would be Dean walking around, getting shakas and fist bumps from strangers, high school girls hoping to get him to their beach party, Mom and Dad letting him lie around the house, all because for a few months he threw a ball through a hoop with other boys and got it in more than he missed. Noa, if he came home, too, would have his own room— they'd move me to the couch, guaranteed—and would mostly be in there alone, right, or in the garage like he'd been before, or out and away, seeing what new laws of the universe he could bend.

Summer break in Hawai'i would be me with a job at a mall or a fast-food place or maybe at a hotel. If I was lucky. Whole ocean between me and climbing. Between me and being an engineer. Between me and Van.

"Come home," Mom said, on the phone.

"And do what?" I asked.

"Whatever we need you to do," she said.

Sometimes I don't know if the fight finds me or I find the fight. Especially with my family.

"You mean sweep up the lanai, get Dad a beer when he wants, maybe even bag groceries?" I should have just shut up. But there was me and there was the rest of the family. "You don't need me for that," I said. "Someone already has that job."

"You don't ever think before you talk, do you?" Mom said. "You're the only one that's like this."

"Like what? Independent? Guilt-free?" I said. "If this is about money, I can make more here. And spend less. I'll send you a check every month, if you need it."

"It's not about the money," she said.

"Mom," I said. "In Hawai'i? If you're not making bank like a lawyer or something? Everything's at least a *little bit* about money."

I knew what it was really about. She could see what the main-land was doing to me, okay? What it was giving me. Big-sky space, opportunities, and oxygen to burn and burn and burn bright.

"I talked with a couple of your dad's friends," Mom said. "Kyle and Nate—them, you remember?"

I had no idea who these people were. "Sure," I said.

"They've got a few engineering jobs. Some work they're doing over in Pearl Harbor, one of them has a solar-energy company in the industrial area."

She had me there. That *did* sound good, right, at least compared to anything else I'd get, late as it was in the semester. I swear, it was almost like no one in all of San Diego had a job. Offices full of consultants and advisers and part-time-appointment-only business cards for hire.

"You tell them thanks but I got it," I said to Mom. "I can make it work here. I gotta go. Studying. It's almost exam week."


BUT WITH HAO AND KATARINA AND VAN, when the end came? You'd think there'd be speeches, right. Since it was before summer break and it would be months until we'd see each other again. We'd become each other's habit, as much a part of the morning and night as brushing teeth. And just like that we'd cut ways for long enough that it almost felt like we wouldn't be quite the same when we came back. But no one really said anything about it. We just rolled out of the two piles we'd made of ourselves, me Van Katarina Hao, our ripe tangle of denim and brambles of hair and hot-mouth yawning. Around us on the tabletops and counters a few beer cans gone halfsies, grease-freckled pizza boxes, the television remote by our toothbrushes. This was the us left over from the end-of-year parties and the party after those parties. Smearing now our stink all over the room and each other. We had different planes or cars to catch and there were hugs and *see you soon*s. Van was heading home and Hao was heading home and Katarina was heading home. Then the medicated weather of summer San Diego opened up yellow and orange and polite in front of me and me alone.

I found what I needed to stay. Students here always rented their lives out over summer. They went to six-week language school in Nice or volunteer vacations in Oaxaca or wherever else the tear-away flyers in the student union suggested as a glossy possibility. And left behind? Their work-study jobs. Their three-person close-to-campus houses. An easy fit for a short time for the leftovers. Like me.

That was the summer I learned: almost anything becomes tolerable if you get yourself a routine.

One. Wake in the morning after two or three snooze buttons. Sit up in the blue sheets that haven't seen a wash cycle since the day they were bought. The right mornings I'd pour myself into my running clothes and quick-step down the front stairs and run good splits in the sticky cold fog. Gasping for oxygen through a sucking wet shirt, way before breakfast. Bowl of cold milk and no-sugar cereal, a piece of fruit. Walk to my first job, an office job, fresh and hot clean from a shower, my legs stretching with the afterburn of the run.

Two. Choose between maybe too tight or maybe too low-cut, maybe it's dowdy or maybe it's infantilizing. But you have to wear something appropriate to the campus office job, okay? Elevators and office foyers, hallways. Dark, ridged, rounded wood. Me pulling from stacks of printed papers, efficient-fingering the data-entry key combinations. Form e-mails and easy chatter with my office-mates—there's one other, a haole girl junior who takes smoke breaks every twenty-five minutes. On her return the first thing she always does is gather her textured, fake-leather purse in her lap, crinkle free a piece of gum, and bend it onto her tongue. It's that smell and the sharp citrus of whatever they put in the bathroom hand soap. And she'll ask where I got the blouse. The earrings. The necklace I hated but wore anyway. And on and on and on.

Three. Tuesday Thursday Saturday I hop a bus to Romanesque

to wait tables for the dinner shift. Four hours of walk-running to the kitchen and back, memorizing and then scrambling and rememorizing the orders of patrons. Remember the specials, the allergen considerations, wine lists, and ironed white shirts and ass-sucking black pants, of course those help me get tips. Even with a body that feels as tita as mine.

Weeks go by, right, me not even knowing what the date was, just the day of the week. Which shifts I was working. Some nights I'd split sides of the couch with one of my dull roommates, the kind of haole girls that were up-and-coming members of the Future Trophy Wives of America. Bland as saimin without the sauce. Other nights I'd get itchy hands and grab my climbing shoes, find a closed-down crafts store or bricked-up condemned industrial block, and climb and climb and climb. Slip my toes into cracks or the ledges and dimples of architecture. Hook my fingers into dime edges, get up off the ground and breathe terror.

But mostly it was time like a dull buzz. Routine and sunup sundown hello goodbye. Time like a filament made incandescent by a weak electric current.

If Van was here, I thought, that filament would get so hot it would pop. If Van was here, there would always be something to laugh about, right? Something we'd make, some new experience I never would have guessed I'd do but that would suddenly seem to say more about what I wanted to be than anything that had come before. If Van. If Van.

That summer there was this one time Noa called me. I was walking from the bus stop to Romanesque.

"Dial a wrong number?" I asked, when I answered.

"Come on," he said.

"Bad joke," I said. "I was just surprised that you called."

"Yeah, I know," he said. "Me, too."

That was weird. "Okay," I said. "I'm heading into the dinner shift, so make it fast."

"You're a cook?" he asked.

How many times. "I wait tables, Noa." And it wasn't that he was forgetful or stupid or any of that, right. He just didn't care enough to remember. It was him and what he was doing, that was all that was in his head. "This is why I don't tell you anything, because it's not worth it. What's up?" I asked.

"Nothing," he said.

"You called me to say nothing's up," I said. "Great, thanks for the call, Noa, you can do this anytime—"

"Remember how Skyler's hand was when he came back to school? After New Year's?"

Something in his voice, like how Van was sometimes. How I was sometimes, when we had the right chemicals in our veins. Everything expanding. The memory of Skyler's hand jumped into me. I'd never seen the hand again myself, after he blew it up. It was only that I'd heard there was something off about it, when they uncovered it in the emergency room: The skin was too smooth. The perfect shape of the fingers. *Kinda different, almost like it's one statue girl's hand or something,* is what Dean said. "Everyone thought it was too pretty."

"Like a sculpture." Noa laughed. But just as fast, something went tight and quiet in him. "You don't believe that was me, do you?"

If he was just calling for a verbal handjob. My shift started, like, two minutes ago. "Noa, I don't—"

"It seemed like you were always the one just playing along. Dean believed. Of course Mom and Dad did. They saw . . . they saw other things, too. But you never believed, did you?"

"Why are you asking me this?"

"I'm seeing all these things out here. The people I'm with in the ambulance, the people right on the edge—there's all this light and thread that makes up our bodies. It almost feels the same as the 'uke. Like when there's a voice and the strings humming from a chord, I can do that now, with a human body, the bones and the heart and the lungs, I can make it sing—"

I laughed at that. "Sorry," I said. "I shouldn't laugh, you just—you sound a little nuts."

"There was this addict—" he started, we'd been talking at the same time, but *a little nuts* just hung there in the air.

"Noa," I said. "It's okay—"

"No, I get it," he said. "You're right."

"Maybe you should spend less time in the ambulance," I said. "Take a break or something."

He cleared his throat. "What makes you think I can?"

"You can do whatever you want," I said.

"No I can't," Noa said. "You can, but not me."

Part of me was tired of him this way. When he acted like he was the one suffering, when really all the rest of us were having to deal with what it meant to not be him. Who knew what he was going to be able to do with his abilities someday, while I had to check my watch and see I was late and late meant maybe getting fired and maybe getting fired meant I'd lose the wad of tips I always went home with, the only real money I'd make all summer, okay?

"Hey," I said. "I gotta go. Time to indulge ridiculous gluten requests and pretend everyone is my friend for the next four hours. I didn't mean anything by laughing, Noa. I'm sorry."

"I know," he said. "It doesn't matter."

"I can listen, I swear," I said. I don't know why I got apologetic at the end. It seemed like something was slipping away.

"I know," he said. "I know that."

We said goodbye and hung up.

I tried again later. I tried with him and Dean at the same time, party call. I wasn't good at stuff like that—it quickly became an obligation. But Noa was gone by then, anyway, or at least it felt like that when he'd talk. Like he was back out in the ocean among the sharks, bobbing alone. I could see him there, the waves and tides and gods dragging him around. But I'm in the water, too, I wanted to say. And there are plenty eyes on you. No one's watching to see if I stay afloat.

BUT SOON SUMMER BREAK WAS OVER. Everyone came back: Van and Hao and Katarina. Like nothing had happened in the two and a half months apart, because nothing had happened. It couldn't have been more than a week into that fall semester and Van had something for me: did I want to check out this uppity party she had tickets to.

"Except," she said, "I don't *have* have tickets."

She clarified: "There are these boys we have to bring. They have the tickets."

So we went to Connor's house, paint-chipping trim and a Corona sign in the window, right, a mashed and faded couch on the porch. Lacrosse stick leaning against the electricity meter.

"You're kidding me," I said.

Van shrugged. "They have tickets. Connor's got a body like a swimmer."

She was one step ahead of me on the stairs. I slapped her ass, hard enough that it stung us both. Her muscle, my hand. It was all we needed to say.

The festival was in Ramona, its front entrance was a large white tent surrounded by fuzzy gold globes of light and cream-colored linen and enveloped in a fog of constipated pleasantness. All these haoles of a barely wrinkled age, prevailing interest rates and the latest *New Yorker*. We stood on green grass, me and Van easily the youngest two people there. Like, it almost looked illegal.

Van was wearing a sleek black top, shoulderless on one side, a pair of immaculate white shorts with gold buttons. Me in this blue dress that I guess could be little except the way some parts of it stretched wrong on me.

At one point we were separated. Sean and I were out on the bluff. Below and distant, pinched hills bearing what looked like mesquite and bougainvillea. A truck from the thirties or something, strategically placed off the bluff, casks in the back cocked just so, right? It was so disingenuous, it might as well have been a movie set. The high humid sonata of the crickets. Grass crinkling under our shoes.

"You're going to say something," I said to Sean, "and it's going to ruin this goddamn moment."

"What?" Sean said.

"You see?"

He laughed. "I swear, Kaui." His teeth were the white of new snow, his skin was dark brown, knotted and roped through with muscles I didn't even know existed until I saw him with his shirt off. He'd been a gymnast and then he was studying—I shit you not—sports marketing. But he answered me the same so often: *You're crazy*, or *What am I going to do with you*. He didn't know a thing. It was like talking to a sack of hammers.

"Wine's good, though," he said, finally.

"I can't tell," I said. "It all tastes the same to me."

"Huh," he said.

"I'd die for a beer right now. Literally die."

He smiled. "Right. So—Connor tells me you're studying engineering."

"Yep."

"Sounds hard."

"Yep."

"Engi*nerd*. You ever heard that one? That's what we used to call engineers. I mean, not all of them. And not you, obviously. Only—"

"I get it," I said. Just for the hell of it—because it was, like, polished and jumping with strength, the sort of dark brown that reminded me of boys back home—I stroked his right biceps. I could maybe do this, I thought, wondering how much wine it would take. More than I was willing to put in me.

"Cheers," I said. Tilted my wineglass back, and swallowed.

While I was drinking, something caught my eye. I turned to focus on it. On the far side of the bluff, Van's voice had come up. She was talking to Connor. I couldn't make out the words. But I could see his weight shift. Leaning with his chest out, like he owned her space. But those things never worked on Van. Instead, she finished her glass of wine in one pull. After she got it all in her mouth she looked at him straight and spat the wine into his face. Then she placed her glass on the nearest cocktail table and walked back into the tent.

I started walking after her. "Stay," I said back to Sean. "Or go to him. Whatever."

It was much hotter in the tent. As if something large was sleeping just above the crowd. And it was starting to smell, in some corners, a little like armpits. Everyone's voices inside were excited. I found Van by the snack table. She was stacking cheese on crackers and chomping them down. Plus holding another glass of wine.

"You spilled your wine out there," I said. "On Connor's face."

She laughed. "I guess I'm clumsy when I drink wine."

She crushed crackers and cheese into her mouth. "Think it was a good idea to come here?"

"If you wanted to be fancy, we could have just gone to something fancy in the city," I said. "Swing-dance clubs downtown."

"Do I look like I swing-dance to you?"

"You do right now."

She shrugged, crunched another cracker sandwich. "We're going to leave school one of these days, probably faster than we think. All over. We're supposed to be women out in the world—office heels and bank accounts. I don't know."

"Are you kidding me?" I said. "Talking to Sean is like talking to a crash-test dummy. I'll stay in school and get another degree."

"But he has good arms, right?" Van asked.

My turn to laugh. "Right?" I said. "They're, like, lickable. I want to rub my— Aren't you lactose-intolerant?" I asked, watching her pinch more cheese into her mouth. Cracker dust stuck to her lips, even after she took a sip of wine.

"Kaui," she said, as if tired, "just eat some of this ridiculous food with me and have a fucking glass."

FORTY-FIVE MINUTES LATER we were in the bathroom. Van was bending at the waist like she'd been punched in the gut. I was struggling to get the zipper down on the back of her shorts.

"You have to hurry," Van said.

"It's caught on all this thread, Van, I'm trying," I said.

She shuddered. Slapped my hands away. Started backing up toward one of the bathroom stalls. "Oh God," she said. "This toilet is going to get it. So are my shorts. God, I'm going to shit all over myself."

"Just let me," I said.

She doubled over again. Her eyelids clamped down. "Hurry up!"

She looked at me quick. There was a flex of panic in her face and she backed all the way into the stall. Still doubled over and stress-breathing. I knew I had about ten seconds. She was fumbling with the zipper. Gritting her teeth. As she shifted and struggled her calves flexed. I stepped into the stall with her, smacked the door closed, hitched one of my legs up on the toilet's valve—it was one of those weird metal things, like a miniature fire hydrant—and jerked down on the zipper on her shorts. It burned sharply in my thumb but didn't move. Van groaned.

"There's, like, a turtle head coming, Kaui, it's going to be all over me in a minute—" I clutched at the shorts' waistband and pulled down as hard as the fabric would let me. Something ripped and the shorts got below her knees and Van slammed herself down on the toilet seat and the volcano in her guts erupted. I flinched, banging my elbows against the stall door.

"Can't you just—" I started, but there was nowhere to go, and Van grunted and let loose again. Wet sounds crackled out of her bottom. She was pressing her hands against the sides of the stall and panting as the food jetted out of her in one endless run. I was still holding on to her legs, where the shorts had stopped. I wanted to cover my nose, to back away, but it was already over. Van shook with laughter. A stench steamed oppressively out of the toilet.

"Oh my God," Van gasped. "I don't even smoke, and I feel like that deserves a cigarette." She laughed. I did, too.

"How was the cheese?" I asked, tears in my eyes, although it was hard to know what from, the stink or the laughter. "Worth it?"

"Worth it," Van said, forearms on her knees, hanging her head. "Definitely worth it. God, my ass smells terrible. Who knew." I let go of her shorts and stood. From up there I could see the hunch of her back. Gentle knuckles of spine. The big and small of her breathing. Her shorts puddled around her ankles, the explosion of shredded fabric and mangled zipper track. Just then the main bathroom door groaned open, followed by the sharp clack of a pair of high heels. Whoever the woman was, she didn't make it far. After a few seconds the heels retreated. The roar of the party came up, then swung back to silence with the closing door.

"Exactly," Van said, as she wiped. "Run for your life."

But we did need to leave. "Let me try this zipper," I said. I squatted again, and when I shifted my weight, my left knee, the purple-brown spatters of scar on top of my dark-brown skin, that knee pressed against her shin. I left it there. Van had finished wiping. I tried the shorts, their zipper, but after a few pitiful jerks I gave up. The wine was letting me know how much of it I'd really had. My head throbbed from the effort of pulling and I let my skull roll forward onto Van's shoulder. Then sideways into the scoop of her collarbone. We paused. Breathing: my head, her neck. I lifted my head slightly and our ears touched; our necks, hers damp. I lifted my head, knowing what I was moving for. My lips drifted across the small hairs on her cheek and then into her mouth.

Sweat stippled her upper lip. She opened her mouth slightly, me, too, and we pressed ourselves together. Her lips were way softer and more foreign than I thought they'd be and there was a short wet flash of our tongues meeting, thick and warm with spit, plus the cooked pocket of our breath. I prickled, all over my face. Our lips stayed together. Pressed harder. Then we disconnected.

Soon we were single file on the dusty road away from the parking lot. A purple dusk was coming. We put our thumbs out into the yellow beams of headlights coming from behind, stripped off our shoes, and walked backward so we could see the faces failing to pick us up. Eventually a car whined to a stop alongside us.

They were an older couple with ashy hair. Neck wattles checkered with creases and liver spots. She had a long face like a horse and lipstick so bright her lips didn't look real. His hands were on the wheel, and all the way up to his blue golf shirt his arms were wrinkled with dissolving muscle. But they were smiling and said they'd remembered what it was like to be in a place like this, young and broke. They said they'd take us all the way.

We got in and the car creaked down the dirt tracks that led out to the blacktop road.

We hadn't said a real word to each other since the bathroom. I still felt Van's lips on my own. Their perfect curve and the way they were soft and sticky with a little of her lipstick. I can still feel them now, anytime I want to remember. You can talk about a thing over and over. Or see movies or listen to songs that you think say something about it, right? But still it's nothing compared to the whirling jump of blood in your chest when you find, at last and at least for a moment, someone that wants you as much as you want them.

Van shifted her legs around. It made the leather seat groan. Her hand was spread next to her leg. I slid my hand out so that my fingers touched hers. The delicate ridge of her cuticles, so light I might have imagined them. She took my hand full into hers, our fingers zippered up together.

"Kaui," Van said. Like she'd discovered something.

The car bumped off the dusty lawn-road and met the hard, straight asphalt. The blinker clicked, over and over, as we leaned into the freeway. We were touching, me and Van, all the way home.

# 10

# DEAN, 2008

## *Spokane*

SIX A.M. LIGHTS ARE UP AND WE WORK THE LINE, LOAD-ing all the time. It's all cardboard boxes everywhere, rumbling around metal trays and chutes, underneath there's gears and rubber belts, bunch of whirrs and clanks and clatters. That's the thing I'm inside for my eight hours, loading and loading and loading. Everything across the belts and into all the open backs of the trucks, or else you're working farther back, forklifting or roller-carting pallets of stuff, making all the stacks neat and fast with the *sthunk sthunk sthunk* of cardboard stacking on itself.

Loader, that's me, right, but I was training for a driver job, figure I make a little bigger paycheck and get outside, so I got for do a few ride-alongs and see how deliveries work. This was what, April. Of course one of the first routes I'm on goes right to the university and I was all, "I'm not going in there." Carl, the driver, said, "The hell you talking about?"

The way he said it I could see the tooth that was missing, far right side just at the edge of his always-chapped mouth. Him every time with his skin like a pirate, not shaving for days and days. What a bald-ass, chewed-up haole. First day I went for a ride-along with him, Carl gleeked the last of his dip into a 7UP can with the top peeled off and asked from under his weird blue eyes, "What are you?"

I was like, What.

"I figure it's like you're black, but I dunno. You have Chinese eyes and hair like this one girl I used to know. She was a Jew, I think."

I figure would've been bad to false-crack him right then so I just said, "Hawaiian Filipino," the same I had to say to everyone, everywhere, except back home.

Then we was on our second run together and I bet Carl already couldn't remember what I was. Us at the university and me still in the passenger seat in the delivery truck. The back side of the union was where we'd parked, where all the deliveries got done, and Carl was already starting for the back of the truck while I was still trying for figure out if any of the students going by was people I knew, or if they knew me, which was what really mattered.

"Help me stack all this," Carl called from around back of the truck. "It's always faster with two."

For maybe a minute I was thinking I could probably just duck down right there, sit on the floor, and curl up, but I'm six five and there's no way you can keep me hidden anywhere. And anyway I never liked hiding, so when students started walking past I just tried not for make eye contact with none of 'um. But I don't think nobody even looked at the delivery truck—I know I never did when I was a student—so I was probably more invisible than I ever been before. I hopped out and went around back to Carl.

"Yeah, I'm here," I said.

"Kid wants a participation medal," Carl said, stacking the bigger boxes on the handcart he'd set up. His bald head was all sweat and shine.

"Used to be I was at the student union all the time," I said. "Late-night snacks and like that. I never really been around back like this before."

"Yeah, yeah, I know all about your story, superstar," he said. "Everyone does. Well, now you're around back all right." He chin-pointed to one of the biggest boxes in the back of the truck. "Lift that one there."

We rolled the cart in toward the union and Carl went on about all the ways to be a top driver: Never ignore the GPS driving directions because the GPS is always right, park wherever the hell is closest to the entrance, just hit the flashers and unload, and always always *always* lock the back before you make the drop. More time you shave from the route without breaking the speed limit, the more bonus you can pick up at employee review.

We struggled the cart up the small hill at the loading dock, Carl was still talking. We went by all the weeping milk from the garbage overflow next to the tied-tight stacks of cardboard, Carl was still talking. We took the heavy freight elevator crashing and squealing to the second floor, Carl was still talking. Then it was the mail room, mostly staffed by work-study students, and so of course, even though had been two years since my last game, the girl and guy at receiving fully recognized me.

Chubby plain Jane with her caked-makeup cheeks and moled neck, and the guy with pink dyed hair that was starting for wash out, sharp-ass nose, and two thick earrings in one ear. Yeah, I can see the thing, when it happens, still. Them with their eyes up and on me like I'm just another delivery guy, then there's this flex moment, where they're like, Isn't that Dean Flores? The guy *smiled*, even. Like he couldn't wait for get off shift and tell his friends, Guess who I saw at the mail room today, no, *at* the mail room, delivering packages. He'd say it all happy because of how it was when I was starting two-guard and he was just another punk haole student at the school, and now here we are. I couldn't let him get away with it.

"The fuck you looking at?" I said to him.

Punk's smile dropped through the floor. I seen the fear. "Sorry?" he said, like he didn't hear me.

I was about to say more, but then Carl frowned at me so hard his face went like a raisin. "Boy," he said. "Get the last of the stuff."

I stared Punk down, though, just a minute more, so he knew what was what. Then I went back around the corner, to the door we'd come into the mail room by, got the last few boxes, brought 'um back. I could feel Carl watching me the whole time so I didn't do nothing but what I was supposed to until we left.

"Trying to get fired on your second ride-along?" Carl asked, us back in the truck and the engine grumbling and the fibery smell of cardboard and old coffee all around.

I shook my head but didn't apologize.

"You know that guy?"

"Nah."

"This gonna be a problem, you doing a route through here?" Carl asked. Gave me one of his hard looks, one of his dad looks.

"Let's just drive," is all I said. "We're losing time."

**ASK ME HOW IT HAPPENED.**

How do you have the world by the nuts and then let go.

Shit is so simple anyone that's not as dumb as me would've seen 'um coming. That sophomore season when I took over, our team went late in the tournament, made it all the way to the Final Four, with me leading in scoring and third on assists, double-double as easy as pissing in the shower. After a season like that, how could I not recognize what I was?

Howbout the party in me started small and got bigger, just a little here and there and then epic, all the time epic, blackout epic. Howbout reggae, howbout pass the dutchie, howbout freshman girl hips and my hips and everyone in the living room when the bass drops. Howbout those days I was missing the beach bad and wanted to bring all the aloha back. Howbout if you try hard enough you can make the beach show up anywhere, even Spokane in the off-season, a little beer a lot of beer couple other brown boys and good beats, girls down to their hot pants and scooped-out necklines and we go. My grades was barely enough through spring semester and summer. Howbout I can see now, can't nobody do it that way, not for long. Howbout I remember when I should have started for pay attention, when summer league started and I tried for all my mongoosing on the court, dipping into the flow, and something felt syrupy slow and numb. But I was only twenty, how could that be? Howbout island love can only do so much, at least for me, since there was arguments at practice with Coach, always telling me what to do and I swear half the time he was wrong, even Rone and Grant and DeShawn, I dunno what happened but soon wasn't none of 'um talking to me, and me right back at 'um. Get your shit together, you're getting sloppy, you're getting slow, you're getting fat. Used to be I was a razor, sharp and flashy bright, till I went and dulled myself.

NOW IT'S JUST DELIVERIES. Whole string of 6:00 a.m.'s go, me with more ride-alongs. Boss is saying maybe I get to start on my own. Don't even have to help the loaders, maybe just a little bit, stacking everything the way I like it in the back of the truck, which I get all kapakai the first few weeks, like putting the big boxes for the closer addresses too far back in the truck, stacking all the crates wrong so that I'm always reaching bent over, like that. But I learn. I bet no one thinks I can, but I do. And Carl must have said something to someone for real about the university because I never gotta go that way again. I guess that's his route anyway.

There's the fuzz of the cardboard boxes, when I hold one I can feel 'um in my fingers like little hairs on some pet I gotta take care of. There's the flex and *whank* sound when I step up into the back of my delivery truck, then all the angles and edges and the silver shine of the walls inside when the sun's coming up and I'm delivering. I'm delivering.

Plenty times after work, me and Eddie and Kirk-guys all met in the back of the parking lot to tailgate, like we were headed to a ball game or something, but it's just all us getting off our shift and chilling, just for a minute. Before some of the guys gotta run home to the edge of town in whatever small little house they're all crammed into we stand around the back of Eddie's car, far side of the parking lot, cracking beers from the trunk.

"Anybody going to the game tonight?" Eddie asked.

It gets all quiet.

"Right," Eddie said, not looking at me. "Sorry." His shitty little child-molester-looking mustache and squirrel cheeks, raising his can, everyone else did the same. Guys is slamming their beers since they gotta get home to their families, except a few guys that chilled and drank slow, like we was at a bar and trying for make it last so we don't gotta order another, just stay and listen to the music.

# 11

# NAINOA, 2008

*Portland*

A SEVENTEEN-YEAR-OLD GIRL WITH A COLLAPSED LUNG was breathing no oxygen but death, I kept her alive. A construction worker with a severe incision of his left forearm, dropping into hypovolemic shock, I held him together. Parks in the ceaseless damp of a late cold spring and their gray alcoholics, stripping their clothes in a fever of hypothermia, so drunk and cold they were delirious, how desperate their heart thumps were, body cores falling below ninety degrees as they grew waxy, fetaled underneath benches, I kept even the coldest ones alive. We got the hemorrhoid calls and the imagined myocardial-infarction calls and the stomach-flu calls, yes, the street-corner raving lunatics and juvenile fistfight losers, we got their ambulance calls again and again, every day and all the time, the dull act of standing on stoops with supposed patients while we ran through the symptom list of everything this mild illness, that tickle of the chest, this *I don't feel right* might be, but when the significant ones came, the ones me and Erin wanted but never confessed we wanted, the way our lungs and hearts and skulls were roaring with adrenaline when we arrived to another bloody, screaming scene, when those came I was getting better every time, pushing further and further into the borders of death's country.

I poured myself into work. Inside the rig, the rush and struggle and the essences crowding inside me were like a habit now, always rubbing me for attention, saying, Just a little bit, just give me a little bit, every day, so that soon visiting Khadeja and Rika and helping with elementary-school projects, opening bills and taking out the garbage at my apartment, groceries and laundry, is it movie night at Khadeja's or gym night by myself, all were just footnotes to the next time an ambulance could catapult me to a dying body.

Weeks and weeks passed as this. The chaos of being on shift, long stretches of meaningless work, easy calls we didn't need to be at, then the harder calls with true accidents, fingers lost in a meat slicer in the back of a bright white supermarket deli, a pathologic humerus fracture from a domestic ladder tumble of a cancer patient, low-speed bicycle/car interactions . . .

As I began to understand myself, to learn what I was capable of, these basic traumas became things I could repair, even as I was masking the repair, so that by the time the patients had made it to the hospital in our ambulance, their bodies were set on a trajectory to be fully healed, but not so quickly as to be a miracle. I can only imagine the number of ER doctors that pulled back bloody dressings only to find the wound underneath far less severe than had been described in the paperwork.

For a time Erin said nothing, but eventually she stopped me outside the front of the station at the end of one of our shifts.

"You have to tell someone," she said. I smelled her cola-sweetened breath and our compost-heap body odors from another long shift.

"Tell someone what?" I asked.

"Don't insult me," she said. "We can't just keep on like this."

"We?" I asked.

That flex in her jaw. "You," she said.

"Describe it," I said. "What this thing is we should be telling people about." I watched the station cleaners chuck giant popcorn-ball-shaped garbage bags of medical waste into transfer bins.

"You're doing things to our patients."

"And what are those things?"

"Putting them back together, I don't know."

"So you're going to tell someone, 'Nainoa's doing I don't know'?"

She tucked her hands into her pockets and shook her head.

It was the end of the shift and my skull was angry and crammed with sharp dehydrated headaches, I wanted her to see this, to accept she didn't know what I was, leave me be.

"I know you're doing something," she said.

"I'm doing my job."

"That's the problem," she said.

"What?"

"Not like that. I just mean"—she cleared her throat—"is this the best place for you?"

"Erin—"

"We're in one of the worst parts of the city," she said, "and I still don't think we help as much as—"

"Spit it out," I said.

"You shouldn't be in this station," she said. "You should be in, I don't know, a war hospital or a—a—Calcutta. Where there are thousands. Millions."

"I'm not Jesus," I said. I'd seen the strand of gold she wore around her neck, coming on shift or going off it, the delicate cross, the ash on her forehead in spring.

"I didn't say that."

"I want to work here."

"No one wants to work here," she said. "Except people that can't go any farther. We're just Band-Aids. Think of all—"

"The people I could help, I know, you already said that. I appreciate your perspective on my life," I said. "It means a lot, especially coming from a girl whose sole accomplishment off shift has been to binge-watch whole television seasons."

Erin's brow furrowed, her jaw flexed as she turned so that I could see the profile of her face, she watched the city two streets over, the plastic bags hooked by the air, the gray-cracked property lot stitched with weeds. "Wow, okay," she said.

Inside me the storms of all the animals and humans I'd touched were churning, so that, yes, I was standing on a sidewalk, concrete holding me up and air that smelled of dryer sheets in my lungs, me talking with her, Erin, yet also I was the panting ribs of the graveyard owl from Kalihi that knew only green *hunger sleep shit fly fly breathe hunger breed breed fly hunt breathe fly* and red *fight fight take fly fear,* and also I was the old woman I'd treated on an earlier shift in Portland, who had collapsed on her walk to the park and her blue flashes of *forty years waking at the certain side of my husband our curled mornings under the sheet,* the orange and pink and brown *cradling of a child to my breast its sleeping in a warm milk-drunk state* and the long white pain of her regrets that streamed so fast among the others, a roiling mass of lives, all inside my body all at once, every one of my patients. They all stayed resident and never left my skull, and though they would come and go inside me in waves, the intensity of them was rising in a rush after these last few months, since the night with the addict. The more I understood what we were all made of, the more everyone I'd touched stayed inside me, still crying out, showing me their injuries over and over and over and over and over.

"Don't pretend you know what this feels like," I said.

Erin put her hands up. "I'm sorry I said anything," she said, then pivoted and started to walk away. "See you around."

I wanted to stand there, to think about what she'd said, but I knew if I did she'd realize she'd had an effect on me, so instead I gathered my wallet and phone, a few other things from my locker, and started out for my apartment by foot, I'd catch a bus on the way when I needed, but first I had to think.

Erin wanted me to be something more, the same as my family always had, the same as I did, as well. But I couldn't, I wasn't. I was only here. It was that I didn't know enough yet, I decided. I couldn't move on to something else because I hadn't yet mastered what I was, and if whatever came after this asked more of me than I was capable of . . .

I was turning these thoughts over, barely stopping for crosswalk signals, jaywalking in slants across busy thoroughfares, when something caught my eye. I'd passed two buildings, the alley between them, and saw the asymmetrical slab of a dead Labrador, resting a hundred feet down the alley.

I had no idea what had happened to it but I was certain it was dead, felt the rigor mortis running along its torso, as unyielding a curve as a frozen hillside, and when I touched the body the colors I felt inside were barely more than whispers of violet and midnight blue. The dog was long dead. I searched inside anyway, all along the body's length, finding the jagged wound of the broken skull, there but crushed by something I could only assume was a tire. Even with my eyes closed and everything in me pouring into the dog's body I knew I couldn't do this, the body wasn't listening the way they normally did, eagerly awaiting my vague explanation of how to make themselves right. I thought again of what Erin had said, what my family had always alluded to, what I was supposed to be, I flexed myself harder, trying to encourage the life to show itself again, just for a moment, so I could harness it. Something in my head popped, went bitter, bursts of fire and twisting ache all along my back as I bore down, how can a skull recognize itself, to want to be whole again, there was nothing, then the echo of nothing.

I dove further in, I forgot myself. All blackness, could I start something, I tried and failed, it was like yelling into the bottom of a lake. I pushed harder, my whole body gripping the idea, the want of life, can I make the life here again, you're going to come back. I gasped, opened my eyes briefly. The same gray alley and stained stucco walls, my vision splattered with the patterns I'd been seeing inside, then came chill swamps of sweat at my armpits, neck, crotch. I gathered myself again, closed my eyes, flexed everything.

There was a spark, something shifted in the dog's body, the trickle of electricity that was all that was left of a life, it was something at least, it was in the dog again when it hadn't been a moment before, and I held it with my mind along with the injuries—the skull fragments, the messy smear of teeth and jaw bone—and pushed harder. The electricity flared then faded, the dog went dark in my mind and my whole skull hurt, the teeth I'd been grinding, something behind my nose made a crepitus sound. I wouldn't let it go, no, having resuscitated something of a soul. My hands were still there, somewhere, holding this animal's body, the legs that had padded softly and flexed and shot the often desperate hungry body between the dark barrels of trash cans, the hot relief of recently parked cars, legs that supported a trembling, casual defecation, legs that had cupped and tapped and batted trash and rats and kittens, this animal had tasted joy and terror and time, I could bring it back. And the spark inside became a steady trickle of light, and the trickle became a flood, and brightness coursed through the animal's body like a city waking from a blackout.

I opened my eyes. The dog's skull was sealed and it lay there, gently panting through its thawed fur, as warm and leathery as a boot left in a sunny mudroom. It stood, shivered, shook its head so hard its ears made slapping sounds against its perfect skull, then trotted away, leaving the alley.

I wanted to call out to it, to ask the dog to stay, could I take it home, but exhaustion rolled over me so fast that I collapsed on my ass and fell over sideways onto the ground, closed my eyes.

I woke with the frost of the alley pressing up into my ribs, clavicle, patellas, lips gritted with road filth. I was lying in the same place where the dog had been, only now the sun had shifted behind the buildings completely and there was no warmth in the alley, I composed myself on my knees and shivered, again and again.

Never before had I saved something so far gone, human or animal. Death looked just as I'd expected, silence and a hollow darkness, and from that place I'd pulled back the lightning of life.

I squatted on the concrete, leaned against the clefts of

mortar in the brick wall, birds shot across the gray above, I smelled the happy-hour grease of a kitchen heating up, roving packs of baggy boys passed at the far mouth of the alley, a delivery truck backing halfway toward me from the other end with its incessant beeping. In my pocket, my phone lit and buzzed. A message from Khadeja:

*Hungry for some dinner?*

With all the things banging around in my brain, the galaxies of exhaustion, I still answered, probably too quickly, *Yeah, you at home?*

The answer came back as quickly: *Wasn't inviting you over, just asking if you were hungry, haha.*

"The hell," I said out loud, but just as quickly she wrote, *Just kidding. See you soon?*

*I hate you*, I sent back. *Let me get a shower first, my 'uke. Be right there.*

And so I went, on wiggling quadriceps, deltoids hived with weakness.


WHEN RIKA OPENED THE DOOR for me the television was on, puppet animals gabbing at each other, then a flash to trembling cartoon numbers that counted down from ten, then two bright puppets entered from opposite sides of what appeared to be a public-housing street.

"Mom's making curry," Rika said, turning back to the screen. Her schoolbag slouched in the corner by the love seat.

"Don't you have studying to do?" I said.

"Come on," Khadeja's voice called from the kitchen, "people have been telling that child what to do all day. Give her a little freedom."

"Freedom to watch television," I said.

"Yes," Khadeja called out. "You could maybe come in here and help me."

"But you're doing such a good job," I said.

Only a skeptical snort from the kitchen.

"Sounds like trouble," Rika said to me, without turning from the television.

"She didn't say anything," I said.

"Yeah," Rika said. "You're *really* in trouble."

I mussed Rika's hair, even as she protested and tried to escape. "What do you know, anyway," I said. "You're six." I headed to the kitchen.

And it was Khadeja, her strong cheeks and bright eyes, intricate Arabic earrings dancing against her dark-brown neck, hair pulled back in that same Afro bun. Down to a white V-neck but still in her black office pants, her thick thighs pressing through. She was evaluating the curry, as if it had insulted her.

"How's it going in here?"

"Curry's a little off," she said, but when she turned and saw me she stopped. "Jesus, Noa."

"What?"

"You look exhausted," she said. "I know I'm not supposed to say that, but seriously."

"Thanks," I said. "You look fat in those pants, as long as we're being honest."

She laughed. "Sorry. But, Noa, you look like you ran a marathon and only ate cigarettes the whole time." She hid a smile behind her hand. "I can't believe I just said that." In the living room the television babbled on and on, more puppets and some sort of giant animatronic elephant, it seemed they were talking about what makes rain.

"Are you still here?" Khadeja asked. I hadn't realized how long I'd been staring at the distant screen. Khadeja came so close to me, one of our shoulders brushed, hers smooth and warm as a cheek.

"There was this dog today," I started to say. "It was—" Khadeja placed a palm against my stomach, eyebrows raised in concern, all at once I wanted to tell her everything. But I remembered the last time people knew me: all the neighbors that had heard and suddenly and always after needed me, the small stacks of cash my parents would bring in . . .

I shook my head. "Never mind," I said. "I make it sound worse than it is. It's mostly allergic kids eating peanut butter, cats stuck in trees, people faking heart attacks so they can get out of jury duty."

The smile she gave was flat, polite. "I'm right here," she said. "I can listen."

"I know," I said, but I didn't say anything else.


AFTER DINNER RIKA did her normal game of trying to avoid a bath and bedtime, was clever about it, asked after the 'ukulele I'd brought over, if she could hear me play it.

"It's too late to play now," I said to Rika. "You only want me to play when you're avoiding something."

"'Ukulele," Rika said. She chanted it, I refused, she hollered it out loud, 'Ukulaylaayyyyyyyyyyy, I stood and mugged my face, she scrambled from her chair and grabbed the 'uke herself, began to strum it terribly. It was a fifteen-hundred-dollar 'uke, more than that, a graduation gift from my parents for Stanford, I never did know how they'd afforded it, and all the answers I'd imagined since tore my heart so bad I played it even when I didn't want to play it, and it said for me the sharks, the graveyard, everything my parents thought would come after. I mugged and moved, Rika ran, down the short hall, made it to the corner of her room, tried to strum again, but I was there too quickly.

"Give it," I said to her.

"It's mine now," she said, not even holding it right, upside down, missing the frets, missing the strings when she tried to strum. "I'm the best 'ukulele player in the world. Like way better than you."

I snatched it on her next attempt, and cradled it in one arm. She reached for it and I turned to shield, wait, I told her, just wait. I strummed the chords, twisted the tuning pegs. "You knocked it out of tune." Just then I felt Khadeja arrive in the doorway behind me, just her shadow and the vanilla-floral scent of her.

They both knew to listen when I had the 'uke, I knew it was one of the things that made me for Khadeja, I knew that. I did this often at their place, made music, sometimes after dinner, sometimes after Rika was asleep and it was just Khadeja and me in the living room, Seagram's we'd cut with ginger ale, or just as often sober, I'd pull out the 'uke and play, sing well enough for it to work, warm honey. It did things to me, to be that sort of person for them.

I played a few songs, right there, right then, "Guava Jelly" and "Leaving on a Jet Plane," each chord better than the last, the extra notes I could stick in and make ring longer, I warmed to it, Rika wanted "Somewhere over the Rainbow" but I said I was sick of it, played a version of "Bring Me Your Cup," ran that into "Stir It Up," the way I believe Marley would have liked it, his hoarse and wailing voice, it was the best end for all of us, when the last chord went down I said to Rika, Enough, enough, now, it's time for your mother to give you a bath.

"Why is it always me?" Rika asked. "You never take a bath."

"Me and your mom do sometimes," I said, grinning at Khadeja, the horror in her face. I chucked a few chords. "That's how babies get made."

"In the bath?" Rika asked.

"No," Khadeja answered. "Well, sometimes. Listen," she said, "I'll tell you when you're older."

"I'll tell you tomorrow," I said. "I'll draw you pictures."

"Cool," Rika said.

"Nainoa," Khadeja said.

"Bath," I said to Rika, practically giggling, then stepping out of her room, toward the bathroom, so that for a moment I was in the black of the hallway, looking for the door frame in the dark.

How many nights did we make like that? How long was I stupid enough to believe we were indestructible? But that's the problem with the present, it's never the thing you're holding, only the thing you're watching, later, from a distance so great the memory might as well be a spill of stars outside a window at twilight.


SEPTEMBER THEN, I flipped to the six-to-six overnight shift and somewhere after midnight we got the call, a mother thirty-six weeks pregnant in early bleeding labor, in a car accident on the way to the hospital.

"Great," Erin said after dispatch broke away, after the static and just us in the rig, her hitting the switches to start the siren shriek again. "Sounds bad."

"It's only potential premature childbirth and high-speed blunt-force trauma," I said. "What's bad about that?"

"When we get back to the station," Erin said, "remind me to have you push the water cooler through your anus. Then we can talk about childbirth and easy."

"I've done that water-cooler thing before," I said. "Ask Mike."

"You're disgusting," she said. "Just drive."

I drove and the rain came down in strange pulses, pouring, then spitting, then pouring. Traffic was already backed up on the freeway, a quarter of a mile before the accident, so slow to part we might as well have gotten out and walked. When we finally arrived the car was facing the wrong way on the street, accordioned and blistered with airbags, spatters of glittering glass, all of it soaked with rain. A much larger truck had skidded to the other side of the road, the front barely crunched by comparison. The driver of the truck was sitting with his back against the lane divider, his legs curled up close to his chest, muttering something to the interviewing police officer. We stepped out into the blare of all the traffic headlights, the night so strangely quiet in a pure way, the tap of the drizzle on our jackets, smell of pine mulch spilled from the pickup truck bed, the pink-orange blossoms of the road flares lit by the police. We approached the car.

We saw her, although even now it's hard to recall as exactly as I'd like, the position of her body, and was she really still breathing, which was the frame of the car and the fabric and which was her own body, the tang of bile and the deep arterial blood, almost black, the poisonous smell of burning metal, electronics, but we were able to extract her, neck collar and get the gurney underneath her, even as some of her leaked onto the car seat, then the concrete, then the pure white of the gurney cloth.

Erin was murmuring to the mother and I had my hand on her body, trying to find the sources of the blood. There were raw, clawlike scrapes on her face and neck, her chest where the cotton shirt had been shredded through. Now I was sensing her, the life inside her body was like the center of a forest fire, all I could feel was the red evacuation and orange breaking and tearing of blood vessels and subcutaneous tissue, her torqued spinal column, then the sudden blue flickers of the child inside her, its infant essence fading already.

I was in the back of the rig, hands on the body, we weren't more than half a block from the wreck before I screamed at Erin to stop the ambulance.

"Are you kidding me?" Erin said, turning to face me, her hands steering the rig in a lazing slalom between the vehicles on the road in front of us, even as she watched my eyes.

"We take her to the hospital and the child dies," I said.

"Fuck that," she said.

"They'll have to choose between the mother and the child," I said. "You know what they'll choose."

"That's their job."

"I can do more," I said.

"No," Erin said.

"I'll keep them both here," I said. "No one has to choose anything."

Erin shook her head.

"Erin," I said. "You know me." It was all I had. *I* didn't even know me, but I had to pretend to something greater, and to invoke all the gory hours Erin and I had been through. We lurched to the side of the road and stopped. Erin jammed her palms into her eyes, saying fuckfuckfuckfuck, which I suppose was the best she'd give me, us stopped near a building, and the ambulance lights whapped red and blue and red along the windows.

"Three minutes," Erin said. She punched the steering wheel. "That's all, you hear me?"

I returned to my examination, the baby's essence fading, the mother's as well, her body less a fire now and more a lava river, molasses and a soft hum, the vibrations churning through my hands. I couldn't find the spark, the life's desire. Everything was falling apart at once, it was too much to hold, I had the vague sense that both of their lives were ready for flight.

Again I let my mind enter her body, I searched for the spark, the same as what I'd seen before, it was there but going. I was trying to find them both, the mother and the child, to hold them at once and then shove everything broken back together, as I'd done with the dog in the alley. But nothing happened; it was quiet. My brain was clenching so tight that there was a tearing feeling below my waist, a sheet of something hot on my own quadriceps, only later was I able to identify it as urine, rusted with whatever had been beaten out of my kidneys by the force with which I tried to revive the lives underneath my hands. Still I couldn't find inside the mother any source of light.

"Almost," I lied.

"No time," Erin hollered. "I'm driving."

There, did it flicker, there was another, a distant lightning bolt at the edges of the mother's horizon, I sent everything I had at it, every part of me that could wrestle with her life, convince it to contain itself, to begin the repair, even as I tried to imagine what that repair would look like: start with the gashes and ripped places, seal them, begin the amassing of platelets and the thatching of fibrin protein, clot please clot please clot, and your oxygen to the child, and the volts to their hearts and brains so that everything still has the hum and pump that I feel no longer, and the wounds again, stitch yourself, stitch yourself, the light went out.

"Wait, okay, wait, please, you're cold. Not yet," I said, "you're cold. Not yet." Then the vague knowledge that the rig was moving. The shrieking sirens. I was outside of her again, resident only in myself, looking down at the mother's body and beginning the resuscitation techniques they train us in, the only thing left.

By the time we arrived at the hospital the mother's blood had flowed arterial dark, then slowed, skin ashen, uterus wall still curved where the child was silent inside her. Every revival I'd attempted—defibrillation, chest compressions, rescue breaths—was met only with chill and limp apathy from the mother's body. We'd jerked to a stop at the emergency room, Erin opened the doors and sobbed at the sight, it must have been the gray and blue colors of the mother, even as the crew of nurses rushed the rig, a wave of clatters and yanks and cracking voices that broke over us and pulled away the mother's husk to what I already knew would be her final resting place.

# 12

# KAUI, 2008

## *Indian Creek*

THAT FALL WE LIVED IN THE LANDSCAPE. WE CLIMBED on the fringes of crusted mountain ranges once plowed by glaciers as big as cities. We set our toes and fingertips on razored bits of stone and slipped ourselves into the veined cracks of sheer walls of limestone or granite or basalt, all of it ceilinged by a thunder-brained sky. I felt the first people in those worlds. The earth that generations of Shoshone had lain on was there still, underneath our tents, right? Frigid air that cycled off the snow-caps, what had once been of the Kiowa's breath, passed through us the same.

With Van, with Hao, with Katarina, suddenly I wanted

fright-fest runouts at Smith Rocks. The Totem Pole in Australia and El Potrero Chico in Mexico. The Salathé Wall in Yosemite and El Chorro in Spain. The more we climbed the more it got in deep. Under my skin.

And something even better happened. Those hard-climbing nights I'd collapse in the wet-dog smell of our tents and plunge into black oceans of sleep. I'd dream of what must have been Hawaiian gods. Women as large and distant as volcanoes, their skin dark like pregnant soil, dolphin-kind bodies thick and slick and full of joyful muscle. Their hair tangled and tumbled down into the trees until I couldn't tell the vines from their locks and their eyes were golden or blue or green without white and smoldering. Everywhere they touched the land, the land grew into them, skin blending with earth, until you couldn't find where one ended and the other began.

I guess that was when I danced. Or at least that's what Van told me every time the dream happened, especially at the start, right. She said I'd be deep in it: On my back out cold, sleeping bag slipped to my hips, dancing hula in the tent. Arms locked and pointing forty-five degrees, periodically sweeping across my body, hips rocking in 'ami or knees going in 'uwehe. She said she had to duck and flinch so I didn't smack her with my gestures.

She asked what did I dream about. There was no point in explaining the women—it would just sound stupid—but even explaining the ambience wouldn't work. It felt like I was being dragged, like I was in a riptide, thick cords of current carrying me to a nameless destination.

INDIAN CREEK will never be the same for me, because of what we did there. It was the start of the end, I see that now. It was our fall-break trip. Indian Creek with its sandstone cliffs going copper in the early sun. The smell of coins, strong from the distant lake. Hao and Katarina were there, but we'd started to pair off for our climbing in the same configuration, more and more: Hao and Katarina, me and Van. Me and Van. We climbed like it was a conversation. She was elegant and precise. Fatigueless. I was powerful and dynamic—big sweeping moves and hard lock-offs. And we displayed those things to each other, she responding to me and me responding to her, so that we were pushing each other, even as we admired. We were turning each other into the sort of people we wanted to become, creating the sort of experiences I never knew I wanted until I was having them.

"You need to flow more," she called up to me, as I worked my way through a hard series of locks on a finger crack. "Settle into the flow. You shouldn't have to try most of the time, only at the crux." And I was like, Sometimes I don't want to flow. In those cracks in particular for me it still went like a war. I'd fumble among the smallest gashes in the rock and all the muscles in my back would be yanked through with strain and I'd have to squeeze and quit breathing and grit my teeth to pull through. Van up there before me on the sharp end of the rope like a liquid snake. All spread knees and leg flagging and delicate camming. I'm the hula dancer, you bitch, I wanted to say. Then I *did* say it, and she laughed, right? Because we knew each other.

I'd finally taken to climbing well enough that it had all the danger I wanted. The second day in the Creek I took a fifty-foot fall from a splitter crack. The seasick feel of plunging through the air, rope slack and rippling in the air below me. Falling and falling until the rope finally caught on two shaky pieces of gear that left me dangling just above Van's head. Had those pieces pulled, I would have broken my back. Neither of us said anything for a long time. Okay, I just hung there, trembling from my belly out.

"We should have brought more number twos," Van said, all chill and clever.

"It's better this way," I said. "Consequences."

It's what I wanted. Take me and Van: I didn't know what we were and there was something in the not knowing. In playing at the edge. Climbing was the same. Again and again we did it, teasing the edge of disaster. The consequences made us into something that was completely known when we walked around on campus, right? It spilled over into classes. I was building off those first semesters, establishing myself as one of the best students in every class I took, stoked to be understanding the mechanics of the world: what I could build with my brain, the sciences. I could make buildings or bridges or engines if I wanted. I had no questions now of what was inside me.

Except with Van. It had been a month and a half since the wine festival and I was cramped with want for her. Our dorm room was a pressure cooker: casual bumps or grazes as we handed each other pens or textbooks or the remote, or when we passed on the way to our lofted beds.

The week before this trip, she'd come back from the shower, closed our dorm-room door, and dropped her towel. I was on my bed, knees kinked up and reading my *Statics & Dynamics* textbook. T.I. was playing in my headphones—*Paper Trail* had just come out—which I remember because I can't hear "Whatever You Like" now without being yanked back into that moment, her body. Mint and flowers, the white smell of soap, even. It was never her body itself that I cared about. The surface or whatever. It was how she wore it: tension and flex, asymmetric, solid. I remember a few things. The rooty tangle of her barely groomed crotch, the thickness of her wrists and forearms, the thin veins sprung by the climber's muscles. The flex in her neck. She just stood there naked. My insides kinked and kinked. Then Van crouched and pulled underwear out of her drawer and rolled them on over her clean skin.

In any chemical solution made up of two or more parts, there's a solvent and a solute. I knew this. I studied these sorts of things all the time, okay? The solvent does the work, creates the acidic burn. I told myself with Van I was the solvent sometimes, but I wasn't kidding anyone. Mostly I knew what it felt like to be dissolved.

Now we were at the Creek and in our tents under great spills of midnight stars, me and Van in our tent together, across the campfire from Katarina and Hao, whose banter we could faintly hear. They never stopped talking, but it was like a brother-and-sister thing. Van turned to me in her sleeping bag.

"You going to dance hula again tonight?" she said.

"Shut up," I said.

"Don't get all moody," she said. "I like it."

I shrugged, because I couldn't think of how else to not react. "I don't control it," I said.

"Almost everything's like that, isn't it?" she said.

I made a skeptical face. "Yeah, I don't think philosophy's your thing."

"I'm serious," she said.

"So am I." I grinned.

Then Van leaned over and kissed me on the cheek, as easy as a European good night. We were all sunscreen and salt and campfire stink. Two days of hard-climbing grime all over us. But I could feel her lips through all of it, a surprise still soft and unfamiliar.

She pulled back and without looking at me unzipped her sleeping bag to the toe box. Slowly I did the same to mine. I sent my hand out into her bag, drew my palm down along the length of her body, starting at her shoulder. Instead of looking at her face, I watched a space past her, the corner of the tent where I could see the glow of Katarina's and Hao's lamps. I let my hand follow the curve of her. Down to her hip. She grabbed my wrist. Tucked it under her shirt, my hand on her belly. She exhaled and pulled my hand farther up, shifted herself against it, and there was the small warm rise of her tit. Her stiff nipple played between two of my fingers. She exhaled again. She'd worked her own hand down under her waistband, into her underwear, and began moving it there.

"Keep going," she said, through a flushed face with closed eyes. Her other hand was still over mine, moving on her nipple. I did it. I mirrored what she was doing, my hand inside my underwear, all the way down. My head went swirled and hot. My belly, too. We settled into a rhythm of stroking ourselves and each other. Me all her and her all me, right here, right now, until what had been clenched inside me unspooled in a rush.

I don't know if I danced hula in my sleep that night. There wasn't music in my dreams. But I remember what I felt. I was a seedling under the soil, pushing up. I was a hungry muscle, flexing through the dark earth until I broke in to the rain and sunlight.

It made sense later. At the end.

# 13

# NAINOA, 2008

## *Portland*

FIND ME IN THE PRODUCE AISLE, LOST BESIDE THE FISTS of broccoli, the slick knots of yellow red orange green bell peppers, I could stand there or I could stand anywhere and it wouldn't matter, because it came for me anyway. It hit me at Khadeja's place, trying to read to Rika or tell a joke in the living room, it struck me on the bus, riding to the gym, it stung me when we turned out all the lights, lay low, and Khadeja reached out to knead my neck, it clutched me and it wouldn't let me go, that moment, the mother's body, the delicate but desperate child inside, when everything departed.

I had failed, and in my failure I had killed a mother and her daughter, because I was too stupid to know my own limits. I hadn't just undone what they were, but what they'd ever been—what was the point of those memories now? could the husband kiss the memory of his wife? could he palm the memory of the swell of the child, could he feel the memory of the kicks?—and then of course I'd taken everything that might have come after, sleepless midnights in a newborn house, school plays, national-park vacations with shitty selfies. I'd taken what the father could have been, I'd taken what the grandparents had earned, even the lovers and angers and jokes the child would never have, years in the future, the artifacts it would have made: songs or stories or even text messages. I'd taken it all.

And what I had been given in return was a leave of absence, not because anything was suspected (nothing was, Erin had said what I thought she wouldn't, I was exonerated), but because I was unable, in the hours and days after, to be anything like myself. The company said, *Take as much time as you need*, which I knew meant no more than a month. Yet a month came and there I still was, barely leaving my apartment, certainly not making it all the way to the station.

Khadeja would be doing things such as putting on earrings at the full-length bedroom mirror, taking off a dangling pair and fastening simple X's, then going back to the dangling pair, and she'd say, "Am I right?"

"About what?" I'd say.

She'd let her hands drop, then consider me quietly. "You haven't been listening."

"Sure I have," I'd say, and try to convince her, badly, that I had been listening, and she'd start again, with whatever thread she was on, and I'd declare, "I'm going back to the station today."

"Do you like the X's? They look like crosses. I don't want people to think I'm Christian," she'd be saying. Then: "And I don't think that's a good idea."

"Being Christian?"

"Going back to the station." Her hand would find my cheek and she'd look me right in the eyes; at the time I thought it was dramatic, but now I understand it was completely honest, in a way that I never had been, then or since. "You need time."

"*They* need *me*," I'd say. "It doesn't matter what I need."

But I didn't go. One morning after I'd slept over I sat at the table next to Rika, watched her dark-brown legs in their polka-dot socks dangle and kick while she stared at the back of the cereal box and two-handed her glass of orange juice, another school day.

"How come you're so quiet?" Rika asked.

"I'm thinking about what comes next," I said.

"I go to school, duh."

"After that," I said. "For me."

"You go home and feel sad, right?"

I smiled. "Something like that."

"Mom said you're going through things," Rika said. "She said, 'He's going through some difficult things, try to under-stand.'" She tried to say the last part in a deep voice, but it came out sounding ridiculous, there was a joke in there somewhere, normally it would have come to me easily, but humor had be-come a foreign language I'd once been fluent in and was now left searching for the simplest nouns and verbs: it was all there somewhere, just out of reach.

"Your mom is right," is all I could manage, instead.

AND I DIDN'T go to work and I didn't sleep more, I stole a

handheld from the station and brought it back to my apartment, spent the days listening to calls come in, ALOC announcements and vitals summaries, dry dispatch and bored paramedics, descriptions of disaster scenes, and I hoped to hear a mistake, something like the one I'd made. Fumble the neck stabilization, I'd think, get the intubator stuck on the vocal cords, forget to check the pupils for dilation. The colors came for me, the gold and green and silver pulses of the dying owls in Kalihi with their *hunt hunt fly eat shit eat sleep hide hunt fly fly* and the poisoned dogs with their purple and brown *drag drag stand bite breathe bark whine breathe drink drink drink cramp go go go* and the patients here, the storms of yellow poison through addict veins, the dark-blue memories of last shared dinners or long mornings in bed before someone was hit by a car. Over and over and over and over they came for me.

"Oh," Khadeja said, and I jolted, turned to see her. I was standing in the living room of my apartment, the handheld pressed in close to my ear. "Oh, Nainoa."

"What?" I said, then I saw her eyes. When her gaze swept over me, the room, all at once I recognized the blotched burning of my irises and that they must be cracked and red, I felt the raw hairs at my throat and cheeks from days without shaving, the ripe grime collecting at my armpits and feet, the scatter of torn bags of table crackers and licorice, four pint-glasses of half-finished water, the smell of the whole place: wet cows and corn chips. The sudden arrival of the recognition of significant time having passed, of having grown older, how many days I didn't know, but each one like this.

Khadeja closed the distance to me in a few fluid strides, slipped a hand against my neck, so that her thumb rested just in front of my ear. "Nainoa," she said again, as if trying to wake me up. I was still holding the handheld against my other ear, she reached for the arm that held it and gently closed her hand over my forearm.

I jerked my arm away. "Don't," I said, and pressed the handheld closer to my ear again, even as the static exploded and a voice calmly called out a call sign, acknowledged they'd take the call that came in about a bicycle-automobile interaction, possible C3 spinal fracture.

"Nainoa," Khadeja said, and she was in front of me, no matter which way I turned, and she reached for the handheld again, this time she had a good grip, I pulled but she pulled back, and the unit slipped free and went spinning away like a top, thumping to the floor. She clutched me in a bear hug, her face buried above my clavicle.

"I'm sorry," she said. "I'm sorry I'm sorry I'm sorry." When she could tell I wasn't going to move—when I neither collapsed into her, reciprocating the embrace, nor pulled away—she raised her head and wiped away tears. "I can take you out of here," she said. "Can I do that?"

I shot my arms out so hard they broke the hug completely, Khadeja stepped back, and I gripped her right biceps in my hand, began to crush. "What can you do?" I said. I gripped harder, she had no idea what I was, no idea, I gripped harder, imagining the burning and the squeeze, a blood pressure cuff gone too far, wanting to go all the way, for the veins and capillaries in her arm to pop, I wanted the pressure of my grip to transfer everything inside me into her, so that she could feel, but that was impossible. "You can't do anything."

She jerked her arm free. Her eyes went sharp and she tilted

her head just slightly, glaring at me. Both of us taking big breaths, her gaze going from knifepoint to rounded stone to puddle as wetness gathered in her eyes and started draining in long runs down her cheeks, she didn't wipe this time, just stared and stared. She righted her posture.

"Do that one more time and I'm gone," she said, but the agreement was already between us before the words left her mouth, because she could see that I realized what a mistake it was, what a mistake I was, and that whatever violence had been in me had departed.

"Nainoa," she said again. "I want to help you. Can we do that?"

But I didn't answer, the colors came and went, *run run fly eat flee eat sleep run fly there is my baby where is my husband here is my body wasting away on your gurney*, and the mother and the child and everything I'd destroyed, Khadeja, you would never feel any of it the way I would, I am on an island in a dark ocean you will never be able to cross. I remained silent.

Khadeja's face fell; she'd been angry, righteous even, but it was gone. She was trembling as she stepped backward, opened the front door, closed it gently on her way out. As soon as the door closed I stepped to it, leaned against its cheap, prickly grain, feeling her on the other side as she paused, then moved away from me, down the sidewalk, and into the street.

I was still standing there when evening came, the room growing colder and dimmer, I walked about and turned on the lamps, recognizing my living room more and more as the lights came up, the dilapidated couch and stacks of trash mail, the milk-crate shelves of books, and there beside them, the 'ukulele.

Just as I did in our garage all those years, just as I did at

Stanford especially on the hardest days, just as I did at Khadeja's house, I went to music. I opened the 'ukulele case, ran my hand along the instrument's koa body, the colors flaming against the light of my living room, windows still open and thumping with moths, but October waiting in the air already.

I ran through a few scales to warm my knuckles and wrist, let the strings heat and ring. I started with the sort of songs that always made people living-room-excited, "Creep" or "As My Guitar Gently Weeps" or "Aloha 'Oe," but there was this version of "Kanaka Wai Wai" by Olomana I came back to sometimes, a solo one I learned from an uncle back home, I came to that one with floating fingers, strummed the strings harder, sang a little even, mine not a throat meant to sing at all but if there were a time to sing I suppose it was then. I could imagine the slack key accompaniments and the rich sad voices of true Hawaiian singers, I strummed and tried. I remembered the shreds of rain forest that made their way to us, from the palis all the way down along the gulch to the fences that separated warehouses, the gulch that barely trickled until the rains came, then roared. I remembered pink clouds above the Ko'olaus at sundown, perfect temperatures by dinnertime, all of us kids at the table, farting and joking and ignoring our parents' orders to eat, eat. I remembered Sandy Beach, the waves pitching up into sucking walls of water striped through with different shades of glassy blue, the concrete smack of the waves coming down but me and Dean diving deep, holding our breath, our skin hot and brown from the sun, our skeletons accepting what the tide did to us, and then the time Dean had held my ankle to force the competition to go on, and I'd almost drowned. With the memory of water came the sharks, the rough snout that split into a terrifying cave of teeth, but then the gentle gathering of me in its mouth, the hypnotic muscle of the shark's body weaving through the water. I played and I remembered all of this, and the memories became a calling, not a voice but instead a very distant urge that set in my sternum and started to spread like medicine until it was pulling at my mind, directly.

Home. Come home.

I didn't finish the song.

# 14

# DEAN, 2008

## *Spokane*

THIS ONE DAY I GOT A CALL FROM NOA I WASN'T EXPECT-
ing. Used to be we planned our calls, back when Kaui was doing
like Mom said and making all us kids conference-call once in a
while, *You have to stay connected out there trust me the mainland
will try and break you apart.* Except on those calls, it was mostly
Noa and Kaui trying for see who's got the most Ph.D. vocab-
ulary. Half the time I could put 'um on speaker and go back
to cleaning my toenails or whatever while they jabbered away,
forgot I was there.

But after things went bad at the university, Noa started calling me more. At first I didn't know what he was doing. Wouldn't

even ask me about basketball or what I was gonna do next or none of that, the way everyone else did. He just started talking about his day.

He would say stuff he didn't want to say while we was on the phone with Kaui. We'd talk about work and girls and all that. I think I was the first person he told when he'd started checking out Khadeja, and he'd call and say, Man, I went by their house and Rika was running down the hall naked, just got out of her bath and she's trying to escape, and even though I'd spent all day with sick and broken people in the ambulance their house would light me up inside like a Roman candle. And we'd talk about Hawai'i little-kid days, how we used to wrestle at the park like we was MMA champs, or the weird kids down the street that always smelled like fish and ate their boogers, how I used to make them give us candy and then split it fifty-fifty with Noa, partners in crime.

After a while it got so that on the calls Noa started slipping in these comments and questions about me, way after everyone else had stopped talking about my future. He'd say, There's so much you can still do with your life. Maybe basketball isn't the only thing. I'd be like, You don't understand, if there's no basketball, there's no me.

And so he'd say, Well, you can still win, then. You just need one good break, he'd say. You'll get lucky, just keep working hard on the practice squad.

It was hard for figure out how to take what he was saying. It lifted me some, but it wasn't enough. For real, more he said the right things, the things I wanted for hear, the more it made me go the other way. It was like I was still fighting with him: if he was going for be the better brother then I was going for push him off. It got all tangled up with how I was feeling about

Coach and the team and how basketball was feeling sour, so that
I wanted to burn all of them, and that's what I did, all the way to
the end, when I got cut and dropped out.

Didn't stop Noa, though. He kept calling, even after Kaui
stopped enforcing the group phone calls. Sometimes I hardly
said anything, Noa would just talk, but it still did something for
both of us, just to be on the same line, just for a little bit.

But this one time he called and even now I wish I could do
'um again. I didn't do what needed for be done.

"What's up?" I said when he called.

Right from the start there was a pause. "Nothing," he said.
"Just thought I would call."

Oh, man, I thought, one of these-kind calls. I started watching *SportsCenter* again, but it was all hockey highlights, haole
guys bashing each other's brains against the walls while, like,
moms and dads got their kids on their shoulders, cheering with
blood flying in their beer and everything.

"What are you doing?" Noa said.

"Just curing some cancer while I figure out how to make nu-
clear energy with my ass," I said. "How 'bout you?"

"I don't know," he said. He took this deep, wet breath.

"What, are you crying or something?" I said, and Noa said
he was, yeah, and said it this weird way. Like he was talking to
the empty air, not me, didn't matter who was listening. "Noa,
brah," I said. "What is it?"

"I just," he said, "I made a mistake."

"A mistake," I said. "Like calling one girl another girl's name.
I done that this one time and you shoulda seen—"

"They were here, then they were gone," he said. "I almost did
it. But I shouldn't even have tried."

And I said what the hell, because I had no idea what he was

talking about, and he said that there was a car accident, a pregnant mom in the one car, she'd died on the way to the hospital, while he was trying for save her. The baby was gone, too.

"You did everything you could," I said, which, I wasn't even there yeah, but I knew my brother.

"You remember New Year's?" he said.

"'Course."

"I thought that was the start," he said. "I thought I knew what was coming."

"Noa," I said, but then nothing came after. And on his side of the phone there wasn't nothing, either, just something cold. Might as well he was calling me from inside a refrigerator.

"What do you think I am?" Noa asked.

"What you are?" I said. "A smart-ass, is what you are."

"No," he said. "You know what I mean."

"Like what you got inside you," I said.

"Yes," he said.

"Whatchyou want me to say?" I asked. "Aren't you doing what you're supposed to? Fixing people like you did back in Kalihi? Isn't that what it is? Or you're, what, gonna be a badass kahuna emperor, like Mom thinks."

"What if they're wrong?" he said. "What if it's not just supposed to be me?"

"What?"

"Did you ever feel anything yourself?" he asked. "From the islands, from back home. Or even after, in Spokane."

When he asked again, for real, this feeling came inside me. Back then I didn't know what the feeling was, but now I do. I was scared, is what it was. I thought if I said yes, if I said I believed, that it meant it was true, what Mom and Dad and everyone back home had thought about him, and what they'd thought about me. All the old anger came foaming back up. "Shit, Noa, you tell me," I said. "I thought you was supposed to be the smart one."

Something went stale in the call. Like he pulled back, I could feel it. He sighed. "Sorry," he said. "I didn't mean it that way. I've just got this feeling. I don't think all of this is about me. I need to go home to find out."

I didn't say nothing, so he filled the space. "You believe in destiny?" he asked.

I only had to turn my head a little and I could see the last pair of basketball shoes I got at the university, custom-made, so that they matched our jerseys. "What," I said. "Like you show up at the right place at the right time, and everything gonna go the way it's supposed to?" Those shoes was still mostly new, stuck in the corner under some old magazines. I snorted. "I don't believe in none of that no more."

Noa coughed, cleared his throat. One of those forced ones. "I figured you'd say that," he said.

You take me back to that call now, I'd do it the right way. I'd be the man I was supposed to be, not the boy I was. But I wasn't ready yet, I guess. I shoulda been.

Give me that call back.

"Good talking with you, man," my brother said. And then he hung up.

# 15

# NAINOA, 2008

## *Kalihi*

FOR THE FIRST FEW DAYS WHEN I ARRIVE HOME, MY PARents believe what I tell them, which is that I needed a break, that I'm on vacation, and will return to Portland soon. We have vacuous dinners together, full of easy pleasantries, where I'm able to lie about my life with Khadeja and Rika and they talk about uncles and cousins and different hānai family in the islands, gossip and trite news to fill the air. There's katsu and teriyaki and saimin and Zippy's chili, shave ice and Leonard's Bakery and even the classics, pōke and poi. Blue-sky noons when both parents are at work, I make my way through concrete Honolulu, the cacophony and open-market whirlwind of Chinatown, the quiet fury of the homeless city in Kaka'ako, the polished bougie product of Waikiki. I'm home but I'm not home.

Khadeja calls me, over and over, I don't answer. She starts calling Mom, Khadeja's clever that way, street-smart, relentless, and while she calls less often as the weeks go by she doesn't stop.

I visit the island like I'm a tourist. *Arizona* Memorial, Sea Life Park, Hale'iwa, Aloha Stadium Swap Meet. Just to walk around in crowds, to have faces I don't know and don't want to caroming around in my mind, feel the collective rhythm of conflicting desires and states of being, to try and think of Hawai'i as a place that I don't owe anything to. I get sunburned like I never used to and then I get brown again the way I was, nothing else changes.

On the third week, Mom stops me as I leave the bathroom, my breath still cool and thick with toothpaste. "You have to talk to her," she says, meaning Khadeja.

"No I don't," I say. "She doesn't understand."

"She wants to," Mom says.

I shrug.

"You know," she says, "since you've been back, I know you've visited some of the old places. Does it feel like it did when you were a kid?"

"When I was what?" I ask.

"When you were young."

"I don't remember that," I say.

"Remember what?"

"Feeling young."

For a moment it's clear she thinks what I'm saying is ridiculous, and I believe another day or a different child—Dean or Kaui—and she'd say, *Get it together, drama queen*, with all her salt and thickness. But she pauses, she's searching my face, the same way Khadeja had, but there's something bigger in her, more insistent and unflinching, as if she can see the me I am now, but also all the versions of me that were here, with her, for so many years. "What's happening?" she asks.

She doesn't say anything, I don't, either, at first, but then it all comes spilling out, what I had been learning to do with myself in the ambulance, how I'd been close to unlocking all the mechanics of human life, but at the same time starting to resent the patients, their weaknesses, how I'd been stupid and arrogant and wasted the life of a mother and child, that I'd left Khadeja and Rika behind.

"I hate this," I say. "I hate what's in me."

"What's in you," she says. "What's in you is a gift."

"It should have been given to someone else," I say, my voice louder. "You're so grateful for it, maybe you should be the one to have it."

A slanted smile on her face now, she won't break her gaze with me. "You know, I could have left this place years ago, even after I met your father," she says. "I could have gone to the mainland, too. Just like all three of you keikis. I had excellent grades."

"Why didn't you—" I start.

"Don't interrupt me, Noa, not now," she says. "I've been to the mainland, I've traveled to San Francisco and Chicago and New York City. There's something here, in Hawai'i, that's bigger than all those *Lifestyles of the Rich and Famous* places. It's what woke the night marchers. It's what pulled you from the water and sent the animals to die with you, what gave you all these gifts."

"Gods," I say.

She shrugs. "That's one name for it."

"All the stories you told me," I say. "Some ancient relative, floating above me in the clouds, turning into an animal when I need it, guiding my destiny. I don't feel anything like that."

"I don't know the rules," she says. "Listen. I'd lift it off your shoulders if I could, Noa. There are so many places and people that need what you have." She seems more sure of herself the more she talks. "But I believe you can still be what's needed."

"It's like you haven't been listening," I say. "I don't want to do it anymore."

The slanted smile she had earlier comes back, as if she's in on a joke that someone told her behind my back. "So you're done," she says. "Fine. But tell me. You could have gone anywhere after what happened in Portland. So why did you come back here?"

"Free food," I say, halfheartedly. "Free rent."

She shakes her head, she knows, I didn't even have to tell her. "It just felt right," I say. "It felt like what I needed to do."

"That feeling," she says, "it's something speaking, Noa. So listen." She gives me a quick hug. "We're glad to have you home."


**AND SO I LISTEN, I DO.** I leave the concrete parts of the land, I find the parks and the valleys and the oceans, I let green and blue and gold songs scatter around me in the dawn and dusk in wild places. Illegal trails and vacant strips of sand, all the hidden places I knew about as a teenager, places kids would go to smoke a joint to the roach or play with each other's bodies or realize a dare. I walk and I catch the bus and I hitchhike, crisscrossing the island, until it happens.

There's a morning when I'm on the windward side, a steep trail somewhere between Makapuʻu Point and the tide pools after. There's a slice of sand that plunges into midnight-blue water and I slip into it, let the current drag me into the deep. Ocean swells roll in above my armpits, rock against my shivering torso, the water below me clean and clear.

The pull had been strong, to come here, to get in the water, the call was almost its own gravity, it doesn't take long before I see what's been waiting.

The sun is just risen, and I can see four lashing shadows in the water, headed directly for me, slowing to a liquid glide as they close the distance. They are sharks, and for a moment my body shoots with fear, I should go, I should go, there's still time, but another part of me is done with fleeing, and that part of me makes a stand. I tread water gently, and the sharks begin to circle.

They go clockwise, gray reef sharks, and I name their parts as they pass, snout, pectoral fin, dorsal ridge, caudal. Snout, pectoral fin, dorsal ridge, caudal. They circle sleepily, barely dancing their bodies. Their eyes find mine and my stomach wells with fear and excitement.

I reach a hand out, the circle closes just enough that I can touch each one as they pass, their bodies are ice-slick, thick with potential violence, and when I touch, something blooms at the point of contact, travels the length of my arm, a channel of feeling that is the same as what I felt when I worked in the ambulance, only now I don't see inside anything, but rather outside myself: Waipi'o Valley, its rivers, then lo'i paddies of kalo stalks growing plump and green, swarming the valley bottom, and there my family is among it all, with many families, on the beach sand or along the river or standing among the trees. The figures of our bodies become shadows and warp and diminish into the paddies, the river, the bay, as if we are made of the same water, beating into the current with the same motion the sharks are making now, everything blending into the other, it all flows into me and I flow into it.

My eyes are open, the sharks are gone.

It's just me, floating chest-deep in the ocean, cold water, warm sunrise, but I know where I have to go, where it all began of course, the valley.

# 16

# MALIA, 2008

## *Kalihi*

IF A GOD IS A THING THAT HAS ABSOLUTE POWER OVER us, then in this world there are many. There are gods that we choose and gods that we can't avoid; there are gods that we pray to and gods that prey on us; there are dreams that become gods and pasts that become gods and nightmares that do, as well. As I age I learn that there are more gods than I'll ever know, and yet I have to watch for all of them, or else they can use me or I can lose them without even realizing it.

Take money: my grandmother's grandmother's grandmother, Kānaka Maoli that she was, had no use for paper printed with the silhouette of some faraway haole man. It gave nothing. What was needed was food from the earth, housing from the earth, medicine from the earth, a sense of one's place in the system. What was provided and what had to be cultivated. But ships from far ports carried a new god in their bellies, a god who blew a breath of weeping blisters and fevers that torched whole generations, a god whose fingers were shaped like rifles and whose voice sounded like treaties waiting to be broken. And money was the name of that god, and it was the sort of god that preyed on you, made demands and laid its hands on you with such force as to make the Old Testament piss its pants.

We were made, eventually, to pray to it, whether we wanted to or not. Your father and I still pray to it now.

Take language. ʻŌlelo Hawaiʻi, which was not written, only passed from one mouth to the next, less letters than the English that soon roared over it, and yet it contained more mana of Hawaiʻi than anything that foreign tongue could twist itself into. What do you do when *pono*, a healing word, a power word—a word that is emotions and relationships and objects and the past and the present and the future, a thousand prayers all at once, worth eighty-three of the words from the English (righteousness, morality, prosperity, excellence, assets, carefulness, resources, fortune, necessity, hope, and on and on)—is outlawed? When our language, ʻŌlelo Hawaiʻi, was outlawed, so our gods went, so prayers went, so ideas went, so the island went.

Take you, my son. You are not a god, but there is something that moves through you that may be one. Does it revive what came before, or build something new? I can't say.

But when you returned from Portland with a broken hope I did my best to help. It's hard to guide what you can't feel, and there are so many days in this modern Hawaiʻi in which I don't feel anything. But when you are near, there is something, just under the surface, that I can feel. It is bright and warm and ready, but I can feel it, like a gentle swell of the ocean that contains a million pounds of power underneath.

And so I encouraged you to visit the valley, it's true. I trusted in what you were feeling, and that to follow that feeling would hopefully bring forth that which was inside you. See that? Hope can be a god as well. It's something that can be prayed to.

# 17

# NAINOA, 2008

## *Waipiʻo Valley*

TWO DAYS OUT AND I'M STILL WALKING, STILL FEELING the call, the gravity, ever stronger every day. I'm here, the Big Island, heading up out of Waimanu Valley, second valley after Waipiʻo, heavy with the feeling I will find something, just around the next turn, just behind the hala trees and on into the gritty mud of the trail, all the mosquitoes and flies tickling my skin, scattering from my slap.

The sun hasn't broken through and the gray smears of cloud rush past, the gusts make the bushes sizzle. I'm nearing the ridge, the point past which almost no one visits, out of this side of Waimanu and into the valleys beyond that have no name, it is said to be a broken and impossible path. I step up into the mist and muck and swing my machete, and I walk and I hack, knowing if I keep going something will be revealed, that I can finally understand what I should become.

At dusk it's clear that I'm not alone. I've been bushwhacking for hours, stomping and slashing, the folds of my shirt flapping with sweat, when I break through a heavier section of branches into a clearing. It's more space than I've felt since the morning, and I can smell the eggy metallic scent of a lit camping stove. Fifty feet away there is a shack, the boards lepered with moss, the tin roof copper with rust and blanketed in leaves and twigs. There is no window on this side, but I hear a murmur of voices and so make my way across the clearing.

When I am close enough I circle around to the front of the shack. It has an official bearing, perhaps a building once used to shelter park rangers or trail crews or rescue workers. The front wall has collapsed in sections, complete chunks gone like a house in a war, so that you can see through large holes into the room inside, it looks warm and dry, and even if the wood floor is rotting, it's certainly soft.

Pale fluorescent light flashes through the holes and I hear the voices clearer now, a European language of some sort. The light turns full into my face and I hold up a hand to shield my eyes against the blast of white.

"Yes, okay, hello," a man's voice, thickly accented, comes from the inside of the shack. "What does he want with the machete, don't come closer."

"I heard you from the trail," I say. It sounds apologetic, but the light remains blinding in my eyes. I step toward the door.

"Stop," the man says, and I do.

There is a series of whispers that slash back and forth between the man and someone else, a higher and rounder voice that sounds like a woman.

"Can't I come in?" I say. "I've been sleeping in the dirt for the last two days. I'm very tired."

More whispering.

"Maybe tell us something."

"Tell you what?"

"From where you are coming, what trail you were on, these things maybe."

I sigh, leave one hand up, still blocking the light from hitting my eyes. "I'm from here," I say. "I grew up in Honoka'a."

"And the—"

"—I've been on the trail starting at Waipi'o. It gets very thick coming out of Waimanu. I've had to hack my way out to get here."

They whisper again; I don't wait, I don't care, I pitch the machete through one of the holes in the wall and the clang of it on the floor stops their discussion. "You keep it for the night if you need it."

With the blade out of my hands, whoever's inside is satisfied. The light swings away from my face and I'm able to step up to the front door and enter. Bare walls, grim-frosted windows, a small wooden table where the man and the woman are sitting.

Even above the thick smell of mildew, I can smell the couple. It's an organic stink, like a pile of compost in the sun, lemon peels and old coffee and vinegar, and I can't help but think, *Fucking haoles*. It's the way Dean would have put it if he were here: he'd always bought the local perception of white people— hopelessly ignorant, awkward, dirty—and as much as I resist the stereotype, sometimes it smashes itself in my face. The man with his dark, tangled hair pulled back into a stumpy ponytail, a pubic beard crawling his throat, hunched at the table like a new kid at school, then the woman's blond hair, hacked boy-short, frames her mouth, a crooked fence of teeth I see while she whispers. Both are vaguely athletic, piercings across their faces— all their ears, he the eyebrow, she the nose and lip—and they have dark-blue circles of sleeplessness around their eye sockets.

Their camping stove, basically a small metal fist, continues hissing. Battered metal plates and utensils are cluttered around it. I gesture at the table; they nod and I sit. I slip free from my pack, and when I do exhaustion slides over me, pulls at my eye-lids, I lean my head down into my crossed arms and rest it there, trying not to fall asleep.

"Are you taking a meal, perhaps?" the man asks.

I raise my head and stumble through a response, yes I do eat and I haven't eaten, I have some things here and should proba-bly start, and I unzip my bag and withdraw wadded clothing, finding my own small pot underneath. I've stored some of my meals inside the pot—packages of mac and cheese, tins of tuna, a small, crackling rainbow bag of candy—and they spill out when I open it on the table.

"No no no," the woman says, smiling. "We can eat some with you. It's not needed."

"It's always needed," I say. I offer up a tin of tuna, the man shrugs and slides the tin to their side of the table, then we all sit and watch the pot belch steam.


EVENTUALLY, THE MAN SPEAKS. Our stomachs are full now with the heat of the pasta, tang of tuna. We'd said few words about ourselves while eating, talking first about the trail. They'd started out days ahead of me, their intention to cross all the val-

leys to Pololu, except about a day's journey farther up the trail
its condition became so degraded and unstructured they were
certain it would kill them if they continued. They were Ger-
mans, on the island for another week and a half before visiting
bits of the mainland as they made their slow way home to Mu-
nich. As we talked now the woman, Saskia, loosened up, she
mentioned how much she wanted to see the volcano, asked me
about my "child-time" in Hawai'i. She talked with her mouth
open and scratched her armpit, she was blond, and yet when I
saw Saskia it was Khadeja that was there, not because they were
at all the same but because of the way I could feel her presence
on Lukas, as if the very air between them was filled with invisible threads that stitched them to one another. They could stand
and carry plates away to the dilapidated shelves, or step outside
to relieve themselves, and yet you'd feel each one's attention
to the other tugged along. In it I recognized what I had, too,
Khadeja and Rika, and memories tumbled down and stacked
on each other so that I was playing pool at an ashy bar with
Khadeja just before closing time, watching her lean over the
pool table, the way her lips parted just slightly while she focused
and her fingers delicated the cue, those same fingers she'd use to
brush an eyelash from Rika's eye when we were all on our way
back from a picnic at the park, smelling of sandwich turkey and
lazily full of afternoon sun.

I had a feeling there would be more of this, that their absence
was something that would rest inside me, like the salt underneath my skin, rising out of my pores to sting my eyes when I
least wanted it to.

"Something is out there," Lukas says suddenly, and I'm
pulled from my memories.

"What?" I say.

Saskia says something gentle to Lukas in German, Lukas replies almost playfully, his voice going up an octave. "The land is something," Saskia says, turning back to me. "It is a person and an animal and other things, I don't know." She leans over, places her head on his shoulder. "We don't have religion," she says to me, "but we both say this place is somehow like that."

There's a queasiness of happiness that starts then, quickly, inside me. If these two could feel something, if they think this place is special. "Yes," I say, "there is something here . . ." and I start talking, too fast, the words don't touch my mind before they leave my lips, all the things I've wanted to say about what I'm feeling here. By the time I catch up to myself, I'm saying ". . . it could make the whole world better, couldn't it. If the right person was using it."

They smile, but there's a question behind it, their brows raised and crinkly with incomprehension. There's a sudden flatness to whatever had been between us. "Wait," I say, although no one is doing anything. "I've got an idea." I fumble the bag of rainbow candies from my backpack, tear it softly, and offer the opening to each of them. I turn and pull my 'ukulele from the backpack, open the case. "Have you heard any of our songs?"

I offer the candy again, each of them takes one. Lukas sucks his a moment, then frowns. He says something to Saskia and she spits her candy softly into her hand, motions for him to do the same with his, then cradles both to the jagged hole in the window and ejects them into the night.

"We can hear the songs," she says, "but no more of this"— she gestures to the candy bag—"please."

I laugh. "It's only candy," I say. "You don't have candy in Germany?"

She fetches an elegantly decorated bar of chocolate from her backpack; she peels back the foil, breaks us each a shard of the dark chocolate.

"Here," she says. "We do it right."

"Give us your songs, then," Lukas says, his eyes gleaming. "Tell us about this place?"

I lift my hand, feeling all of it, from the night marchers until now. When what's in my mouth hits my tongue it blooms, dark and sweet and barely bitter.

MORNING COMES, I wake in the corner of the shack, the damp pocket of my sleeping bag. The room is worse in the dawn: the wood everywhere is dark and I can feel the moisture coming off the boards, the swelling steam of decomposition, ceiling joists are bowed, sagging, spattered with the remains of bird nests. The table we were sitting at last night, sturdy enough then, in truth has ragged legs and a warped, bleached top. Rot has chewed through several small spots in the ceiling, and when a cloud splits apart above, through those holes, rods of white light slant down and scatter on the walls, the floor.

I stand, go to the table, where a green plastic bowl waits, heavy with oatmeal. I lay my palm over the top and feel a last bit of heat rising. They left it for me, and I can't help but smile, although there is no spoon. I sit on the creaking chair and listen to the clack of the leaves, I scoop the oats with my fingers, as if they are poi, feeling my body hum to life.

Ever since I'd taken my hands from the body of the mother, the feeling of connection—to the physical world, to the people I talked to or lived around—was gone. Wherever I was, in a crowded room or on an empty sidewalk, in the ambulance or at home, sleeping against Khadeja, I ended at the tips of my fingers and toes. There was nothing shared or passed to another, nothing I took from them, I was alone, all of me wrapped up in the voices and memories and souls of the animals and people who'd passed through me. But now, this morning, that has all quieted, replaced instead by a light, steady tug, a desire, but not a voice, wanting me to join it; I'm home.

By the middle of the day I don't remember all the walking that came between the morning and now. I know that there was exertion, that I stepped and rose and fell with the trail and hacked bush in some places and tramped through the same track that Saskia and Lukas bore down the day before, but it had come and gone without my attention. I'm sweating and thirsty but I don't stop, I can't, the valley is opening up for me, as if in invitation. All the branches bend away rather than claw, the mud firms itself for my feet, the mosquitoes scatter rather than swarm. Every step I take, I bounce back stronger and lighter.

*Here I am*, I think to myself, not as a declaration, but as an offer. This is where I should have been all along, I should have stayed in the islands, worked harder to listen. What did I think I could have accomplished alone, trying to mend broken bodies on the mainland? A whole parade of patients couldn't teach me as much as a place like this; connections are leaping out at me, revealing themselves, without any effort from me. The way my sweat takes the cells of my skin, mingled with dirt, from my body and drops them into the soil, and how the mist drapes the trees and the trees drink of it and then the sun lights it up and takes it back into the air, and how the plants breathe and their exhale becomes my inhale, the same way so many of the people of these islands once pressed their foreheads together in greeting and inhaled the same air, as one.

The path breaks in front of me. A clearing appears off the

main trail and I take it, slipping between the trees. My backpack bangs against the branches, but I continue, push along. I want to see the valley from the sky, I want to see the ocean, it's there just past the break. The ground slopes down toward a lookout edge, and when I arrive it's clear how far I've come. Waimanu and Waipiʻo, distant and massive but closely tactile all at once, clefts of green with curving bays of rippling surf.

I am far above the valley floor and I stand and watch, but then the ground shifts under me. I feel weightless for a moment, as if I'm leaping, then the swerve of acceleration in my belly, a blur of grass and rushing wind, something jerks and tears at my shoulders, my spine is wrung with heat, popping, the yawning of my body swinging, then I see sky, or ocean far below, something snaps, my femur, I'm spinning, weightless again, the air rushes, Oh wait, oh wait—

# PART III

# DESTRUCTION

# 18

# KAUI, 2008

## *San Diego*

AFTER ME AND VAN AT THE CREEK, I WAS MOVING LIKE A bullet train on fresh rails. I started telling all my engineering professors that gave out group work that I didn't want to be part of a group—boys after boys after boys and always the same, me fighting each one of them for a voice—so I'd do all the work myself, even if it was four times as much, okay? I did all the work and stood at the top 1 percent of all the hard classes.

Me and Van (and Hao and Katarina) would climb buildings at night if we couldn't get away from campus. Sometimes me and Van would sit on the floor of our dorm room with our backs to each other, right, while we scribbled in our notebooks, read and highlighted our chapters, our shoulder blades running over each other the way I wanted our hands to. But we didn't go as far again as we had at the Creek. It was like we were at the top of the diving platform, eyeing the water far below that could soak us, could cool us, but we didn't leap. We were back to something less, but not nothing. I could feel myself run to a fever by it, fighting to keep myself from flat-out begging for all of her.

One night there's a call from Mom. It's about Noa, of course. Only this time it's different.

"What do you mean he's missing?" I say. The only thing I knew was that he'd had some sort of accident at work. Someone had died on his watch and maybe it was his fault, so he was getting space and time to deal with it, gone back to Hawai'i. But home should be safe, right? That's the point of home.

Mom explains the trip Noa had taken to the Big Island. A walkabout it sounded like. Hiking all the remote and sacred spaces in the valleys near Honoka'a.

"He was called there," she says.

"Called?" I ask. Not this bullshit again, I'm thinking.

"The 'aumakua," she says. "He was feeling it strong once he got home. The valley was where he needed to be."

"You're searching for him now?"

"We're flying out tonight. Dean's coming in soon. The county has a search-and-rescue team started up."

"I'll come home," I say.

"No," Mom says, "you're not leaving school."

"But you just said Dean is coming home."

There was a sigh from her, like I was being stupid. "He's not in school anymore, Kaui," she says.

"Oh," I say, stripping all emotion from my voice. "This is that you've-gotten-an-opportunity-we-never-had speech, isn't it."

"Watch it," Mom says.

"It's like you know what I want, and then force me to do the opposite," I say.

"Everything that got you to where you are, the mainland, a university," Mom says, "it's not just you making your life happen."

"Of course it is," I said. "It's the only thing that is."

I figure that does it. Let's go, yelling or maybe cold quiet fury, Mom can do both. But she says the strangest thing, I'm still thinking about it later, when it's all done.

"Oh, Kaui," she says. "I know you. I *was* you. Stay there. What happens if you're here, and don't finish the semester?"

"I don't know," I say. But the more I start thinking the more I see she's right. It'd take another semester to get caught up on whatever classes I missed, at the very least. Which means another five digits of debt. It would hurt. I could do it. But I knew what would happen in Hawai'i: Noa would come back from the valley, probably flying on a unicorn that was farting rainbows, and he'd shower more miracles on the family, news stories and donations flooding in and another round of perfect golden light. If I went home I'd be nothing but a spectator, at best, okay? I wasn't worried about my brother.

And what hits me then is relief, big and strong. I'm not going home. They don't want me. Relief relief relief. What sort of shitty sister does that make me?


I TELL MYSELF this is what everyone wants and not just me. And actually, does it matter if it's only me that wants this? I get back to work. Days with just my books and classes, all platonic with Van, wondering where and how we'll finally jump. If it's my move or hers.

But something about that call changes everything, I swear. A curse or something. It all stops. Van stops coming back to our dorm room, and she doesn't answer when I call. We'd scheduled ourselves to take one of those bullshit requirements together, Christ and the Crusades or whatever. I figure I'll see her there, ask her what's up, right? But she doesn't come to class. I send her one text message and make myself not send another.

I go itchy with want, thin on sleep. I feel her fingers in mine. The jolt of her laughter. The way we could be both hard and soft on each other. Her sandy voice calling out as I climb one exposed cliff after another. Up, up, up. All night this all goes through me, the four hours of sleep I get. I slip up on my latest Structural Designs homework set, score a 70 percent, barely on the curve.

*Not like you*, the professor notes on my exam.

When I talk with Hao and Katarina, ask about Van, they shrug and say she's acting different, won't talk to them, either. Two days after the call from Mom, I wait in the student union, just around the time Van normally comes by for her coffee. I fold myself into a corner love seat, across from the announcement corkboard. Okay, she comes along soon enough, backpack hooked over both broad shoulders. Hoodie navy blue and logoless. She has a wide, lazy stride, her bob tangled and unbrushed, her small overbite peeking out between sips of coffee. When she gets closer, I stand up.

She stops. "Kaui."

"Hey," I say.

"What's up?" she says. Glances to the side. "I've got class."

I should take it easy, right? I know. Find the gentle words. But my heart is too strong. "Bullshit."

She scowls. "What?"

"Something's going on."

"I have class," she repeats. She starts walking. I don't say anything right away, just start following her out of the union, into the parking lot.

A skateboarder rumbles by. His wheels grinding over the rough concrete. We both watch him go by. His white cotton boxers muffining out of his slouched jeans, the burred outline of his wallet wearing through his pocket. We watch him like he's the best skater in the world, following his passage with our eyes, saying nothing.

"How come you haven't been coming to the room?" I say.

"I just needed a break," she says. She sips her coffee. So many times she's done it I've followed the liquid through her body: around the pink warmth of her mouth, down her freckled neck, into her chest, spreading behind her navel. But now when she takes a drink it's just a thing she's doing while not looking at me.

"My brother's gone," I say. "He went down into a valley and he hasn't come back." I don't know why I'm saying this, except that it feels like it might bring her closer to me. Just a little bit. "Like, we don't know how much food he has, or if he has a map or anything."

She jams a hand in her pocket. The skin pressed bloodless where it meets the jeans. "Sorry," she says. "I guess we never really talk about our families, do we? He played the 'ukulele," she says. "I remember that."

"*Plays*," I say. "Van, fuck, this isn't helping."

"Sorry," she says again. "I don't know what to do." She starts to move toward me, right? With this stiff and uncertain opening for a hug that makes me want to puke.

"Quit it," I say.

She starts kneading her own neck with her free hand.

I figure I might as well just say it, okay? I'm not delicate and can't pretend it, especially not with Van. "Don't act like you weren't in the car with me coming back from the wine festival," I say. "Don't act like you haven't been in the tent with me. Our dorm room."

I watch her. To see what she'll do now. She keeps kneading her neck, then sets her mug down on the curb. She ties her hair up. She bends and grabs her coffee. "I was drunk at the festival," she says. "I don't know what I was thinking. It was just a thing. Connor's such a douche and when I spit on him . . ." She laughs. "Everything after—it was just—I'm done with guys for now. But that doesn't mean I'm gay."

And I think: Is that what we are? The sour-stinking nights crushed in dorm rooms and hallways with all the other coeds, five beers deep and spinning but always staggering off together. Right. Joking about other people, sharing our headphones and snacks, slouching into each other's shoulder in front of the television. Then the rock climbs, the mountain treks. One of us leading on the sharp end with the rope dangling down behind. Up, up. Taking the long falls, right. Her coming out of the shower naked, us changing in our room with no hesitation all the times after. The way our bodies found their way to each other, again and again, that moment in the Creek when we dove into something hungry and basic. It's not like I spend all my time thinking of Van's body, our sex, the physical mechanics of us, okay? It's how there's a bright burst when I see her, how everything is all of a sudden coated in this anxious, hopeful warmth. We own each other. Gay? It's just a word, a syllable, a checkbox. Whatever I am I don't fit inside it.

"I'm not gay," I say.

"Oh, Kaui." Van smiles a sad smile. "It's okay."

"It's okay yourself," I say. "Jesus, you should see the shit I've done with boys. Don't act like you know me better than I know me."

"You're probably right." She reaches out for me, then stops. "Sorry," she says. "I should have quit this all sooner. I don't know. It felt good, because it was you, but it's not—it's not who I am."

I go cold all over. I rub my arm and turn away from her just slightly. "Fuck," I say. Just the one word.

"Kaui," Van says. And I hear it all even though she doesn't say it, right: Kaui, don't do this. Kaui, you sound pathetic. Kaui, we don't talk about love. You do that with someone else. You and me wreck the world, not the other way around. Kaui, get your shit together. I hear her say all that, but she doesn't move her mouth.

"Listen," she says. She has a look on her face I've never seen before. It's sad, and—and—

Oh. Is it pity?

My guts are about to unkink completely. I'm afraid I'll shit or puke or both. I have to get away. I turn to go. One step. Then another. Then another. Don't run, I say to myself. Don't run. But get away.

"Hey," she calls out. "Come on, stop."

But I don't stop or speak or turn. I keep going. Past the mission arches with their tall, swooping shadows. Past the yawning glass façades. The quads and sand and stairways. Sometimes you know when a day is going to stay inside you for a long time. And I feel the morning chill that is way too cold for the season.

# 19

# DEAN, 2008

## *Spokane*

BEAT HITS HARD ENOUGH IN THE CLUB AFTER ELEVEN, making my ears all fuzzed along with the dirty tilt I'm getting from my sixth shot, I think. Me and the boys at the bar, this one with its restaurant on the other side and the sports TVs, and in between the spinning color lights and a little stage and dance floor like the place can't decide which one it is, bar or club or restaurant. Waiters trying for get around the few couples all grinding half faded on the dance floor.

But the stuff coming out the speakers is good enough, and Travis and me and Billy-them been doubling down since the late happy hour, and soon enough that's me doing the dumb grind on the dance floor with this Middle Eastern girl or something crazy mixed, hair like a lion and perfect lazy eyes. Her lids is halfway the whole time we're talking and who even cares what the words is.

Most the time we're just with our hips so close we can feel the loose change in each other's pockets. We rock and grind and sway and come apart, then back together, I'm pissing hoses of water into the toilet, lime-green walls all scribbled with tags, then shots at the bar with Travis-them, hollering hoarse at each other over the music, how the hell did it get louder. Then we're back out on the dance floor and soon enough I'm telling my boys there's this thing I got for take care of, her hands are in my back pockets, knuckles to my ass, and we head for the door, past her open-mouth-O friends and the red and pink glitter lights hitting the sides of the bar.

We're in the taxi and then back at the house, kicking aside the junk mail by the front door, then through the dark living room with last night's dishes still around the television, and straight to my bedroom.

She laughs just a little while I'm licking that space at the base of her neck, she's saying, "You're crazy, you're crazy, this is weird, I never—"

"It doesn't matter," I say. "Maybe you never, but I always."

She's laughing again, only now we're pressed against the wall with our pants dropped to our feet, trying to work our way around our underwear instead of taking 'um off, then there's sheets tangled around our legs, us on the mattress, I got her calf up on my shoulder and she's holding her other leg in the air and pulling me into her with her hand, we settle into a rocking rhythm, in and out, over and over and over and over and over.

She's still there in the morning, when my phone explodes with noise, it's way early and it's Mom and I'm like, Goddamn.

The girl from last night's hand limp on my ribs when I roll and answer the phone.

"Sorry to call early," Mom says.

"I was just doing some push-ups," I say.

"Your voice," Mom says. "You sick?"

"Yeah," I say. "A little, yeah."

"Well, I'm sorry I had to call, then."

"Call back?" I ask.

"I can't," she says.

NOT LONG AFTER I make the other calls I gotta make, airlines giving me a bereavement discount, up in the air and we're almost done flying, because I can see O'ahu below, Honolulu in the night. It's funny, used to be I thought it was the big city, buildings taller than, like, ten stories was something special, streetlights and boulevards and all that, but now when I look down it's small, lights crammed into one tiny little corner of a place that's black with midnight water and hungry valleys. Doesn't look nothing as big as Los Angeles or Seattle or even Portland, where the sparkling goes on so far you can't see nothing but the bright.

I don't wanna be in Hawai'i. Last time I came back was so bad—it was just after I got released from the team at the university, when my scholarship was shut down—I kept running into everyone I knew and all they could remember was the newspaper articles and local news-channel sports coverage of the university, the tournament, local boy making it big on the national stage. Strangers remembered more about what I did in this or that game, all the way down to whether it was a crossover or a soft layup or a fadeaway or whatever. Every person had the same questions and I had to give them the same goddamn answers over and over: Yes, I remember that game; no, I don't play no more; things didn't go so well at Spokane; yes, my family is doing good.

And now I gotta come back like this. Mom called telling me that Noa went missing while he was hiking on the Big Island, long solo trip like a walkabout or whatever. She said he'd seen some things and had to go figure 'um out, and he told her where he was going but not for how long, and then he was gone and then it was a week, another week, no word, and she went to the cops.

The woman next to me's been sitting down the whole flight. The haole-est of haoles: a weird white sweater-jacket and stretch khaki pants, a splatter of freckles in the sag lines above her titties, and this crazy upturned nose and accent like she's from a farm or something. I can already see her burnt to a red sizzle in the Hawai'i sun, forced to drink mai tais at another stupid Waikiki beachfront bar.

She sees me looking at her. "Our first time," she says.

"I totally couldn't tell," I say.

"Are you happy to be heading home?" she asks.

"Of course," I say.

"I've got a question for you," she says. She turns and looks at me, blinks twice. "Do you play basketball?"

This question. Every time.

The overhead announcement ding goes. We all lean back. The air outside cuts and roars and the plane shifts and falls to the ground.

UNCLE KIMO GETS me at the airport with a face that's closed and tired and might as well we're going to a funeral. We sling my bag into the back of the truck cab and start driving for his place. The empty Big Island: it's black out and the road is narrow, and up along the hill we're going to climb there are large empty spaces with lights of towns all clustered in between. Uncle Kimo puts on some Bob Marley and lets it ride and we just go that way, windows cracked, us quiet, the island jumping out at us in the headlights as we ride.

At some point Uncle Kimo turns down the music and starts talking about Noa and how from what he knows Noa came home to Kalihi all bust-up, same as how he was from when we was on the phone, after the pregnant lady died in the ambulance with him. I guess he seen something while he was on Oʻahu with Mom-them that made him want for come back to Big Island. When he came back, he didn't come see Uncle Kimo or any of the other ʻohana, and no one knows exactly what happened. Only that he was gone for too many days with no calls and how finally Mom went all 911.

They been looking for him in the valley ever since. It's dangerous since they never found him in Waipiʻo, or even Waimanu, the valley after, which they figure means he went past Waimanu, which is bad, because it gets serious after there. The trails get worse and worse and they're full of savage animals and hidden cliffs and bust-up, dead-end side paths and they been looking for three days now, going as fast as they can up and down into each valley, hopping in Zodiacs to get around to Waimanu, helicopters and county search and rescue and everything.

Uncle Kimo says it's still good to see me, didn't remember I was so tall. Then he turns back up the radio and stares straight out the windshield. There's reggae songs on the station, about bottomless pits and pressure drops and rising up. It hits me: islands like Jamaica maybe know more about the way things are than half of this country. I keep thinking of the conversation me and Noa had on the phone—I can't help it—our voices and what was underneath 'um, and Uncle keeps driving.

"IT'S GOOD TO SEE YOU AGAIN," Dad says when we get to Uncle's place. He's been back up from the valley for a few hours. It gets dark down there and you can't find your ass with both hands, especially since the clouds are almost always out and covering the moon. So he had to come back up. Dad's body's changed since I was here last, he's got a little more thick to him, starting for get that old-football-player look where a solid packed lump starts to slide over the belt buckle. He's letting his mustache grow and there are scars and lines on his face I don't remember seeing.

"Look who finally made it back to his home," he says, and I'm like, Damn, Dad, getting right into it. I thought he'd wait but I guess he's ragged from searching and a little pissed.

"It's a long trip," I say.

"How many years it been now?"

"Shit, Dad."

"Tree," he says, counting out three fingers. "Been tree years."

"Always you could have come to Spokane," I say.

"Like there's money just lying around for that."

"I got nothing, either," I say. "Just maxing out my credit cards with flights like this. Gonna be working one year *at least* before I can pay this flight off."

"Still yet," Dad says, "I bet a guy like you can find something somewhere."

"No," I say. We're on the lanai, leaning against the railing. Out in front of us the land slopes down to trees clattering and swaying and the ocean way down below the cliffs. A truck booms and rattles on the highway somewhere. "Only thing I'm rich in is haoles," I say.

He's fully got a grin creeping up his cheeks. "Eh, you still shower at night, or what?"

"Sometimes."

"I heard up there they don't shower for days. Just rinse off when they feel like it. Shower in the morning."

"One of my roommates, his feet are so stink," I say, "smells like dirty milk or something."

Dad finally cracks up. "Stupid-ass haoles. But you're not showering, too, yeah? You shower in the morning sometimes, I bet.

"Hey," he says. "You wear your shoes in the house now, yeah? I bet you get a fanny pack."

He keeps going. He lists more, all the fantasies he's got of haoles: oily faces, precise pronunciation, butter in their rice, them being all hurry-up about everything. Says that's me now, too.

"You like Frisbee. You throw Frisbee with your friends."

"Dad"—he's really getting into it now—

"You got sandals, yeah? You brought home your Tevas? You brought home your sunblock? You—" He lowers his head onto the railing, giggling I swear just like a girl. He has this high, silly laugh, and that thing catches you and grabs you, and I don't know why I don't laugh with him, but I don't laugh, I just watch him laugh, and I don't think he's okay, something is wrong.

THIS IS THE DYING SEASON, but that next day I don't say nothing about it. Back in Spokane it would be starting, the leaves like pennies falling from the trees, the air bleeding-knuckle cold, and Hawai'i doesn't have seasons like Spokane, but either way I don't want Noa to be a part of this time of year. We're on the trail now and so cold and tired, all of us. This is the far side of Waimanu and us up on the trail leading out of the valley, a steep slope like all the others, but the trail is mostly gone, just a trickle of mud through all the mess of trees and bushes.

We've got a county search-and-rescue crew with us, two of them with their sharp blue uniforms and buckle-covered backpacks with kits and maps and flares, then they've got their dog, and it's out front now, snuffling and pulling us on.

Dad and Uncle Kimo and the rest of them come next, me right along with them, all us muddy to our ankles and tired to our teeth and mostly just scared we're going to run up on Noa's body every time we can't see in front of us.

So we hack, and we walk, and we hack, we push the branches back from our faces and the leaves is running their itchy blades along our clothes and our feet slurp the mud. The slope steepens, so that we're really having to push up and lean forward with each step, and it's hard to find good footing so that we don't just slide back down after stepping up and pile more mud on ourselves. There's a tangy sweet smell of overripe guava, and it mixes with the horseshit stink of the mud, coming on the cold wind. Clouds been pushing down into the valley all day, and now they're really getting black and all brainy. The SAR crew stops and sits their dog. Everyone knows what's coming.

"We don't have much light left, and it looks like it's going to start raining," one of the SAR crew says. She's haole, her hair braided in a knuckled ponytail and her blue baseball cap pulled down low on her face. "I think we're going to call it for the day."

"Fuck that," I say. "There's still light. I got a headlamp."

Dad is standing there, too. His eyes has these folds of skin under them with lines all sharp and broken. He leans against a tree and lets out a long breath. When I look at his hands on his thighs I can see they're all shaking like he's run through with electric current. I see it and I think again: *Something is wrong.*

Uncle Kimo has his hat off and runs his hand through his thick black hair. His gray shirt is sweat-dark all across his chest. Everyone looks like they want to sit down, but there's nowhere to sit because everything is mud and there's just this narrow little trail.

"We have to make sure we can make it back to the valley floor so the chopper can come grab us," the SAR lady says. "And I'm not running Pomai all night." She gives the German shepherd two good, whumping pats on the side.

Then rain starts falling. First it's just a few spitty drops, but it starts to pick up until there's a tapping drizzle.

"I'm staying," I say.

"We're all going back down," Dad says. He stands back up off the tree he was leaning against.

"He's still up there somewhere," I say. "Not like he gets a break just because it's raining."

"We have to go back," the SAR woman says. She turns the dog. The dude with her, the other SAR guy, who's Japanese but pretty big and cop-looking, turns, too, and steps back down.

"I'll sleep on the goddamn trail," I say, but I'm already talking to their backs, everyone else going back down the trail. Leaving my brother or his body—no, my brother—to whatever this storm brings.

"Pussies," I say. No one listens.

By the time we get back to base camp the rain is coming

down gray and steady and the clouds washed out any of the sun. The tents are all up close together under some other trees, out past them there's the lake and plenty bushes.

Dad's talking with Uncle Kimo-them about running the Zodiac around to Waipiʻo Valley so they can get out and grab some more gear, and the SAR team's all off talking together near their tents, and so I'm just standing alone, in the small rain under the ironwood trees.

For the first time I'm really starting for think Noa might be gone. Already I been thinking about all the things I wanna say sorry for, all the times I tripped him or pushed him or made anything in our house a weapon I could try on him when we was small. All the times I wanted for make him think I was the one with all the mana, even when we both knew that wasn't true. There was this one philosophy class I been in at the university, where the professor was talking about force. He said people think force and power is the same thing, but really force is what you use when you don't got power. I think about me and Noa and I'm like, I been using force my whole life. What does that make me?

The SAR helicopter is coming in for its people. As it comes down, the blades whack through the air and each beat hits me in the chest, going all the way through, out my ears, even though I'm probably three hundred feet away. The helicopter's striped all yellow and red and it's not a Blackhawk or like that, the ones in movies, it's smaller, a beetle without wings. It's loud. Each beat cracks the sky and then underneath that there's a silvery whine. The grass all washes back and flaps at the edges. The SAR team and their dog run to it with their heads ducked, their jackets snapping in the wind and the rain, and the lady in front, the one with the dog who told us we had to stop looking for my brother, she's clamping her hat to her head, and she and the guy behind run with that funny ducked-head, creeping-robber run, and they climb up and the blades run faster and crack harder, and all the grass leans away as the SAR team rises up and swings outta the valley.

# 20

# MALIA, 2008
## *Kalihi*

ME AND AUGIE BOTH HAD TO COME BACK TO KALIHI A week ago. We left the Big Island to return to our another-day-another-dollar life, not our choice, because I know my son is still alive, somewhere in those valleys, and I want to be there when he makes it back out. But we would've lost everything—our jobs, the pathetic rusting house we rent, our junker car—if we'd stayed on the Big Island another day. So we'd stuffed back up our duffel bag and suitcase and stood in the gravel outside Kimo's place with the early-morning bird burbles and chirps, the cool vanilla skies.

"We gonna find him," Kimo said, the white of his eyes browned from all the sleepless nights in the valleys, bushwhacking and tramping beside Augie.

"Yeah," Augie said. "We going to, one way or the other."

"Nah, come on," Kimo said, placing his meaty paw on Augie's shoulder.

"You know," Augie said, "maybe not. Maybe he's gone, yeah? Maybe one of the valleys swallowed him whole."

"Come on," Kimo said. "No be like that."

"Or maybe," Augie started—I could see him trying to hold his face, and not let it break—"if he's gone, we can try again." He grinned, reached out, and goosed my ass. "We can make another Nainoa, yeah babe?"

And then he broke with laughter.

"You dirty, panting dog," I said, laughing with them. "Always thinking about burying your next bone."

"I cannot help," Augie said, and giggled. "Let's go inside real quick for something, Malia. Ah, Kimo, try wait here for five minutes."

"Augie!" I said, but we couldn't stop laughing, all of us.

That laughter carried us through the truck ride with Kimo, through the ranch hills and leaning trees and back sides of the valleys in Waimea, past the fingernails of beach and black flaking lava fields of South Kohala. But eventually we had to stop, of course, at the concrete and screaming engines of the airport, where it was impossible to not feel like we were abandoning our child. The plane took off and we arced along the clouds and landed back in a Honolulu that that seemed to have become both empty and dangerous. Everything could take something from us now; we had so little left.

I am still here, I remind myself. I am still here, and so is my son, I swear it.

DAYS WENT WITH NO NEWS, only that Dean and Kimo and a few others are still searching, and here I am now, driving my bus back to the station at the end of another shift. Empty and large, shuddering and cannonballing along the night roads. The most peaceful time of my day. I like to ride dark, turn off the seat lights and the cab, so that it's just the instrument lights on the dash. There's something soothing about the sheer weight of what I pilot.

I'm halfway down the Pali, almost to the Nu'uanu turnoff, and from between the trees, below the sloping green shoulders of the Ko'olaus around me, Honolulu is swelling into view, the yellow-and-red haze of lights in the night.

The bus headlights sweep brightly ahead of me, showing asphalt, more asphalt, then guardrail, and then they catch a figure on the highway ahead. It is a man, stooped and almost naked, only a malo cloth wrapped around his hips and boto, then barefoot and bare legs and bare chest, dark-dark skin. He wears a lei po'o on his head, leaves spiked out in a crown, although his head is tilted strangely to one side, his eyes in black shadow.

I start to brake, then blow the horn. The man just stands. His whole body slips and shudders, flickers like a television signal that's partially interrupted by bad weather, then jumps forward to ten feet in front of the bus. I see the salt crusting his chest, his palms lashed with purpled skin, the sort of rope-handling scars we never see anymore. I slam the brakes and there's a terrible squeal and shake and then the surging of my body thrown forward against the seat belt. The bus jerks to a stop.

I didn't feel anything I didn't hit anything I didn't feel anything. The headlights show an empty road ahead.

Holy shit.

I pull the bus over and press the hazard lights. The blinkers
*tick-tock* away. The brakes spit air, *shishhh*. I throw the door
lever, the flap and squeak as the front door folds open. I step
down each steel stair and into the thick night air. There's nothing caked to the front of the bus, no dents or bloody smooches
or burst body.

I look behind the bus, where the remains of the man should
be if I ran him down. He's still there, a black silhouette stark
against the pale reflection of moonlight on the highway. But he
flickers again, shudders and twitches, and then there is only a
pig, hip-high and thick with fur and mud, which bellows and
squeals and grunts off the highway, into the ferns and trees on
the side of the road.

Headlights come. A car blows past me and the bus, shoulder-
parked on the highway. I stand for a long time, hoping the ice will
leave my spine, hoping the tumbles of my pulse will mellow. I'm
reminded of how it felt that night so long ago, Augie and me in the
valley making love, then the night marchers. This man was not a
night marcher, but I know he came from the same place, the edges
of the natural world, which humans never have access to. I can
feel the heavy press of sleeplessness on my skull, that I'm almost
delirious with sleep starvation and the numbing of the bus route.
I stay that way for I don't know how many minutes.


**I'M SLOW COMING HOME.** I feel thick and dumbstruck. If I saw
what I saw then I wonder why it happened now, so many years
since the last ghost we'd seen, hundreds of miles away on the Big

Island. I wonder what Augie will say, what I can tell him—he believes much less than I do, it seems like everyone does—and I realize I'm hoping that telling it will somehow make it true enough that it wasn't some half-crazy dream.

By the time I get the bus to the depot and drive our rattling Jeep Cherokee back to our house in Kalihi it's as dark as the night will ever get. I park in our driveway and I bang through the front door of our house. All the lights are on, so is the television, but quickly I can tell Augie is not home.

Of course.

It started happening soon after we got back from Honoka'a and the search for Noa. Augie has been getting up early—two, three in the morning—and then he walks out of our house. I don't know where. He leaves and comes back hours later, creaking through the house to our bedroom and bringing with him the trail: leaves in the hallway, the dank smell of earth and ferns on his skin. His knees popping when he eases himself to the edge of the bed, where he often pauses and I can feel the jumps of him crying silently.

I haven't said anything to him about it yet. I don't know why. This secret of his walks feels so delicate between us, as if the entire weight of what we're becoming rests on a few thin threads of privacy. But, then, he also believes Nainoa is dead; I know our son is still alive. We talk about it indirectly but never come at it full in the face. And so he walks and grieves, alone. Augie has never let me see that part of him. There's always his laughter or his brow split with worry and labor, but never the ragged teeth of full grief.

The thought comes to me all of a sudden: *God, these men.* Why is it they always pull their hurt up inside themselves, gulp it down into the quiet corners of their soul, clench it like a muscle?

Nainoa did it—does it—with his valley retreat, but before that how he'd shut down on the phone, a flat voice and easy words, *Everything is fine over here in Portland, just another day of car accidents and domestic violence,* but when you saw him play his 'uke you knew he had a heart ready to burst. And Dean does it, too, with all his slick talk and joshing everyone, a tough front with simple answers, but his eyes are always glimmering with the shine of his basketball memories. He never hit me again after that first time—was never violent in the house again at all—but that didn't stop me from remembering that he'd become someone capable of losing control. And now here's my husband. He's all jokes all the time, of course. When we first started together I loved it more than anything. He'd joke and giggle and the giggling would bubble over into my own lungs, until we were both laughing to tears. I've learned that laughter is the first wall he puts up against the hurt of the world. The walking he's doing now is what comes after that wall is smashed apart.

But now I am here, and he is here, standing at the door, letting it creak closed behind. His lids are heavy, his eyes cracked with red, but those great cheeks of his are still strong and round. He's wearing a shirt that grips his chest, and there's the outward stretch of cotton from the solid brick of his belly, the one part of his body that's grown slowly, but steadily, since we've been married, and an old pair of faded jeans that are about to go at the knees. The sun-heated shine of his dark-brown skin, even at midnight. He steps out of his slippers and wipes a hand across the thin mustache he's let sprout.

"Where were you?" I say.

"Out," he says. "Out out out. Out . . ." The sound drifts. He walks past me to the kitchen. I feel the argument starting to rush hot to my face as I follow him into the kitchen.

"Will you talk to me, for once?" I say. "You don't talk to me anymore."

His head's in the refrigerator. It's like he didn't even hear me, his fingers drumming the top of the refrigerator door.

Who knows how many seconds he's like that, staring into the refrigerator. I swear I can feel the cold from it looping through the whole room. But he stands, the door open, his fingers drumming, long beyond the time it would take anyone to look through the whole refrigerator. "There's nothing in there," I say. A jug of milk, always—always—on its final third; limp lettuce that we've been stretching for well over a week; a cheap plastic tray of huli-huli chicken with its glazed and blackened skin that Augie's been nibbling at for the last two days; half a bag of carrots; the last beer in a six-pack, the plastic rings looped around its neck like it's the last catch of the day; and then the ketchup and mayonnaise and four eggs and the other little things, none of them whole.

"There's never nothing in here, yeah," he says finally. "Just this little chicken," he says, pointing to the leftover huli-huli. "Little chicken. Little chicken little chicken little shit little chicken shit." He says that last part so that you can almost hear an "e" in it. *Shet.* I hear him whisper *chicken shit, chicken shit,* just barely audible. There's a serious look on his face, as if he's looking at the first page of a test for a class he wished he'd studied better in.

He scratches his belly, his shirt piling up on his wrist. The prickly sound of his fingernail over his hair, and he's looking at the kitchen wall. I wait. Sometimes Augie gets to what he wants to say the long way, talking about sports and a fishing trip and the color of the awful shirts at Hilo Hattie's, or how many tourists he saw down by Kalakaua Avenue when he went to see old friends that lived just off Waikiki and then suddenly he'll be talking about how he loves me and missed the way my hair fanned out across both our pillows at night.

But it doesn't happen. Augie shakes his head, something he's remembering that he won't say. The realization comes to me: he is cracking, inside; I'm losing him.

"You heard that?" he says. He pivots toward the hall, our bedroom the rectangle of light at the other end, where the ceiling fan is creaking out a constant beat. "Like a song." And when he says that there's a flicker of recognition in my head, of what I've just seen, and something now that feels the same. There's the smell, the same smell the man on the Pali left behind: wet ferns, thriving soil, seedy and brown and spicy, a lawn after rain, a field being harvested. It's coming off Augie.

"Hey," I say.

Augie starts moving down the hall, only says *Mmm?* over his shoulder.

"Augie, stop."

He disappears into the dark bedroom, and I follow, stopping at the doorway. Augie is sitting on the bed in the darkness.

"Where did you go?" I ask as gently as I can.

He starts rolling his shirt off over his head.

"I was walking," he says, his lips moving through the threadbare shirt. "All up the way, with the water. Up the way. Toward the clouds, the Pali.

"Farther back you go, bigger the houses get here, yeah? You and me was gonna get a two-story house, big lanai on top, watch the sunrise. Watch the sunrise. You remember? Here comes the sun, we gonna watch it from our lanai?"

It was a dream he and I had, a vacation we went to the same way people come to these islands, something they store away for their cold and bitter city winters, the blue-and-gold-and-soothing beauty of something possible in the near future: us on the lanai of our own home, high in the hills, looking down at the island's green ridges, the ocean after.

"We never getting that house," he says. "No no no, chicken shit, we only getting this chicken shit"—he has his shirt off, and he flings it toward the closet doors—"closet, tiny bed, this stink, old, beat-up chicken-shit house. We gonna die just like this."

It's the most clarity his voice has had since he's walked in the door. He's coming back into focus. The smell that was here is leaving just as quickly. His hand on his knee is trembling. I kneel down and grasp it. He won't look at me. I move my knees forward and hug against him, my shoulder under his chin, and a sob jerks from his chest. Another. I want to tell him immediately, what I saw on the bus, how it gives me so much hope. Even now I can feel, the two are connected. What is it he walked to in the night? What is it that's trying to reach us?

"Stay with me," I say to Augie. "Please, Augie, please. Stay with me. Stay." I say it over and over, as if it's the music he heard, as if it's what's been in his head all along.

# 21

# DEAN, 2008

## *Waipiʻo Valley*

FOUR WEEKS IS HOW LONG IT'S BEEN, YEAH, WHICH means no job left for me back in Spokane, soon not enough money for my part of the rent, but I don't care, I go down and up to the other side of Waipiʻo, into Waimanu and beyond. For real I can run the whole trail now, and this morning I'm on at dawn and by the time the first surfers is splitting the ocean at the mouth of the valley I'm most the way up the other side, on the Z-Trail, my legs going like pistons. Below me there's the whole green valley and the lines of waves rolling in, one after another, cracking across the sand and stone and scraping back out.

I'm still searching for Noa, all alone now after the SAR team and family and friends had to stop. Sometimes Uncle Kimo and some of his friends come along, but I move so much faster they just get left hours behind.

For most the time since I left Hawai'i it didn't matter what Noa was, because I was all basketball. But when I fucked that up, what was the point of me? Just making beer money at a package-handling company, waiting around for what? But when Mom and Dad had for go back to O'ahu, or else lose their jobs, and we still hadn't found Noa yet—there they were on the back lanai at Kimo's place, both of them with swole faces, red no-sleep eyes, quiet because every time one of them talked they'd just cry—never mind my bad job and ratty little room in Spokane, they needed me again. Here I am. I can still do this, and who knows what it's gonna make me after.

I keep moving. Over the crest of Waipi'o, through the thirteen gullies after that, the cold coming off the streams. When I cross each one I can feel the sore curve of the river rocks on the bottom of my feet, then after there's mud that sucks at my ankles, stinks like pig, but I keep moving. I speed up, even. Gotta get to the far side of Waimanu and start searching there again.

Steep miles, me down the front side of Waimanu, into the valley, mostly empty except for a few tourists stupid enough to hike here in the winter. Hala plants and gray sand and black-egg rocks the size of refrigerators. All these haoles squatting out by the edge of the ocean, or back by the dirty lake, or the cold-ass waterfall. Makes me shake my head every time. Welcome to Hawai'i, dumbasses, here's wet rocks and shitty camp food in an empty valley.

I go more miles. Up the other side of Waimanu, right on time. I shove a PowerBar into my mouth and chew, my jaw clicking by my ear. I already searched all of these parts of the trail, so mostly I'm running through here. Machete slapping on the outside of my backpack and the *ruff ruff ruff* cotton sounds of my jeans. My ankles is strong still from basketball. That's one thing I got. Plus I figure I lost plenty weight, from all the running and hiking and small food since I been searching. No more Korean ribs and white rice. I feel light as hell, moving like a mongoose again, like I got a basketball in my palm.

But then I slow down. This is the new part of the trail for me. I've checked the back of the valley, near the waterfalls, I've checked our old campsites and down along the coast. I spent days checking through what looked like little side trails he might have followed, hacking back the new growth, crunching over stiff weeds and heavy grass. Yesterday I found this dying old cabin, I think it used to be from the state-park people or something. Holes in the walls and the ceiling and a sagging floor. He wasn't there, no sign of anyone, even, but it was as far as I got before I had to turn back.

This time when I reach that place, there's something tugging me hard. Got a flow feeling, almost like when I was mongoosing on the basketball court back in the day. Everything around me bends away out my vision and there's just the one thing, only this time instead of my body moving between players it's my body moving between trees. The leaves lean away, the ground not sucking me down or rolling my ankles but holding me up, boosting each step, and the vines and the grass I swear start pulling back so this whole new path opens, through the dirt and bugs and green.

It's a clearing. The trees and grass go right up to the edge like they didn't use to stop, and at the edge there's huge cracked plates of dirt and mud and even rock that's all chewed off, like it recently broke, and there's a steep slope for maybe thirty feet before it breaks again into a straight drop a thousand feet into the cracking surf.

And down that slope before the straight drop I can see this funny lump, poking upside down from some of the dirt. Takes me a minute, but I figure out what it is: a hiking boot. I can't reach down the slope by myself, too steep, guaranteed the whole thing would pitch me into the ocean. But there's a tree small enough I can hook my legs around 'um, like I'm riding a horse upside down. I lock in and swing upside down and the dizzy comes into my head, like syrup. But I hang down the slope and can reach the boot, the dirt all torn and the loose plants going below it, over the cliff. I snag the boot with one hand and pull myself back upright. Sit away from the edge. Inside the boot there's some plants and mud and yeah, just like that, brown stain of old blood, all along the ankle and heel.

I take a knee. I see what's right there in my hand, the answer. I check down the slope again. There's all this colored fabric sticking out from where I yanked the boot out of the dirt. I set the boot down gentle, then I hook my legs around the tree and go upside down again, reach out for the fabric. When I first grab it, the cloth doesn't come. So I yank and dig and yank and jerk and whole scabs of mud shift and slide away and pitch over the cliff, I hear cracks and hissing. I pull one last time and up comes a backpack. Orange and red and just like Mom and Dad described to the SAR, back when we first started. I pull it up into me, all these ropes of heat and pain along my arms from pulling, and then get myself right side up. My skull is spangling from the upside down.

I sit cross-legged and set the backpack in my lap. It's ripped open in a couple places, and when I lift the main flap a food wrapper, like from a trail bar or something, flashes like a knife blade in the light and curls off into the air. There's a few muddy clothes inside, then part of a camping stove and a few nylon bags with cords and stuff, and when I shift those aside, there's his 'ukulele. It's in a soft case, but when I unzip the case the 'uke is there, clean and true.

I set it down like it's a baby. Next to the boot, where I can see the rusty bloodstain, and behind and far down, the surf cracks and rips against the cliff.

"YOU'RE BACK?" Uncle Kimo asks, when I come out of the room at his house the next morning.

I can't say nothing, I can't make my voice. I shake my head.

"Eh," Uncle Kimo says. He's looking at me serious. "Eh, Dean, what happened, brah?"

I'm shaking. I can't stop shaking, it's like I'm run through with that volt that hits at the end of a good session at the gym, the way I used to get after double overtime, just shook with light and juice, ready for jump. Only this one is different, got a blue feel to it, like I know it's one that's going come and go and wreck me whenever it feels like it, and I reach out and touch the counter and I start for say, *I think I know what happened to Noa,* but the words don't come.

Why can't I stop shaking?

I go back into the room and bring the boot, the backpack, the 'ukulele, set 'um on the table. Scabs of mud flake down.

"Okay," Uncle says, and he blows a good breath. "Okay."

Maybe we wait awhile or whatever, Uncle just thinking, then he says, "We gotta get some people, we gotta go get the body. Your parents, too."

"No."

"No?"

"There's no more body. Just got one place where there was a landslide, broke off into a cliff. There's nothing else."

"What do you mean," Uncle Kimo says, "nothing? Gotta be something. You went down farther, or what? All the way to the bottom of the slide?"

"There's nothing," I say. "Past where the boot and the backpack was buried."

"You have to—"

I tell him I'm not doing nothing else, not another thing. I don't have to do one more fucking thing. All this time I been here. Before and since, while everyone else went back to everything they had, I'm in the valley almost every day, sinking down into the mud and shit and centipedes and coming back up, climbing the long wet shining asphalt out Waipiʻo, where I kept seeing the bent guardrails and the busted, black frames of wrecked cars down in the forest below, drunks that went off the road and died making themselves into comets, their leftovers rotting in the trees, it was only me still out there, still searching. All for nothing.

Back when the sharks first gave us back Noa, I was the first one for reach him on the boat. I don't talk about it much. That time it was crazy quiet when the sharks came at us, the crew leaning over the railing, seeing the lead shark nudge Noa up against the side of the boat, not biting, not thrashing, just placing him as close to us as they could. Then the captain and his deckhands with their ropes and loops plucking my brother up, and the sharks dropped back, darker darker darker shadows until they became the deep blue. I was right there. The deckhands and Dad pulled Noa over the rail and I bear-hugged my brother hard, while Mom came out of nowhere and tackled us both. Got so that all three of us were crushed up together and there was the smell of mustard and potato chips and fruit punch from our lunch, our pulses beating on top of each other, and our arms and legs crushed together, me and Mom and Noa, like so you couldn't figure where one of us ended and the other started.

I was supposed for be the older brother, but after that day it was like every day he was growing up faster, until it was like I was the younger brother. And now here I am, carrying the last piece of clothing to touch his blood. Uncle Kimo's standing there, looking at me with liquid eyes that's all shining and trembling.

"You gotta call your mom and dad," he says.

"I will," I say, and he looks like he doesn't believe me, because Uncle's a smart man.

"Let me do it my way," I say. "I found him, not you."

"I know," he says.

"No you don't," I say.

Uncle Kimo starts for say something, then he stops. He leaves me there and wanders out to the lanai, then past it, out into the yard, with his hands up on his head like he's trying for get breath after a long run. I go the side table, where he's still got a landline, and white-knuckle the headset for who knows how long.

I start for dial Mom. I hang up.

I start for dial Dad. I hang up.

I start for dial Mom again. I get to the last digit, but I stop and hang up.

Uncle Kimo had come back inside, now he's watching me from across the living room.

"No one answered, Uncle," I say. I get up from the table, grab my shoes, and go to the front door.

"Where you going?" he asks.

"Out," I say.

He crosses his arms.

"I can call when I get back," I say. "They're always up late."

"Don't go thinking you can take my truck," Uncle Kimo says. "I gotta go back office after lunch."

I wave a hand over my shoulder. "Great, thanks for the help, Uncle," I say. I'm out the front door, down the driveway, up the hill, and thumb-out on the highway. Start walking toward Hilo, and after like fifteen minutes a car pulls up ahead of me along the shoulder. The driver's this old hapa-Japanese guy, clothes like he's been working in a garden, and he asks me where I'm going.

"Anywhere but here," I say.

"You have to have a destination," he says.

No I don't, not anymore. I almost say it, but keep it inside instead. "Hilo, then," I say. "Thanks."

IN HILO, I walk around Bayfront and watch the ocean and the breakwater. The water's all gray and murky, same like Waipi'o Valley after a storm, only this is a long curved bay, with barges and cruise ships out by one end, where the harbor is, and even farther past that, Coconut Island and the hotels. I watch the trees above me, their spiked fronds clattering lazy. All along the Bayfront road there's these small-kind old-school businesses, hand-lettered signs and everything. I go into the first bar I can find.

The bar's big enough and almost empty anyways. I sit right at the bar and get a beer, it goes down fast and cold with a couple flexes of my throat.

I order another and the bartender's like, "Easy, Hawaiian."

"Yeah yeah yeah," I say. "I'm not driving anyway, howbout I do my thing."

"Just go easy."

"No worries," I say. "Nothing gonna happen. I'll be like the son you never had."

"I got three sons and had to kick them all out the house," the bartender says. "So."

I laugh. "Well, I won't let you down."

"They said that, too."

I raise my hand like, Enough, and the bartender goes over to polish the chrome part of the counter. Then I figure, this cheap little place, I bet that part of the bar is plastic, fake chrome everything. I almost say that, too, but I'm not that stupid. I bet his sons would have said that.

A few more beers go, a couple guys come in and sit down at the far end of the bar. I figure they're from construction, because they both got on hyper-yellow shirts and when one guy raises his arm to signal for a couple of drinks you can see the sharp tan line on his arm. I keep drinking and they keep complaining about their wives or how it's hard to catch good fish too close to the coast. After a while they're still going: *She always trying to get me to change something, my shirts or my haircut or whether I watch football on Sunday.*

One of 'um looks over at me. Then they go back to talking to each other.

I stand up and go over next to their stools, lay my hand on the guy's shoulder. He's got these small ears and meaty cheeks with some Okinawan-style stubble.

"Eh, mahu," I say. "Why the fuck were you looking at me all funny just now?"

He shrugs his shoulder out from under my hand.

"You heard me or what?" I ask.

"Go home," he says. He doesn't turn from his drink or his friend.

"Oh," I say. "Only you were looking at me just now like you wanted my phone number or something. Guys looking to make a new fag for yourselves?"

The one guy, the one close to me, sighs, like a dog trying for sleep on the floor. "You're all buss already," he says. "Go home."

Then to the bartender, "Eh, Jerry, maybe you should cut this guy off."

"Your wives sound like real bitches," I say. "Give me a few minutes with 'um. I'll straighten everything out. Straighten 'um out to the tips of their toes."

Both guys laugh and I think I hear the bartender laughing, too, until he says, "Brah, pay your tab and go piss on a wall somewhere."

I take a bunch of money out my pockets. I know it's all ones and not nearly enough so I flutter 'um over the bar, tell the guys to go suck some goat balls, and push myself out into the afternoon.

Something's not right. It's hard for tell where I am. Sun's like a headache and my legs is not totally listening to my head. There's the white stone pavilion in the distance, the round one over by the bus station. I try for turn my body toward it, find something in between to aim my legs at. Got the light post at the intersection, so I make it there and grab the metal and wait for the light to change. Feels like I'll fall off the planet if I let go.

The light goes to a walk signal, but someone grips my shoulder and twists me around. It's the construction moke from the bar. He swings his fist up into my chin and there's a white explosion in my eyes and I sit down hard on the curb, but I don't fall all the way over. Just sitting there like I'm relaxing, and the moke stands over me.

"Not so smart now, yeah?" he says.

"I'm still plenty—" I start saying, but I figure why finish talking and stand back up and punch him in the throat. He makes that *huuuuh* sound everyone loves to hear from the person they just hit. The moke staggers back and his knees go all chicken-wobble, but he doesn't fall down, too.

Whole thing feels good. I want everything broken.

So when the moke comes at me again I drop my hands and wait for his next punch. He gives it, and there's a black crunch and my head sparks again and I tilt and pitch and my shoulder blades smack the sidewalk. I open my eyes and I'm on the ground and there's the sky and then grass and cigarette butts and plastic wrappers and the moke's boots, stepping forward. I hear traffic go by in the street behind us. He punches me two more times. My skull feels like it splits open on the concrete each time and there's all sorts of dull throbbing after. Got red spots dancing in my eyes.

There's someone shouting and tires screech to a stop. More voices saying things to each other before the moke says to someone in the street, "Get back in your car." I think it's happening behind me. "I just talking with my cousin over here," the moke says. "He fell down."

Mostly my eyes are pointed at the sky, where gray breaks up into blue every now and then, but here comes a shadow over me. It's the moke standing there, leaning down into my face. "Not so funny now, yeah?" he says, fresh beer fizzing off his breath.

"Thank you," I say. I start noticing the hurt, places where it feels like I'm ten inches thick on my forehead, must be new lumps forming. My tongue is like a fully dead whale. "That was perfect," I say.

"You sick fuck," he says. Then he's gone and it's just sky again. I close my eyes. Someone comes asking if I need help and there's another voice—a woman's—saying, "We're down by Bayfront, over by the bus station. Yeah. Some sort of fight. He's bleeding a lot."

That first voice asks again if I need help. I keep my eyes closed and just listen.

THERE'S AN AMBULANCE that comes but they don't take me anywhere, it's just cuts and bruises and swelling, I still got my brain. They close all my cuts up right there on the curb, give me some cold-ass gel pack I can press over my lumps, and I cannot believe it, but I make the next bus. Driver doesn't even flinch when I get on and he sees my bust-ass face. Plenty empty seats, I find one on the sunset side and lay my head back against the sagging headrest. Smell the ashtray stink, hear the old vinyl creak when I squirm in the seat. The inside lights drop down and we leave Hilo.

## 22

# KAUI, 2008

### *San Diego*

GOD, PLEASE LET ME FORGET THIS WINTER. FIRST CAME
December, an ugly end to the semester. Me and Van like strangers in our dorm room, functioning off the smallest working vo-
cabulary we could, one-word answers to each other. Trying to
be in the room only when the other person wasn't. Each time
we were forced into that tiny space, it felt like something was
strangling me, right? We tried our best to get ourselves out of
tune, so one of us was coming while the other was going and we
were only there when the lights were out and we could sleep

away our shared space. Finals in Vector Calc and Physics III and materials in front of me like a guillotine, trembling above the bloodstained chopping block.

In the middle of that hell Mom called. It was over. Noa was gone. Dean had found a landslide that ended in the sheer edge of a cliff into the sea and that was what had taken Noa to death. We had his backpack and a wrecked boot and that was it. I talked with Mom on the phone and I talked with Dad on the phone and I talked with Dean on the phone. No one had any opinions about the world. The calls were full of quiet space. I think we were focused on breathing. Take this breath, then the next. Each day I tried to sort out the words and symbols in my homework, work that was supposed to be my best shot at becoming something, while all around me the things I'd thought would survive were extinguished. Van gone. Noa gone. Classes next. Let it be.

But I made it through, in the end. All of it.

Now it's winter break. Dean's back in Spokane, he doesn't know for how long. We didn't have the money for me to fly home in the meantime. I mean we didn't have the money but we did have the money, because I could have floated another flight on my credit cards. But I'd about maxed that out with climbing trips and stupid school things, and flights to Hawai'i in winter are murder, even from San Diego. So it's a shit winter break and I start it with a few begged shifts at Romanesque again, which is lucky for me: the first day I go in there, the day before I'm about to get kicked out of the dorms, I meet a waitress named Christie. Her other job is at a hostel front desk. The hostel helps Cali-fever Euro gap-year kids see America, it's not supposed to be for broke college kids who normally live up the street. But

Christie lets me rent a bed for the rest of the break at a higher rate, vouching that I'm just passing through if the hostel owner asks. Most days I catch the bus down to the beach in the middle of the workday. Shiver in the kiss of the chilly sun once the fog burns off the sand, or stay put and bum caustic liquor off the generous Euro kids at the hostel, who are overwhelmingly blond and stupid happy for America. I eat saimin and cheap knockoff cereal and Dollar Menu specials that I double up on and refrigerate. I have one of the bussers at Romanesque saving scraps for me. Look at me, Mom and Dad, I learned how to hustle through osmosis, all those years at home with both of you on the edge of economic cliffs.

On Christmas I call again to talk. It's gotten harder with my family now. Each of us with our own language of death and grieving and no avenue for translation. There's this weird thing where I don't get to talk to Dad as much as I used to—whenever I call, Mom has some reason he can't come to the phone. It's weird, okay? Our phone calls turn into a board game where no one knows the way to win but everyone knows the way to lose: talk about Noa. So we talk about the weirdest stuff instead. The price of milk. The new route Mom has been driving with her bus-driver job and what the traffic patterns are like. What sort of shoes make my knees not feel like they're filled with cement by the end of a shift waiting tables at Romanesque. I explain what a hostel is.

It goes like that, but I keep calling. Christmas is no different.

"Downtown Pizza, how can I help you?" a voice says.

"Hey, Dad."

"We don't have Dad, but we do still have some turkey pizza. Special today, for Christmas."

"I thought this was Hawai'i," I say. "Can you put some pineapple on there?"

"Pineapple!" Dad says. "Shit should be against the law."

"So should bad Dad jokes," I say. But I smile anyway.

There's this pause after I say that, and then Dad's voice is lower than a whisper, almost. Moving swishy and fast and I can't understand what he's saying.

"Dad, what?"

His voice is still calling. The air in the call between us shifted. I can feel it, like ears popping when you come down from altitude. He's not on the other end.

"Dad—"

"Hey, honey." Mom's voice now.

"Mom, what's happening?"

"Nothing."

"I mean with Dad."

"Your dad's, uh, there's someone at our door he had to go talk to."

There's this squeamish fist that clenches in me. I know she's lying. "Mom," I say.

"How's the break?" she asks. "Are you doing okay up there?"

She's done this before and today's not the day to make it something more, right? I let it pass. "Sure," I say. "I guess. Glad I made it through another shift without spitting into anyone's food."

She laughs. "Trust me, I know how that feels," she says. "But you have to go away from yourself. You go to work, imagine it's Kaui you're hanging up in the closet, not just your backpack, your change of clothes. That's you, locked away until the end of your shift."

"I know how to survive," I say.

"Good," Mom says. "It took me a long time. A *long* time."

"Yeah, well," I say, "it's only like this for a few more weeks, then school starts back up."

"Lucky you," she says.

And *Oh Christ* is what I'm thinking. *Here we go again.*

"Can we not do this on Christmas?" I say. "I'm—there's no one here, Mom. It's just me."

"You're right," she says. "It never gets any easier, Kaui."

"I know," I say.

There's this pause. I realize our cadence now would be that she'd ask about Noa. Every time before this that's what it would be, but there's nothing to ask. We both know everything there is to know about him now.

The call ends. Soon enough everything in my head grinds apart under another stack of days in San Diego. Hostel, Romanesque double shift. Hostel. Shitty foggy mornings and waiting tables. Hostel. All of my time is chunked up into surviving each place: surviving the shifts and surviving the chasm of quiet and solo that comes after.

The mainland Christmas–post-Christmas bullshit comes in one big tide of gimme gimme gimme and all of a sudden it's New Year's. I'm on the last call at Romanesque and catch the final bus home, right? We're passing people in the street: rumpled black cocktail dresses and flapping loose ties. All of them chasing last call up the boulevard. Horny or hilarious or ecstatic. Colored lights and fireworks and Top 100 Moments on the hostel's television when I return. I wonder: What am I doing? Is it Van or Noa that did this to me, or did I do it to myself? It wasn't so long ago I felt I'd cracked open the shell of life and found a bright core of happiness in the middle. But so quickly it seems like it's crumbled.

God, please let me forget this winter. Please let me forget

this winter. Please let me forget this winter. And time goes. Good, okay. The new semester arrives. Van comes back.

The first night we're both back in the dorm it's quiet, me and Van with our headphones on, staring at our laptop screens. It's a replay of the end of last year, right? We're sitting back-to-back at our desks by the dorm window, each trying to pretend the other person isn't there. Smell of one of her candles burning, tarry and spicy. Suddenly I feel her hand, cupped and patting my shoulder, trying to get my attention. I wonder what this is, if I should hope. It feels like there's something softening between us while my heart goes *Okay, okay, okay.* Then I slip my headphones down and turn.

She locks her gaze on me; her eyelashes are long and easy. Seems like she's been getting more sleep, all the creases gone from her face. Fuck, she's already killing me. I turn completely sideways in my chair.

"What's up?" I ask.

"Is he dead?" she asks.

I surprise myself with how fast I answer. "Yes," I say. "He is." The words just float there.

"Okay," she says. Then she gun-points her finger at her headphones, down around her neck. There's something humming-birds-in-syrup in the sound coming from them. "Ever heard this song? I bet you'll love it." I shake my head no and she slips the headphones off her neck. Places them over my ears.

Common's "Drivin' Me Wild." I have heard it. But I don't tell her that and I let the snare snap and Lily's high and slippery voice run against Common's verses. I start nodding to it, lean over sideways in my chair so I'm in Van's atmosphere, right? I close my eyes; I don't need them. There's her smell and the headphones hugging the music to my head. That's it. When it's over, I say, "Good song."

"I have the whole album," she says. "You remember the one before?"

"I do."

We go back to our classwork, scribbling pens and tapping keys and the flap of textbook pages. Neither of us put our headphones back up. When I'm done I stand and go to the mini-fridge under my lofted bed. Get the milk I stole from the cafeteria and pour it out over the last of my cheap bulk cereal and sit, cross-legged, in the middle of the carpet.

I'm crunching the first bites of cereal when Van leaves her desk and joins me on the ground. She nods her head to the bowl. I pass it over. She takes a bite and then passes it back, our fingers glancing when we exchange the bowl. I scoop again and crunch and swallow and pass the bowl back. She cups it in both hands, has another bite, passes it back. The spoon rattles in the ceramic. I scoop again and when I bring the spoon to my lips I can still taste her there. Her warmth. Her flavor. I swallow it all down, the milk and the cereal and her. It feels like we're praying.

"Okay?" she says.

"Okay," I say.

I'd never felt Noa's death, really. Not the way I thought I was supposed to, heavy and dramatic. Until right now. It comes down on me like a wave jacked up to its full height and me the shore. Jesus Christ, he's gone. He's completely gone. No more phone calls with his hyper-intelligence that pissed me off. No more living link between how we were in our hanabata days, giggling and reading on the couch together. No more is there the idea that we could get back to that or something like it in the future, something bigger and richer. No more bright pride from Mom and Dad—if not for me, then at least I could still live off the warmth even if I wasn't the firestarter. No more no more no more. Someday I would be the same. And everyone I loved. Nothing.

I'm dumb with impact. When I almost drop the bowl Van reaches out to grab it, and our hands meet. Strong and steady.

"Oh," is what I say. I'm not sure Van hears it. I don't want her hands to move.

And they don't.

THE FEELING SETTLES. The loss becomes as much a part of me as anything. There's no time for it to take me over. I'm locked back in my work, climb back out of the hole of last semester, top of my class in thermodynamics, swing a few climbing sessions indoors with Hao and Katarina and Van. A weekend comes a few weeks further and we're out on beach bikes after dark, the four of us. Mist sticks to our cheeks and eyebrows. The road pulses up through the handlebars. We cackle and whoop and blow down the street like we just came off our leashes. I guess we did: a little bag of coke that Van came up with and a few pre-party beers at Katarina's place and then the idea of a bike ride to the house party we heard about. We swerve through the hours at the house party, thick boom of music and rusty voices cackling in the cramped angles of a house, hours where I'm above my bones.

The house is full of people we don't know but plenty of people we do. At least their faces. But even if the faces are ones we know the people underneath are—I don't know—there's a sameness to so many of the people at these parties, desperate to get the right stance, the right clothes, the right picture. This idea of a perfect night they have and can never live up to, so they do it again, right? Over and over.

We bump against all these people and find our spots, inside the house and out. We dance and nudge each other's elbows and hips and drink what we brought in our backpacks and stumble in one pour out the back door.

There was some sort of idea to all get back to Katarina's place together, see what damage we could do to ourselves there with more beer, some movies. But they left without us when a designated driver emerged. Now it's just me and Van again, okay, our skulls whirled with booze. The way she was right after the wine festival, the bathroom—when she said she didn't feel about me the same way I feel about her—that feels like it was a mistake, that what's happening now is really what we are. Yes, I think I'm emerging, just a little. From whatever storm rolled in with my brother's death.

I take Van's hand. I'm surprised when she holds mine back.

"Your hand's warm," she says, drifting in her drunkenness. And I'm not sure which of us does it or if both of us do it but then we're moving back into the house party, together.

Back inside, the smells: mint and the leftovers of cigarettes. Fresh-cut lime and steamy beer. The halls are crowded and people might be staring at us like they know what we are, what our holding hands really means, but I don't care, okay? We're on the dance floor again in each other's arms. Then we're in the kitchen, where a ripped bag of tortilla chips is leaning into a puddle on the Formica counter. We scrabble two shot glasses from behind the sink and slip ourselves a vodka each. I don't taste it—there was blow earlier. Off the top of a bathroom counter. We're dancing again, each with a thigh in between the legs of the other. Then we're on a set of groaning stairs that lean us into the walls, the railing. Three or four people coming down as we go up but we just push past. A hall we find an empty bedroom in, the sheets and comforter half poured from the mattress. An obvious wet spot in the middle of it.

We stand and stare at the room, turn around to all the walls. Like it's an observation deck.

"That last shot," Van says. "I can't feel. I can't feel me it." She giggles. Pokes her own cheeks, her lips, and when she touches her lips they bend and I can see the lines and curves and how pink they actually are. I laugh and poke her cheeks, too. In the half-light see my brown hand against her paler skin. Then I lean over and lick her lips. They're cracked and salted, they're curved, they stink. But she opens her mouth just a little and accepts me. Our mouths are wet with each other. I hold the taste, and tell myself, This is how you will remember.

"Mmm," she says.

My head is heavy. Freighted with all the things I've done to it. I lean in to Van, who's just as unstable, and she leans back into the wall. I feel all the places we're connected, the same, the density of us.

She rocks with me for a second, but then she goes stiff and pulls back. "Nope," she says.

I pull away. "What?"

"It's gross, Kaui," she says. Her eyelids droop but there's something in there, something hard and mean. I tell myself I don't recognize it. "I told you." She laughs. Her hand comes up and pushes into my face. "You're so gross."

Everything in me falls off a cliff. I don't move, right. Try to think of something to say. Van moves to the bed like it's taking a lot of concentration to operate her body. She collapses on her back.

"Van," I say.

I back into the door and strike my funny bone on the handle. The hit sends a metal, buzzing echo along the nerves of my arm. I fumble open the doorknob and step into the hall and the bright headache of light. I can feel the hot shame coming to my eyes already.

"Hey," a boy's voice says as I start to close the door. A pale, thick arm reaches over my shoulder from behind, palms the door to keep it open. I turn around. It's Connor, Van's date from the wine festival. There are two other guys behind him, leaning against the wall. They don't even bother making eye contact.

"Downstairs you two were ready to party," he says. "Still ready?" He drops a hand to my waist as if to steer me. Sour beer and menthol-heavy cigarettes stinking off his body.

I clear my throat and slap his hand off me. The other two boys stand up from their leans against the wall. One of them has a hand in his pants pocket, adjusting himself.

"Get the fuck away from me," I say. "All of you." I say it loud and long. And again. So that everyone can hear. Especially Van. All the way back in the room, passed out on the bed. There's this moment where no one does anything, not me, not the boys. They move past me like the cars of an express train and no stopping for miles. When they pass me, I run, taking the stairs out of the house two at a time, without falling. Without slowing down.

There's the dizzy throb of the chemicals in my veins and the sick fist of my stomach clutching and unclutching as I think about me and Van. I was practically begging for her. And what came back from her, that sharp meanness—I start to wonder if there have been other nights. Her and Katarina and Hao without me, where maybe I was the joke that was riffed between them around the table.

It's twenty or fifty or a million blocks later when the cold air cracks open my brain with clarity and I see. Jesus, she was alone in that room. Barely awake. Three of them.

I move fast, the sidewalk rocking and swerving with each leg running. I don't really know what's happening with my legs and an edge catches part of me down around my feet. I pitch into wet grass and crack a knee. I'm up and holding a fence to try and lever myself forward faster, with balance. A few blocks later I pitch into the sidewalk again. When I try to stand there's a pair of curbside garbage and recycling bins that I lean into, and all three of us go over with a sparkling crash of glass and sliding cardboard. I get right and run. The street yawns forever in front of me, on and on. But I make it to the back door of the party house. People are laughing or oohing or holy-shitting when I get back inside. Bodies and words, but I paw through whoever's there and make it: the stairs, then the door, but the door is wide open and there's no one inside. Van is gone. The boys are gone.

Back outside and into the street, where behind me there's no one I want to recognize and in front of me is a smattering of golden house lights down the block. The dark empty pavement smooth and slithering into the night.

# 23

# MALIA, 2008

## *Kalihi*

TWO NIGHTS NOW SINCE DEAN ARRIVED FROM THE BIG Island with the last things to touch you when you were alive— your backpack, your hiking boot—and tells me the story of your fall. The minute he described it, I knew it was nothing but true. If I'm honest, I'd felt you gone for quite some time, but told myself I was wrong, that I had no idea.

But of course I knew. You are gone.

It's an impossible thing to explain, motherhood. What is lost, the blood and muscle and bone that are drawn from your body to feed and breathe a new life into the world. The bull- dozer of exhaustion that hits in the first trimester, the nauseous clamps of the mornings, the warping and swelling and splitting open of everything previously taut or delicate, until your body is no longer yours but something you must survive. But those are only the physical. It's what comes after that takes more.

Whatever part of me flowed into you from my body, it turned us tight into two people that shared a soul. I believe that of all my children. Fathers will never understand the way you get deep in us, so deep that there's a part of me that remains, always, a part of you, no matter where you go. For all the sleepless nights you bludgeoned us with your mewls for milk, for all the car rides you screamed through, the scrapes and cuts and shrieking afternoons at the mall, feverish nights I'd have to hold you to my chest and feel the butterfly flap of your lungs trying to fight off the fever, the shit stains on the sheets Christmas morning and the broken wrist on our anniversary-dinner-reservation night . . . despite all that, there was still something of unprecedented perfection underneath. You'd wake in the crook of my arms with the whites of your eyes alive with brightness and wonder, drinking in every new thing as your impossibly smooth skin pawed at my cheek. Windowsills we rocked by. The fuzz of your first hairs under my nose as I nuzzled you in your sleep. How open your face was at the sight of the first caterpillar we found in the earth, how you squealed laughter when we blew on your tummy, or the days where we'd get the whole family under the comforter at five in the morning and snooze, drinking in each other's dreams. The whole world was there, in your face, beaming out of your perfect brown skin. Everything was made new, over and over. It shook me with something so holy and complete I didn't need a prayer to know there were gods with us, in us.

Never would we imagine anything but our lives ending before yours. It could only be you to tug the sheet up to our neck and tell us it was okay, that we could go now, that we'd done everything required. It's how a parent's life should end. But it never will, not for us. Instead, we usher you first to the other side. This is what we do when we put you into the earth.

It's not your body, of course. We'll probably never have that. Instead it's a lei of pū hala flowers in blazing orange, the biggest lei I can manage, strung so long with hala that it's as solid and heavy as a book in my arms. To make the lei, I skewer each hala key and thread it through, the same as how your loss runs through me. Between them I string lauaʻe fronds, to decorate, to make it spike and prickly against whoever touches it. So it goes. I pierce and slide.

It takes hours, me alone in our bedroom, but there are no tears. Just the work of my hands. Pierce and slide, keep stringing. That's all.

When the lei is finished we drag ourselves into the car— your brother, your mother, and me—and head east, to the Kaiwi Trail.

Out of the car and down the paved trail we go, to the point where the grass grows gold with drought and the trees are short and lashed by wind. We leave the paved trail and the host of easily pleased hikers for the rougher stuff, thorns and thistles and a sandy wash that slopes down to the ocean and ends in the crumbling steps of a small lava field. Black ridges being lapped by waves, and the wind howling across our backs, where the saddle of the low mountains cradles the sun to sleep behind us.

We stand at the rockiest spot, all seafoam against the lava rock shore. There's a pillar of rock that refuses to be worn down, Pele's Chair. We stand at the base of the pillar and watch the waves roll in.

These days without you have been damaging your father. He

talks to me less and less, spends more time drifting at night, walking like a stoned monk into the forests. Whispering his chants. There's less joy in his body when he moves around the house. Less clarity. I am terrified that he's leaving me.

But today he's here, he's made the hike with me, as has Dean. The three of us at the base of Pele's Chair with the hala lei. I wish I knew the right song, the proper chant, the ways of the kahuna that might help this be more.

"Okay," I say to Dean and your father. "It's time."

There's a pause in all our breaths. Then one inhale together, a breath we lock up as long as we can. It escapes us. Then we step away, to where the lava breaks to soft soil. And there we scrape until the earth gives enough space to let the lei rest. It's warm, it's dark. It will keep you.

Do you remember the tiny curl of your fingers, the dimples on the backs of your hands in that first year of your life? The complete contemplation in those fingers as they wrapped around mine. Hours of your frogged arms and legs against my chest, both of us deep in sleep. Your downy cheek against mine.

Now we are on our knees, your father and brother and me, and we place the lei in the pit and the soil slides back over it like an eyelid closing that will never open again.

FOR A FEW DAYS none of us want to do anything. Quiet blankets the house in Kalihi. We come, we go. Work and home. Cheap cereal. Saimin and fried eggs. Microwave pizza. Fast showers and stacks of bills past due.

Khadeja has been calling our house, the same as she has since you went missing. I don't know how long the two of you were together, but there's something fierce there. It's good, knowing that you bridged that gap with someone, before you left. It's difficult telling her. But, much like me, I get the sense she already knew the answer before she asked the question.

"Is there anything I can do?" she asks.

"Nothing," I say. "We put a lei in the earth for him. I'm sorry you weren't here."

"I'm sorry, too," she says. "It's just with Rika, my job . . . it's not easy to move around, like it was before."

"I know," I say. "But we'll always be here, if you ever want to come."

"I understand."

She'll call again, or I'll call her. We can keep this connection, let it be something.

DEAN EXTENDS HIS plane ticket back to Spokane as far as he can, playing with the dates to minimize the fees, most of which we get waived for bereavement, until finally the date comes.

"I'm useless here," Dean says. "Better I go back Spokane."

"And what, toss more boxes?" I say.

He flinches. I already want to take it back.

"Won't be that way forever," he says.

"You can do at least as good here."

"I cannot. You know how it is. Up there get plenty different ways for make money. Not like here."

"This is your home," I say. "Is money all that matters?"

"I can't do nothing about how it is," he says.

"This is your home," I repeat.

He keeps his eyes so they don't find mine. Out the window, at the floor, anywhere but where I can see him.

"I gotta go," he says. There's not much for him to carry in his bag, but he takes what he has. We drive to the airport.

MORE DAYS GO, BLUE and stiff and long. But there's a morning I wake, Aloha Friday, after trade winds have blown apart the night's storm. The leaves are wet and fresh and there's a clean salt in the air, as it would be just after a wave breaking.

We don't have to stay this way.

Your father and I coordinate our work schedules and get a Saturday off together. Then we call Crisha and Nahea, Keahi and Mike-guys, friends we don't see as much as we should, call them down to Ala Moana, us with our hibachi, and we pot-luck with mac salad, fried rice, and Crisha gets us steak that we ginger right on the hibachi, Keahi brings two long blue cooler trunks of Kona and Maui Brewing like he's royalty. In front of us, past the edge of the trees and down on the sand, small waves crumble and hiss in sandy blue. People play catch with their dogs, sleep on towels. Behind us there's the peak of downtown buildings, glimmering office glass and clean white concrete we've never been inside and speculate about while we grill and get un-steadily mellow off the beers.

How many stories do we tell? How long are we laughing when Keahi can't find an unlocked bathroom and is running up and down the frontage sidewalk with his hand clamped on his crotch? We nod our heads and wonder who that is on the radio, turn it up. We let the sun rain down on our brown bodies, get sea-washed salt in our hair and eyes, jump off the rocks into the torch-blue ocean like we're young and tight-bodied.

There's aloha yet, to keep the rest of us alive.

# 24

# MALIA, 2009

## *Kalihi*

Garkins Properties LTD
5142 Hinkleston Place
Portland, OR 97290

February 10, 2009

Dear Mr. and Mrs. Flores:

This letter is to inform you that one of our property tenants, Nainoa Flores, has an overdue balance of rent; as the cosigner for the tenant, you are now responsible for the amount owed.

The tenant is currently in breach of tenancy due to the accumulating size of the past due balance. This is the third such notice our offices have sent you. Unless full payment is received promptly, the tenant will be required to quit, vacate, and deliver possession of said property on or before the end of the month, February 28, 2009. Should the tenant fail to do so, we will take such legal action as the law requires to evict the tenant from the premises.

You are to further understand that we shall in all instances hold both the tenant and you, as a cosigner, responsible for all present and future rents due under your tenancy agreement.

Thank you for your cooperation.

# 25

# KAUI, 2009

## *San Diego*

MORNING LIKE AN ICE PICK TO THE FROST OF MY BRAIN, I wake as always after a few hours knowing I need to keep moving. The couch I'm sleeping on is Saad's, a guy I knew from the climbing gym, who I helped out with homework back in the day. I've been creeping in through the front door after dark with the borrowed key. Then morning, my alarm before he and his roommate are up so I can leave without seeing anyone.

Sometimes I take the floor instead of the couch. If I want something hard. Sometimes that's what I deserve or what I want to make myself feel, my bones and something hard. It makes me feel like I'm camping, like I'm back in Indian Creek.

Fingernails jammed to the quick with chalk and the grime of splitter cracks. Me and Van under nylon tent ceilings, right, huddled up against each other while the bears outside snuffle around our tents.

I'd dumpster-dove by the dorms and fished out a half-done bottle of Vicodin. I couldn't believe the luck and I put as many in me as the Internet recommended. Took a ride on a warm syrup version of myself for hours, right?

Now. Up from the couch. Saad's family is a million years ahead of mine. The place stinks of their wealth. The furniture shines like it's been buttered. The drawer handles all thin and chrome. The doors are heavy and sit at whatever angle you leave them, glide open and closed the way I imagine the gates of a castle would. If someone were to ask me what money means this would be what I would say: The world feels like it will stay under you no matter what you do.

I check the fridge. Like something might have appeared overnight. Right. It holds a plastic-smelling pitcher of filtered water, a six-pack of Pepsi and nine beers, margarine and sriracha, a fogged jar of pickles, and polished, empty crispers. A box of baking soda gashed open in the corner. In the cupboards the same crackling bags of natural cheese curls and graham crackers, chocolate frosting and vegetable chips. These guys are barely better off than me.

I stop by a mirror. I mean I guess it's worth looking every once in a while. There I am: natty Hawaiian hair that I start bunning up the minute I see it in the mirror, that nose thick and flat from bridge to tip, the muscles in my arms and legs looking softer. With my arms up I can see my middle and it is not flat. And even in San Diego I've lost some of my brown.

But I am here. I guess. Okay.

Everything has been wrong since the house party, Van, where I left her. I always feel tired even when I manage a complete night of sleep, right, and I'm afraid around every enclosed space I'm going to see her, or those boys, or someone else that knows. I have a feeling word has spread everywhere and people are already looking at me different, even people I don't know.

Most school days I find my way to class without seeing anyone that knows for sure, and it's easy enough to dodge everyone because I mostly chose morning classes. But some days it doesn't matter, I still end up seeing Van or Katarina or Hao and have to dodge into the nearest building. I'm like a cockroach, right, scuttling into my dorm room when the lights are off, scuttling away when the morning comes, same for Saad's place. Then in the back of the class, where I can see everyone in front of me. It's been this way for maybe three weeks. But here's the thing: I'm not even sure who knows what, since we were all faded and stoned.

But I know the most important what, I know what I am now. I wanted Van and when I couldn't have her I left her to the animals, Connor and his friends. Until that moment I was certain I'd been moving forward—past Nainoa, past the ways my mom and dad have failed to understand or even want me, past the islands altogether. Now there is no direction but down.

I change for the first time in days and my shirt has layers of grime, light and salty, laked around the pits. I've got my climbing pack stuffed with underwear, tampons, toothpaste, my laptop, a flask spattered with a few last licks of whiskey. No razor or foam, though. At first I was like, I really need to shave all my hairiness. Like I'm some sort of good girl, right?

When I roll the fresh shirt over my head something happens. It's not me in the mirror and I'm not in the bathroom. I feel myself standing on a grass plateau, all green swells and curling wind and those ancient women of hula. All of us in our pa'u skirts of bristling kapa. I feel the scratches all along my waist and my body naked otherwise. Lei po'o poking my forehead. My thick hair is miles long, reaching to my ass. My skin is dusted and salt-crusted and girded with gristly muscle. The ancients, hula: all those years since I've felt it this way. We are in the field, me and two lines of women, the pahu drum going like the fist of Pele in an earthquake. We dance and chant. The sky's an up-turned bowl of bright heat, more white than blue.

And then my phone rings and I come back to the Kaui of now. It's Dean on the line. I mash the buttons to send him to voice mail. When I do I see that he's called a few times already. But I don't care. I'm not calling anyone anymore. Not Mom or Dad or Dean or Van or any of them.

Dean calls again, ugh. I can see this won't stop. I pick up the phone.

"She finally answers," Dean says.

"She does," I say.

"Kill you to answer your phone? Could've been we were all on fire or something."

"Are you on fire, currently?" I ask.

"Fucking right I am," he says.

"Dean."

"What?"

"I don't have time for your boners. You would only call this much if you wanted something."

"Why there's gotta be something I want?" Dean asks. "Man, you're just like Mom. Maybe all I want for do is talk."

"Well, let's talk, Dean," I say. "Let's chat. Let's fraternize. Let's holler back."

He's quiet a minute. "You drunk or something? And why are you whispering?"

"Stoned, actually," I say. "And I'm whispering because I broke into someone's house. Proud of me?"

He laughs. "Goddamn."

I put the phone on speaker so I can finish fixing my hair, use the scraps of makeup I have to clean up my look at least a little. "So, what, you need something, right?"

"How come you never been calling Mom-guys?" he asks.

I look down at the floor where my shoes are. The puddle of my BO-infested shirt, the orange painkiller bottles peeking from my backpack's open top. "There's a lot happening over here."

"I bet."

"You have no idea," I say.

"Yeah, well," Dean says, "lot happening in Portland, too."

"Portland?"

Before I can ask more, Dean starts in. He says they're taking Noa's stuff. He says Noa's rent wasn't paid and the next in line to pay it was Mom and Dad.

"You know what that means," he says.

"You can't just empty someone's house if they don't pay their rent," I say. "There have to be court orders and things like that. It's impossible to evict someone these days."

"They called Mom." Dean says it like a shrug.

Due process, I say. Tenant's rights, I say. Reasonable opportunities to repay back rent, I say.

"Look who's the house lawyer all of a sudden," Dean says.

"*Law & Order* marathons on cable, twenty-four seven," I say.

"Shut up already," Dean says. "You gotta stop clowning, this isn't a joke."

"Okay okay," I say. "Calm down. Did you call a lawyer?"

"I don't got time for fight, Kaui," Dean says. "I gotta fix this. Mom called me."

The way he says that last part: Mom called *me*. As in, Let me handle it, right. As in, I finally get to be the good one. But there's blame in it, I know. For me going back to school while he stayed and bushwhacked alone in the valley. I take in the room around me: boys' razors crusted with old bloody foam; last year's Swimsuit Edition magazine in the reading rack by the toilet, sopping bathmat crumpled in the corner. I see it all laid out before me, okay? This day and the day after. Me couch to couch, away from Van and Katarina and Hao. Living out of my backpack since the start of the semester. Drifting off into some rat's existence because of what I've done, or didn't do.

"Is Noa's address the same?" I ask.

"Same as it always been in Portland," Dean says. "Why?"

I hang up. I jam everything I own that's on the floor back into my bag and tie my shoes. I leave Saad's key in the mailbox on my way out.

# 26

# DEAN, 2009

## *Portland*

USED TO BE NOA HAD THIS WAY OF MAKING YOU FEEL stupid without even telling you what was stupid, like he could just talk about how steel gets made or what the Latin blah blah was for "nerve" and you didn't even have to say nothing one way or the other, and still you came away feeling like he said you was a dumbass. And all morning I been thinking about what he'd be saying if he was here with me, looking through the windows of his apartment and checking the doors for the fifteenth time and being like, I'm locked out. Didn't even think about how I'd need keys when I got the call from Mom and came busting down here off hitchhikes and bus rides, figuring, I don't know, the door was going be wide open or the landlord would be here painting or some shit. Noa woulda had something for say for sure if he was here, but he's not, and I still feel like a dumbass. I don't even got another place for stay if I can't get this door open.

I jerk on the door handle again, just for feel the door frame shake and hear the force of metal on metal. I pull and pull and the door squeals and flexes hard enough that it curves at the edges. But nothing breaks. I sit down on the front steps, thinking about what I gotta break and who's going get called when I do it.

There's a car I never noticed, parked across the street. Small and silver and simple. Driver's door pops and this lady steps out, unfolds herself to full, thick height. Tight cornrows sweeping up her head, Afro puff ponytail in back. Got on this slouchy black top that slides down one arm so you can see how her shoulder glows. Her shoes clack on the concrete as she comes up the walk.

I know her even if we never talked before. "It's you," I say.

Whole time she got her eyes on me, not hiding. I give her that. "Your mother called me," she says. She stops in front the steps where I'm sitting. "This really happening?"

"She called you for what?" I ask.

"Noa's," she says. Points at his door. "Said he was getting evicted. Or, at least"—she frowns—"his things."

"Yeah, but I mean," I say, "dunno what she thought you could do that I couldn't."

She smiles like I'm some kinda joke. I let it go. "Dean," I say, giving a hand to shake, which she does.

"I know," she says. "Khadeja."

"I know," I say.

We let go the shake.

"I called the Sheriff's Department. They said there's no way out of this unless we paid the forty-five hundred that was due."

"Shit," I say. "You figure if I take him on a date maybe he'll let it go for less?"

She looks me up and down. "Not dressed like that."

"I give good back rubs, though," I say.

"I'm surprised how wrong Nainoa was about you," she says.

"Whatchyou mean?" I ask.

"He said you were supposed to be charming." And she straight-up laughs at her own joke.

"Come on," I say. "No be like—"

But now this moving truck creeps around the corner, says *Branton's Hauling* on the side. It stops like it's thinking. Then the truck moves forward again and stops again. It comes right up to Noa's curb like that. There's two dark shadows of heads inside the cab. I can hear the power steering shudder and whine, the click of the truck falling into park. Then two guys get out in tight blue jeans and, like, carpenter's jackets or whatever. Both of 'um haole with haircuts like soldiers and faces like kids and I almost want for be like, Which way to the gay rodeo?

They see us at the doorway and stop, talk to each other for a second, then the one with brown hair and a bent nose walks up, hand out palm-down, like I'm a dog off the leash he gotta make calm.

"What, haole?" I say.

He's all, "Sorry?"

"I said, *what*," I say. I nod at how he's walking at me. "I'm his brother. I don't bite."

He stops walking. Crosses his arms. "We got some stuff we gotta take out of here. All of it, actually."

There's another pickup truck of guys that show up and park

by the moving truck. Five of 'um. I step down from where I was, out from under the eaves, so everyone can see all six foot five of me. "Go home," I say.

"BOYS," KHADEJA SAYS, "what do you say we talk about this a minute."

Funny thing is these guys might as well be guys I worked the packing line with back in Spokane, or when I'd do some of the landscaping stuff on the side. I think they figure that out, too, because there's this moment where we're all like, I know you, aren't we on the same side? But then that all goes away.

"Our job is just to start emptying the place out," the other guy from the moving truck, the one with the lighter hair, says like an apology.

"You got guns or knives?" I ask.

"Dean—" Khadeja says.

"What?" someone says.

"Only way you're getting in."

But they got better than guns and knives, because just behind that second truck was the Sheriff, who I didn't see. Now he's out on Noa's natty lawn, Sheriff shaped like a bowling pin, including the white skin and red neck. Arms crossed over his chest with his gun coming off his hip, him all leaning like his dick's weighing him down. "Don't make this harder than it has to be," he says.

What can I do?

I get out of the way. Khadeja walks straight over to the officer and starts talking. Repo guys get busy taking things out. Whole big group of 'um, like this is just another day, following their system, bigger stuff first and one room at a time, marching in and out with a few grunts and words back and forth like I'm not even there, and Sheriff's drifted back to his car to sit down and jaw on his gum.

I watch the big stuff come out, but then things start happening. They're tossing clothes onto the sidewalk by the handful, faking jump shots and baseball pitches, mostly I think because they seen how I stood down when the Sheriff came calling.

"Surf's up!" some prick worker calls out, and one of Noa's Quiksilver shirts comes out the door like a gut-shot bird, flapping into the muddy ground. I see that shirt and I'm seeing us and beaches and Kalihi, me and my brother, Noa. I'm listening to us on the phone when I still had a chance at the university.

I was saying to him, I'm about to quit this bullshit team.

No way, he said.

I was all, This is like it's high school all over again. Coach talking about benching me like he's got extra talent just lying around. Fuck those backups, they can't ball like me.

Who ran things at the tournament? Who almost went all the way? I was First-Team All C—

I didn't realize, Noa said, you turned into such a pussy.

I was all, What?

Basketball, he said. You've been hunting like a shark for this, your whole life.

I was all, Man, now you're getting all up in my face like everyone else.

Then give up, he said. Do it. No one's even going to remember a few years from now.

The hell, Noa, I said. I thought you was my brother.

You weren't listening, he said.

What?

You ever think about the sharks? he said.

Of course, I said. Every time I see you.

Maybe when the sharks pulled me up, he said, it wasn't just me they were saving, you understand? Maybe it's about our whole family.

And I never felt the gods Mom was always talking about, but I did feel something right then when he said that, and for a while after. I got lifted. Stepped out the door after the call was over and everything was bright and mine. You can take the drugs and sex and basketball, just give me that feeling one more time. I had my last good game the next night, playing outside myself like my whole body was new.

That's my brother, that could do a thing like that, and no one here's got any idea.

So now. I start carrying his stuff back in from the lawn.

Khadeja comes back over and starts talking like she thinks she can make me stop. Even tells me to stop and think about what I'm doing.

"You're not solving anything this way," she says. "Let's just take what we can."

"Fuck that," I say.

Workers don't figure it out, what I'm doing. The first few rounds of stuff they toss out, I'm getting handfuls and putting 'um back inside, and when Khadeja sees I not even listening she sighs and pinches her nose and steps back down to the sidewalk. Pulls out her phone to make a call. I take a bunch of clothes and some chairs back inside, even while the repo guys is still bringing other stuff out, but then we start bumping into each other. Ends up I'm at the door with desk drawers that I'm bringing back in, one in each hand, and two guys is carrying a futon out, and we meet at the doorway. The one in front has his back to me, but looks over his shoulder to check the clearance and sees me. We both stop.

"Move," he says, his face red from holding up his side of the load.

"Nah," I say.

The worker nods past me and tries for smile even while he's straining. "Looks like someone else has a better idea."

I turn and Sheriff is coming up the sidewalk, saying, "Now, son, you think about what you're doing here for a minute."

That's when I see something past him, out in the street, that makes me smile. Sheriff thinks I'm smiling at him and he says, "There's nothing funny about this. I'm not joking."

But I'm not smiling at him, I'm smiling at what's behind him—past Sheriff, past Khadeja, out by the street, no joke, it's Kaui standing on the sidewalk, backpack slouching off her Notorious *Ready to Die* hoodie.

One of the movers passes by her on his way back from the truck and she says something to him. The mover talks back at Kaui over his shoulder. Khadeja moves toward them, saying, "Everyone needs to calm down before this gets ugly," but Kaui already dropped her backpack and now she runs past Khadeja and the repo guy, up the sidewalk to the stairs where I am, but she goes past me and right into the one guy in the doorway holding his side of the futon. I see her hands before she uses them on him and the futon falls and booms and so does the guy. I'm still holding the drawers and I don't remember how I put 'um down to make fists and I'm still trying for remember five minutes later, now, with my wrists pinched in handcuffs in the back of Sheriff's car.

Kaui's in here, too. The Sheriff's car smells like too much Armor All and gun oil. Got some crackled voices going on the radio. Kaui's to my right and handcuffed just like me, her breaths raging out so hard they snap into fog against the window. The car's heater is off and the damp-ass winter is leaking in through the doors.

Just now I'm starting for remember what happened, how when the futon fell it was like the bell at a boxing match and everyone was happy for finally do something violent. We just started pounding on each other until the Sheriff waded in and broke it up, hog-chained me and Kaui, and heaved us into the back of the car one at a time. Now he got Khadeja talking to him on the lawn. She's doing that thing where she's extra polite and upright and all that, holding her hands together down low like it's church and the Sheriff's the preacher.

The movers went back to carrying Noa's life out the apartment: the milk crates of books they chuck out so that the books flap and scatter on the wet grass, shrink-wrapped bricks of good saimin and bottles of shoyu, picture frames with the pictures still in them, tumbling and rolling and cracked all up on the grass and sidewalk. One of the movers got toilet paper jammed into his nose to stop the bleeding from my punch and another one with his lip getting fat from where Kaui put him down, but they keep working. Soon all the movers is coming out the house empty-handed, and they push and kick all the heaps of Noa's stuff off the grass and onto the sidewalk. The last guy for leave the apartment stops at the edge of the lawn and looks down. I see him pinch up a sock from the grass like it's something dead and filthy and drop it on the sidewalk in one of the heaps. There's a clipboard with a clean bright clip that one of the repo guys talks over for a minute with the Sheriff, then they get back in their moving trucks and drive off.

When the repo guys is gone Sheriff strolls over to us. Pops the driver door in the squad car and talks to us through the wire mesh between the front and back seats. "I could make this very ugly for you," he says.

Kaui snorts.

"I could get the paperwork started, get statements from the movers, set a court date," he goes on. "I'd make it so you couldn't even get back all this"—he points to everything the movers threw out—"no matter how much of it you wanted."

"Officer," Khadeja says.

He looks back at her. Some sort of understanding, but like he still going warn her about who's wearing the gun. "I know," he says. He turns back to us and gestures at Khadeja. "She told me who he was."

"Who?" I ask.

"Your brother," the Sheriff says. "That doesn't justify any of what just happened," he says, "but." He unlocks our doors. "Get out," he says. We do and he pops off the handcuffs. There's a rush of happiness in my wrists, just before the ache. He's all something something something don't make me regret this. His car door whacks closed, then the chatter and rev of his Challenger engine, and then he's gone down the street and there's no more noise. We see what's in front of us.

"So I forgot to say hello," Kaui says to me. "How's Spokane?"

"Total shit," I say. "How's San Diego?"

"Warm shit," she says. "Khadeja, right?" she says to Khadeja.

"Yes," Khadeja says.

But after the joke we're still standing there with Noa's things all over the sidewalk, the rice cooker and the boxes, the Quiksilver shirt and the rainbow of dead books.

"The hell happens now," I say, "with all this stuff."

Rain comes as the answer. It's like a breath letting out, so soft and quiet might as well we never knew a breath was being held in the first place, and the water fizzes down. It cobwebs on Kaui's and Khadeja's hair, barely taps my skin. We can't even hear the sound of it hitting.

Kaui looks up at the sky. Then it just pisses down on us: the rain gets fat and hard and roars on the roofs. Me and Kaui and Khadeja run through the yard, swearing and saying no and clutching at everything we can hold and trying for get 'um all back under the eaves of the apartment and I check the front door but of course it's locked tight. Kaui's got a cardboard box she's trying for drag back to the front steps, the brown lawyer boxes with one handhole on each side. The lid's come off. I can see the photos and albums getting soaked dark by the rain. Kaui's all tugging at the lid to get it back on and trying for drag the whole box with one hand, and now one of the bottom corners is running deep into the dirty grass and zippering apart the mud. Khadeja drops some clothes she picked up and starts on the other side of the box. I run into the yard and we get the lid on and haul it back together. I feel the prickle of chicken skin under my jacket, under my shirt, under my bones.

In the yard all Noa's stuff is just getting destroyed. The gray cushions of the futon, the wrinkled lumps of clothes going shiny wet, a floor-length mirror catching mud splashes from the dirt. We're done, this is all done.

"I'm fucking freezing," Kaui hollers over the rain, but she's not saying it to me, she's yelling it into the yard, into the sky.

I know Noa's got neighbors next door, I seen their faces peeking out behind the window curtains when the Sheriff and the repo team was here, but they're all inside with their warm orange lights on, acting like they don't know what's happening out here. I start testing the front windows on Noa's place with my palm, then reach down for one of the lamps to break the glass, but Kaui sees me and rolls her eyes.

"What are you, a caveman?" she says. "We break out a front window and everyone will know what's going on. Cops right away," she says. "Wait here." She disappears around the side of the duplex.

"Don't," Khadeja says. Kaui keeps going.

Few minutes and the front door rattles and clicks open.

"Come on in," Kaui says.

Khadeja looks at each of us. "I just talked that officer out of arresting you and this is the first thing you do?"

"We've got no other choice," Kaui says.

"Of course you do," Khadeja says. "Don't break in."

"And what?" Kaui says. "Let Noa's things rot? Freeze our asses off in the yard?"

"There's a—"

"We've got nothing," Kaui says. "Nothing." She shoulders the door open wider. It's all she's gotta say.

"I can't," Khadeja says. The rain roars louder. "Even if I wanted to—and I don't—I can't be this kind of stupid."

"I can," Kaui says. She looks at me.

Khadeja doesn't say nothing when I go.

Inside's all dark and empty. Nothing in the living room but white walls and bare dark carpet. The air's already gone flat and cottony like the apartment's been empty for years.

"Get in here," Kaui says, and slams the door. She crouches down and peeks over the edge of the front window. "I think the neighbor saw. She definitely maybe saw us."

I go to close the curtains, but Kaui says no, that would make it obvious we were inside, since the curtains wasn't closed when we came in. I see Khadeja running across the street, Afro full of rain. Bends down into her car and shuts the door.

"Just stay away from the windows," Kaui says. She ropes her hair tight in her fists and twists until water gushes onto the carpet. She shivers hard, like a horse coming out of a river.

We open the front door one more time and haul in a few of the things we'd saved. When I look across the street, Khadeja's gone. From the stuff we saved on the front steps there's a gym duffel and garbage bag with some clothes I guess he was gonna donate and that box Kaui was dragging before, with photos and albums and like that.

When we rip the garbage bag and check in the gym duffel there's almost no chance anything is gonna fit on us but we try anyway. We each take two or three trips back and forth from a bedroom, taking clothes from the bag and duffel and trying 'um on. Kaui ends up with these black dress pants that she's practically busting out of—they're Khadeja's, I guess—and she's got one of Noa's sweatshirts on, some no-brand red hoodie. I ask why she didn't try on more of Khadeja's clothes and she said nothing could really fit her on top, because of the, like, hooded climber-kind muscles she's got all up her back. I got the same problem but way worse, there's a pair of Noa's sweatpants that's baggy enough that they get around my waist, even though there's tons of tearing and popping sounds when I do it. The cuffs hit somewhere on my calves. I get one of Noa's rain jackets, the thing's big enough that when I put it on it's almost like a shirt.

I'm busy laughing in the mirror when Kaui says, "Look at this."

I go over to her, careful to crawl under the front window. She's got the picture box cracked open and she's holding a picture, Noa and Khadeja at the beach. Khadeja's all leaned back on her arms in the sand, carameling in the sun with the same swirling set of cornrows running up her head to a Afro ponytail in the back. She's laughing at something we can't see. Doing it with kind of this mana, like she's not gonna be laughing if she doesn't want to, and there's a spray of water on the small rolls of her belly. "Well, damn," I say all soft.

Kaui sighs. She snatches the picture back. "God, Dean."

"What?"

"Does every female relationship you have start and end on the tip of your dick?" She doesn't even wait for me to answer. Just goes back to slapping her way through the stack of photos and shakes her head at me. There's a scrap of paper comes off one of the pictures. *Khadeja*, it says, then a phone number. I slip it before Kaui sees.

"There's you and me," I say. "That's a female relationship with no dick."

She flips through more pictures. "Like that's something," she finally says. "You don't know anything about me."

"Whatchyou mean?" I say.

She stops flipping through the photos and looks up, across the room from us. "Twenty-four point four," she says, and I know right away, points per game, and I try for say but she goes on in this tired voice, "Twenty-four point four. A blend of carbohydrates and poly- and mono-unsaturated fats, along with normal servings of the food pyramid, total up to three thousand calories for a peak-performance athlete. Nahea, Reese, Trish, Kalani, in missionary, doggy, sixty-nine, cowgirl, and money shots, respectively. USC and Arizona scouts at the Lincoln Invitational, UT Austin and Oregon scouts at your opening game at states." My points per in high school, the diet Coach had me on once we knew I had a chance at college, some of the girls I did in high school, scouts at my high school games, I don't even have for think any of it. I just know it when she says it, *That's me*, all those facts wrapped around me like my skin. She turns her eyes on me. "I could keep going."

"Yeah, well," I say. "Still wasn't enough."

"What's that supposed to mean?"

The box where she got the pictures from, I can see other Noa stuff in there—the Stanford diploma he got in less than three years, few newspaper articles about big science and math scholarships he got, chemistry competitions and mentions in the Stanford magazines and all like that, a pile that just keeps going—and part of me still feels like starting there, telling Kaui, It's us versus him, remember? But something about all that is gone now in both of us. Used to be me and Kaui didn't even have for say it to each other, you could tell we was both burning about Noa, all that he got that we didn't, but came a time we stopped talking like that. I could almost say that was the only thing me and Kaui had, especially with how she's talking now, but that's wrong. While we're sitting here I get this feeling. It's just like what I'd get at Spokane, when I'd go back on the court way after the interviews and the showers, when there was no more music and no more crowd, no more rush. From the locker room I'd cross the curved hall with the polished concrete floor, had the glass cases with trophies from the fifties and black-and-white pictures of haoles in high and tight shorts playing basketball, and I'd open the door into the bright-ass court, and there was the facilities crew digging garbage out the chairs and sweeping up all the crowd shit from the game. See it that way and it's easy to figure, the court is just a building and the game doesn't matter, not to everyone. It's the same now, with Kaui: she's been on the other side, another world, the whole time.

"I get it," I say. I cough, just to get another sound out, to not stop. "I was famous. But I been paying attention to you, too."

She purses her lips. "If you say so."

"Like," I start, but I don't really know what's gonna come out, since I don't actually know much about her, but it's too late to stop now, "I know you—I know you like girls."

Her face. Just for a second it's like I threw a bucket of ice-cold water on her. But she fixes it fast, back to something that's supposed to be tough or whatever. "Dean, what the hell?"

"It doesn't matter," I say.

"I *know* it doesn't matter," she says. "I don't need you to tell me that."

"No, not like that," I say. "I'm saying I bet there's plenty people it does matter to, yeah?"

She's sitting on the floor with her legs straight out, but now she slides both her legs up so her knees is bent to her chest and she can hold on to 'um. "Of course," she says.

"Make a list, all those people," I say. "I'll kill 'um. Even their dogs. Matter fact, I'll do the dogs twice."

She busts out laughing. "You'll slay them with your incredibly bad math skills?" she says. I know she's joking, but it doesn't feel like that.

"Bad joke," she says, I guess when she sees my face. But when I don't say nothing, she lifts back up some of the pictures and starts going through them again.

I kick the box she's taking pictures from. "Don't act like that," I say. "I was the one that had for stay down in the valley, looking for him for weeks, mosquitoes and cold nights camping in the rain, while you was studying at school. I was the one that had for see where it happened, then go tell Mom and Dad after."

She puts down the pictures. "Sorry," she says.

Sorry sorry sorry, I think. Everyone's always sorry. You're not the one that fucked up again and again and again.

"What was it like?" she asks, her voice quiet.

"What was what like?"

"Him," she says. "Dying."

I lean my head back against the wall, next to the window. There's still weak light coming in. "You mean—"

"—I mean the place. Where you found him."

There's the valley. It was going from hot to cold to hot again, since the clouds was moving fast overhead, but I was all sweating from the trail, and the ground was ripped up and smeared, like someone had started for sweep the whole world off the edge of the cliff but stopped before they was finished, and I go to the edge and look over, there's crampy ropes coming in my stomach because I see fabric and reach for 'um, the blood all squeezing my skull when I hang upside down for extra length. There's the backpack in my hand, there's the boot, there's the blood.

"Dean," Kaui says again. She scoots herself over and touches my shoulder. Everything goes out of me.

I say one sound, more like a breath: Ah. It gets something going. When I got there—to where he fell—it was like for just a minute all of me and all the valley was touching each other. Had a feeling like I got before on the basketball court. A chanting sound somewhere. Like when I first got to Spokane, or like that one Hawaiian Night game during the regular season, when I got that green feeling, like I could feel all the old kings right inside me, coming across the water.

"You ever think you felt things the way Noa felt 'um?" I ask.

"What do you mean?" Kaui says.

"Sometimes I get this feeling," I say. "Or I used to, anyway. Where it was like I was me and then I was something bigger than me, all at once."

I check her face and the yes is right there, I can see 'um. Like maybe she didn't get just what I got, but she got *something*. Hell, no, Noa wasn't the only one. Makes me smile, even.

"It's funny," I say. "Noa told me this one time he thought the sharks wasn't just for him. I never really believed him . . ." I wait just a minute, try hard to feel it. To *listen*. But there's nothing.

"I think maybe I missed it," I say. "Like it was looking for me, same as him, and I never figured out how to answer 'um."

Kaui starts talking, but a shadow moves over the window next to us. It's big, like we can feel the person in the room already. Kaui's on her feet and checking the peephole. "Oh, no," she says.

I'm all, "Who is it?" but she's already backing away from the door. I hear keys jingle, then grinding in the lock.

I stand up. Kaui shoves me with her hand, says, Go go go, and there's no more talking, we just start for run.

# 27

# KAUI, 2009

### *Portland*

GO IS WHAT I SAY. OR THINK I SAY. WE'RE UP AND FREN-
zied. We grab whatever we can—our wallets and my backpack,
two of the smaller photo albums—and bolt. The front door
opens. There's a voice but we don't stop to listen. We reach the
bedroom I broke in through, window still open. I heave myself
out. Fall into the slurping lawn that runs behind the duplex. My
backpack's open, so painkillers and wadded tissues and sticks of
gum and tampons spill out. I gather what I can, jam that and the
photo albums in the backpack.

"Around the corner," I say to Dean, and we go around the

corner. Except when we do we practically run into the Sheriff's chest. He trips backward and a hand goes to his gun, he's calling, Stop stop stop. We explode the other way, through the yard toward the gap between a garage and another house. The rain is spitting into my eyelashes. I can't blink it away, things go blurry. The Sheriff's hollering behind us. We hear the jingle of those keys. We keep running, but I'm clenched for the shooting to begin. They always shoot at people like us.

But we make it to the gap and out the other side. Noa's sweatshirt is swimming and sucking on me, too big and getting wet. When we don't hear the Sheriff, I stop and look back the way we came. He's far away, running to his car. My hair is starting to drip all over me. My breath smokes in the cold.

"Go," Dean says, and we do, again. Only I don't realize he means different ways: when I break across the next street, Dean goes for something kitty-corner, through a yard, and by the time I realize it, he's already on a fence, scrabbling halfway up and over.

The Sheriff's car comes hot down the street, lights boiling bright. No sirens, which makes it feel nothing like a movie. It's real, we're real. I turn and run my way. There's a break between two houses and I go for it. Dog growls crack out and roll over me, bounce around the walls on either side, but whatever's there I can't see and nothing lunges. I don't stop. There's a tire squeal. A metal crunch. It's all behind me. What I see is in front of me, the wide-open land past the houses.

I'm out. It's just an empty lot. So much space and air it's like the world's taking a breath. Stacks of lumber under blue tarpaulins and little wooden stakes stabbed into the cold dirt, orange ribbons twirling from their ends. I leave the lot and turn onto a new street and run another block and cut through to another yard. There's no sound at all. I heave in oxygen. My left backpack strap is loose and I yank it down tight on my shoulder.

Right beside me is a set of patio furniture. The sort of thing most of my classmates in San Diego probably own, modern and minimal and violently expensive, right? Like, there are all these plates of gray stone in the ground, making up a walkway that goes from the patio through the lawn to the driveway. In the driveway is an idling car. There's no one inside the car.

I hear the Sheriff's siren. Howling now. The part of me that wants to run is grabbed by the part of me that's smart and it says: You see what you need. Go slow. Act like this is your neighborhood. Like this clean white sedan with butter-leather interior is your car.

And then it is. I pop the driver's door, slip into the seat, crank the car into reverse. Funny. You think a thing like car theft is something incredible, all complicated screwdriver technique and dark parking lots and hammering pulses, okay? But it's as easy as flicking a switch.

I back out of the driveway fast and gun the engine down the block, screech the first turn so that I feel all my insides swing. But then I say again: Go slow. This is your neighborhood. You're on the way to the grocery store. I start looking for Dean. I turn a few more corners, try to see anything I recognize. Easy slow loops across each block. I think I'm generally going toward where we separated. The Sheriff's siren goes again. Not here, but closer. I keep thinking of how when I saw the police lights and knew they were for me, right? My heart moving the same as the lights, skittering and spinning.

Dean comes out from behind shaggy hedges in front of me. He's limping with his head down, chest naked and wet where Noa's raincoat blooms open. One hand is clutched on the waistband of Noa's sweatpants, which he can only keep halfway up his ass. I pull up close and honk and roll down the passenger window.

"What are you doing?" he asks.

I imagine how it must look. Me, his enraged sister, sleep-starved and food-starved and panicked, rolling up in a white luxury sedan with a 109.5 *The Prayer* bumper sticker, stinking of floral air freshener. "Get in," I say.

He's in the passenger seat and we drive down to the end of the block. This doesn't feel real. I'm watching a brother and sister try to escape, catching crime, making the wrong choices. But it's not me, nothing to do with me except to try and tell them *no*.

"You stole this car?" Dean says. I turn on the windshield wipers. For a second my view is completely clean.

"It was there," I say, and shrug.

I stop at a sign that says *Stop*.

"Are you kidding me?" He's looking around. He says we'll get arrested for real now, we have to dump the car. But I say no. We're going to get out of here, the whole state and the whole continent and all of it, everything that started from before that fucking kiss, the climbing and the culvert and every square of earth Van and I ever stood on together, and the sharks and the news and all the parts of Hawai'i that killed my brother.

I'm still driving.

"We can catch the bus, we can hitchhike. We can *walk*, even." Dean's pinching his nose. "Not this."

I stop at another intersection. The road we're on goes long, and down at the end of it you can see a busy street, a row of businesses. Bougie clothing stores with gossamer fabrics and jaunty mannequins, I bet. A six-dollar coffee shop. The avenue and the buildings and the sky all the same shade of gray.

"Go if you want," I say. "I know the way back."

Dean's quiet. He chews his lip and shifts in his seat so we can share a look. Something funny settles in his eyes, right? Scared but then dead calm, almost relaxed. He lunges for me and then darkness and something jamming into my chest and he's pulling me, his knee cracks my skull, and buckles or knobs jam and scrape over my ribs and hip. Every edge of me is hitting something but my brother keeps pulling, pushing. I'm folded up. His feet and his hands as he's jamming me under him and crawling into the driver's seat. I figure my back will hit the passenger door, but it's just air. Sharp slap of my shoulder on asphalt. Water and light and my backpack pitches out in front of me. I'm out of the car, in the street. By the time I'm able to stand up, Dean's in the driver's seat and piloting the thing forward with the passenger door still open. And there's the Sheriff's car, coming straight at him with the lights and siren. The Sheriff's car swerves sideways, screeches to a stop across both lanes. Dean's blocked.

While I'm standing there another cop car blows past me. The engine yelling. The car filling whatever exit Dean had left behind him. The brake lights go when the officer sees that they've got him.

# PART IV

# REVIVAL

# 28

# MALIA, 2009

## *Kalihi*

PICTURE THIS, THE MOTHER AND THE FATHER STILL living after you're lost, where every day feels like a fog: no way forward, no way back, no idea which is which, everywhere the cold heavy colorless feeling of floating, alone in the middle of nothing. Picture the work they do anyway, the father heaving the luggage from the belts to the shuttles to the airplane bellies, steel flashing in fluorescence, the blast of sun and clean high burning smell of jet fuel, the dull rumble of departures and arrivals. The mother with the hours of torque on her back as she captains the city bus from salty beachside streets into the cool green orderly neighborhoods and back again, glass high-rises downtown flashing like knives, the shudders and bangs and shoves of the road. This way and that. Picture the call that arrives, it is always a call, this one about the other son, charges and detainment in the county facility while awaiting arraignment, the policies and procedures as foreign as the land—Oregon—on which they're being implemented. Picture the incapability, the lack of money and work schedules and the distance, and how the mother and the father have nothing to do but listen from afar as their daughter describes what's coming.

Picture the father's mind, drained as a reservoir in a drought, now comprehending another loss, the other son, who was perhaps farther away than the father ever thought, more than a phone call, more than a plane ticket, and getting farther. Picture the animated glitter of a healthy mind at work, and then that same mind—the father's—locking up, sputtering and choking on circumstance. Going black.

Does the wife see? She sees the start, the long night journeys, the husband's whispers to ghosts she does not know. But she cannot see it all, cannot know exactly how the madness seizes the husband at his place of employment. Perhaps he staggers from the luggage line out into the striped grids of the tarmac, the flight patterns, and endangers whole crews and passenger loads and himself. Perhaps he wanders instead to the chain-link fence, desperate for the midnight mountain prayer garden he's been digging; perhaps he just sits, and sits, and sits, and mutters to himself in the break room while the luggage piles up and spills over on a shorthanded day, the other luggage handlers screaming his name, demanding he get back to it. The wife doesn't see this, she only sees that his uniform stops leaving the closet, that their car stops leaving the Kalihi curb of home, and the bank account starves.

Picture the corporate conversation, the mother begging, something she thought she'd never do, the airline company executive saying, *We're sorry, we can't. He wasn't fit to work here anymore.*

Picture the mother, the wife, now the last bones of the family. Hard and old and cold, holding everything up. Let's not call it hope. It is a labor of sorts; that is all. Picture her as she realizes she can no longer go to work, because of the father, the constant observation he needs, and her employment goes almost as quickly as his. No money from him, no money from her. This means, in the city, they are dead.

There's only one place left to go, back to the Big Island, the land of your birth, where family still resides, your father's brother and his successful business, extra buildings on his extra property that can house the diminished count of us.

If she doesn't beg, exactly, there's still a quiet resignation to the mother. There's still a kneeling, and opening of the palms upward, asking for something to be placed in them. Hands that used to push and take and grip their own way through the world.

Picture what we've become without you, my son.

Can you see it?

## 29

# KAUI, 2009

### *Portland*

BECAUSE THE ARREST. BECAUSE THE SECOND COLD POLICE
car, my brother in the back. Because I couldn't enter the station,
had to hide and peek every now and then at the white walls and
the steady shot of the clerk's stamp on paper, case closure after
closure. Because the last talk with Dean, in person after his arraignment, when he'd kept his mouth shut about me—before I
had to head back south—we sat in those plastic spine-stabbing
chairs at the table, what could we say? Because our eyes filled
with a wet history, and we knew there wouldn't be another vis-
itor until his release, if then. Because another punch of poverty, no way to make bail, seeing what we can't do as a family,

again and again and again. Because I had to watch while the guards corralled him back to his cell, through the thick blue-white doors, heavy with locks and screens. Because I walked the rain-gleamed Portland downtown. Because that night, the cold gnawing through all of me, because the only dry doorway was by a parking garage, because the backpack that held the last physical pieces of Nainoa's life became my pillow, because the plunging in and out of sleep. Because the stabs of ache all along my side: hip, ribs, shoulder. Because again the dumpster diving, this time for food, no college throwaway painkillers, right? Because the shelter after, the steaming rows of bunk beds in the homeless shelter, the mutterings in the unlit corners, the hunting knife I stole from the locker, its duct-taped handle, gripping it under my pillow. Because the morning lines: dingy porcelain bathroom, watered oatmeal, small television picture jumping, cartoons. Because the mouse blackened the cat with dynamite, pounded the cat as a peg with the sledgehammer, buckshotted out the cat's teeth, each one tinkling as a piano key. Because the phone call, after my mother telling me she had failed Dean, had failed all of us if this is what we were, because she said I had to go back to school—"You're the only one now," she said, "you're all we have left." "But I can't go back," I said. "Mom, I just want to come home. Can you get me home? I just want to come home." Because she found the money somewhere, somehow, her own form of magic, I came back to Hawai'i.

From the air the gas-burner-blue ocean pounds wave after wave into the crusted black slabs of lava on the Kona coast, little scoops of white-sugar sand beaches and coconut trees. The sun golden and everywhere and hot, even from inside the plane. We lower and we lower toward the ground. In the ocean below there's an explosion of water and a humpback whale heaves itself free of the sea, vertical, twisting in the spray, two blue-gray dorsal fins and the smiling snout. Barnacles and knots of scabby skin. It twists and stretches as if it could keep going, right through the sky, never stop. But instead the water spins off it and dissipates into mist and the whale's breach ends when it hits the water and throws up a giant sheet of foam.

A prickly feeling all along my arms and legs and I get chicken skin: This is it. This is Hawai'i.

They meet me curbside at the airport, Mom and Dad rolling up in a pickup truck I don't recognize, a white and lifted Tacoma with a rack in the bed and knobby tires. I'm sitting on a lava rock wall under a shady tree, close to one of the lei shops. Smell of plumeria and orchid. Pinks and purples and yellows. Mom hops out of the truck and comes around to the curb, looking me up and down. Like she needs to check and see if I'm damaged goods, right? I don't ask her what her conclusion is. Finally she hugs me, holds on, longer than I expected. And I hug her back, longer than I expected. When I pull away Dad's still sitting in the truck.

Mom lifts my backpack from the concrete. "Not much in here," Mom says.

"What's up with Dad?" I ask.

"He's—" Mom stops. We both stare at him. He's not really looking toward us. Off instead to the voggy sky. "You see him," Mom says. "I don't know."

When I approach the window to get into the back seat of the truck's cab Dad sees me. There's a flicker of recognition, but it fogs over. He doesn't smile or say hi or get up out of the truck. His lips are going, soft and smooth with some never-ending whisper.

"Fuck, Mom," I say. "Why didn't you tell me?"

Her lips go flat, pressed hard on each other. "You think you could've done anything?"

"Maybe," I say. "What have *you* done? Anything?"

She drops my backpack on the ground where she's standing, ten feet back from the truck. "There's space for you in the back seat," she says, and goes around to her side.

The truck swings away from the airport, up the road toward Hualālai, distant volcano gone green and brown all the way to the cloud-scudded peak. Then we turn northwest and the road tracks the coast, the broad table of old black lava flows surrounding us. The ocean curling into the shore. Up the hills are the bristling thorns of kiawe trees, and after we drive far enough, the hills become the desert grass of Waikoloa, right? All the while Dad just going, lips whispering or quiet and eyes blinking out toward the island. The skin near those eyes striated with a tired sort of anxiety.

"Is he always like this now?" I ask.

"He still breaks through here and there."

"Have you taken him to a doctor?"

"Good idea," Mom says. "I've raised three kids and been an adult for most of my life, but I didn't think of that. A doctor." She says, "Let me write that down."

"I just wanted—"

"They couldn't do anything for him, Kaui," she says. "Just tests. That was their idea. This or that drug for a few months, have him come back to get tested all the time. After I got the bill for the first visit I never went back."

We pass through Waimea and it's twenty degrees colder, fog and sideways rain from the wind, right? Like, people holding their hats and leaning their chests into the ripping gusts when they get out of their cars.

"Who takes care of him while you work?"

"I work nights," she says. "When I go, Kimo checks on him every now and then."

"You leave him *alone?*"

She shoots stink-eye at me. Then goes back to watching the road. Okay, the windshield wipers flap and squeak. "He's usually asleep for all of it," she says. "It's the only way. Otherwise we don't make any money."

When she says that I think about me at the shelter. After Dean was taken, right? Me calling from the shabby lobby, handwritten signs and a sour sweaty mildew smell underneath the tang of bleach. *I just want to come home.* And there was no hesitation from her when it came time to pay for the ticket. Now it was clear there must have been a million calculations in the back of her head. An endless accounting of what it would take.

We come down from the peak of Waimea, eucalyptus and skyscraper trees, where I roll the window down just to breathe the Hāmākua air. The hissing of the cane fields. When we reach Uncle Kimo's place there's this huge grassy fenced-in field, the fresh-painted wooden eaves and clean picture windows facing out, down his property, toward the hills that end in cliffs of the northeast coast.

At the far edge of the property there's a smaller house, a little lanai facing that same ocean. None of the elegant finishes you'd find on the big house. But, like, it's not slowly decaying the way our Kalihi place was. Mom takes the road leading to the back door of the little place.

I catch her watching me. Waiting for my reaction. "What?" I say.

"I had to sell our computer to get back here," she says. Throws the truck into park. "Before you say anything."

"I wasn't," I say.

"You get him inside, and take your bag. I'll go drop the truck back off at Kimo's."

**WHEN I WALK** into the small house with Dad I almost start. It's mostly the bareness of it. There's nothing on the walls. The cabinets are unpainted, the walls not more than primer. A faded rattan papasan chair in the corner, a mismatched pair of wicker love seats. A wobbling dining table that's some sort of composite-fake-wood thing. Jesus, is what I want to say. Has it always been like this?

There's the distinct tapping splatter of liquid hitting the floor. Okay, I turn and see Dad with a hot sheet of piss down his pants.

"Don't—" I say. But he can't *not*. Which means he does. When Mom comes in I've just started to get his rubber slippers off.

"Towel," I say.

"No," she says. "Get his clothes off."

"Me?" I say.

"He's already splashed you. It's on your jeans and feet."

She's right. But still.

"We spent years wiping your ass," she says. "This is nothing."

"No way," I say.

She takes two strong steps toward me. The movement re-minds me of what she used to be: all-state basketball and the thighs and back to go with it, right? But it's not that there's a threat. She just wants to be close enough that I can feel her words.

"Kaui," she says, "this is how life is here. Which means it's yours now, too, for as long as you're here. Help me the fuck out."

I start with his shirt. I find he's able to help, it's a pattern his body knows. He pulls his own arms through the sleeves. After the shirt I see his back and chest. His arms. Sprayed with small mosquito bites and old scars, purpled smooth scratches on the brown tree trunk of his body. After his pants I see places where his hair has been worn thin. At the bulge of his calves. At the peak of his thighs, from the rubbing of jeans and shorts.

"I can finish," Mom says. "I'll take him to the shower. You don't have to learn it all in one day."

I'm grateful and don't argue. I watch her walk him to the bathroom. He can move himself mostly, but that's about it. Like, he pilots his body and leaves us to the rest of it. I think of what he used to be, a man that could lift a piano with one or two other guys. Ironman football all those years ago. Then the felling of canes, the carving out of clean flat spaces in our old yard with a machete. Shirts stretched tight against the bulk of his chest after he'd hefted rocks and thrashed weeds. After he'd wrenched another year out of our rusting cars. I see all that and I'm not sure if I can do this, being here.

That night we eat a simple dinner, Spam-and-rice furikake. There's a bit of fresh papaya we scoop after. We talk—like, I know my mom's mouth is moving and I'm moving my mouth— but I'm not there. I'm three thousand miles away. Earlier, I'd sent a text message to Van, *hey*.

The reply was a long time coming. *People from the university came by, said they have to start sending your stuff home.*

*Yeah*, I typed. *Gonna be here awhile.*

*Hard at home?* she asked.

*Hard everywhere*, I said.

Minutes went by. The screen flashing with a picture that showed she was typing something back. Then it stopped. Then it started again, she was typing. But it stopped.

*How much do you remember from that party?* I asked.

More typing and stopping from her. Typing and stopping.

*You left me,* she wrote back.

*I came back,* I said.

*Only after Katarina and Hao,* she typed. *Fucking Connor was trying to get on me. I barely remember all of that but I remember who was there when I needed it.*

I squeezed the phone so hard I could feel it in my shoulders. I was drunk, too, I almost typed but then didn't. I typed, *I'm sorry,* but deleted it all. I typed, *Do you remember how you called me gross and did you mean it,* but I deleted it all.

I turned my phone off after that.


**AT NIGHT MOM GOES TO WORK.** Cleaning offices in Waimea and Waikoloa. I sleep on one of the love seats in the living room, or else on the floor with a few towels underneath me to soften the wood, and tonight I'm just starting to fade when there's a thud, doors closing, the swoosh and clatter of the screen door. I sit up, turn on the lights, and see Dad heading out into the yard. Okay, so I squirm into clothes and make for the lanai, to follow him. But he doesn't go far. He's there, cross-legged. Just outside the rectangles of light the house windows throw on the grass in the darkness. Him sitting there like a monk in the dark, right? I don't speak; he's not going anywhere, not hurting anyone. I watch as he bends forward and presses his ear to the ground. He stays that way so long I finally come off the lanai into the grass with him, talking, saying, "Dad, you need to get up, what are you doing? It's cold out here." But he stays down, even as I speak. Me saying, "Dad, let's go back inside, I'll get you a glass of water." But he won't rise easy. He stays bent in supplication.

Just listening. Eyes squinted, lips just a little open. Finally I stop tugging, I stop talking. I lean into the grass myself, ear to the ground, facing him.

I don't hear anything.

And Dad's whispering, "Listening, listening, listening."

"Okay, Dad," I say. "Okay." I reach for his shoulder.

He gives me a stink-eye, bats my arm away. Sits back up completely straight.

"Listen," he says. "Listen, listen, listen. It's not just a dance."

It's the first time he's talked in a regular voice since I've been home. I have nothing ready.

"It's not just a dance," he says again.

The hula. Ice stipples my arms and legs. "What's not just a dance?"

"What they look like when they come to you?" he asks. "You have to listen. Like me."

"Listen to what, Dad?" I ask.

But something's changed, okay? His face goes slack like he's seven beers deep, but of course he hasn't been drinking anything.

"Dad," I say, "stay with me."

But he doesn't.

# 30

# DEAN, 2009

## *County Correctional Facility, Oregon*

IN HERE AFTER THE SENTENCING AND YOU'D THINK IT'S all ass-rape and gang shanks, but for real it's the quiet that's violent. Most minutes in jail is like this:

And in between get the light-blue-and-white walls and that's it. County Corrections, light blue and white, light blue and white. The two colors that's everything in here. Underneath the light blue and white I can see the writing we all put on the walls while we're dying, while we're hurting ourselves in here, because that's what you *really* do in jail, hurt yourself, and even when they paint over 'um, the words sawed in with the shaved side of a spoon we palm out the dining area, we just do it again, all the crazy coming out of someone's skull while they sit and shrink against the thin mattress, and some of it's garbage like *Yabba dabba doo* and some of it's for real like *God gave Noah the rainbow sign, no more water but fire next time.*

You cannot keep 'um down, the good or the bad, either way they come up still through all the layers of paint people put on.

The room is five steps from the door to bunks and it's four from wall to wall and in between get the cold steel no-lid toilet and the cold steel barrel of a sink and all in the air get the cold steel stab of my memories. Get my bunk, it's too short but it's the top, a plank built straight into the wall and turned sideways so my feet touch one wall and my head touches the other, and above and to my side there's just this thin block of a window.

First day in, they had us all in stalls and bending over, the officers like, I wanna see the top of your mouth from behind, boy, and we turned and bent and bent and spread our ass cheeks cold. They was looking for drugs and checked us for everything else, toes and feet and fingers and teeth. When it was done we got in our scrubs, light blue with the pink sleeves, thin and fuzzy, and our haole-style bad sandals like we're in a old-folks' home. After getting in my new uniform I came into my room and it was empty and I was thinking it would be an easy one eighty days until they brought Matty right behind me. I'd been in the room maybe two minutes and there he was, carrying his sheet to wrap the mattress, curly blond-boy hair all blown out like he just woke up. He had cankles all chipped with scars and way-freckled arms with stretch marks and a rounded back like maybe he'd been strong at something once but he'd sort of forgot about it. Here he comes escorted to the room. I was all keyed up and ready for throw and thinking about all the movies I seen. Specially the prison scenes.

The fuck you looking at, I said.

Matty stopped. Right at that door. The guards in their tree-green uniforms stacked behind him, saying, Keep moving, keep moving, and saying to me, Stand down if you don't want to go into iso. And Matty stopped and grinned at me. But it wasn't evil. It was fully chill and wrinkled and he said, Boy, don't give me none of that gangsta rap shit. Like you're Fifty Cent up in this motherfucker.

And he was right. And I laughed.

Me and Matty don't talk much. When we're in the room we're both up in our bunks and reading, or doing push-ups on the floor, where the cold on the concrete comes up your hands into your arm muscles, or else we're taking turns shitting on the toilet while we try not for look at each other.

Watch out, Matty said one time, way in the deep black of lights-out, while he rustled to his feet and headed for the toilet, tonight was taco night.

One hundred and eighty days minus time served. That's what I made. Arrested on February 26 and arraigned the day after just like that. I thought there was, like, you go to the police station and then you get released and come back for a court date, but—between the forced entry and the car theft and the buds on the counter?—I wasn't going nowhere. April 15 is this morning, and so I get one hundred thirty-two to go. That's the best I ever been at math right there, look at me subtract. You get good at all kinds of things in here.

February 26, after I got Kaui out the car and drove straight to the Sheriff like I was gonna deliver something. Sheriff and then his backup coming after, both in their tight lumpy black coats walking slowly around my driver and passenger sides, blue and red lights from their cars flashing in my eyes. The crunchy wind coming through their radios and them talking down into their coats while they walked the car, looking in at me. I just kept my hands up on the wheel and tried for breathe slow. I remembered every story I heard about how not to get shot.

Me and Kaui didn't have no time for talk. We could have run again, yeah, ditch the car and go for the streets. But I dunno, it's just I reached a point where I was like, Fuck that, I'm not gonna run away anymore. Me and her had been talking, before, about Noa, the sharks, what he'd felt and what we'd felt, and whether some of what he was, if it was in us, too. Like maybe just because he was gone, everything didn't have to be over. But you look at her and what she's been doing, and you look at me and what I done?

Easy answer. I did what we all needed.

Kaui saw the whole thing happening and I felt bad for her, but this way was the only way. She got all this shit she learned in school, about how to build things. How to make things. Wasn't right for her to be the other things, the police and the pakalolo and the stealing, the running.

I swear. Me and those cops. That was the worst part, the waiting after they stopped me. Had the feeling they could do whatever they wanted and wouldn't nobody stop 'um. I just watched while they was checking out the car. I could tell Sheriff was figuring out the car was stolen, he'd written a bunch in his

book and pinched the radio clipped to his shoulder. I still had on
Noa's sweatpants that I couldn't barely keep at my ass, they were
so small. The seams all cutting and biting into me.

Sheriff made a motion, like, roll down the window. I did.

He was all, You just keep those hands on the wheel.

I am, I said.

Where's the sister? Sheriff asked.

She was fighting me the whole time, I said. Had to get her
ass out the car. I dunno where she gone.

He was all, I thought this was going to end okay when I let
you go.

Yeah, well, I said, you don't know me.


THERE'S AN EDGE on the side of the sink in this cell. I read
somewhere that when Muay Thai fighters is training, they roll
and tap sticks on their shinbones to kill the nerves, make the
bones strong and so they can't feel pain. How nothing hurts
after. So when I walk back the three and a half steps from the
door to the bunks I swing my shin into the edge of the sink.
Just a light tap. Killing those nerves. Three and a half steps, tap.
Three and a half steps, tap. The first times I'm shinning the sink
like that, I feel the tap all the way up to my teeth, this confetti
pop of pain like I'm seeing my veins all red in my head, needles
on my bone. But then after I do it enough (three steps, tap, three
steps, tap) the pain dulls down.

"Ayo, ayo," Matty says from his bunk. "Rocky." His voice all
smooth and even. He could be a radio announcer. "Howbout
you knock off that training until the morning. It's dark o'clock
up in this bitch."

"I thought you was asleep," I say. I'm still facing the door, with its window and the low lights outside it, coming into our cell. There's that cold going up the bottoms of my feet but my shins is way hot and a million little lines of hurt pumping with my pulse.

"I was *trying* to jack off." He says it like it's something he gotta check off a list. "It's hard when someone's kicking the fucking sink."

I smile in the dark. I still got my back to Matty and the bunks, but I smile all the same. "All right," I say. "Get back to it, player." At least he's still got the sheets up over himself. I walk back over and climb up into my bunk up top and right away a soft, steady creak starts up from below, bucking and swaying through the frame. You gotta be kidding me, Matty, but I can't do nothing but lie there until he's done, yeah, so I'm straight staring at the wall, thinking maybe if I look long enough, I can read some more of the words there, even if there's no lights.

"I GUESS YOU can't really tell me how it is in there," Mom says on the phone. Twelve minutes left, since I talked to Kaui first.

"It's boring, Mom, I swear to God," I say. "Don't nothing happen. We just sit and sit and sit."

"Television?"

"Yeah, get plenty. It's funny though"—I almost laugh—"before, when I was working warehouses and all that, on the weekends all I'd do sometimes is watch TV. But now I hate it."

"Don't they have you working? I feel like I read something about prisons being used for free labor camps."

"Yeah, we get all that. But there's like a whole system for getting on the teams outside, right, the ones that get, like, forest work and all that. You gotta sit inside for some of your time at first, only the guys that's been here a little while with good behavior and all that. My turn's coming soon maybe. The guards is assholes about it, though, and it's one of the first things they take away if they can."

"Oh."

"Yeah, so maybe I don't want it. I dunno."

"I see." She does a small cough. Just to pass the time. I can hear some thumps in the back, the crumple of a paper bag, makes me think of grocery stores and how there's so much light and space in 'um, and how it was before, at J. Yamamoto.

"You can't let no one else get something on you," I say, "not while you're in here. You get it? Once someone's got something on you it's all over, you lose."

"You'll be home soon," Mom says. It's what she says every time she can't think of nothing else for say.

"How's Dad?" I ask. "Kaui's saying he's . . . I dunno. There's problems."

"Your father," Mom says.

"Right, Mom," I say. "Who else?"

"He's fine."

"Mom."

"We're surviving," she says. "It's the same out here for us as it is in there for you, Dean."

"Same for you," I say. "The fuck it is."

"No, no," Mom says. "I didn't mean it that way. What I mean is that . . . I know you're not telling me how it really is in there."

"Maybe not all of it," I say. I even smile when I say it.

"So we both edit," Mom says. "That's what I'm saying."

"Okay," I say. "Yeah, okay."

"If I had ever known this would be where you'd end up, Dean," Mom says, starting that same thing up again.

"Mom."

"I should have done it different back when you were in school—"

She goes for a minute, same old same old, since every time I been on the phone with her in here, so I stop listening. Eight minutes left now. Part of me wants to tell her it's okay, but part of me doesn't. How messed up is that? Like I want for her to know that yeah, maybe it should have been different back in high school days, maybe she shouldn't have been so sure about Noa and the 'aumakua. Maybe she should have been more sure about *all* of us.

"Nothing we can do about none of that," I say. "It's all done."

She says something off the phone to Kaui and then there's a weird robot-glitch sound of the cell-phone signal going bad on her end. When she comes back I say, "Hey, Mom."

"Yeah?"

"I think maybe I'm going at it alone in here."

"Dean."

"When we get to talking there's all this stuff from outside that comes back in here," I say. "I don't need all that right now. It makes it harder, you know? Plus it's like people can smell 'um if you're missing things outside, if you're hurting."

"It's not a good idea," she says, "to not have us in there with you."

"Nah," I say. "Best idea I ever had."

"Dean."

Like she can scold me now.

"Let me do it my way," I say. "You don't have a choice."

That's the end of it.

BUT CHECK WHAT does get to me from outside: There's the yard, right, with the fences and the concrete court, lap track around it, little spits of yellow summer grass out in between them. Basketball court—hell, yeah—and jail might be shitty but the backboards is solid and the rims, too, plus there's a net. I been listening to that kiss sound when the ball slips through, all these days since I first came out to the yard for rec time. Balls are fresh and pumped up, and it's maybe sixty days in before I let myself step out on the court. Two prison guards stand at either end, just by the hoops.

Some of the guys is in torn-up shorts or denim-style, looking all gangster with headbands and shit, it's sort of hilarious how hood they look. I been watching these guys stumble around each other and throw elbows and pretend they're Jordan and it's not even close, I'm way on top.

"Knew this tall motherfucker'd be out here someday," Roscoe says, I don't know him so well. He's got a thick Mexi mustache, rolls with one of the gangs in here.

I keep my head down, don't make eyes. Guys in here is like dogs that way.

"Brian's knee is all beat up anyway," one of the haole guys from the other team says.

"Fuck you it's not," that's Brian.

"You can't jump higher than a pregnant hippo," says the guy.

"Look who's got big words all of a sudden," says Roscoe again. He nods, chin up, at the guy that was talking. "Been reading in the library, GED-ready, huh, Toni Tone?"

"You bet," that guy, Toni or whatever, says. "Been reading up on how to school your ass, too."

And they go back and forth, jokes about who's been studying what and whether they even know how to study anything if they can't beat his team, check the scoreboard, all that garbage.

"Howbout you take a break, Brian," I say.

"Right after you lick my balls," he says.

"You be careful out there, Weston," one of the prison guards calls out. "Sounds like you're looking to lose some rec privs."

There's *ooos* on the court, everyone stands a little taller like it's basic training with the drill sergeants. We're all smart-asses, yeah, until the guards start talking.

Brian steps off the court, keeps his hands folded out in front of his pants like a good little schoolboy. Someone bounces me the ball.

Even just to touch it. Been a long time, feels like, since I had this. All that time I was back in Spokane after I got cut: I didn't touch no basketball, not once I wasn't dressed with the team. I figured that was it, all retired from basketball, and then once I was slipping—beers in the parking lot, buds and late nights, all the television couch time, no running—I didn't want for feel what it would be like, me all slow and heavy on the court.

But now I got the basketball in my hands like what. And I feel the flow the second I'm holding it. Like all my muscles are ready for the jump, every part of me. Like some sort of lion. King again, me across the water. Only this time I wonder if I can really listen, if I can reach from here to there.

"You don't check the ball in and you don't bring it up," Toni says to me. Toni the haole dude with his gorilla-hair chest, wannabe pretty-boy face. "You play center, tall boy. Pass it here, I'll start us up the court."

I smile. "Why don't you clear on up there," I say, waving up the court. "I'll bring it."

"Give me the ball," he says.

"Clear on up there, boy," I say, and there's some other guys on the team, some brothers, and I know they see something and smile, because they're telling him the same, Clear on up, let the man go, let's see how it rolls. You can't pass for shit anyway, someone tells him.

I get started.

Maybe I'm slow somewhere still, yeah, but not on this court, not right now. I'm liquid, is what I am. We go for another twenty minutes and I'm all over the court like I ain't never missed a day of practice, like don't no one understand how it feels. I get the ball and cut between two boys, shoulder off their hack fouls, tomahawk the ball in so hard it almost bounces back up into my face and I hang on the rim. I thread passes down low to the brothers and even Toni, slip it between suckers' legs, even get a crossover. Kids are slow in here, too many drugs, too many for- ties, too many weights and not enough running, and now they're all mine. I fadeaway-jumper kiss it in off the glass. I find my three-pointer and I murder 'um with it whenever I feel like it. Automatic. Yeah, I miss a few, okay, more than a few, and soon enough there's heat and ache in my knees and back, like I'm an old man for the first time, but whatever, it's nothing. I'm here. I'm now.

Everyone knows who I am when I leave that court.


**DAYS GO A LITTLE EASIER AFTER THAT.** At the tables, on the work crews, guys is nodding at me, giving me space, and since I don't run my mouth or pull any stupid stunts, not beating my chest like some moke or getting smart, there's respect. It comes on silent and steady and sometimes it even sounds like disre- spect, when guys is all jawing at me, saying this or that about the court, but even then I know they say it because I'm the one to get after now, yeah. Even some of the guards is like that. There's a couple that work the yard more than others, Officer

Trujillo, he'll nod and say some stuff low to his friend when I pull my slick cuts and drop a fadeaway. I see him nodding and all that.

Which I think is what helps give me the other idea. Later, I'm back in the cell and it's those three and a half steps again, all the memories like obake haunting me, and I'm tuning my shins on the sink again. Three and a half steps, do it. Three and a half steps and make my bones sing on the steel.

Matty goes, "What you need is some OC. You could kick that sink all night and not feel a thing."

I stop kicking. "Already getting so I don't feel nothing. Or it's like my brain sees the pain coming and shuts it up." I can feel the flex in my jaw, though, from gritting my teeth, that's for sure. But I don't tell Matty that.

"On that OC, though," Matty says. "You ever did it?"

"That's that show with haole girls and boys, yeah? Rich ones or whatever in Hollywood."

Matty laughs. Like he fully *cackles* after I say it.

"Oxy, son," Matty says. "I'd give my left nut for some in here. Just one run of it, man, I swear. Flatten this whole place out into one quiet line I can sleep through. I miss it more than my mom."

"You telling me you can't get that in here?" I say. "You ask around?"

"First thing I did when I saw somebody," Matty says.

"Back in the day, like high school? I'd get you that easy," I say. "And I don't even know what it is. But still I coulda got it for you."

He snorts. "Look who's dreaming of being Santa Claus."

"I coulda got it," I say. "I swear."

And just like that it's there, the whole concept. Trujillo nodding after my game, Matty hurting for some drugs. Whole idea falls in my lap.

**SO THE NEXT TIME** we're on the yard and Officer Trujillo is the one getting the game shut down at the end of rec time, I'm the one holding the ball that gets to hand it back to him. I went like ten for twelve on the floor, had this mean reverse near the end that had everyone like *oooooooh*. Officer Trujillo is standing there and he says, "Time for the ball, Flores."

Him in his khaki uniform, mustache and goatee like every hair is exactly where he wants it, eyebrows and all, marine-style haircut. All I need is a little friendliness. Used to be I could make anyone friendly.

"You guys work real hard in here, you know that?" I say.

"The ball," Trujillo says.

"I mean I bet the hours is long, guys like us giving you a hard time all day," I say. "I only seen a little of the crazy, guys shitting and pissing on the floors and stuff, fights and all that. Heard Crazy Eddie tried to give one of you guys hep C by spitting on you."

"You don't know the half of it," Trujillo says.

"I'm from Hawai'i," I say.

"The ball," Trujillo says, holding out his hand.

"I'm from Hawai'i," I say.

"Don't make me ask again," Trujillo says.

"What I'm saying is, like, when was your last vacation, yeah? I know all about vacations, what they cost and all that."

"Flores," Trujillo says, like he's tired and I'm in between him and his bed, but he's not angry and he's listening, and that means

I done it right. Okay, I never won a trophy in Spokane. Not the Big One, after all those years. All those hours and palu and sweat and hurt. Me and Mom and Noa with that fight in the kitchen, all the silent fights after. Me flying off to that goddamn ice storm of a state, all for basketball. All for number one. In the end there wasn't nothing to show for it. Long time in here I was sorry—sorry Mom sorry Dad sorry Noa. That's what I was saying in here every day in my head until now and there's no sorry left anymore. I got other things to win.

Do you believe in destiny, is what Noa asked on the phone that one time. About what we're supposed to be, if it's written from the start.

That maybe what he felt in the islands and what I felt on the court were the same thing, and I could be like he was.

It's too late for that now, Noa. But I can still be what we need. There was basketball, now there's this. Both supposed to end in money.

"Listen," I say to Trujillo. "Howbout there's a way I can help you out with that vacation."


AFTER THAT IT WAS EASY. Look. When I was back in Hawai'i I knew some guys that would do things, move things, without really thinking about it. That's how I could get what I needed back in high school, these guys already understood was all sorts of things out there you could have if you just had the strength to take 'um. I still know guys like that. That's where this starts. Then it goes to Trujillo.

Next thing you know Trujillo and probably one or two other guys is bringing things through, doesn't take much of a markup to make it work, they even got some space at the commissary to store some of it, since it's not like they can just walk into the office with boxes full of used panties from people's girlfriends and cocaine, like that. No one knows about the commissary thing except me and Trujillo and his guys. But I mean, it's not like this is max-security federal with guys in face tattoos and life vows to MS-13 or whatever, it's got plenty knuckleheads like me, made a few dumb choices or whatever, or guys that just can't keep it together.

Mostly, anyway, you figure. But then one day Rashad sits down next to me at a lunch table.

"A few of us figured we'd let you know straight," he says. "Wild Eights is talking about how maybe you should close up shop."

"Wild Eights," I say.

Rashad laughs. "That's right."

"Like those two fat guys always hanging over by the track at rec? Then there's that one dude with the big ears—"

"There's almost always a few of 'em rolling through County at the same time. Usually it's the new guys since it's all low-level things. But still."

"And I take your story on it because . . ."

Rashad had been getting cough syrup through me and Trujillo, another satisfied customer, had some sort of recipe that was getting him as stoned as a rap star. So I guess there's that.

"Listen, man," he says. "There's this guy I know."

"There's this guy everyone knows," I say. "Everyone got a guy they—"

"*Listen,*" Rashad says. "His name's Justice. He's, like, legit. Wears suits, clean fingernails, and all that."

"And?"

"He doesn't come down here," Rashad goes on. "But he's got guys you can call, they know how to talk to guys like the Eights. Before shit gets serious." He rubs the back of his neck. "Matter of fact, it already is serious, you just don't know it yet."

"So this thing's turning into, like, *Blood In Blood Out* all of a sudden," I say.

"Just saying," Rashad says. "Probably wouldn't even come to that in here, shanks made out of spoons and shower mobs. That's not Justice's style. Anyway, Negroes in here is just trying to get out, you know? Shit ain't Death Row."

"And what," I say, "you're telling me how come."

"Those Wild Eights motherfuckers got their own they help out and that's it," he says. "They don't want to share. Not like you."

I let a breath go through my teeth, yeah, I can feel the whole thing turning. "I'm not a criminal," I say.

Rashad laughs, his sharp nose and those happy teeth. Kid could be a model if we wasn't in here. "I know," he says. "Me, too. Even Kevin.

"Right, Kevin, what you in here for?" Rashad calls out louder.

"Couldn't prove nothing," Kevin says. Dude might as well be in one of those heavy-metal bands, haole boy with his long sharp beard and hyped-up eyes. "Nigger couldn't prove I was choking him."

"Love you, too," Rashad hollers. Turns back to me. "See? No criminals in here. Just perfect gentlemen."

I sit there, like, forever.

"You want to call?" Rashad asks.

This is another one of those times, right? Just like the car, me and Kaui. Where there's the one side and the other side, and you take the wheel or not.

"People needed things," I say. "I got 'um things. That's all it was gonna be."

"Yeah, well"—Rashad raises his hands, then lets 'um back down on the table—"it's more than that, now. Your choice."

## 31

# MALIA, 2009

## *Honokaʻa*

THERE'S THE REMEMBERING I DON'T TELL ANYONE about, the remembering I do every day, alone, like this: tucked in the bedroom, burying my nose in the last of your clothes that you left with us before you went into the valley. The shirt is my favorite, because it was pushed farthest back in the drawer, and some of you clung to it, so that I can still smell you strong in the cotton.

No one can tell me not to do this. Not to be close to you this way, to have your scent and think about my son and the hole you've ripped in me that feels like it's doing the opposite of closing. Howl, I want to tell that hole. Swallow the entire world, swallow me, too.

But for just the little bit while I'm here, with your clothes, if I don't smell too close and I don't keep my eyes open, it's almost like you're back, and we're in Honoka'a before that boat ride and the sharks, when your father still had a cane job. We had so many jokes! Dirt and school grades and bills didn't matter. The news didn't matter—

"What are you doing?"

It's Kaui's voice. You plunge away and I turn to face your sister with open eyes. We both stand still. My hands still on your shirt, which I bring down to my side.

"I could make something up," I say, "but I think you can see what I'm doing."

Her mouth opens, but she closes it and crosses her arms.

"You're judging me," I say. "Don't judge m—"

"No," she says.

"You'll have to be a mother before you can understand the craziness of it," I go on. "Until then—"

"Mom! It's not that."

"When it's your child—"

"You're not listening," she interrupts again.

I ask her what it is, then. What she saw.

"There's nothing wrong with missing him, Mom," she says.

"It didn't seem like that when you stepped in the door just now," I say.

"It's nothing," she says. "I was just surprised."

"I don't believe you," I say. "I see the way you're looking at me." And my voice gets louder.

"Nothing," she says. She scratches her arm and looks away.

"You walked in and saw me smelling his clothes," I say. "And then you gave me a look."

"You'd never do that if it was me," she says. "That's all."

"You mean—"

"I mean if I was gone," she finishes. "If it was me that was dead."

"What do you think?" I ask her.

"I don't think you would," she says.

Sadness rings through me, sudden and clear. I ask her if she really believes that, and she says of course she does, that she's believed it since she was young, at Kahena, invisible, she says.

"Oh, Kaui," I say. "It's not like that at all. Of course we'd miss you."

She keeps her eyes away from me, looking at the floor or the wall. One arm crossed over her chest and grabbing the other shoulder. She mm-hmms my answer, softly.

"Did you ever think," she says, "maybe he wasn't what you thought he was?"

I'm still holding your shirt. I can still remember you, all of you, the sharks, New Year's, the neighbors, the graveyard, the way there was a feeling in those things. The edge of some brightness I haven't felt since you've been gone.

I shrug. "He was special," I say. "Don't you think so?"

She doesn't answer. After a few quiet breaths, she leaves the doorway.

Your sister. There's a lot about her I still don't understand. So much judgment going from her to me. I see it in her eyes when she comes home from the farm, when I've spent hours with your father, listening to his whispering and finding myself watching the small television more and more, anything to drag one hour into the next until I can make my way to all the offices of professionals that need cleaning. She sees me that way and I can tell she thinks I'm lazy, physically and emotionally and mentally.

Maybe she's right. In my best days I don't think so, but this isn't one of my best days.

In the other room, I hear her saying simple sentences to your father, that his bath is ready, that she can help him through all of it.

# 32

# KAUI, 2009

## *Honoka'a*

I START MY DAYS DIFFERENT NOW. JUST ME AND DAD running down the shoulder of the Honoka'a-Waipi'o road. It's one of the ways I take care of him, right? It seems good for him. *I* seem good for him. But I don't tell anyone that, okay, maybe not even myself most of the time. I hate so much of this—being home, being something like a nanny or a nurse. It isn't what I was supposed to be. It isn't what I'm going to be, someday. But it's what I am right now.

The first weeks were bad between me and Mom. Lots of cold stare-offs and her making me do things for her—help cleaning, help cooking, help budget shopping with the little money she brings in from cleaning, right. I'd do a bad job, slam things, complain. She'd ask what did I want her to do—I was the one that begged to come back here—and that she'd tried to keep me on the mainland, where I still had a chance.

And that was true, but I don't belong in San Diego anymore. It's almost March, almost spring break up there. I've sent too many messages to Van. Plus I even called once, my heart going so hard in my throat I thought I'd vomit. But she never responded. She's probably blocked my number by now. I deserve it.

SO THIS IS IT: I'm here, a fucking housemaid and a nurse. We run. There goes the *pat* of our running shoes on the blacktop, right along the guardrail, with the spills of green below and then beyond ocean and horizon. My father's mind has gone away to someplace young, the way he's running. He's looking ahead and his eyes and cheeks are tight with memory of a body that could do this. Now he's brown and touched by age—moles, deep creases, scars—and thicker than he should be. He's got his old high school football shirt on, heather gray with *Dragons* across it in Kelly green, and shorts that are definitely too short, okay? Under his shirt you can see his broad middle ripple with each stride. But the old Augie is there somewhere and we've been running ourselves off, him and me. Sweat stains in patches across his chest like calico. His hair clumps and splays from the morning heat and where he's swiped his hands. He's still got his trimmed little mustache. These days mostly me or Mom do the trimming.

He's running and I'm running and I see his eyes looking far ahead. Or far behind, right? He's thinking of when he was the one in the Friday-night games. Ironman football. Tight end and linebacker both. We pound down the blacktop hills and the long straight flats of the road to Waipiʻo with all the stalks of cane hissing and bowing. Long shadows from the eucalyptus planted on the mauka side. The beat of our breaths and our sweat. The dark smell of the soil. Pink-blue sunrise.

"HE'S NOT GETTING ANY BETTER," Mom tells me, when we're home, and Dad's on the porch, staring out at the ocean, out past the hills and Hāmākua cliffs. Uncle Kimo has left for work for the day. I don't even know what day of the week it is. "Actually, I think he's getting worse."

Me and Mom standing at the kitchen counter. Hands wrapping coffee mugs. The steam curling and vanishing, same as our thoughts. Okay, there are two versions of Dad, I know there are: The one that we see now, that is something like a dream trapped in a body. And then there is the Augie that was once a cane-truck driver once a husband once a luggage handler once a father. I've seen them both since I've been home, is what I tell her.

She smiles. It's a sad smile. "Me and Kimo figured the same thing with us. Some days your father would spark back to who he was. Like a switch had been flipped, and he was almost normal. But then he'd fall back. After long enough, it stopped being both ways."

"He didn't use to go for runs with *you*, did he?" I say. "He's still in there, Mom."

"Maybe," she says.

"What else can we do?" I ask. "It's not like we can just drop him off at a care facility somewhere."

"Don't insult me," she says. But there's no teeth behind her comeback. Shit, maybe she did think about just dropping him off once. She's looking at her palm. As if it has a message written on it, right? Finally she leans her chin into her hand, cups her jaw.

"He's better now," I say. "He's better with me."

She shakes her head. "Go ahead and think what you think. I should know better than to try and talk you out of it."

"Listen to yourself," I say. "You're acting like you're giving up."

She examines her coffee. The sweet steam of our mugs blows over us. The day is coming full across the lanai. The trade winds and their nightly showers left the plants damp. Now they're as green as anything could ever be. Okay, I want to tell my mother I'll keep trying. I want to tell her she should, too. But it's a conversation we've had a million times, and the only answer that ever comes out of it is that we're never going to have another miracle. I want to scream: Where are all the island gods now?

But she wouldn't hear me. She never hears me.

IT'S TUESDAY, which means I go to Hoku's farm. He of the jowly sunburned face and broad-brimmed straw hat. He of the paint-stained, mud-stained, knee-patched jeans and the sort of easy paunch you get from drinking too many beers at pau hana time. I started working for him after that day he found me in the grocery store.

THAT DAY I WAS just standing there in the store, staring at the surprising varieties of paper towels, when he'd started talking to me. "You're Malia and Augie's daughter, yeah?" he'd asked.

"Yeah," I said.

"That was your brother, then, d'kine that fell."

"It was," I said. "They never found him, though."

He nodded. "Sorry for your loss."

I shrugged.

"Some people was telling me you're looking for one job," he said.

Shame and distrust prickled my ears. I'd forgotten how people talk when they all know each other. Honoka'a. "Maybe," I said.

"Wow, no smiles or nothing?" he asked.

"I'm not your eye candy," I said. "My face is my face."

"Okay, okay," he said. "Simmer down, Hawaiian, easy. I got this farm I trying for get going. Maybe some aquaponics, maybe some of the normal stuff, lettuce and papaya and like that."

"Okay," I said.

"I need people."

"How much?"

"How much what?"

"How much do you pay?"

He coughed. He rubbed the back of his neck. "That's the thing," he said. "I just getting going."

I almost slapped him. "You're looking for free labor, so you find the girl whose brother died?"

"I mean," Hoku said, "there's stuff I trade for with a few the other farms, they give me their leftover harvest, like that."

I hate to admit it, but that did get me listening. If there's one thing that we pay out the ass for, it's groceries. I could already hear the conversation with Mom: You went away to college and came back to work for *what*? But it's not just the food that we'll be getting. It's the other part, too, for me. The work. My hands, my head. Making things again, building toward something be-sides bedsheets and towels and washcloths for Dad. Sometimes people make me feel sorry for wanting more, the same as they did back when I was growing up. But that day in the grocery store I didn't give a shit. "How much free food?" I asked.

He shrugged. "More than I can eat."

"Looks like you've been trying to see how much that is." I waved in the vague direction of his belly.

He actually laughed. "I like you," he said. "Way salty, this one."

SO I WORK. Mornings I'm at Hoku's farm. I dig and plow and plant. I trench and lift and wheel and throw. I blister and splin-ter and ache to the stiffest. There's chicken shit and centipedes that get in my shoes and this warm stink that settles in my hair, right? It's so hard to get out that I let it stay. Seems like it says clearly what I am now anyway.

By late afternoon I head home. Most days that means slog-ging up the hill to the Honoka'a-Waipi'o road and hitchhiking it. I carry my machete to and from. Not like there's much of a danger out here. Small slow days with small slow people on the road. If anything I'm the dangerous one.

The first few days when I come home, there's Mom at the door, seeing me in my mud-streaked clothes and nothing in my hands. No check or cash or pluses for the bank account. And she does that one sigh I used to think was reserved for Dean and Dean alone, another behavioral report or study-hall re-quirement, right? Only now it's her daughter, another moneyless day in the fields, so a long slow exhale from her nose. It seems to blow around the entire house and fill all the space between our sentences. But eventually I bring home the first weekly exchange. Two backpacks and a rice sack of rainbow leftovers, lettuce tomatoes kalo papaya. I thump each one softly onto the table when I take it out. So she can hear the weight. So she can hear the reality. It sounds like an answer, even if I hate it.

## 33

# DEAN, 2009

### *County Correctional Facility, Oregon*

WHEN THERE WAS THAT LAST PHONE CALL WITH NOA AND he asked me what he was I never thought about asking the same question about myself. Now I know the answer: what I am, is good at being the bad guy. Funny all this time it took me to figure 'um out, but when you look back at everything from the start, shouldn't be no surprise.

It's like this: People in here need things and I know how for get people what they need. There's plenty guys in here that's down for whatever. I got some clout now, so I spread the word and my new friends do what they gotta—threaten and flex, bribe, play boy-toy games, I don't care—to get Crazy Eights off my back and keep 'um off my back. I give my people their cut. So I got my friends and Justice-guys outside these walls getting stuff to Trujillo and whoever's with him, bringing it inside to me. Like I'm Amazon dot com or something. I still get heat from Eights sometimes but the more our agreement works for Trujillo the less I gotta worry. There's a new normal and that new normal is two hookups, Eights with their people and me with everyone else.

Days go where I think about Mom and Dad and Kaui on the outside, everything they need, and Noa gone away now. Long time I told myself things was gonna be different. Maybe all that was a dumb fucking dream from the start. Maybe it wasn't never supposed for be anything but like this.

And that thought hits me fully true. And I know what I gotta do. When we get our walk time, I head to the phone and make a call, one of Justice's guys, I don't know his real name. On the phone he says he's Paul.

"Hey, my man!" Paul says. He sounds as haole as can be. "I hope you're . . . getting by in there. Doing your time, right?"

"Yeah, speaking of," I say. I gotta figure how for tell him my idea. "Feels like it's gonna be longer than I thought, you know? Some days I think I might do something stupid, get in trouble, just for stay in here."

He's quiet. Thinking. "Well, slow down," he says. "You do what you gotta do. I'm not there, so I don't know what it takes. But think about everyone out here, you know?"

That's him saying, *We appreciate your services, but don't stay in there too long.* It's good, I figure. Means they think I can do bigger things on the outside.

"Yeah, you're right," I say. "Just been thinking about my

family, too, you know? I wanna have 'um proud of me, when I get out."

Which is me saying, *I need to get money to my family.*

My money.

Our money.

"Yeah, I hear you," Paul says.

Once the bank account gets big enough to mean something, it's going straight to Hawai'i. I know Justice-guys can help make that happen.

After the call, I start figuring how for get a little more time in here. There's all sorts of rules to break, and you know that's one thing I'm good for.

Yeah. I can do this.

## 34

# KAUI, 2009

### *Honoka'a*

NOW IT'S JUST MY HANDS. THE EARTH. THE SWEET STINK of chicken shit steaming in the soil. Tang of clipped grass, the heat of growth coming off the field. Five weeks now I've been doing this, right? Hitting Hoku's farm early-early, staying home nights with my dad while Mom works cleaning shifts. Okay, I used to hate waking up so early. But I've started to enjoy these first hours the best. The air is fresh with unbreathed oxygen and my ears are stuffed with pure quiet. Pale-yellow glaze on the fringes of the sky. Light chill where I can feel the hairs on my neck, below my bunned-up hair.

It's just Hoku and me working his little farm. We weed. We

turn soil and introduce manure. Other natural fertilizers. We move rocks. Clear cane. I like the way the machete feels. The way a hacking strike makes the stalks clap before they fall. The hiss and clatter of moving a set of stalks, the way something more organized and ordinary appears underneath the cane when we clear it, when the ground is just the ground. Waiting to be turned. Hoku has a narrow, long yawn of land out here. At one end he built a corrugated tin shed and stretched a tarp over six poles for a garage and workbench. At the other end our grooming meets a fence and the stalks and bushes that lean over it. Okay, Hoku wants to try and get these fields ready for a crop as soon as he can—I don't know if to start selling it or so he can start eating again, or what. I never see him with food. The only water he drinks is whatever beer is on sale at the grocery store. We don't talk much. He just gives me directions, and I even surprise myself when I mostly follow them without a word. We till. We weed. We saw. We hammer. We sweat. We splinter. We work.

I'm tilling and I'm gone. Zoned in the tang of gasoline and clipped grass, the drone of the engine, and the buck and dive as the tiller spins down the soil. I'm something like asleep until I see her toes in front of me, about to go under the tiller blades.

I flinch and pull the tiller up short. There she is. A broom of black kinked hair. Sun-dark skin and blunted face of an original Hawaiian. Bare-chested and thick-titted and all broad belly, glittering with a day's work of sweat. She stands facing me and doesn't blink. Completely statue, okay? Not breathing.

Then she takes a step.

Hula dreams, I think. That's you.

She takes another step. A weight pulls all my guts down: I have the distinct feeling she wants to harm me.

"Wait," I say.

She takes another step.

"Wait," I say again, and start to step backward. But I'm still holding the tiller's handles, the engine still *pockpockpock*ing and droning. The breeze absolutely dead. There's a smell that was never there, the strong smell of keawe-wood smoke. Like out of nowhere there's a forest on fire right behind us. But it's only the woman and even in the time it took to understand the smell is her, she's moved again. She steps through the tiller, stands between the handles. Which puts her right between my arms.

I jump back from the handles and start to say— But suddenly I feel like I'm thin and strong and old, like a bird made out of leather. I've walked a million miles. There is a child on my back, wrapped in tapa cloth and smoothed bark-rope. It's easy—I've carried whole generations this way. I'm ascending alongside the cold mineral smell of a stream, up the muddy trails to the mist and scraggy peak of a mountain ridge. Could be the Koʻolaus or the Waiheʻe Ridge or anywhere at all in Hawaiʻi, right? I'm hefting kalo in bunches, hairy roots tickling my wrist. When I look around I see there is no sugarcane here, never has been. Plants that are dinosaur-height and mad with color. The muscles of their roots, tendrilled through the rich earth—but there's something like a sudden impact on my lungs and eyes and then Hoku's voice calling, *Hey hey hey.*

Blue. I'm looking at the sky. The cool grit of soil on my back. My mind dilates; I'm waking up. And, okay, here's Hoku above me, blocking out the clouds, shirt slouching off his chest as he bends forward. He kneels to my side, glances up and down along my whole body. "What, drugs or something?" he asks. I can smell the sour mix of coffee and hot dogs on his breath.

"I just thought I'd lie down for a second," I say. "You know, do some cloud gazing." I roll over, kneel, stand. My vision pin-wheels. "You normally work your slaves to death, or what?"

"You only been working for an hour," he says. "Still morning."

"I know what time it is," I say. Which is a lie, right? I'm not sure exactly where I am.

"*I* not working you," Hoku says. "*You* is working you."

I stand on the flat ground and feel the tilt and swerve. The sun is white and everywhere. "I'm fine," I say. "Let's get back to it." And I do, okay? But the tiller and the dirt and my skeleton don't feel like they're even in the same reality.

After what seems like a reasonable amount of time, I sit on a folding metal chair that's stenciled with *Property of Honoka'a High School* and drink a glass of tap water in the shade.

"Stop looking at me," I say to Hoku. I take another swallow of water.

Hoku stops doing whatever he was doing and walks over to me. Leans against one of the workbenches. He crosses his arms and wants to know if I have cancer.

"Nothing's wrong," I say. "I'm fine."

"You not working for me if you gonna die in my field," he says. I ask him where else he'd get labor so cheap. He laughs. "In Honoka'a? I sneeze and it hits someone without a job."

I snort, but he's right.

And he starts a nagging interrogation. Every illness he can think of: Cancer? Heart murmur? AIDS? Sickle cell? Gonorrhea? Asthma? Tumor? Chronic laziness? And even though I answer no to all of these things, it doesn't matter. Something about his eyebrows. His jaw. Either I tell the truth or I'm never coming back here.

"I don't need this," I say.

"Then go," he says.

We both just stand there. He places his hands on the work-bench and leans forward on locked elbows.

"I'll see a doctor," I say, and shrug.

Hoku yanks on the brim of his wide-brim, woven hat, but it can't go any lower on his head, right? Stands back from me.

"Go home," he says.

"I can't," I say.

"Why's that?"

I can't tell him what I've seen. They are there. Finding me when I close my eyes. Women who can only be Kānaka Maoli, skin joyfully dark and thick with work, proud cheeks and eyes full of the old island ways. The salty, fruit-tinged stink of their sweat takes over my nose. They dance on a hilltop. They dance in a valley. Kaholo, 'ami kāhela, lele, 'uwehe. They reap in bundles with hands plunging into dark-brown soil that gives and gives and gives. Something is alive all over my body now. Something like a hula that won't stop dancing.

"There's something here," I say. "I can feel it. Something big."

# 35

# DEAN, 2009

## *Portland*

WHEN I STEP OUTSIDE THE PRISON IT'S NOT AT ALL LIKE
I was thinking. It's a flat paper-colored sky that got enough light
to make the wet flash off the sidewalks but then it's dim enough
it still feels like I'm inside. Might as well I'm in Spokane, it's the
same sort of feeling, where you can't tell October from March
and you just know some of the brown is leaking from your skin
every day. I'm on the steps outside County Corrections and I'm
back in Noa's clothes, got his skinny-ass sweatpants ending at
my shins and the waistband knifing into my hips and tearing
with each step and the hoodie I have to keep open 'cause it ain't
zipping up ever. I feel like everywhere I'm about to rip.

I'm out. Nobody to escort me, or some sheriff or county worker or whatever to chaperone me from this place to the next. I got a thick plastic bag with all the stuff I was carrying when they brought me in: wallet, one penny, two quarters, receipt from a 7-Eleven, credit card, cell phone. I wonder who got to smoke the joints I had, bet it was one of those fucking cops and his wife or something. Now, out here, there's tan pebbly steps in front of me and people in the street below with their briefcases and kids waiting for buses and construction workers at the end of the block with some buzzing machine scraping metal over the wet blacktop.

But my cell phone's dead and Justice never sends his people down here for a pickup, it's the one thing he was saying about getting out. I gotta make my own way to him. Almost feels like a test. And I fucking hate tests, I got no idea what for do next. I swing one hand into the pocket of the sweatpants. Got a paper scratching at me and when I pull 'um out, no shit, like an answer from God, the paper says *Khadeja*, and a number. Hell, no, is what I'm thinking.

But it's cold and I stand there long enough and the no goes to yes. Bad idea. But I do 'um anyway.

Back inside I ask to use the phone and the lady on the other side of the bulletproof glass pops her gum and gives me a dead look.

"I bet you get that question all the time," I say.

She's all, "Every one of you people that comes out those doors. Plus people coming in off the street. There's families, too . . ." She shakes her head.

"I like your braids," I say. "You do 'um yourself?"

She laughs once, ha, smirks like, come on. "Like I've got three arms and eyes on the back of my head that can see where to do it all?"

"Oh," I say. "But I mean, looks good, those red braids and your dark skin, don't be like that."

She pops her gum and gives me the dead stare again.

"You know you kinda look like Oprah, though," I say. "You ever hear that? Got that same no-nonsense look, yeah. When you gonna quit this job and get something better?"

She does that one-sound laugh again, ha, rolls her eyes. She strokes her braids. "You don't even know how fast I'm leaving this place." She shoves the phone up close to the glass. "I tell you what, you get one call," she says. "Two minutes."

"Whatchyou doing later?" I say while I'm grabbing the phone, but I almost start laughing even when I say it, and she starts laughing, too, she's all, "Like I'm finna take your prison-clothes-wearing ass to Cheesecake Factory or something." She points to the phone and makes deuces with her fingers. "Two minutes."

When Khadeja picks up I say, "It's Dean, don't hang up."

"Who?"

"Nainoa's brother."

The line goes quiet.

"Don't hang up, I said."


AFTER, I'M STANDING OUT ON THE STEPS, I figure Khadeja's not coming even though she said she would, but then there she is, pulling up in her little sedan, wearing her black pantsuit and her hair out in the full Afro, not like the cornrows in front with the Afro puff in back I seen last time. I try for take a step toward her but something happens.

I have to keep pulling on Noa's sweatpants, because they can't stay up, but it's more than that. Almost it's like I don't wanna go from the prison, like it's scary. I stop and turn and there's that prison and I'm fully sad, how crazy is that. Feels like I'm leaving home, or at least a place that made more sense than most other places I been, which means it *is* a home, I figure. Around me now there's all this space and noise and light and everything that comes after Noa, just waiting around the corner.

But I blow out a breath and take a step, then another. At the bottom there's Khadeja. She's got a worried face.

"You're walking slow, did they hurt you in there?"

I snort. "It's prison. Whatchyou think?"

And she's all playing with her key chain, watching it spin and dangle. She stops. "I'm only here because of Nainoa," she says. "So don't give me any of that attitude."

The anger comes on me in one big flex. "Look at the good girlfriend," I say, "here for him now, not like back when he was hurting real bad and needed someone and you was out the door. Lucky him."

She looks me over. Down, up, down. Then she presses the accelerator and the car jumps forward, throws my hands off the frame, and she keeps going, driving down the street away from me. I cross my arms and wait, like, Yeah, right, she's gonna drive away without me. But then she's almost at the end of the block and I start running, those torn-ass sweatpants tearing and ripping even more and me holding them up with one fist, plastic bag of everything I own flapping and swinging and me calling hey hey hey and her brake lights go red.

She rolls the window down when I get there. "I'll take you one place you need to go and that's it."

Rain's been spitting down, on and off, but I let it hit me. I wanna feel the drops on my skin. It's prison that does that, I want to tell her, that's what started this whole argument, it's not me, it's the inside that does that. But I figure no way I can tell her what it's like in there and have her understand, and probably it's gonna be like that with everyone else now, too, and when I figure that out with the rain in my face I'm like, You see that, there's a me that was in prison that no one else is gonna know for the rest of my life.

"There's a time limit on my offer," Khadeja says.

I pop the door and get in.

MY ONE STOP is to a big-and-tall on MLK Boulevard. We didn't say nothing while we drove, just listened to all this music on the radio, there'd be a song and I'd be like, Crazy beat, or, She got a high voice, and Khadeja would say, That song's been on the radio for months. But me all like it's the first time, so after a while I stopped saying something about the songs. Most of Portland I never seen, either, so all the streets and neighborhoods is something new, but it's just a city. Bright glass buildings and suits and ties and then blocks where round-hip Ethiopian mamas are walking white babies in strollers and then bombed-out blocks where there's old brick walls and boarded windows, Chinese take-out boxes and ripped bags of kitchen garbage all over some sidewalks and alleys, and plenty places—under freeways and up against the fences and in the parks—got people sleeping by shopping carts lumpy and overfilled with clothes and boxes and milk jugs, like a dollar store threw up into 'um.

I get out the car. Stopped raining, so Khadeja rolls the window down and I lean back in and say, "I know you didn't gotta do this, so thanks." Even though I want to be like, You left us at his apartment and then we got fucking *arrested*. I think she sees how I'm thinking about that day again and she says, "So this was your one stop?"

I raise both my hands away from my body, showing all what I'm wearing, like what do you want me to do, and when I do Noa's torn sweatpants swoop off my waist and puddle at my ankles. She laughs at my naked-ass thighs and then covers her mouth against it. "I can't go anywhere like this," I say. I bend to lift the pants back, and while I'm down I hear the sucking thump of the window closing back up and the clunk of the door locks and then Khadeja's on the street standing next to me.

"I want to ask you something," she says.

I get all crushed in my throat, I figure she gonna ask more about what it was like inside, guys screaming crazy shit until they went hoarse in the middle of the night, the ass-rape and salad-tossing and dick-sucking that was being forced on guys, and me sometimes scared I was next, but also how outside Khadeja's car there's way too much space and noise and things coming at me from every side. All of it rushing at me at once while I'm standing there. Me feeling like I need a small room to back into so I can see what's coming from the front only. Must be there's a look on my face that I don't fix, because Khadeja closes her mouth.

She rubs a thumb over one of her eyes. "You know what? Let's not do this here. We can just drive for a minute."

I don't know if it's what I want. I already got this list in my head of what I got for do next: get new clothes, burner or a pay phone or some other way to call Justice, then see what he can do or who he knows can help me with a place to stay.

"I'll bring you back here," she says.

Standing there looking at Khadeja I realize for the first time how tired I am, and how safe it is in her car, so I just get inside and lean back in the seat and let the car thump and glide through easy turns with the clouds sliding by the glass and the city just going and going until we're at Noa's apartment.

We park across the street, the lawn's trimmed all nice and sharp and the big picture window in front got the curtains closed. There's no light behind it. We sit in the car and stare at the apartment and don't say nothing and I feel my brother gone by the weight of everything he was holding up that's coming down on me: Mom and Dad going broke in Hawai'i, all the shit our family went through to get us out here, to opportunity, everything we already owed before we even got started. I turn the radio up a little bit, nod along to the beats, no way I'm gonna cry in front Khadeja, even though all around my eyes is hot and stinging.

She wants to know why Noa left, that's what she asks me now. I can't figure out how for start, so I just tell her about everything I know about Noa, one big long rush of it, the sharks and him back home, kid like a legend, then from when we was at college and after, all I can talk about is whatever Noa told me on the phone or what I could figure out from talking with Kaui or Mom—them later. And all the while him having to figure out his abilities, the gods and what they wanted or whatever. The path he was supposed to take. The more I talk about it the more I realize he was probably way lonely. Lonely in a way that never made sense for me until I was in lockup.

"If the one thing you are gets taken," I say—I'm not even really thinking when I talk, the words is just coming through me like they was always there—"if the one thing you are, the part you always figured would be your best, if that gets taken away, the next day . . ." I shrug. "The next day it's like you're carrying around your whole future like a dead body on your back. Right in that place on your neck, between your shoulders. Hard for anything to feel right, when you're like that. For Noa? After the ambulance, the pregnant lady that he lost?"

I put a fist up against the car window, press the side of it on the glass. Cold and clean. I say, "It all had to hurt, something deep."

"Did he tell you that?" she asks me.

"Nah," I say. "Let's just say me and Noa got some things in common."

We just watch his apartment a minute. Like he's about to come out the front door or something.

"I didn't even know him that long," Khadeja says. "That's what I've been telling myself. But I can already tell he's going to be stuck in me somewhere as long as I'm alive."

"Yeah, well," I say, "used to be I thought he was a asshole." She turns at me looking all shocked. I'm like, "Oh, what, he didn't never do that thing where you start talking and then he interrupts whatever you're saying to explain the thing back to you all dictionary-style? Like he's an online assistant ready with all the facts and figures you're too stupid to know?"

She laughs. "Maybe once or twice."

It's good, doing this. Makes it hurt less. Plus, it's all true.

"Once or twice, my left nut," I say. "Shit was happening all the time when we was in high school." I play with the switch for the car window, pushing and pulling just enough that the switch doesn't start the window either way.

"I don't mean to insult you," she says, "and I know I'm not part of your family and family has its own way of working inside, where no one else really sees it. But it seemed like a lot was expected of him. Maybe too much."

And I'm all, like, she thinks she's better than us? Man, maybe her and Noa *was* meant for each other. "You're right," I say, "you don't know nothing about my family."

"I didn't say that, I said—"

"I heard what you said," I say. I'm about to blow up, part of me that right away wants to break things, make this a big fight. *Same old Dean*, Mom said. But I don't this time. I fix myself.

"Used to be I thought like that," I say. "How it was Mom and Dad that pushed Noa too hard and that was what killed him. Then for a while I figured wasn't no one that pushed Noa like he pushed himself, and it was probably just because he got such a big head that he messed up in the ambulance. But now"—I shake my head—"maybe it was all of that. Probably little bit of everything. Mostly it was just shitty luck."

"I'm sorry," she says.

I grunt so she knows I heard her, but that's all. A car goes by us in the street, haole lady with her hair all done up like a fancy vase and some toy dog yapping in her lap. The dog's bow is the same sick bright pink as the lady's jacket. When the car's gone I ask if Khadeja seen it. She giggles.

"She does *not* live around here," she says. The street is empty for a minute, but then this guy that's maybe a plumber or something drives up and parks and keys into the apartment next to Noa's.

"Long time I wished I had what Noa had," I say. "You never knew what he was going for be in the end, you know? He was turning into, like, a superhero. Who doesn't want that?"

She doesn't answer. I keep going. "But he's gone," I say. "And the rest of us is still here and hurting. That means we gotta do what we need to keep living."

She asks what that means, what I'm gonna do. I don't tell her what I been doing since I been inside, how all the money I made was going back to the islands, straight into Mom and Dad's bank account. And that was only when I was on the inside. Now that I'm out here, and can put in work with Justice for real? "I need to get to a phone," I say.

"You can use mine." She digs her phone out her purse and hands it over toward me. I look at it a long time. Once this phone calls that one, there's a record of it somewhere. "I better not," I say.

"Oh," she says, and takes it back. She checks her watch. Clears her throat. "I should pick up Rika."

"Yeah," I say. "Better you let me get going."


SHE DRIVES BACK to the big-and-tall, pulls up to the curb.

"Are you gonna be around?" I ask her.

"Around for what?" she says.

"If I wanted for give you something. College money for Rika or whatever. Like how Noa woulda wanted."

She's just thinking, staring at the street in front of us. Then she says she'll be around, I can find her if I want. She leaves it that way and I let it hang.

"Alright," I say. "I guess that's good enough."

While I'm sitting, I been thinking. I figure there's no way my credit cards is still working. I'm nobody, is what that means. I dunno what I do now, but I know I can't stay in this car anymore.

I step out the car, close the door. When it thumps back into place, just like that the sky opens up and you gotta be kidding me, rain starts for come hosing down. I raise my hands, look up at the clouds.

Khadeja rolls the window down a crack.

"It's always fucking raining," I say to her. "When does this stop?"

"Sometimes it seems like it never will," she says, and puts the car in drive. "But then, all at once, summer comes. Wait until you see how it feels."

# 36

# KAUI, 2009

## *Honoka'a*

THIS NIGHT IS ONE OF THOSE NIGHTS WHERE THERE'S NO sleep and I say to myself: I'm not thinking of San Diego, of Van. But what is it, then, that wakes me. There's a feeling in my belly, cool and thick, like I swallowed concrete, right? A weight of failure, of leveling off, of climbing to the peak and seeing there's nothing next but descent. Small farm. Broke family. Single and lesbian, or not, who even knows. Half a college degree.

The house is mostly shadow. But okay, I love that about where we live. No light pollution choking out the spokes and spills of stars, the natural black balm of late night. I step quiet through the small hallway outside my bedroom. Feel the bits of sand on the floor stick to my feet. Minty-blue glow of the oven clock.

The screen door to the lanai is wide open, which it never is. The ripe, shit-seedy smell of pakalolo drifts in through the gap, spreads in my nose. There's Mom. Sitting on a chair with her feet up in it. Like, her big body folded in on itself, elbows on her knees. She has a joint lazy-pinched in one hand. Smoke twirling up from the embers.

"Couldn't sleep?" I ask.

She shifts her head. "This small-ass house, and you're still always surprising me," she says. "I just got back from my shift."

I slide the screen door closed behind me. "Nowhere to go when you get home," I say.

"Truer words never spoken."

I sit like her, folded forward. Hug my knees. "Let me have a hit."

Mom looks over at me. She gently opens her mouth and a curtain of smoke slow-rises from her lips. Tumbles over her nose and bloodshot eyes. "No," she says. "I'm not stoned enough yet."

Okay, I'm about to snatch the joint from her hand and cram it whole into my mouth, fire and all, when she laughs. She passes it over. "Should've seen the look on your face," she says. "It was like you were about to rob me with a knife."

I pull the pakalolo into me, let it creep down the tube of my throat. Heat the sacks of my lungs and make everything expand. Lift. Mellow.

"You've always been tita like that," Mom says, taking the joint back. "At least I did one thing right."

She smokes a deep one, right? The tip of the joint pulses orange white orange, the fire breathing all on its own. Coqui frogs go on with their drippy whistle song in the green outside.

"You know," I say, "I didn't know you smoked."

She chuckles. "Lots you don't know about me," Mom says. Smoke tusks from her nose.

"You're not the only one," I say.

"Really?" Mom says, fake-shocked. She passes the joint back. "My daughter has secrets?"

"What started it?" I ask.

"What started what, the secrets?"

I nod to the joint in my hand. "Smoking out."

"Boys." She laughs. "I was fifteen, at a football game. Parking lot with my two friends and their boys, plus all their friends. I think I was the only one who hadn't smoked out yet." She plops her hands on the crown of her head, right? Leans back in her chair, tilting it up on two legs. "God, there was this one surfer boy there, passing the joint. You only had to see him from be-hind to get horny. That ass."

"Jesus, Mom," I say. "Not when did you *smoke* the first time, although great, I love thinking about you having teenage sex. I meant what started you smoking up *tonight*?" I don't really need to ask, though. She's got Nainoa's 'ukulele right by her feet. I drag another deep hit from the joint and my fingers go thick with heat from the burning. I pass the joint back to her.

"Your brother sent us some money," she says.

"Dean?" I ask. "Money? But he's—"

"You're smart, Kaui," she says. "Think about it for a second."

Mom sits the chair legs back down. Looks out over the side of the lanai, the pitch into darkness and the float of headlights every so often going by in the distance, out by the road, tires exhaling long on the pavement. Trees nearby us lean and clatter.

"We failed you kids," Mom says. "Big-time."

"No," I say.

"Yes," she says. "I thought maybe if we got you all to college. If we got you all to the mainland." She waves with her left hand in the vague direction of everything behind us. Other hand holding the joint. "But now look."

"Maybe it wasn't you," I say. "You ever think that?"

She snorts. "Even I'm not that stoned. Everything you are now is because of us."

"You think that?"

"I do," she says. "Dean was only ever a basketball player. We didn't push him hard enough to be anything else. Noa died because"—she clears her throat—"we didn't understand what he needed. When he came home . . . Maybe we never understood."

The joint burns down in her fingers. She barely notices.

"What about me?" I ask.

"You're here," she says, like it's obvious. "Taking care of your parents."

"Only until things are better," I say.

"I think," she says, "things are better."

I laugh. "What, just now all of a sudden?"

"It was a lot of money from Dean," she says. "Not enough to buy our own place or anything. But the bills are going to be paid for a little bit. When does the next semester start? You could take a few summer makeup classes—"

"I'm never going back," I say.

She's thinking a second. The joint must be cooking her fingernails. "I guess I shouldn't be surprised," she says. "That was the same thing your brother said."

"Like you understand, anyway," I snap.

"Well," she says, "explain it to me."

"Maybe I don't want to tell you," I say.

"This isn't easy," Mom says, "having you home. It took everything we had just to get you to the mainland."

I don't say anything, right? Not for a long time. There's no place to start. Even if the memories weren't lockjawing me, which they are. "I left a friend," I manage to say. "Left her in the worst place."

Mom nods. She says okay. She says she understands that. Meanwhile I'm sitting there, jerking back against sobs that keep coming and I try to clamp down. I tell her about the party. Van. But once I start, once I'm opened, I don't close: I tell about the culvert, the sleep piles we'd make in dorm rooms. The perfect nights of drinking and drugs and dancing and hollering. How all our outdoor trips felt, the brittle frigid clench of mountain summits at dawn. The ageless hot dust of canyons gold with trapped sunlight. The shit Van would get us in. Dares, velocity, climbing, risk. But it comes back to the party again and again in my head and so I tell her about it. The party, the room.

"I wanted to leave her," I say. I say it again. I wanted to leave her. I wanted to hurt her.

"Those boys," I say. I palm tears from my cheeks. "Those boys were like fucking wolves and I left her."

The house pops and creaks and flexes around us. It's blue and dark out there. I ask Mom if love ever made her feel alone. If it ever made her feel like she was starving in a room full of food.

She laughs. "Only every day." She leans over to me, across the gap between us, so that the side of her head touches mine. Okay, I can feel the bone, the scratchy shift of hair on hair. We lean in to each other more and more heavily. I'm, like, ugly crying, I think. Tears run down me. She whispers something, but I can't hear the words.

"I never thought I'd be the type of person who would do that to someone," I say. "Now it's exactly what I am. Forever."

Mom nods. "It's always like that."

"What do you mean?" I ask.

"Whenever I've made a choice in my life, a real choice . . ." She leans back from my head. Touches my shoulder just for a second. "I can always feel the change, after I choose. The better versions of myself, moving just out of reach."

It's exactly what I think. So there's nothing to say. I saw at my nose with my forearm. Palm more tears from my eyes.

"I'm always losing better versions of myself," she says. "I don't know. You just have to keep trying."

She cries then. We both do for a few minutes. "God, I'm tired of crying," she says, finally. Stands and juts her head toward the kitchen. "You want a beer?"

"I want fifteen," I say, laughing. And I wipe my face again and again. "Let's just split one." She goes. I hear the fridge smooch open and closed. She comes back and sets a beer bottle down next to my ankle and then gently lifts the 'uke onto her lap.

She asks do I ever think about dying. About what's there, on the other side.

"Of course," I say. "Especially since Noa."

"And?"

The answer doesn't come as quickly as I thought it would. "Most of the time it feels like there's nothing after this," I say.

"That part doesn't matter," Mom says. "Or it doesn't scare me. If there's something on the other side or not. It's the getting there, you know? That last minute when you're leaving, still living in this world even as it's closing up around you. You have to do that part alone."

I don't have anything to say.

"I thought about doing it, you know," she says. "When Augie was at his worst, just after Noa."

"Shit, Mom," I say.

"That's right," she says. "Razors, pills. Kimo's hunting rifle. A rope from the ceiling."

It's like she's naming old friends, people she's spent a lot of time with. Part of me wants to know how far she went. If she had the thing in her hands. "I'm glad you didn't," I say.

She laughs. "Gee, thanks." She shifts in her chair and almost drops the 'uke, right? A lurching move to catch it.

I jut my chin at the 'uke. "You ever play it?" I ask.

She considers what she's holding. Like the idea had never occurred to her.

"I only know maybe one or two songs," she says. "Better your father."

"He's asleep," I say. "And anyway I don't think either of us would want to hear whatever he plays these days."

Mom's thinking. I bet she feels what I feel. That something is turning in us. What we are to each other. After all this time away, the island can still never be anything but my home, and I can never be anything but her daughter.

She starts playing the 'ukulele.

There's a pop and chuck to the song. Off-tune chords a little bit. It's sad and slow. Or it feels that way; but she keeps going and it catches in my throat and my fingers and my hips. I stand and it begins: a hula. I don't understand what's happening. My body does not feel like my own, it feels as if I'm just a passenger in the shell. The song Mom plays isn't made for hula, it's too slow and choppy. I lose the beat and move away across it and come back and lose it again. But something keeps moving me. Stop, I want to tell Mom, but something won't let me speak. My hands drift and ripple and harden. My hips roll with my bent knees. The chords chuck. Mom's fingers are picking up speed, adding second and third notes along with the chords so something thick and intricate is rising from the strings.

I don't understand, I want to say again, but I still can't speak, right? Something keeps sucking the sound from my throat.

Mom moves the song to another. She starts slapping a beat on the body of the ʻukulele. Slapping and rolling her knuckles on the body like it's an ipu. Then she goes back and jams out a few chords. So hard I worry the strings will snap. Then while they're still ringing in the air she's slapping the ʻukulele body again, tapping and slapping and rolling.

The song has become kahiko. The ancient hula form.

And the song asks: What are we doing here. In this land.

In my mind I see: Water finding its way from the top of rain-pounded gulches in the mountains to the leaves of green kalo in the valley. To the thirsty earth. I see fish and flower beds and symbiosis. My hands in that same soil, tilting the balance ever so slightly, and the green roaring back.

The song asks again: what are we doing here. Take the balance we're building at the farm, I say. Say it with my hands and hips in the hula. The song is asking and I answer. Make my palms flat and press them down through the air as I rock my hips and step slowly, and turn back. I'm not working hard but I'm dizzy, motion-sick. Something is in me. Mom goes harder on the ʻukulele. She's slapping and knuckling the body. She's hitting chords and notes all over the strings, right? It's the farm, I answer, it's the land, what we can be and what the islands can become. In the hula I pluck from the air like I'm plucking kalo. I sweep down and across my body like rain through the dirt and rivers. The old ways again, land feeding, land eating. That old hum. I pivot on my heels. Mom goes on, the song is swelling with a rainstorm of notes and a beat that's turning before our eyes. I've never seen her play like that, so fast and precise; it's not sad anymore. I see my hands as I sweep with them. My hands. Stained again to the quick, this time with soil instead of the climbing chalk they'd been dirtied with in San Diego. I roll my hips and shoot my feet out and back to the beat. I drop to my knees and turn my arms each way before setting them down. I bow. Mom strikes the last notes, faster than the notes she started with.

There's a rip tide of silence. I slam my ass back into the chair. Like, almost break it, almost fall over. The sensations of where I am start to creep back into recognition. The coqui frogs go.

"Mom?" I ask. "What just happened?"

Her eyes are larger and whiter than before. "I don't know," she says. "I've never played that before in my life." She cradles the 'ukulele back down to her lap. Opens her hands and wiggles her fingers. As if to be sure they're still there.

I ask her did she see it, too. Did she feel it.

"Yes," she says.

I think of all the other hula that had been in me. From that first night, the cafeteria, to college and Van, to this. *Alive alive alive*, goes my heart.

"Kaui," Mom says slowly, "what is happening on that farm?"

## 37

# MALIA, 2009

### *Honoka'a*

THESE DAYS I TRY NOT TO HOPE TOO MUCH. I'D STARTED
to believe that, whatever gods there are, our future isn't tied to
them, not our present, not our past. They've become nothing
to me, without Nainoa. And isn't it foolish to expect anything,
one way or the other, anyway? Isn't that the thing that's always
undone people? And yet here I am, hoping again, itchy with it,
because of what happened in the music last night. Something is
happening down here, I don't know what, something of the gods
and Nainoa and us. So I'm here, sitting in the unlined bed of Kimo's
pickup with my daughter, our backs against the cab as we face
rear to the road behind us, passing a thermos of coffee back and

forth, the faint taste of its plastic like opening an old refrigerator, underneath that taste the good rinse of the Kona beans,
we pass it back and forth when the truck's not bucking through
the graveled potholes of the farm road. We have bandannas over
our noses and mouths to block the dust from the ride, making
us into bandits, or the Bloods and Crips on Kaui's rap albums.
Through the bandannas everything smells like old cotton and
coffee, and we lift the cloths up enough to sip the mug, then
drop the bandannas back over our faces and pass the thermos
to each other. Road dust churns in our wake. The truck bucks
again and again. We take a corner a little fast and Kaui almost
tumbles over, sloshes coffee on her fingers and the thigh of her
jeans. "That fucking fuck," she hollers.

"You mean your uncle?" I ask.

"Yeah," she says. "Fuck him and his driving. He's trying to
kill us."

"Pass me the coffee if you're not going for it," I say. Just as I
take a sip, we hit a smooth section and I drink long, smack my
lips, make an *ah* sound after I swallow. "That wasn't so hard. I
don't know what you're complaining about."

"Whatever," Kaui says.

"How far down is the farm?"

"Almost there."

And then we are. Clearing the final corner, I see that the
high grass and old cane and eucalyptus trees are chopped back
and away and there's a flat, wide field of a hill, the domed glass
greenhouse in the center of the plot, pipes kinking up and down
into the ground around the property like a half-buried skeleton, a smaller shed to the side. Raised platforms all around the
greenhouse, a riot of elephant-eared taro rising from each platform. A man with a wide-brimmed, tall woven hat, old-school

Hawaiian country-farmer style, sand-colored boots and grubby jeans, balding shirt, strides to the truck.

"You're late." He nods to Kaui.

"Sorry," Kaui says in that flat way she uses on me, too, when she wants me to know she doesn't mean it.

"I bet," the man says. He's got curly whiskers patchy all over his chin and dark cheeks, thick eyebrows, serious stares; Hawaiian-Okinawan, I figure.

"You probably just finished shitting anyway," Kaui says. She hands him the thermos. "Was it a soft-serve morning, or more like a German sausage?" She hops from the pickup bed with her backpack and snatches the thermos back. I swing each leg over the tailgate and step down off the bumper.

"This the 'ohana, then, yeah," the man says to me, to Augie. Augie gets out of the truck cab. Kaui chatters for a minute with Kimo and then the truck starts off, Kimo's arm cocked out and throwing a shaka sign before the truck bucks through the first dusty turn and is gone.

THE MAN IS HOKU and he shows me the farm, what he and Kaui have been doing. It's all aquaponics and biodigesters, build-outs just getting started for a solar array and micro-windmills that hang like tree leaves and spin the smallest breezes. He explains it all and I'm in and out, not catching all of it, not so interested in much of what he's saying. It's a farm, what is there, really, to understand? The whole time we're touring he's got Kaui at work already, shoveling cow manure into a large black cylinder that she tumbles with a double-handed crank, or she's out pruning plants and wrestling with pipes. She's got her hair lashed up into a topknot, body flexing with each punch of the shovel, eyes squinting against the threads of the pipe, the back of her black T-shirt already calicoed with sweat.

Hoku laughs. "You don't get it, yeah?"

"Looks like a small farm to me," I say, fingering the leaves of one of the taro plants. "Kalo" is the other name for it, the one I prefer, the one that makes me think of night marchers and Pele and 'aumakua, and there you are again, waiting in the part of my heart that rests until everything is quiet, then suddenly jumps.

"Everything gotta start somewhere," Hoku says. "Everything big starts small."

"You ever actually do work yourself?" I say. "Or you're mostly a full-time tour guide?" I give him an acid smile. Kaui is wrenching on another pipe, arms going like the inside of an engine, broad and strong and full of sun like her keiki days. I remember. Augie is standing next to her, hair ruffled by the wind.

"You charming, just like your daughter, yeah," Hoku says. "Easy, Hawaiian. I was just showing you around quick one time."

"Uh-huh," I say.

"You don't get it, yeah?"

"What is there to get?"

"Your daughter. I hate for say it," Hoku says, "but she figured this out."

"Figured what out?"

"The whole thing," Hoku says. "The way to chain it all together, plus this new stuff she's making. All the designs." He talks again about aquaponics, the biodigester, the kalo feeding from the waste of fish feeding from the plants, and on and on: a cycle, he says, twirling his finger. It's everything at once, the whole system feeding itself without intervention.

"Right here," he says. "It's perfect." He steps off the raised platform under the shade of the materials shack. "But girl's, like, selling everyone on it. Gonna change everything in farming, I tell you. Just gotta make 'um work bigger. She got plenty ideas now." After a few steps toward the place where Kaui is working, Hoku turns back. "You not coming?"

It's almost as if a switch has been turned on: a warm excitement and guilt juicing through me at the same time. She didn't get this capable overnight. These abilities—she'd been doing something extraordinary, all those days when we were watching Noa instead. Bit by bit she got bigger. Quiet and furious. We never really paid attention, did we? Now look at you, Kaui.

"I'm going to stay," I say. "Just a minute. Give me a minute."

"Yeah, okay," Hoku says. "Stay in the shade, grab one drink from the cooler if need."

"Right," I say, shading my eyes with my hand so I can see her better.

He goes the rest of the way out to my daughter and together they move from one task to another: slicing open parts of a large black drum—a water tank or something else—adding rubber pieces to it, fitting pipes, dragging scrap metal upstream, and then Kaui and Hoku talking about how to make something from it, her fierce gaze locking on an engine they have set up on a board straddling two sawhorses. I've never seen Kaui this way, never *felt* her this way: the whole farm, the whole situation, like an extension of the tendons and muscles of her body.

But then I notice Augie. He's not standing with her anymore, she's given him space, and so he's standing off by the aquaponic section, the huge, crowded bins of growing kalo. He does a strange thing then: he leans over, pressing his forehead gently against one of the elephant-ear leaves, and as I watch he leans farther and farther into the plant, until the whole front of his head has disappeared into the stalks.

There's a feeling, a deep green feeling, and a music. I feel my-self lifting, it's almost as if I'm in my body and outside it at the same time. Something's happening.

"Augie," I say, starting to walk toward him, even though I know he won't answer, it's pointless, "what is it?"

Augie holds a hand up, his head still lost in the stalks and shadow, the leaves draped over his shoulder as if consoling him. But when he holds the hand up, there's something about the ges-ture, two fingers barely apart, two other fingers closed, that's more deft than he's been for quite some time. A controlled looseness, is what it is. Faculties. He pulls his head back out.

"Babe," he says.

I almost trip on myself. *Babe*, a word he hasn't said in such a long time, so long I'd forgotten what it meant to hear it. We had always had us, Augie and I, and our time together had always felt like a braiding, a braiding of our essences against each other tighter and tighter no matter what was being torn down around us. More than anything, what I'd missed most all these months was that feeling, and I realized it was the feeling of home.

"Babe," he says again. As if we'd never missed each other all this time. "I gotta show you something."

I want to speak but say nothing. I step closer to him. His hand grasps my arm just above the elbow and pulls me into the kalo—and when my forehead touches the leaves I feel it.

It's the same as what was there last night, in the song with Kaui, buzzing through my bones when I played the 'uke. Where I touch the leaves and stalks, I feel a thousand voices, chanting. Yes. I grasp the stalks, I bury my face with Augie. The chanting and the singing. I know the language even if this is the first time I hear it this way, a language of righteousness and cycles, giving and taking, aloha in the rawest form. Pure love. The chant grows

in numbers, the way talk at a large gathering of people shifts
from individual conversations into a babbling hum, so that what
I'm touching now is more than voices, more than a chant, it's a
hum of energy, and I can feel the hum extending into everything
around us: the kalo in the field, I feel its green hunger for sunlight and the clamp and flex of its body against the damp soil
and the way it is drinking tongues of water that find their way
to it from the fish, and the fish, the trill and beat of their tails,
a constant rock this way and that as their bodies muscle their
dance through the water, then the mud on the edges of the tank
and past it the grass, all of it raising up and feasting on the sun,
the heat, the rain. It echoes back until it's almost too much to
bear, too much to fit into one mind. I'm starting to lose myself in
it, it's raging around me, it's starting to drown ideas I have even
about myself, where I am, my name—

Augie's rough hand pulls me back from the leaves. There he
is, examining me, his eyes gentle and full, the way they used to
be. *All* of him is there. "You felt 'um?" he asks, and I tell him yes,
yes, of course I did.

"Been there this whole time, yeah," he says. "You didn't
know."

"What's been there?" I ask.

"All of that," he says. "All of it."

I realize, finally, what it's been like in his head all this time,
how if this is what has been in there, in its most loud and central
form, roaring over every part of his mind . . . it would unmake
him. How it started slowly and came on bigger. That he felt it
on O'ahu while I didn't, that there's something Kaui felt, too,
something that she awakened on the porch, her and Noa's 'ukulele, and now here we are. She unlocked it. This place, this land,
unlocked it. A wall of chanting sound storming over everything

else, a demand from the island to be realized—no, released—
this way. This is just the start, isn't it, but this is everything, all
of it from the beginning. Stick me in the heart with a spear, the
way I understand Nainoa for the first time. It must have been so
lonely, all his life, with all of this.

"Augie," I whisper.

"What?"

"Right now," I say, "is it you?"

"I don't understand," he says, but I don't need him to answer.
I can see. Oh my Augie, I kiss him. Push right into him and feel
his chest, the way the muscle has thinned to a shallow dish over
ridged bone, but still it thuds with blood and breath—I press
mine against his, and our teeth click as I shift my mouth over my
Augie, let my lips slide sloppy into place, us breathing together.
He's here right now, all of him, and it is enough. Something is
released.

"Oh my God," I say, pulling back from the kiss, and I laugh.
"Your breath stinks."

# 38

# KAUI, 2009

## *Honoka'a*

WE BEAT OUR RUN OUT ON THE ROAD. AND THE ROAD IT beats us back. The chopping pattern of our running shoes on the blacktop, me and Dad on our eighth mile, and with each stride the earth drives back into our bones and muscles. Sugarcane and eucalyptus scroll by and occasionally, farther out in the fields, there are rust-cancered mill houses and zinc storage-sheds getting swallowed by leaves. Scrubby green unused farmland tilts down toward the faraway cliffs. Okay, and then beyond, the blue ocean flickers with whitecaps from the trade winds. We keep running and we keep hurting, right? Through our toe bones. Through the knots of our calves and the stiff bands of our thighs. All the way up through our bellies goes the beat. *Tff tff tff* is the sound. Each time we stride now there's a sort of gasping from both of our throats. I bet that's the wrong way to run, losing breath like that. But I don't care about being wrong. Or losing breath. I just want to go.

Okay, still running, me and Dad, just like we did at the start when I came home. Back when I figured maybe just running would make him better. You run hard enough and long enough and everything inside is muted under the torrent of your body moving blood and oxygen and your head buzzes bright. Back when I first came home I was ready to get lost with Dad. And I did some days. Some nights.

Then the hurt unlocked itself, Dad and the land. Now whole days go where he's like he was before. There's no muttering, okay? There's no set of staring eyes, as empty as the rusted sheds we're running past. There's no shitting himself or wandering off into the dark green. No. We have all of him now: *Pull my finger,* he ordered at dinner on Saturday. And after our run yesterday morning he said: *I been running so hard I think your mom gonna die.*

Who, by the way. Mom. It hasn't been since my hanabata days that I've seen her like she is now. For a while a part of her had given up. She'd lost everything and was only continuing to wake up because it's what she'd always done. Or maybe she thought there was something in Dean and me that she could live for. I don't know about that. But I do know Noa will always be her favorite; it wasn't even about Noa, really, or at least not just the person. For Mom, Noa was a son but he was also the legends that came with him. How those contracted everything that hurt us—the broke years, the move to the city, the shit jobs she and Dad had—into a single point of purpose. And that purpose was so big she didn't have to understand it to know she had an important part to play. Big destiny is a thing you get drunk on.

*Tff tff tff.* Me and Dad still pounding down the road. Something shifts and crackles in the trees when we run by, where the bushes and branches are spiky and low to the ground. My own sweat is wetting my eyelashes, tickling the muscles in my neck, and the road humps up hills and rolls down and curves away. Orange late light. We keep running.

Okay, nothing's the same now when we run. Now I'm not looking to lose myself. I'm looking to expand what I've made. I call it a new ahupua'a: the old system resurrected. When the island was ali'i split in stripes top to bottom and everything produced was given to everything else: fish from the sea traded for sweet potato from the plains grown from water from the ridges. Only now me and Hoku have enclosed the whole thing in a smaller space, plus incorporated photovoltaics plus water reclamation. It trades and feeds among itself, see? The kalo and the fish and the flowers. Much from little land. It's going to change what these islands are, I swear. When we first started talking about it. When the articles were in the paper and the island airline's in-flight magazine, people started coming around. Tita earth mamas with toenails like cracked roof shingles and vana-hair armpits, koi tattoos, and whole farms they were building, just like us. Guys with kinked hair that fell to the middle of their backs, dark-skinned chests that are just plates of muscle. But it wasn't the news that brought them. They'd been called, too, is what they said. That same voice, the one that came to me like a hula, that came through Dad like a river. All the people that came to us had been hearing it. Driving them to make what they had. And so all us Kānaka Maoli and all our noise? Even important people are coming around:

*After all*, the county councilwoman shrugged, *we have to do something with all this land*. Me making visits to the legislative hearings, to universities, joined by other farmers and fishers and speakers of the old ways.

"See that," Dean said on the phone last night. Like I was just figuring out something he always knew.

"Oh Jesus, Dean," I said. "See what."

"Noa was right, wasn't he," Dean said. "Wasn't just about him. Even from the grave he gets for be a know-it-all."

I couldn't help it, I laughed.

But what about you is what I asked him then. Does it call you now, too.

"You know what," he said. "You wanna talk about calling. Try listen to this." And there was a tumble and thump from his side of the phone, an underwater sound. A sound I knew meant he was moving the phone, then moving himself. Then there was a rush of city sound so loud it almost turned into a white-noise rainstorm: car horns, sirens, the cracking of wood pallets and doors. The boom of heavy things tumbling into a dumpster. The long grind and roar of a city bus. Hisses and clatters. Voices. Then those sounds faded and the phone thumped, moving again. A television voice rose, something about markets and expected quarterly growth, predictions of valuation, and then he was back on the phone, right? And his breath. "You heard 'um, yeah?"

"I heard noise," I said. "That's not what I'm talking about."

"Noise," he said. "That's *money*," he said. "That's me finding ways to make it."

He'd been sending more money as he made it, deposits showing up in Mom and Dad's account on the regular. Mom never asked where he made it, and I didn't, either. I bet the answer was not as bad as we imagined. But we didn't ask, because maybe it was worse.

There was a creak of leather on his end of the line, thump of something closing. The whole time we talked I bet he was moving. He's always moving. I wonder if that was the worst part of prison for him, the way movement was taken from him.

"How's Mom and Dad been?" he asked.

"Better, every day," I said. "All of us."

"Look at you," he said. "Maybe Noa wasn't the only superhero."

"He never was a superhero, Dean," I said. "That was the problem. No more saviours, okay? This is just life."

"Huh," he said. And then: "You know, I still think about Waipiʻo," he said. It was like I could hear him shaking his head over the phone. "I was down there way after everyone was all back home. The helicopters and dogs gone and me just hiking for find Noa. Up and down all those trails. I kept having one feeling like maybe he was just around the next corner. Just right up ahead of me. Same as when we was kids, he was always ahead of me. Even the last time, like he took the fall because he was so far away from where everyone else walks.

"Part of me gonna stay down in the valley like that forever. Just chasing him. Part of me ain't never coming back up. You know?"

While he talked, I moved through the little house we have now, on Uncle Kimo's property. I stepped onto the lanai outside our side door. Felt how, like, the hapuʻu ferns and the banana trees and ironwoods made their own atmosphere. And it was different than what there was in San Diego. But just like that how quickly I was back there. Van and all those parties, those climbs. Those drives and climbs and the culverts. And Van. And Van.

"Yes," I said. "I know exactly what you mean."

He didn't say anything.

"You're not coming home, are you?" I asked.

"Home," he said. Like it was a word he'd heard before but still didn't know. "Whole time I was back in Hawai'i," he said, "I run into people and they're all 'I remember when you scored thirty-five against Villanova, last-minute bank shot,' or 'Back when you was playing for Lincoln I remember going to all your games.'

"That's all Hawai'i is now, yeah? It's the me that I was before. There's that and there's the valley and everywhere Noa. I can't beat it, sis. That's it, that's Hawai'i. I can't beat it."

Give it another chance is what I told him. "You'd be surprised," I said, "what this land can do to you."

"Nothing surprises me anymore," he said.

Oh, Dean. Such a butthole, still. Once upon a time it would have made me angry, right? But I figured what he needed then was just a little credit. Just a little bit of being the best.

"Hey, Dean," I said. "The money you sent us, that first time. It got here just when Mom needed it most. I mean really needed it. She was almost gone. Did you know that?"

He inhaled then. Sharp and fast. Voice cracked a little when he spoke. "Ah," he said. "Okay."

"And I remember that day in Portland," I said. "I remember who took the wheel. At the end.

"But you don't have to keep doing whatever you're doing now," I said. "We're going to be okay."

"Oh, yeah?" he asked. "What about all the farming you got started up now? Not gonna be cheap, try and turn that into something big."

Okay, he was right—even with potential investment from

the county or state, governments never had real funding for people like us. I said as much. And I could already feel his money moving over the wire. Like the muscle of an ocean current.

"Yeah," he said. "See that? It's what I'm saying. We're not okay enough. Not yet."

I realized that this would always be a difference between me and Dean. After everything that had happened to this family. Everything we'd seen and felt from Noa. The echoes of it in ourselves . . . I only wanted, finally, to understand. Let the money fall where it may, you know? But there was no settling that way, not for Dean. For him it had to be *his* hand, taking as much as he thought we needed to wipe away everything that had happened to us before. To guarantee it was all over. But there wasn't enough money in the world for that.

"There's way more I can make, like coming out our okoles," he said. "Whatchyou think about that?"

"I think Mom wants her only living son back," I said.

He was quiet a long time. But he was there. I knew he was.

"Let me think about it," he said. "Meantime, I keep sending money. Plenty more. I gotta go."

I wanted to tell him no again. No more money, just him. That we'd be here, when he was ready. But he'd already hung up.

# 39

# AUGIE, 2009

### *Waipi'o Valley*

**AH. HA.**

I feel the breath of life in the valley.

Ah.

Ha.

Four days and four nights we have been here where it started. Waiting. Malia doesn't know for what but I do. All around is the blow and the hiss across the kalo and the stands of ironwoods and farther back the kalo that came up with the rain that drops every night from the clouds which have carried other rains to other places in these islands. No rain is coming this night and I can feel the clear moon like a mother watching me from a house that someday I must return to.

I am returning now.

Malia is here and Kaui is here and we are on the far side of Waipiʻo near the start of the trail that raised my son up to death. Our tent is set back off the beach the polyester zipping and clapping in the wind and I am outside the tent in the black air walking as I do now because of the voices. Stronger here in this part of the valley. They are growing in me every day the voices all these days since Nainoa left. They give the colors and the smells to my head colors only that I feel and know but do not have the words for. But I know we are waiting. Malia and Kaui do not know for what but I do.

It happens tonight. As it did those years ago. We have never been the same as we were when we left this place on those engines to go out across the water to Oʻahu with its concrete and its people all of them too many. We were once here with horses riding across the land and when they ran we ran and when they walked we walked and when they took in air and when they stank and when they sweated so did we and each of us was full or empty as the horse. I was once the sugarcane. I was the cane and the clacking and the sugar-sweet smoke of reaping the season when we harvested and started again after the ashes.

I am here on the sand now in the valley. The gray beach sand an open cupped palm on the edge of the trees and the ocean. The water dances in the black and tumbles to me in a wave then draws out and tumbles back again. The ocean is not cold. The sky is wheeling with other suns other histories already over. My feet are in the sand and the sand is in my feet. To my left is the valley wall and the Z-Trail rising up in the valley dark green and black and the trees and the bushes shining from the moon. The trail slashes back and forth across the face of the valley all the way to the peak of the ridge.

The voices are strongest up there I can feel it.

"Couldn't sleep, babe?"

Here is my Malia. She is standing in her sweater with the hood up over her hair and her jeans and shoes. Her blunt nose is poking out from the hood her hair is one long thick curl sweeping down onto her chest. Her eyes are old and looking at me deep with worry.

I try to say what I am seeing. What comes out of me sounds like the kalo growing from the ponds sounds like the roaring of the waterfall sounds like lava sliding into the sea. Malia looks at me her eyebrows scrunched with worry and she says, "Slow down. You're doing that thing again, where you talk crazy."

I try to say again about the voices how they hum. She reaches out to touch me and I close my eyes and start to say again but I can't get through my mouth.

"Babe," she says. Her fingers are on my cheek and I feel each finger feel them all the way down her arm past the elbow and the bones and blood all straight into the hot center of her life. "What's wrong?" she asks.

I try to say to her where I have to go. She stops talking she stops moving. Then she turns to face the trail that goes up the side of the valley does she remember the night when we made Nainoa when we were in the truck on the other side watching the torches rise across the ridge does she remember the night marchers?

"Up there?" she asks.

I nod my head. They are coming.

For me.

She looks at the trail and the moon and I reach and touch her hand which is still on my cheek and try again to say but not with my mouth and now she sees. We grasp each other's hands and she walks back to the tent and I hear her talk to my daughter and then she comes back. All that time the breath of the valley.

We climb the trail in the darkness. Malia has a flashlight but once we break from the trees the moon is white and full and I can see it all. She must know because she clicks off the light. We walk those steps that Nainoa took. I am the centipede thrashing deep under the rocks. I am the burrowed bird tucked sleeping in the tree. I am the knot and flex of the trees. My hand is in Malia's as we climb and climb and climb up the trail.

Faster.

"Slow down," Malia says but she's falling behind. Her breath. The valley's breath.

But I know they are coming. We have to meet them I have to go. They won't wait just for me this night and then I will have to come again. I will have to keep coming until I meet them so now I hurry.

Faster. Malia is gasping and we are running she is falling behind. I turn and grab her and we lift and move over the trail like the air does. I am the air. We are no longer on the ground we are moving above it. Passing above like a thought that thinks of the top of the ridge and I take us past the trees I take us over their shadows I take us to the top. Malia is clutching me and saying "Holy shit, we were flying, we were flying, Augie, what's happening, we're at the top of the ridge," her asking if I saw what she saw but now when I want to say my words are the mosquitoes singing in the forest my words are the leaves shoving themselves up from the branches.

We are on top of the ridge. Down below us is the whole valley and wide away on the other side is the lookout and the road and the yellow lights of the houses and everything we left behind. Back behind us is the green night valley and wind stretching back along the top of the valley to the place where the ridges come together.

But the wind stops.

The trees go quiet.

Scrape all the sound from the sky and this is what is left. The sound of now. This is what we stand in Malia and I on top of the ridge of Waipiʻo.

Then they appear.

Malia's grip twists down on my shirt. I feel my skin grow hot with blood just underneath. I try to say this is what we came for. I try to say that this is so good.

In front of us is the column of Kānaka Maoli each one of them dead. They are men and women and they are both and they are neither. They are dark brown and almost naked the skin all stitched with scars. Their hair is neck-long or longer and kinked like ours and their noses broad as our noses and their faces tight and proud. Over their shoulders are the yellow and red feathered capes. Some wear pounded tapa cloth across their legs. Some wear hollowed gourds as helmets on their heads with huge holes gashed out for sight. Their eyes are nothing but white light a light that goes like smoke.

Night marchers.

Malia says "Oh, God," says it over and over and her voice is tighter and now she has no words and her voice is just quiet but she is still trying to speak and clutching me her heart like an animal that can't swim suddenly in a lake and so I hold her. I hold her and stare at the night marchers and they stare back. Each one holds in their hand a clump of branches. All at once these branches boom and pop into flame. Each one goes like thunder and the flame crackles and sucks and sets. The torches burning bright now white spitting sparks that do not burn the branches.

I kiss Malia's forehead where she is shivering from the sight of the night marchers. I do not know if she remembers them from before from the first time we saw them on the night we made Nainoa but now it is time. I squeeze her hand and let go. I take my place at the back of the line and the marchers turn their sad faces and the endless light of their eyes up toward the back of the valley.

"Where are you going?" Malia asks. I try to say but it is the sound of sharks giving birth it is the sound of birds plunging for the hunt. I know that I am coming back. I touch her head I touch her neck I touch her shoulder and there is something in me that takes her from the ridge and carries her like air back down to our tent at the valley floor. She will wait. I will be back and I will be the only one.

The march begins. Each one ahead of me with their torch raised high and their eyes nothing but smoking lights watching the valley ridge and how it rises. They march and I march with them. I take up branches from the ground as we go. The sky is blasted across with stars and the valley still scraped of sound and in front of me each marcher stepping and holding their torch high. When I have gathered enough branches I think again of Nainoa lost now to us all these days *my son my son* and as I think of him gone from this world and all the gifts that came with him the thoughts streak from my head down through my hot heart and out along my arm into my hand and then the branches I hold burst into flames.

That is when I see what all the night marchers see.

I am the man named Augie and I am the blood that pumps inside and I am the sand that was blown to life with the breath of all our gods and I am the wet mud of the valley and I am the green that grows from within it. I am the shore the drift of the world underwater and I am the shatter the wave throws over. I am the atmosphere that heats the thunderheads and I am the cool rain the thirsty soil reclaims. I am the flex that drives the arm of the wayfinder the planter the carver. I am the beat that drives the hips of the hula. I am the spark that starts the child's heart and I am the last beat from the elder's.

And so it is with Nainoa.

There he is.

He never left us.

Canongate. Here's hoping this final version of the book is worthy of everything the entire team has put into it.

My wife, Christina, and our entire life together. I was writing revisions when your contractions started, and you just kept breathing. We've been breathing ever since.

Benjamin Percy, who was the first person to believe.

Elizabeth Stork, who was the second person to believe.

Parul Sehgal, for masterfully guiding the first workshop I took, and later tossing me the first paid work I got as a writer. Also for letting me hang out with her and Adam, even after they got to know me.

Kathryn Savage: best fiction, best poetry, even better friendship. I'd take a bullet for her.

Emily Flamm, Carlea Holl-Jensen, Tom Earles, the Max Plateau mob. Best Sunday nights I had in DC. Thanks, Em, for letting me crash the party.

Lance Cleland and the whole Tin House family. I'm so glad I walked through the door when you opened it.

Michael Collier and the Bread Loaf Writers' Conference, for the support and honors. My first waiter reading in Little Theater was a gift of joy I'll never forget.

Dad, for telling me, "If someone told me when I was twenty that if I just practiced for half an hour every morning then the sky would be the limit, I'd have saved myself a lot of time." I was listening.

Carolyn Kuebler at *New England Review*, who sent me the kindest rejection letter I've ever received, saying: I see you, I hear you, almost, keep trying.

Katrin Tschirgi, Gabrielle Hovendon, and Catherine Carberry, who welcomed me into their unholy trinity of cool one summer. Forever grateful for the brief time with you baddest bosses.

Those who came first: Lois Ann-Yamanaka, Kiana Davenport, Kaui Hart Hemmings, Kristiana Kahakauwila, Mary Kawena Pukui, Brandy Nālani McDougall, and all the other artists of the islands who preserve and amplify the truth of our land.

For anyone else I may have failed to mention: Just because I didn't

# ACKNOWLEDGMENTS

Duvall Osteen has been with me from the jump. Intelligent, charming, fierce, family. Her and the whole Aragi Agency, a band of women small but mighty, including Gracie Dietshe. All good things for this novel came through the work of Team A.

Sean McDonald, Daniel Vazquez, and everyone else at MCD / Farrar, Straus and Giroux, for more enthusiasm and investment than I ever could have dreamed of, seriously.

A heartfelt thank you to Jamie Byng, Francis Bickmore, Vicki Rutherford, and the entire team at Canongate. Their early enthusiasm, investment, and engagement with this book both shocked and humbled me. Book publishing is often perceived as cynical and in a state of perpetual collapse; I have found nothing of the sort with write it down doesn't mean I don't care, it just means I'm a parent and husband with two full-time jobs besides. Sometimes I forget things for a minute.